THE INTERVIEW

C. M. Ewan is a pseudonym for Chris Ewan, the critically acclaimed and bestselling author of many mystery and thriller novels. Chris's first standalone thriller, *Safe House*, was a bestseller in the UK and was shortlisted for the Theakston's Old Peculier Crime Novel of the Year Award. He is also the author of the thrillers *Dead Line*, *Dark Tides* and *Long Time Lost*, as well as the Good Thief's Guide series of mystery novels. *The Good Thief's Guide to Amsterdam* won the Long Barn Books First Novel Award and has been published in thirteen countries.

Chris lives with his wife and their two children in Somerset, where he writes full-time.

THE INTERVIEW

C. M. EWAN

MACMILLAN

First published 2022 by Macmillan
an imprint of Pan Macmillan
The Smithson, 6 Briset Street, London EC1M 5NR
EU representative: Macmillan Publishers Ireland Ltd, 1st Floor,
The Liffey Trust Centre, 117–126 Sheriff Street Upper,
Dublin 1, D01 YC43
Associated companies throughout the world
www.panmacmillan.com

ISBN 978-1-5290-9553-1

1 3 5 7 9 8 6 4 2

A CIP catalogue record for this book is available from the British Library.

Typeset in Celeste by Palimpsest Book Production Limited, Falkirk, Stirlingshire
Printed and bound by CPI Group (UK) Ltd, Croydon, CR0 4YY

Visit **www.panmacmillan.com** to read more about all our books
and to buy them. You will also find features, author interviews and
news of any author events, and you can sign up for e-newsletters
so that you're always first to hear about our new releases.

For Jack

A fist bangs on a sheet of glass.

Bangs again.

On one side of the glass, all is still and hushed.

On the other side, the air sings with shouts and screams.

A hundred and thirty feet up, in the middle of a city of nine million people, and nobody hears or sees a thing.

CV

Kate Harding
17b Beaumont St, Balham, London
kharding@mycontact.com

I am an experienced PR Account Manager, a graduate from City, University of London with a 2:1 Honours Degree in Media, Communications and Sociology, and a former flight attendant with excellent customer care and problem-solving abilities. My career goal is to secure a Senior Account Manager role that enables me to hone my creative and business expertise and take on more responsibility at a dynamic, industry-leading PR agency with a focus on the travel sector.

EMPLOYMENT

- Account Manager with Simple PR & Communications (September 2021–present)
  At Simple, I have managed a portfolio of clients including Coachman European Travel, HomeSense Holidays and Scandinavian Getaways.
- PR Account Executive rising to PR Account Manager at MarshJet Aerospace Engineering (September 2014–March 2021)
- PR Assistant at MarshJet (September 2013–September 2014)
- Flight Attendant with Global Air (September 2009–September 2013)

EDUCATION

- 2:1 Honours Degree in Media, Communications and Sociology from City, University of London
- Diploma in Air Cabin Crew Level 2
- 9 GCSEs – 4 Grade As, 4 Grade Bs, 1 Grade C

ACTIVITIES AND ACHIEVEMENTS

- I am fluent in French and Spanish. I speak good German.
- I hold an advanced First Aid at Work qualification.
- I run regularly and I enjoy swimming.

1

Friday 5.03 p.m.

The worst thing that can happen to you in an interview is getting caught in a lie. Everybody knows that. It was one more thing for me to stress about as I waited to get inside 55 Ludgate Hill.

'Come on, come on.'

The revolving glass doors were moving too slowly. Anguish tugged at my insides. I darted forwards and back, forwards and back, then finally burst free and bolted for the front desk. There were three security personnel on duty: one woman, two men. Behind them was a back room where I could see a grid of surveillance monitors flickering against a wall.

'My name is Kate Harding.' I was panting, short of breath. 'I'm late for a 5 p.m. appointment with Edge Communications.'

'I see.' The guard nearest to me lifted a phone to his ear. He had a stiff, business-like demeanour. Early sixties, balding with a moustache, dressed in a navy blazer with shiny brass buttons. 'Let me call up for you. Sign the visitor book, please.'

I grabbed a pen, scrawled down my details. My hand was shaking. I could feel perspiration bubbling on the back of my neck despite the cool lobby air.

Had I blown it already? After waiting all day Friday, a

Tube delay had forced me to run here from Blackfriars Station. I'd had anxiety dreams where I was late for my interview. Now it was actually happening.

Then there was my CV. Why had I added that line about swimming? I suppose it wasn't a *total* lie. I used to enjoy swimming. A long time ago, I was a member of a club. It had been a much more sociable way to stay fit than the gruelling dawn jogs I'd been taking around Tooting Common for the past nine months. But if they asked about the last time I'd been swimming, I'd have no idea what to say. It was definitely before my life was upended. Everything was.

The guard set down his phone. 'They're sending someone down to collect you, but they're running a little behind themselves, so they've asked if you could take a seat for the time being.'

He pointed to an area behind me and I spun to take in the lavish atrium for the first time. The lobby was enormous. There was a lot of glass and steel. Acres of limestone flooring. Far in the distance, a group of black leather sofas were arranged near a trio of gleaming elevators.

'Go right ahead. They'll find you.'

To one side of the elevators, water cascaded down over a wall of rippled slate tiles into an infinity pool. To the other, a living wall was filled with plants in varying shades of green. In the foreground, professional men and women in office attire bustled to and fro. Some held mobile phones to their ears. Others carried briefcases or document folders. Most appeared to be hurrying for the exit and, I guessed, home for the weekend.

You used to be just like them, I told myself. But somehow it only made me feel like more of an imposter.

'And if I may, Miss – *good luck.*'

I cringed. 'Is it that obvious? How nervous do I look exactly?'

The guard's two colleagues looked up from their duties and joined him in indulging me with smiles.

'Less than some,' he said. 'You may prefer not to hear this, but they've been interviewing for most of the day. But Edge Communications? I'd say you'll fit right in.'

I wished. Once, maybe, but right now I felt daunted. The glitzy atrium wasn't simply impressive – it was imposing. And just hearing about the other candidates who'd been interviewed before me was enough for my doubts to resurface in a major way.

Not for the first time I told myself that I should have said no when Maggie, my recruitment agent, had set up this interview. Deep down, I knew I'd been too easily flattered when she'd told me that my past campaigns had impressed the team at Edge. Now I found myself wondering if Maggie had lied flat out. And . . . *Oh God.* What if the team had never actually heard of me and this was all a huge waste of time?

No, I told myself. *Focus.*

I knew I was in danger of spiralling. Knew that if I wasn't careful the swirl of negative thoughts would take hold of me and put me in a spin. In the quiet centre of my mind I conjured the calm, reassuring mantra of my counsellor, a wise and worn mother of two I meet with once a fortnight in Hackney: *Now is not the time.*

And it wasn't. It couldn't be. I was stepping out of my comfort zone here – no use pretending otherwise – but I'd lived and breathed this world before. I could do it again.

'Miss? Was there something else?'

'No, I'm fine. But thank you for your help.'

I edged away from the desk, my heels echoing into the void. June in London. There was so much sunlight streaming into the atrium I had to raise my hand to shield my eyes from the dazzle.

Ahead of me, a cleaner in grey overalls was using a noisy handheld machine to polish the floor. I could smell the cleaning fluid he was spraying – something cloying and strangely familiar that conjured up a memory I really didn't need. For a dizzying moment, I could have been striding across an airport concourse again, hurrying towards a press briefing. The stutter of flashbulbs. The clamour of questions. The choking surge of emotions at the back of my throat.

A job interview.

Why was I putting myself through this?

But in the pit of my stomach, I knew the answer to that question. I was doing it because this interview might – or might not – change everything.

2

Joel White's pulse quickened as he watched Kate cross the light-filled atrium. He'd watched her from the moment she'd entered the building. He'd watched her every second since.

He watched her now, and she didn't know it, because he was standing high up on a glass walkway that criss-crossed the lobby far below, just an anonymous employee in a shirt and tie standing alongside a second man in an expensive suit, who might have been a colleague, but wasn't.

The man standing alongside him was thin, grey-haired, grim-faced. He seemed to have shrunk a size or two since his suit was last tailored and his bunched hands were wrapped around the steel banister in front of him, wringing it so tightly the metal squeaked. A high-profile businessman who'd amassed a vast personal fortune, he was a millionaire, maybe even a billionaire on paper – rich enough, anyway, that the distinction no longer mattered a great deal.

'Do you have everything you need?' the man asked, in a voice that was wheezing and constricted, a combination of ill-health, stress and deep unease. Throat cancer, Joel speculated, though he hadn't asked and wouldn't be told if he did.

He also didn't respond to the man's question. Years of conducting interviews, years of applying his own particular skills in locations all across the globe, and still it amazed him how the big beasts of the corporate world could crumble and fall apart when their reputations and livelihoods were on the line. When that happened, often enough, they would turn to him.

'I asked you a question.' The man's voice pinched and strained. 'I was assured you wouldn't let me down.'

Again, Joel ignored him. The bank of elevators was behind them and he turned without comment to press the call button. When an elevator arrived, he paused for a second before stepping in, glancing briefly at the leather folio case the man had handed him and then staring one last time at Kate Harding. As he watched her, he could feel himself changing. A contraction of his muscles. A hardening of his resolve. A low-level burning like acid in his blood.

'Answer your phone when I call you,' he told the man as the elevator doors slid closed. 'I'll get you what you need.'

3

Friday 5.06 p.m.

I was close to the seating area when a woman stepped out from behind a tall plant to my side and took hold of my arm. 'I don't want you thinking I do this for all my clients,' she whispered in my ear.

'Maggie?'

'Sit down. Smile. Let's both just pretend you're not late and I'm not having a fit about it. You can ignore my missed calls when you finally check your phone, by the way.'

'What are you doing here?'

'My job.' Maggie tugged me down into one of the sofas, taking the seat next to me and placing her handbag on her lap. Her handbag was large and no-nonsense, much like Maggie herself. She had a mop of strawberry blonde hair, keenly intelligent green eyes. Her olive trouser suit was generous at the bosom and hips, worn over a plunging white blouse. 'It's Friday evening, Kate. I was in the neighbourhood.'

'Your office is in Dulwich.'

'So I'm protecting my investment. You do know I get a bonus if you land this job?'

I peered at her. In the Zoom calls we'd had on and off during the past fortnight, I'd placed Maggie as just a few years older than me, in her mid-to-late thirties. Now, though, the fine lines around her eyes and mouth told me she was some way past forty.

'Did you think I wouldn't show up?' I asked her.

'It's probably best I don't answer that. You look great, by the way.'

I glanced down, unconvinced, still worried my look was too formal and safe for a company like Edge. I'd gone with a black pencil skirt and matching jacket over a blush silk blouse that had cost far more than I could afford to spend on it. I'd been to my local salon first thing this morning. Nothing fancy. Just a trim and a tidy-up of my fringe. Look closely, though, and you would have seen the insomnia-bags under my eyes, the hollows in my cheeks. I suppose I was lucky that the four years I'd worked as cabin crew before switching to a career in PR had taught me all the make-up tricks anyone could care to know.

'Maggie, the security guard just told me Edge have been interviewing *all day*.'

'Why worry about it? You're the one they'll want. Trust me. They'll have applicants with general PR experience coming out of their ears, but nobody with your background in the travel industry.'

'How many candidates did you send them?'

'Just you.'

I gave her a dubious look.

'*Seriously*.' She seized my hands in her fleshy palms. 'Kate, how many times do I have to tell you this role is perfect for you and you're perfect for this role? I wouldn't have stuck with you if I didn't believe that. Not after you tried to talk us both out of it enough times.'

Her brusque show of support warmed me, even as the doubts rose up in me again. It was strange to think how someone I'd only spoken with over the phone or in online meetings before now had become such a force in my life in such a short space of time. Maggie had been tenacious when she'd first approached me just over two weeks ago, even as I'd told her (less and less convincingly) that I wasn't interested in a new job. I'm not sure whether that said more about how persistent Maggie was or how much of a loner I'd become. Secretly, I knew that if she hadn't reached out to me in the first place, told me I was wasting my talents at Simple, I could have continued in the miserable rut I'd been in for months, maybe years.

'Breathe,' Maggie said. 'Relax. Take a look around with me for a second. Didn't I tell you this place was incredible?'

Together, we looked up at the lobby as the chlorinated waterfall babbled softly behind us.

And she was right. It *was* incredible. 55 Ludgate Hill – popularly known as The Mirror – was London's most recent statement high-rise building. At thirty-eight storeys high, it dwarfed the dome of nearby St Paul's Cathedral, although its signature feature was the way the exterior above the triple-height lobby was covered entirely in silvered, reflective glass panels. From outside the building nobody could see in to the uppermost floors, but I knew from my online research that they offered breathtaking views across the Thames and beyond.

The Mirror had only been officially opened in February, but there were already rumours that the company behind the project was on the verge of going bust. Construction on the site had begun before the global Covid pandemic and now that the building was completed, the business world had changed. More and more people were working from home and that meant fewer firms were looking to rent prime office space in the City. The penthouse restaurant that had grabbed press attention because of its celebrity chef was yet to open to the public, and there was talk that multiple floors remained unlet and unoccupied. That fitted with what I was seeing in the lobby. There were people here, but nowhere near as many as the project's backers must have planned for.

I found that weird. Maybe I was in the minority, but I had zero interest in working from home, and not just because my one-bedroom flat in Balham was dingy and depressing. One of the attractions of the pitch Maggie had made to me about working at Edge was the distraction a busy office could provide. My counsellor had told me it was time to put myself out there, take risks, scare myself.

Mission accomplished, I thought now.

'I still feel bad about Simon and Rebecca,' I told Maggie. 'They've been good to me.'

'And I get that. Believe me, I'd be worried if a client of mine didn't feel *guilty* about leaving their current job. But you're not doing anything wrong here, Kate. You know you're not.'

I glanced down at my hands, not feeling so sure about that. Simon and Rebecca were the husband and wife team who owned Simple PR. I was their only outside hire. I don't think it's an exaggeration to say that they took me on more out of sympathy than need. They'd been incredibly patient as I'd built my confidence back – feeling my way into the working world again – being ready with guidance and advice. I hadn't yet had the courage to tell them I was interviewing for another position.

'Kate, listen to me. It's comfortable where you are. It's safe and I understand that. But you're a star. You know it, I know it. And Edge are the best at what they do. You belong where you belong.'

I managed a half-smile. 'Have you been practising that?'

'Little bit. Did it work?'

I hummed, the knot of guilt inside me still making it difficult to admit – even to myself – that the lure of working for Edge was the main reason I was here. Edge had fancy offices in London, New York and Sydney. They represented top-tier clients and brands across the fields of entertainment, sports and business. There were even whispers of a roster of high-end clients they never openly discussed.

Like the company name suggested, Edge were best known for high-profile campaigns that were hip and wildly invent-ive. The kind of noisy campaigns Simon and Rebecca would roll their eyes at, because at Simple we generally did the same things Simon and Rebecca had always done – targeting traditional media, aiming for an older demographic.

Like Maggie had said, it was safe. And by safe, I knew that what she really meant was 'dull'.

I nodded, poised to thank her for coming, to summon up a show of confidence that could make her believe her faith in me hadn't been misplaced, when my phone chimed from inside my handbag.

'One second.'

'Great.' Maggie threw up her hands in mock exasperation. '*Now* she checks her phone.'

I parted my handbag, removed my iPhone. There was a short text message at the top of my lock screen.

Go for it, Sis. You'll wow them. Guaranteed xx

'My brother,' I explained. 'Wishing me luck.'

Even as I said it, a peevish thought struck me. *It should be Mark texting me. Why can't it be Mark?* But almost as soon as the thought had surfaced, I immediately forced it back down. I couldn't afford to think that way about my husband right now. It wouldn't help. And I knew I should be grateful that my brother cared enough to send me a text in the frenzied seconds he had between patients. Luke works as a cardiac nurse at St Thomas' Hospital. He's my rock. Since we lost Mum and Dad almost a decade ago, within three cruel months of one another, he's the closest family I have.

Beneath Luke's text I could see that I also had two missed calls from Maggie's phone as well as a news notification: *MarshJet Trial Hears Evidence from Family of Deceased . . .*

Too late, I snatched my eyes away, covering up my phone with my hand. My heart contracted in my chest.

Now is not the time. Now is not the—

'Kate?'

My vision darkened, a sudden coolness sweeping in over my shoulders. I clamped down on the inside of my mouth, clenching my phone tight in my fist. Maggie squeezed my hands. Her touch felt clammy and hot.

'Stay with me, Kate. You can do this. Just remember what I told you. They're going to push you, ask you unconventional questions, get you to take part in dummy exercises, even. They're all about doing things differently and surprising you. *It's who they are.* But that's OK. You're ready for this. You're going to do brilliantly, I promise.'

I nodded, forcing a smile, knowing that I was holding back from her. Because as much as I valued Maggie's advice, there were some things I couldn't talk with her about. Things I didn't talk to anyone about except my counsellor.

'Listen, there's a pub across the road from this place, on the opposite corner.' She rose to her feet. 'Did you see it? I'm going to wait for you there. Come and find me when you're done and we can celebrate together. OK?'

I winced.

'Or commiserate, then. But no excuses. I won't keep you late. I'm driving to Devon tonight to see my parents. But I'm in this for the long haul, Kate. We'll find you your perfect role, at Edge or somewhere else if it comes to it.' Her gaze shifted briefly and she nodded in the direction of the elevators. 'Looks like this is your cue.'

I swivelled to see a smiling young blonde woman approaching me as Maggie backed off and drifted away. The woman was dressed in an on-trend jumpsuit over pristine white training shoes. The instant I saw her, I immediately worried that I was wrongly dressed, over-dressed, just too plain out of touch for Edge.

'Kate Harding?'

I stood up, tugging at my skirt.

'I'm Hayley.' She thrust out her hand. 'It's so lovely to meet you. Shall we go upstairs?'

4

Upstairs in the offices of Edge Communications, Joel sat alone with his thoughts.

And the folio case.

He flicked through it methodically.

The case contained everything there was to know about Kate Harding. There was her CV, of course. That was front and centre. But there was much more besides. There was a detailed breakdown of her personal life and family history. Her social media profile. Her financial records and credit score. Her medical records. Her politics. Her passions. Her likes and dislikes.

Her fears.

He stopped on one of the surveillance photographs they had of her, his heart beating slowly in his chest.

It was a glossy colour print. The stock was high quality. The focus was sharp.

Kate was smiling in the picture. Her eyes sparkled. Her skin looked soft and wind-flushed. She was wearing a pink woollen beanie and fingerless gloves, holding a bouquet of flowers outside a market stall. It was raining and Joel could see bright beads of water glimmering in the light from a nearby cafe. But the part that pierced him, perhaps more today than it had with any of the other candidates he'd interviewed in the past, was how he could tell from the way she was glancing away from the camera, her gaze distant and unfocused, that she had no clue she was being photographed at all.

5

Friday 5.13 p.m.

Hayley pressed the button for the elevators. 'Nervous?' she asked me.

I held up my finger and thumb a fraction apart. In truth, I felt sick, dizzy, the knot in my stomach getting tighter and tighter, but I knew I had to be careful here. Hayley seemed nice but she could have been asked to report back on everything I said to her, how I behaved. Making the wrong comment or response right now could kill my chances before I'd begun.

'I'm fine,' I told her. 'Excited.'

'Great.' Her eyes darted away from me for a second. 'Oh, hey guys!' She went up on her toes and waved at two workmen behind me. They were crossing the lobby in paint-spattered coveralls, carrying tool kits. 'All finished?'

'Almost,' one of them called back. 'Should be Tuesday now.'

'Can't wait! Have a great weekend, both!' Hayley clapped her hands, then leaned closer to me. 'We're having a gym installed upstairs,' she explained. 'And listen, try not to stress about today. We're a really friendly bunch at Edge. And if it helps at all, the guy interviewing you is *seriously* hot.'

The doors parted on one of the elevators and Hayley stepped in, but I didn't follow. I was frozen.

'Is there a problem?' she asked me.

Yes, there was a problem.

'I was told my interview was with Amanda Palmer.'

'Oh. No, sorry. Amanda is with a client all day. Didn't anybody let you know?'

I shook my head, searching behind me for Maggie, but she was already on her way out through the revolving glass doors, her attention on her phone. A sudden surge of dread took hold of me. Amanda Palmer was a Senior Account Director. I'd studied her bio on the Edge Communications website. I'd researched her on Google and LinkedIn. We shared similar backgrounds in the aerospace industry. I knew she'd worked in airline management before she'd joined Edge and I'd hoped it might give me an advantage.

Now I didn't know what to think. Was this the kind of stunt Maggie had warned me about, a ploy to throw me off my game?

'Who is interviewing me?'

'His name's Joel White.'

I mentally scanned through the other bios I'd seen on the Edge website but I didn't get a hit on the name.

'Relax, OK?' Hayley beckoned me into the elevator and after another moment's hesitation, I stepped in next to her. 'He's new. British, but he works out of our New York office. It looks like he's going to be heading up recruitment from now on. Half the office are currently trying to find out if he's single.'

'He came all the way to London for these interviews?'

'Yes, but don't sound so surprised. They take hiring here really seriously. Plus they probably thought it would be a good chance for him to meet the London team.' She pressed a button on the elevator panel. 'We're on floor thirteen, by the way. Amazing views, no street noise.'

Thirteen. Normally I didn't believe in bad omens but with the way things had been going for me lately . . .

The doors had almost sealed when a hand appeared in the gap and they bounced apart again.

'Sorry, sorry.'

The cleaner in the grey jumpsuit shuffled backwards into the elevator, wheeling his heavy floor-polishing machine after him. He was a big, brawny man with jet-black hair that was slicked down against his scalp. A pair of headphones hung around his neck.

'Hey, Raul,' Hayley said to him. '*Please* tell me you have some more photos to show me.'

Raul nodded and smiled toothily as he jabbed the button for floor eight. The doors sealed, the elevator began to rise, and he took a phone from his pocket, tapping it with his thumb and angling the screen for Hayley to see.

'Cute!' She smiled at me. 'Raul's wife had a baby girl last week.'

'Zarita.' His eyes blazed with pride as he thrust his phone my way.

For a second, I was tumbling. The photograph showed an attractive woman with dark hair cradling a newborn baby girl in a pink onesie.

Now is not the time . . . Now is not the . . .

I felt breathless. Trapped. Not so long ago, motherhood had seemed to be a pathway I was destined for. One that Mark had told me he was just as committed to as I was.

Turned out the universe had other plans.

'Beautiful,' I managed, aware that the knot in my stomach was unravelling, a hollowness ebbing in.

I lowered a hand to my waist as Raul slipped his phone away. Hayley noticed my reaction and shot me a concerned look. I could tell she was about to ask if I was feeling all right but at that moment the elevator slowed, bouncing to a halt on floor eight, and once the doors had parted Raul manhandled his machine out ahead of him.

'See you,' he called back.

'Yes, see you later, Raul.' When the doors had sealed and the elevator was humming upwards again, Hayley checked on me once more, then motioned towards the space Raul had occupied. 'Raul's a total sweetheart. He's supposed to use the service elevator, but everybody here knows him and he's so nice he totally gets away with it. Did you have any questions you wanted to ask me?'

I dug my nails into the palms of my hands, trying to draw my attention back to the here and now.

'My recruitment agent mentioned that sometimes in the interview process here there can be exercises or . . . ?'

'Oh. Oh, listen, really don't worry about that. I'm sure Joel will explain everything to you. My advice? If they offer you the job, take it. They're a really great company to work for and we have so much fun. I work on reception with a guy called Justin. It's his birthday today and we're all going out for drinks later.'

That was something else Maggie had briefed me on. There was a work-hard, play-hard culture at Edge. The team were young, the hours long, the work demanding. Most people who landed a position here stuck it out for a couple of years to have Edge on their CV, and then burned out and moved on.

That wasn't my plan. I wanted to be somewhere where the challenges were so intense they could consume me. Swallow me. Make me forget.

The elevator arrived at floor thirteen and this time Hayley led me out into a smart vestibule towards a pair of black, industrial-style metal doors. The doors were inset with thin panels of wired safety glass, flanked by fake topiary planters. Hayley took a key card from a pocket on her jumpsuit.

'You've probably heard that most of the building is still unoccupied, which has its perks. Apparently the lease we signed was a total steal. We have the entire floor to ourselves.'

She wafted her key card in front of a metal sensor on the wall. A green diode lit up and she pushed a door open ahead of me.

'Welcome to Edge.'

6

Friday 5.17 p.m.

The contrast from the opulent lobby downstairs was jarring. Edge's reception area had a stripped back, industrial vibe. Bare cement floors. Exposed ceilings revealing ventilation ducts and piping. Unpainted steel girders. Distressed red-brick partition walls.

Directly in front of me was a semi-circular counter clad in mismatched boards of rough-hewn timber. Behind the counter, the Edge logo was picked out in pink neon tubing above a line of metal lockers. The latest Apple desktops were on show and a skinny guy in a V-neck sweater over a checked shirt and tie – Justin, presumably – was talking on the phone to somebody via a Bluetooth headset. Spray-painted across the front of the counter was the Edge company mantra: *Break your own rules.*

'It's this way.'

Hayley strode purposefully to her right and I hurried after her onto the main office floor. The space was almost entirely open-plan. Around the perimeter of the room I could see the building's signature floor-to-ceiling windows, their silvered tint subtly dimming tantalizing glimpses of the London skyline.

'Quick tour.' Hayley waved a hand. 'Workstations, obviously.

We have a clean desk policy. That means all your work has to be tidied away at the end of each day. Any confidential notes or materials have to be filed or shredded.'

To my right, a series of white laminate desks were arranged in horseshoe clusters with low felt dividers separating them. The workstations featured all the usual office equipment. Desktop computers. Landline phones. Lamps. Ergonomic desk chairs. As Hayley had suggested, most of the desks were noticeably low on paperwork and the endless piles of daily clutter I was used to at Simple.

Positioned around the desks were perhaps thirty or so fashionably dressed employees, some sitting, others tapping at keyboards, still others chatting in small groups and cutting glances my way. Most of them looked like clones of Hayley or Justin.

'Refectory.'

Hayley indicated a kitchen area to her left where a row of glossy white kitchen cabinets were lined up against a long brick wall running through the middle of the space. Fixed to the wall above them was a giant chalkboard with a grid system drawn on it.

'That's the master grid,' Hayley explained. 'Everything we do goes on that wall. Every campaign gets broken down into press targets, budgets, execs responsible, all the usual stuff. In the refectory you'll find complimentary still and sparkling water, Coke, juice, smoothies. There's coffee and tea. In the mornings we have cereal, fruit and muffins. Most evenings somebody orders in from Deliveroo or wherever.'

'Perfect,' I said, trying to act like it was normal for me

to work somewhere with complimentary food and drink. At Simple, I generally ate the same sad packed lunch from the same sad Tupperware container at my desk every day. It was one of my responsibilities to boil the kettle and make tea or instant coffee for Simon and Rebecca whenever they asked.

'Sometimes we hold meetings at the kitchen table. But usually we get together in small groups in one of the pods.'

Again, Hayley pointed, but none of the 'pods' as she called them were meeting rooms in any conventional sense. One appeared to be the shell of a classic VW campervan that had been fitted out with forwards and backwards facing seats and a table fashioned from a surfboard. Another was designed to look like the basket of a mock hot-air balloon that was half risen through the ceiling. There were two painted horses from a fairground carousel. A white gazebo with fake plants entwined around it.

'We have a unisex bathroom behind reception. And at the back there you can see our games area.'

Hayley signalled to another young girl and a guy who were playing ping pong at a table splattered with luminous paint. Next to them was an arcade dance machine with flashing lights.

'I'm top scorer.' Hayley smiled over her shoulder. 'And Justin is *amazing* at the climbing wall. If you take the job, you *have* to get him to show you.'

If I took the job. *Like it could be that simple.*

The climbing wall was at the back of the space beyond the games area. It extended all the way up to the ceiling and had the appearance of a giant pegboard with multicoloured hand- and footholds screwed to it. At the bottom of the wall were an array of crash mats and bean bags.

'Unless you're a demon climber already?' she added.

I shook my head. 'I've been abseiling. For a charity thing, at my old job.'

'Did you love it?'

'I did once I reached the ground.'

'Don't tell anyone I said this, but if you have a hangover, those bean bags make a great spot to take a nap.'

As Hayley led me on, I noticed other features she didn't point out. A library area with see-through inflatable chairs. A swing.

'We have more space to expand into in the area behind the master grid. That's where the gym is going. Your interview is in the cube. It's the one totally private meeting space we have.'

She veered right and cut a path between two workstation clusters and several more employees, in the direction of a large glass box in the middle of the office floor. It was about the size of a shipping container, framed by more bare metal girders. The walls were made up of large sheets of glass, untinted this time, lined on the inside with white slatted privacy blinds. All of the blinds were closed.

I raised a hand to cover my mouth and stifle the dry cough I get when I'm nervous. My palms were damp and I wiped them surreptitiously on my skirt.

Then stopped.

A man in a fitted white shirt and slim, dark tie had opened the door to the cube and stepped out. He was athletic-looking, square-jawed. There was something about him. Something immediately *arresting*. He was handsome, yes, Hayley had been right about that. But he also had this presence. An intensity. A focus.

On me.

'Kate Harding?'

I seemed to have lost my voice for a second.

'Joel White. Why don't you come on in?'

7

Joel offered Kate his hand. As they touched, it felt to him as if a small jolt passed between them, like a tiny electric charge. Did she feel it, too?

She didn't appear to, but he did notice that her palm was greasy and he could tell she was embarrassed by it as she slipped her hand free, and he gestured for her to move past him into the cube.

He watched her, and for a curious second he was lost – his hearing warped, a sour taste pooling on his tongue – until everything snapped back again and his focus returned.

Pay attention now.

She hesitated when she was inside, acting skittishly as she scanned the interior to get her bearings. Not that there was much for her to see.

A glass desk with two matching white leather office chairs on either side of it. Track lighting above them. The closed shutter blinds.

The austere environment was deliberate and something Joel had specified. He preferred to minimize signal interference wherever he could.

'I'm sorry to get you here so late on a Friday,' he said now. 'Hayley, can you take care of Kate's bag?'

'Oh no, that's OK.' Kate flinched and clasped it against her. 'I'll keep it with me if that's all right?'

'Of course. No problem, Kate. Can we offer you coffee or tea?'

'Water is fine.'

She motioned to the carafe that was on one side of the glass desk, next to two highball tumblers. At the other side of the desk was a telephone. The leather folio case was in the middle, and that was it.

'Anything else?'

'I don't think so.'

'Then we're all set. Thank you, Hayley. You can close the door on your way out.'

The door closed behind them with a well-greased *click*. In the short silence that followed, Joel felt the air in the room pressing against his skin, his instincts sharpening, his eyes fixed on Kate.

'Sit down, Kate. Please. Make yourself comfortable.'

He moved around behind the desk, waiting for her to take the seat opposite him. She placed her bag on the floor to her right, straightened her skirt, and once she was settled he pressed his tie flat against his torso and dropped into his own chair.

'I apologize for keeping you waiting, Kate. It wasn't my intention. I'm afraid it's been a packed day.'

'It's fine. It gave me an opportunity to get a feel for the building.'

'Do you like it?'

'Very much.'

He nodded, smiling warmly, keen to put her at her ease.

Experience had taught him to keep the early interactions simple. Establish a rapport. Build a foundation of trust. Using Kate's name repeatedly was a technique designed to reassure her. So was taking his time and not hurrying her in any way.

Joel's main purpose right now was to watch her, study her, see how she behaved. Did she blink frequently? Did she raise her eyebrows or move her hands when she talked? If she moved her hands, what did she do with them? Did she clasp them together? What about touching her face or her hair? Then there was smiling. How *much* did she smile? How readily? Did she frown when she was thinking of an answer? Did her pupils contract or dilate? Was there a flicker in her upper lip or her cheek? What were her *tells*?

Back in his formative days with the intelligence services, interviewing witnesses and suspects, spies and informants, Joel had come to think of this stage of his process like the control questions a technician might employ when calibrating a lie detector machine. The difference was he believed he was more intuitive and ultimately more accurate than any machine, anywhere in the world. As did the clients who paid him so handsomely.

'So, Kate. I'm guessing working in an office tower isn't going to be an issue for a former flight attendant like you?'

There. Relaxation. A slight softening of her lips. A small downward hook at the corners of her eyes.

'That was some years ago now,' she said, 'but I think I should be able to handle any altitude sickness.'

He chuckled, nodding in appreciation and encouragement, noting how the smile became crooked, registering a self-effacing shrug.

Anything else? No.

'So listen, I know you were originally scheduled to be interviewed by Amanda . . .' Tension again. The chin tilted up. The brow crinkled. '. . . and I'm sorry that didn't work out, but hopefully you were told I was stepping in for her in good time?'

Her pupils jinked left to right very rapidly. She tucked her hair behind her ear and winced.

'Actually, I wasn't.'

'Oh?'

'To be honest, I only found out when Hayley mentioned your name just now.'

A stirring in his blood. Normally the phrase 'to be honest' was a red flag for Joel. When a subject used it, it was generally because they were about to be anything *but* honest. But Joel knew for a fact that wasn't the case here – because he'd made certain she wouldn't be told – and it was something he'd have to log and remember.

'Well, that definitely shouldn't have happened. I'm embarrassed, Kate. For myself, and for Edge. You must feel you've been thrown for a loop.'

'It's fine. Really.'

She flapped her hand. Puffed out her lips. Overcompensating.

'No, it's not fine. Not by a long way. I want you to know that I'm on your side here, Kate. I want you to do well. And in that spirit, please don't worry that you won't have had a chance to learn anything about me. I'll introduce myself to you from scratch and we'll go from there. Does that sound fair?'

'It does. Thank you.'

'Good. So I suppose the first thing to say is that I'm new to Edge myself, working out of our New York office. My background is in recruitment although in recent years I've also branched out into corporate troubleshooting and crisis management, working all over the world. But I like to think my real specialism is in meeting people like you one-on-one. Interviewing them. Getting to know what makes them tick.'

He knitted his hands together, tipped his head to one side, smiling freely again. Some of what he'd said was even true, though not the part about having come from the States. He'd never set foot in the offices of Edge in New York. He'd actually flown in from Shanghai, under a different name with different documentation. Prior to that he'd been in Hong Kong. A similar assignment. Another interview in a long sequence of interviews. In Hong Kong, a junior employee had been suspected of corporate espionage. Wrongly, as it turned out. In Shanghai, a female executive had confessed to an affair with a senior board member's wife. It wasn't the secret she'd been accused of hiding, but despite his employer's obvious embarrassment at the revelation, he'd still been paid.

Now he tapped his thumbs together, smiling placidly, and this time Kate held his gaze and remained steady as he allowed the moment to lengthen and stretch. He liked that about her. It meant he would know when the cracks began to show.

'So . . .' He reached for the glass tumblers, turning them upright and pouring water into them from the carafe. 'I have a copy of your CV.'

8

Friday 5.25 p.m.

I nodded, trying to keep up. It was weird. I was concentrat-ing so hard on being present in the moment that it was making everything feel hyper-real – almost unreal – as if the interview itself was passing me by.

It didn't help that I kept looping on how badly my palm had squelched in Joel's hand when we'd shaken. And *great*. Now I was sweating under my arms, too. I shifted position, adjusted my blouse.

Did he notice? I didn't think so. And anyway, based on how polite and courteous he was, it wasn't as if he'd let me know it if he did.

Right now his gaze was downcast as he opened the leather folio in front of him. I craned my neck slightly and glimpsed my CV at the top. The paper was crinkled. A few parts had been underlined. One of them was the bit about swimming.

Ugh.

There was also an inch or so of paperwork underneath my CV. The other candidates' applications, I supposed. I got a sinking feeling as I thought about how many other people were vying with me for this position and how much I now wanted it. Joel had probably been just as charming and considerate to them all.

Then he looked up at me and it was as though every single thought I'd been having fell out of my head. He had flat grey eyes, like tiny dulled mirrors, and again, there was something compelling about the way he was studying me with them. I hadn't been stared at so openly in a very long time.

For a second, a crazy thought flashed in my mind. Was he . . . flirting with me?

And then another, even odder thought: did I mind?

His jaw was square, his brow prominent, his dark hair graded short, like his stubble. His shirtsleeves were rolled up on his muscular forearms, the cuffs neatly buttoned, his tie held in place by a silver tiepin. I could smell a faint trace of his cologne. Notes of cedarwood and citrus. For a jolting second, I thought I recognized the scent, but then, almost as soon as I'd noticed, it was gone.

'Your CV is brief and to the point, Kate, but from your background you seem to be an excellent fit for this role.'

'Thank you. I was advised to keep my CV short so that we'd have more to talk about. But I know that my recruitment agent spoke at length with Amanda about my background.'

Oh God. The slight vocal fry in my voice. I was fighting hard to keep my nerves in check but it was a difficult thing to do in the intense hush of the cube. Hayley had been right when she'd told me the space was private. All the noise and hubbub of the office floor had been muted. I couldn't see out through the closed blinds and I was pretty sure the forced intimacy of the set-up was contributing to my spaced feeling.

'Can I level with you, Kate?'

Again, I got the sinking feeling. Had the position already been filled? I really hoped not, but I also knew there was a chance he could have settled on a candidate already. If he'd flown in from the States, he was probably jet-lagged. Perhaps he just wanted this over.

He leaned closer. 'I probably shouldn't be saying this, but I've had a full day of interviewing candidates in here and I've got to tell you, this whole set-up is starting to feel pretty artificial to me.'

Well, at least I'm not the only one.

He cast his hands around. No wedding ring, I was ashamed to have noticed.

'Think about it too much and you start to go mad. I'm a professional recruiter so I know the routine. I ask you the type of questions you're expecting me to ask, and you give me the type of answers I'm expecting you to give, and then I'm required to make a judgement on you, when the fact is I don't know the *real* you at all.'

'Well, if it helps, I'm going to answer all your questions as honestly as I can.'

Actually, that was a lie. I was going to try and answer them in line with the advice in the book I had stuffed in my handbag. *Interview SOS: 101 Job Interview Questions and How to Answer Them.* The pages of my copy were flagged with sticky notes and blocks of text picked out in highlighter pen. I'd been up late the past three nights studying it cover to cover. When Simon and Rebecca had interviewed me, it had been more of a casual chat – mainly because a friend of my brother's, a consultant he worked with, had put in a good word for me. It was years now since I'd been formally interviewed. The last time had been in front of a trio of senior executives before I was promoted to PR Account Manager at MarshJet.

'You know something, Kate? I read this article a while ago – I forget where – but it was all about the science behind first impressions. You'll have heard the same thing, right? The theory goes that we all make hard-to-shake judgements about other people within the first few seconds of meeting them. The way they look. The way they act and present themselves. The first handshake. First hello. We take all that data in, and we crunch it incredibly fast, and we already know, on an instinctive level, how we feel about someone before we even talk to them.'

'Right.' I teetered. 'Then do I get the job?'

He rocked back and laughed, harder than he needed to. 'I wish it could be so easy. Believe me. But we both have to jump through the hoops here, Kate. I'm guessing you already know Edge do things a little differently?'

'It's why I'm here.'

'Well, sometimes when we're hiring, we like to use psychometric tests. Other similar techniques. For the right candidates.' He flipped over my CV and removed a clear plastic pocket from the folio case, sliding it across the desk in front of me. I could see several sheets of typed paperwork inside. 'What do you say? Would you be prepared to go along with that?'

I thought of the warnings Maggie had given me. I hadn't been told this was part of the recruitment process here and I'd never taken a psychometric test before. I didn't, in all honesty, know what they really involved. But I felt comfortable with Joel. I was inclined to follow his lead. And more importantly, I'd picked up on two crucial things he'd said. *Sometimes when we're hiring.* Sometimes. Not every time. And also: *For the right candidates.*

'I can do that, yes.'

'Great.' He dipped two fingers into his shirt pocket and removed a propeller pencil that he clicked a couple of times. 'How about you get started?'

9

Friday 5.30 p.m.

'*Now?*' I asked.

'It's only a short test, Kate. Won't take you more than ten minutes to complete. We'll have plenty of time to talk afterwards, I promise.'

He passed me the pencil.

'Should I step outside?'

'No, there's no need for that. We can both stay here.'

I looked at him, puzzled.

'Relax, Kate. I designed these questions myself. It's completely painless and you won't have any trouble with them.'

I opened the plastic pocket and slipped the papers out from inside. They were neatly stapled and there were only five or six pages. I was conscious of Joel watching me as I flicked through them before looking up.

'Can I ask you something?'

'By all means.'

'What is it you're hoping this will show you?'

'*You*, Kate.' He spread his hands and grinned as though I'd asked him the exact question he'd hoped I might. 'Specifically, your personality traits. The best approach is not to think of this as a test at all. It isn't anything you can fail.

40

It's more like a questionnaire. The idea is for me to get a truer sense of who you are, to see whether you'd be a good fit for the company and more importantly, if the company is a good fit for you.'

'And if we're not a good fit?'

He smiled again. 'Why don't you just go ahead and take the test and we'll see. And be sure to answer honestly, for both our sakes.'

I glanced down at the top sheet of paper.

1. I don't like confrontation and avoid it where possible.
   (a) This is not like me   (b) This is sometimes like me
   (c) This is often like me   (d) This is very like me
2. I prefer working on my own rather than as part of a team.
   (a) This is not like me   (b) This is sometimes like me
   (c) This is often like me   (d) This is very like me
3. I make decisions quickly and stick to them.
   (a) This is not like me   (b) This is sometimes like me
   (c) This is often like me   (d) This is very like me

I lowered the pencil towards the paper, then stopped and looked up again. 'What if I'm not sure what to put?'

'Go with your gut.'

'But with some of these questions, it really depends on the circumstances, don't you think?'

'Make your best judgement, Kate. Trust yourself.'

1. I don't like confrontation and avoid it where possible.

Well, that didn't seem so hard. You'd have to be a complete psycho to *like* confrontation, but equally I could see that it wouldn't do me much good to say that I actively avoided it. Edge would want their applicants to be prepared to speak up when they disagreed or were challenged on something. I circled (b) This is sometimes like me.

I moved on and stuck with answer (b) to question two (I prefer working on my own rather than as part of a team). For question three (I make decisions quickly and stick to them) I went with (c) This is often like me.

After that, I began moving more swiftly through the questions. Joel was right. Even though having him watch me felt a bit awkward, they really didn't take too much thought. Besides, I could hardly go wrong if I mixed my answers up between (b) and (c) all the way through.

Unless . . .

I pressed down on the pencil, almost breaking the lead. I was thinking about what I knew about Edge. They liked to stand out, do things differently. Did that mean they were actively seeking employees who tended towards one extreme or the other? Perhaps it was a mistake not to be circling the (a) or (d) options.

'Kate?'

I lifted my eyes and he shook his head gently.

'Stop thinking about what you think we want to hear and tick what is right for you.'

What was he, a mind reader?

'It's just that—'

'It's OK, Kate. Really. Everyone does it.'

'Everyone?'

'*Almost* everyone.'

Was that a hint? I looked down at the next question.

10. Speaking in public makes me nervous.

I stared so hard at the words they swam before my eyes.

My skin flushed hot and I immediately worried he could tell, which only intensified the sensation. There was that one time – the one that would never go away now – but it was something I knew I had to push past. And the real me – the one I'd told my counsellor I was afraid I'd lost touch with – had always been naturally talkative. You couldn't be an effective PR if you weren't a confident spokesperson. I circled (a) This is not like me.

'Good, Kate.'

I blocked the bad thoughts that were crowding in on me, the sense that I was cheating in some way, and tried not to squirm. Staying still seemed suddenly important because I was starting to wonder if Joel was just as interested in *how* I approached the test as the answers I circled. Now that I thought of it, perhaps that was why he'd wanted to stay inside the room with me.

I pushed on, trying to convey a sense of confidence even if that wasn't really how I was feeling. Soon, I became so absorbed that I almost forgot Joel was there and the next two pages of questions passed in something of a blur.

Until I turned to the penultimate page and read the question at the top.

26. When I am having sex I picture myself with other
    partners.

Whoa.

'Problem?' Joel asked me.

I showed him the page, pointing to the question.

'Ah, yes.' He scrunched his face up. 'Question twenty-six.'

'It's intrusive.'

'You're right, Kate. I apologize.'

'Not to mention highly personal.'

'I agree with you.'

'I'm not going to answer it.'

He sucked air through his teeth and looked pained. I took the gesture as an indication that I was making a mistake.

'This question shouldn't be on here,' I told him. 'It's not right.'

His wince became more regretful. 'Yet I put it there.'

'It breaches all kinds of employment laws and . . .'

His eyebrows shot up, like I'd struck the nail on the head.

And then it hit me. The Edge mantra. *Break your own rules.*

'Why don't you remind me what you answered for question one, Kate?'

I stilled for a second, aware of a buzzing across my scalp as he watched me flip back to the start of the test.

1. I don't like confrontation and avoid it where possible.

I'd answered (b) This is sometimes like me. But that didn't really mean anything. Did it?

'If it helps at all, these questionnaires are strictly confidential, Kate. Perhaps I should have mentioned that at the beginning.'

I flipped back to the sex question. I felt embarrassed by it, exposed. But at the same time . . .

'You're going to read it,' I told him.

'Because that's my role here.'

'Would *you* answer this question?'

He seemed to think for a moment about what the most diplomatic response could be. 'I'm not the one applying for a job, Kate.'

And I supposed that was the point, wasn't it? I wanted to work here, or at least have the option of working here. Maggie had told me again and again what a great opportunity this was for me. I knew she was right. And if this was one of the hoops I was expected to jump through . . .

'It doesn't apply to me,' I said, more quietly this time.

Joel faltered, as if he wasn't sure how to respond to that, but then before he could settle on something to say, I shook my head and circled (a) This is not like me.

The questions that followed were equally crass and bizarre.

27. Recreational drugs help me to relax.

28. I have been violent on occasion.

29. I discriminate against others based on their ethnicity or religion.

I kept my head down and circled (a) This is not like me to them all. I thought I had a handle on what was going on now. It seemed to me that Joel was seeking to provoke a response. Perhaps some candidates would flatly refuse to answer his questions whereas others might just blindly tick their responses without querying the test at all. But the way he'd interacted with me, responding to how I'd challenged him, told me those would have been the wrong moves to make. I also suspected this was the main reason why he'd wanted me to fill out the questionnaire in his presence and I began to feel a growing confidence about how I'd handled things.

On the final page there was one last question.

30. I view psychometric tests as a waste of my time.

I laughed faintly, shaking my head.

'Can't say I'm not intrigued by what you're going to answer to this one,' Joel said.

I smirked, tapping the end of the pencil against my palm to prolong the moment, then again circled (a) This is not like me.

'Are you sure about that?' he asked me.

'I'm sure.'

'Do you need any more time to look back over any of your answers? Or do you have any other questions or notes you'd like to add?'

'No. I'm finished.'

I held his gaze as I butted the pages back together and slipped them inside the plastic pocket. After placing the pencil on top, I went to push everything across the surface of the desk towards him when he raised a hand and stopped me.

'No, that's OK, Kate. You hold on to it for now. Let's get down to it, shall we? Why don't you tell me about yourself?'

10

Joel watched Kate's pupils flick upwards and to the left. Information recall. Here came the prepared response.

'Well,' she said, 'I've always been passionate about connecting and communicating with other people. After gaining an Air Cabin Crew Diploma at college, I worked for four years as a flight attendant on international and transatlantic flights. I loved the lifestyle, and it was an exciting and rewarding career, but I realized I wanted to change course and so, after spending three years studying for a communications degree via distance learning, I applied for and secured a training position as a PR assistant with MarshJet. My work focused on promoting their aeroplane manufacturing business across the world, competing with the likes of Boeing and Airbus, and I rose through the ranks to an Account Manager role. Since then I've also worked as an Account Manager at Simple PR, growing brands and helping to drive sales for a variety of travel companies. Now I'm looking for a new challenge in a more dynamic, higher profile field, which is why I'm so interested in working as an Elite Account Manager at Edge.'

No surprises there. It was basically a rehash of the statement she'd placed at the beginning of her CV. Again, instead of focusing on what she was saying, Joel took the opportunity to study what she was doing instead.

He logged her eye movements and facial expressions. The pauses she took between speaking. He noticed that she was maintaining eye contact, even as she withdrew her hands, and he sensed it was bothering her that he hadn't accepted the questionnaire back from her yet.

'That's a very detailed answer, Kate. I can see you've done your research and preparation.'

He let that hang, careful now to convey just the right impression of being mildly vexed and disappointed by her, as if she'd spoiled the fun they'd been having. Tilting his head to one side, he flipped back to the beginning of her CV in the folio case. The way *he* responded physically was another tool in his arsenal. He could use his own body language to magnify any message he cared to. Such as when he wanted to throw her off her stride, make her doubt herself.

'Prepared answer or not, I mean what I say about working for Edge,' she told him. 'I think I could make a real impact here.'

Interesting.

When he glanced up, her brow was furrowed, her lower jaw extended. A fighter's pose. Maybe this would be more of a challenge than he'd thought.

'You mentioned that you enjoyed being a flight attendant.'

'I did.'

'What did you like about it?'

Her eyes went up and to the left again. Another prepared answer, even after he'd signalled it wasn't a good strategy

48

for her. That was also interesting. It confirmed to him that she was faking what confidence she had.

'All the things you would expect. I liked to travel. I enjoyed flying. But mostly I enjoyed it for the connections I made with the passengers and my colleagues. It was fun putting a smile on people's faces.'

'And the discount travel?'

'That helped. We had a similar scheme at MarshJet. It's one of the perks that comes from working for a company that supplies passenger planes to many of the world's leading airlines.'

'You miss it?'

'Sometimes I do.' *There.* Her eyes went misty, as if she was looking inwards. It was a classic indicator of an honest, instinctive response. 'I miss being in the air. I miss the sensation of take-off and the thrill I got from seeing people reach their destinations. Mostly I worked long haul, and often the people flying with us were taking their one holiday of the year, or travelling to catch up with family. I liked being part of that.'

'Were you ever scared?'

Hesitation.

'No.'

A lie.

An obvious one. He felt a small pulsing behind his thorax, like the throb from an invisible pacemaker.

'Any near misses? Emergency landings? Technical faults?'

She bit her cheek and he saw how the colour instantly drained from her face. She was naturally pale and there was a blue tincture of veins curled up at her temple. If he watched closely, he was pretty sure he could see when her pulse spiked.

'No.' Her voice quavered. 'I was lucky.'

'Speaking of MarshJet, I don't know if you happened to catch the news today, but they were saying—'

'I saw it.' Her eyelids flipped down. Her mouth closed. A trap slamming shut.

Joel felt another hot buzz in the middle of his chest. He could have let the sensation spread, but he dampened it down. Controlled himself.

'Needless to say, I'm as interested as anyone else in seeing how the court trial turns out.'

Now she lifted her chin, straightened her shoulders. A classic reset position. He could see she wanted him to move on. So he did. Momentarily.

'Why the change to PR in the first place, Kate?'

Light bloomed in her pupils, as if she thought she'd made it back to safe ground. 'I think it was really the creative side of PR that appealed to me. Plus I love to organize things. I'm good at keeping on top of projects, sticking to budgets.'

'And by working at MarshJet you continued to work in the airline industry. It was a logical move.'

He dropped his gaze and watched through the glass surface of the desk as she pulled her hands in towards her waist. A defensive impulse. She was picking at her thumbnail, too.

Good. There was definitely something there.

'Yes, it was logical. They were looking for someone who could talk the language of flying with clients and journalists without geeking out. Several of my colleagues were former flight crew, too.'

'Tell me about some of the campaigns you worked on.'

'The most high-profile campaign I helped to develop and implement surrounded the launch of our CruiseFlyer super jumbo. At the time it was the world's largest, most fuel-efficient passenger plane. I helped to secure global coverage in the trade and general press.'

'What else?'

'I was heavily involved in helping to promote our existing fleet of mid-sized passenger jets to a number of European airlines. I also spearheaded a campaign to highlight MarshJet's green credentials.'

A hanging pause.

'And the cabin air scandal? What was your involvement in that?'

She raised her chin, the tangle of blue veins pressing against her skin.

'I did my job. We had evidence demonstrating that our planes were safe and I was part of the team that communicated that. As I said, I'm aware of the ongoing court case, but it's really not something I'm in a position to comment on.'

11

Friday 5.47 p.m.

My temples were pounding. I could feel a clammy coolness at the back of my neck. Somehow things had started to go wrong. Joel's attitude towards me had changed. Or maybe it was me? Perhaps Joel had picked up on my discomfort, amplified it back to me.

It was always going to be tricky for me to talk about my time at MarshJet, but I'd tried to handle things the best way I could. I hadn't evaded Joel's questions, but I had made it clear the court case wasn't something I wanted to discuss.

Not that I didn't get why he would be interested. I also understood that perhaps he thought I could give him an inside track.

For most of the past week, the press had been running stories about how the family of a former flight attendant named Melanie Turner were suing her ex-airline employers, alongside MarshJet, in the High Court in London, in a test case backed by the unions that represented pilots and cabin crew.

Before her death, Melanie had suffered from acute joint pains, headaches and cognitive degeneration that her family believed had been caused by regularly breathing contaminated cabin air. As with other aeroplane manufacturers, the systems on board MarshJet planes used compressed air taken from aircraft engines to maintain cabin pressure. Melanie's family, and the unions backing them, argued that this re-cycled air contained poisonous fumes, and that long-term exposure to it on MarshJet's planes had caused Melanie's illnesses – as well as the acute health problems suffered by hundreds of other pilots and crew.

Whether or not the claims could be proven in court, the personal tragedy that Melanie's family had endured (and my heart went out to them) wasn't something I wanted to dwell on or speculate about, least of all in a job interview. I hoped that was something Joel could respect. It was definitely some-thing I wanted to move on from.

'What do you say we go for a speed round, Kate? A few more general questions.'

I shifted in my seat. 'OK.'

'Where do you hope to be in five years from now?'

A dose of endorphins shot through me and, for a brief moment, I relaxed. For a company that was so hot on innov-ation, the question was surprisingly mundane. But then my doubts swept back in. Wasn't the question a bit *too* mundane? Even though Joel was still watching me closely, I had the worrying sense that he'd mentally checked out, as if his mind was on other things again.

'For now, I'm keen to develop my expertise, maximize my media contacts and share best practice by managing a team in a forward-thinking, progressive agency with global reach. In five years, I'd like to think that I'll have proved myself worthy of further progression, perhaps to a role as an Account Director.'

And . . . breathe.

'I'm glad you didn't tell me you'd like to be sitting on my side of the desk, Kate. What do you think is your greatest strength?'

'My curiosity. I like meeting new people, learning new things, having new experiences and facing new challenges. It's that drive that has brought me here today.'

'Greatest weakness?'

'As you know, my experience to date has been focused on the travel industry, and while I'm applying for a role here as an Elite Account Manager focused on the travel brands you represent, down the line I'd love to explore working in connected areas. I think new experiences and fresh challenges can only make me a better publicist and I can't think of anywhere better for me to spread my wings than at Edge.'

He stared at me without moving. 'And how about personally?'

'I drink too much caffeine.'

That seemed like a safe response. It was an answer that didn't really mean anything. The kind of fun response Joel had seemed to respond to before. Except that now he was peering at me as if maybe it *did* mean something.

'Yet you said no to tea or coffee when I offered it to you earlier?'

'That's because right now I'm working on improving myself.'

I reached for my glass of water and took a sip as if to cement the point. I wanted to distract him, get him to change tack, but instead he steepled his fingers and leaned forwards over the desk towards me, looking much more serious all of a sudden.

'I won't lie to you, Kate. Edge are without question the best at what we do. We work for some of the biggest firms and the wealthiest clients in the world. I think we can both acknowledge this would be a big step up for you, although there's no reason why that can't be a good thing. The point I'm trying to make is that in order to be the best, we have to hire the best and work with the best. Right now, we have a role to fill and we've been searching for the perfect candidate. I think you may be that candidate. So perhaps now is the time to cast aside all the nonsense we could waste time on and focus on the only thing that really matters here: what is it that's so special about *you*?'

12

Joel maintained his intensity as Kate set her glass down.
She looked perturbed, as if she no longer had any idea what
to make of him, which was exactly what he wanted.

'I think that's a difficult question for me to answer without
sounding like an egomaniac,' she said carefully.

'Right now isn't the time to be coy, Kate.'

'OK.' She nodded, gathering herself. 'Then I would say
that I'm dedicated. I work hard. I come up with innovative
ideas and I always push them as far as I can. At Simple, I've
worked with our clients at identifying product placement
opportunities and fresh social media campaigns that have
led to significantly increased levels of business. With bigger
brands, household names, I believe I could achieve great
results at Edge.'

He watched her without responding, letting the pause go
on so long he could tell she was debating whether to fill it
or not. The pattern in her answers was blindingly obvious
to him now. He'd been able to tell from the very beginning
that she'd read one of those corny books on interview technique. She'd been concise. She'd given an example of
something she'd achieved. She'd brought it back to Edge.

This time, when he leaned backwards, he scrubbed a hand

over his face and took a prolonged glance at his watch. Time to crank things up a notch.

'What skills do you think a good publicist needs, Kate?'

'Enthusiasm. Commitment. I think you have to be a very organized person. You need to be able to think strategically. You also need resilience. And creativity, as I've mentioned.'

'What else?'

'Um . . . ?'

'Do you think you have to be a good liar, for instance?'

'A liar?'

'Yes.'

'I . . . No, I think you have to be able to convey a level of enthusiasm for a product or a client you don't always feel, but—'

'Lying, in other words.'

His gaze bored into her. Her lips moved and he could see she was reckoning with how to respond, but he pressed on before she could.

'What's your opinion of Hayley?'

'Hayley . . . ?'

'She brought you in here. You don't remember her?'

'No, of course I do. It's just that—'

'Just what, Kate?'

He saw the flash of disquiet in her eyes. She obviously understood this wasn't something he should be asking her. After a moment's consideration, she sat up a little straighter, raised her chin.

'She seems nice.'

'Does she?'

'I think so, yes.'

'And is "nice" all you think?'

'Well . . . I've only just met her, obviously. But I'm sure she's very good at her job.'

'You are? Why?'

'Because she struck me that way. You mentioned first impressions and that was my first impression of Hayley. She seemed confident in what she was doing. Relaxed. At ease.'

He drummed his thumbs against the edge of the desk, allowing more silence to develop. Did she realize that everything she'd just said was the exact opposite of the behaviour she was displaying right now? From the way she was shifting in her chair, rubbing her hands on her thighs, he was pretty sure she did. And now she glanced over her shoulder towards the door as if she was scoping out her exit.

'Why don't you tell me what you make of this place, Kate? The office layout. The pods. The refectory. All that. Your *first impressions.*'

'It's impressive.'

'Impressive. OK. You don't think it's . . . I don't know. Ridiculous?'

Again, she glanced towards the door. This time, she noticed that he'd caught her doing it and she tried to cover it up, straightening her shoulders, smoothing her hands across her skirt.

'Do *you* think it's ridiculous?' she asked him, raising an eyebrow.

'I'm asking you, Kate. I'm inviting your opinion.'

'The truth?'

'That's what I'm here for.'

Somewhere in the universe, there was a distant ringing clang.

'OK. Then I think it's an aesthetic. I think it tells your staff and anybody else who walks in here exactly what Edge is about.'

'And what *is* that, would you say?'

'That you're energetic. That you're unconventional. Fun.'

'You don't think it looks like we're wasting time?'

'That would be impossible for me to say without spending more time here. But my guess is that in any given week most of the game-type stuff doesn't get used very often.'

'It's all for show then?'

'Doesn't matter if it is. It still serves a purpose.'

'Does it strike you as sinister at all?'

She hesitated, as if perhaps she expected him to backtrack.

'You don't know, or you don't have an opinion?' he pressed.

'I'm . . . not really sure I understand what you mean.'

'Well, what I suppose I mean is that having all these areas to have *fun* and relax, all this free food, perhaps it's just a way to trick our staff into working longer hours. Like we don't want them to leave, maybe.'

'Is that what you're doing?'

He sighed and broke eye contact, glancing down at her CV again.

'Do you worry about your age, Kate?'

13

Friday 5.58 p.m.

'**Excuse me?**'

I was reeling. How had things got so off track? I'd felt as if there was a real connection between us to begin with. Now I seemed to be under attack.

'I'm asking if you think you're too old for the role, Kate. Most of the staff you passed on your way in here today are already Account Managers or Elite Account Managers with us. By the time they're your age, they'll be looking for promotions, or moving on to start their own boutique firms, maybe thinking of starting families.'

For a second, I could almost picture Mark watching from the corner of the room. I could imagine him stepping forward to interject and shield me, tell Joel he was out of line.

'I'm . . .' *Challenge him? Let it go?* 'I'm not sure that's an appropriate question.'

'Oh, it's not. Clearly.' He parted his hands. 'But it is something I'm inevitably going to weigh up when I consider if I should offer you this job, whether I choose to admit it to you or not. Personally, for what it's worth, I don't think your age is anything you need to worry about. So you're female and thirty-one. You could be twenty-five, and what's the big difference? I suppose the question is, has it become a hang-up for you?'

Actually, I was starting to think a better question was, should I punch him in the nose or the mouth?

I knew I had a choice now. I could take clear offence at his sexist attitude and needling questions. Or I could treat it as harmless conjecture, play along, try to recreate the flirty rapport we'd traded earlier.

'You're beginning to sound like you think you're my therapist.'

'Do you have a therapist, Kate?'

So I wasn't imagining it. This was targeted. It was deliberate. Not unlike some of the more out-there questions on the psychometric test, I wondered if it was a tactic that was designed to push me off balance, see how I reacted.

'If I did have a therapist, it wouldn't be any of your business.'

'No?'

'Definitely not.'

'OK.' He rolled out his bottom lip, bobbed his head. 'This company you work for at the moment. Simple PR. Do they know you're here today?'

'I took the day off.'

'But see, that's not answering my question, Kate.'

Arsehole.

'Then, no. I didn't tell them directly.'

'So just to get this straight, what you're saying is they don't know you're here today. You're lying to them.'

This again.

'I'm . . . They've been good to me. They're a small firm

and when I decided to move on from MarshJet, they basically created a role for me. I didn't want to upset them by telling them I was interviewing for another position unless—'

'Unless you get the job. I understand. But your omission is a type of lie, isn't it? You must be able to see that. They think you have a day off. They probably think you're running errands, or maybe you've gone away for the weekend, or—'

'I told them I'm having a spa day.'

'A spa day?'

'I told them I had to use up a voucher my brother had given me for my birthday. Which I do, as it happens.'

'Except not today. Because today you're here. With me.'

Me. I didn't like that. His focus should be on Edge.

There was something different about his smile now, too. Something almost taunting. His eyes seemed oddly disconnected from it, but deliberately so, as if he *wanted* me to see how insincere he was being. I sensed again that he was trying to needle me. That there was another agenda here he was working towards.

'Suppose I call them, Kate.' He nodded towards the telephone. 'Suppose I pick up that phone right now and call them and tell them you're here with me. How do you think they would feel about that?'

I instinctively tightened my hands around the arms of my chair, wondering for a second if I should treat it as a rhetorical question. But then I thought once more of the pep talk Maggie had given me. I'd told him a good PR had to be resilient.

Prove it.

'I'm sure they wouldn't be happy about it.'

'Because?'

He watched me again. Those eyes. I could feel them scrabbling over my skin.

'Because they rely on me.'

'And because you lied to them.'

'No. It's not like that. I—'

'Who *does* know you're here today?'

14

'No one,' she said. 'Other than my recruitment agent.'

Joel's blood was up. He could feel it thrumming through his veins. That burning again, mixed in with the buzzing in his chest. He was so dialled in to her now that he could tell it was another lie immediately.

But an unusual one. He had to give her that.

She didn't look up or look down. She didn't fidget, or swallow. She held herself preternaturally still. It was only in the vaguest twitching of her cheek and the very depths of her pupils that he caught the slightest hint of a tell.

She was good. Better than average, anyway. Joel had dealt with countless CEOs and board members who would have blown up at him by now. There was that one management candidate in Tokyo he'd never forget – the one who got so distressed when Joel challenged him about embellishing sales figures that he began weeping and tearing at his clothes, ripping his shirt clean open in a desperate act of corporate self-flagellation.

'Really?' he said. 'You've told me how badly you want this job, Kate. You've talked many times about how excited you are to work at Edge. And yet you're telling me you weren't excited enough to tell anyone close to you about this interview?'

He watched her lips press together as she pondered her next move. Would she admit to the lie, or double down on it?

'You seem flustered, Kate.'

'I suppose I'm just wondering what this all has to do with my ability to do the job I'm here to interview for.'

Deflection. Also interesting.

He felt a wave of heat move through him as he lowered his eyes to the folio case again, tracing his finger down over her CV. The lie about swimming was an obvious and depressingly common one, but he no longer felt the need to go there. Rather, he allowed the silence to develop for so long that she opted to fill it.

'Perhaps you could tell me something more about the details of the role I'd be doing here at Edge. If I was offered the job, I mean.'

'No, right now I'd much rather you told me about this gap on your CV, Kate.'

'I don't—'

'There's a gap on your CV, Kate. You started working for this agency, Simple, nine months ago. You stopped working at MarshJet six months before that. Now, my maths isn't brilliant, but even I can see that there's a gap.'

Silence.

She stared at him. The wave of heat pulsed outwards towards his extremities as he saw the muscles in her jaw bunch and tighten. Again, her gaze flicked to the door. A kind of desperation in it now.

'It's OK if you quit and it took you a while to land a new job, Kate. Or perhaps it wasn't your decision to leave MarshJet in the first place. You'd been with them, what, almost seven years? Maybe they – you know.'

He made a pushing gesture with the heel of his hand. A squawking noise in his throat.

He noticed that she was physically trembling now. Her lips had thinned, her nostrils were pinched.

'That wasn't what happened,' she shot back, her fingers digging into the arms of her chair.

One more nudge.

'You sound offended, Kate. I'm not sure why. Maybe you need a refresher on what my role is here today. It's my responsibility to look at the information you provided to us, and the answers you give me, and identify any areas of possible concern. Which brings us to this gap. The one I noticed. Now, it's possible you don't want to talk about it because you're embarrassed, or ashamed, or because you're hiding something, or—'

'That's enough.' The wavering pitch of her voice caught them both by surprise. 'I've played your games. But that is enough.'

'Is it? Shouldn't I be the judge of that?'

Her eyes were reddening, wet. She bit her cheek and shook her head. A wounded look of hurt and defiance on her face. Of disgust.

'My husband died,' she said.

15

Friday 6.07 p.m.

There. I'd said it.

And it hurt.

Damn him.

Hot tears pricked my eyes. There was a lump in my throat. My nails scraped against the upholstery of my chair.

I wouldn't cry in front of this man. I refused to cry in front of him.

But the emotion was welling up in me and when it hit like this – *especially* when I didn't want it to – it wasn't anything I could control.

I blinked, taking hold of my wedding ring, rolling it around and around my finger. Mark and I had chosen it together, on a weekend trip to Chicago. It was an inexpensive platinum band but there were so many memories wrapped up in it. A whole future we couldn't now share.

My eyes stung. I glanced down at my hands as if somehow they could help me to hold everything in.

'Mark was killed in the Global Air disaster,' I whispered. 'He was one of the victims.'

I still couldn't say the words out loud without wanting to scream. Mark was everything to me and now he was gone. Taken from me in the most harrowing way imaginable. His plane had gone down in the mid-Atlantic, one of 210 passengers who perished.

In the silence that followed, I waited for Joel to apologize. I expected him to act appalled, backtrack, try to repair the damage he'd done.

He did none of those things.

He just watched me without speaking, his eyes like two misted pools, no hint of contrition on his face.

That's when my anger really kicked in, hot and fast. It was the same futile rage that had engulfed me again and again since the tragedy.

I couldn't believe I'd been made to feel this way during a job interview. I should never have been put in this position.

I looked up towards the corner of the room, blinking. I bit the insides of my mouth until it stung. To think, I'd actually wanted this job. I'd wanted it for all the reasons it was going to be so hard for me to take. A radically different environment. A complete change. *Moving on.* But I didn't want it enough to be poked and prodded and turned inside out for someone else's entertainment.

'Forgive me, Kate.'

Something in the way he said it – the detached quality of his voice – told me he didn't really mean it. Not even close.

I glared at him.

It was too little, too late anyway.

Keep your dignity. You still have that.

'That was insensitive of me.' Again, his words were robotic, lacking any genuine compassion, edging towards contempt. He closed the folio case and lifted it from the desk. 'Kate,

I'm going to step out for a moment, get some paperwork, give you some space.'

My breathing had grown ragged. There was a ringing in my ears. I turned and looked away from him as he stood up from behind the desk and came around to pause beside me.

I could smell his cologne again. *Was* that the scent Mark had worn?

My head swam. I choked back tears.

Then his hand reached out suddenly and for an awful second I thought he was going to touch me, until he swerved at the last moment and lifted the plastic folder containing my answers to the psychometric test.

'Drink some water if you need to, Kate. I won't be long.'

16

Fifteen months ago

'Have a drink of water, Kate. Take your time.'

Time was the last thing I needed. I craved answers and information. I wanted someone to burst into the room and tell me this was all a horrible mistake.

Staring at the water in the glass in front of me, I tried to shut out everything else. My body felt rigid with terror and shock, my heart swollen painfully. My hand was clutching my mobile phone so tightly I could hear the plastic creak.

'This can't be happening,' I murmured.

'We were only notified moments ago, Kate. There's nothing in the media yet and the information we have from the airline is sketchy, at best. There could be other explanations, but with Mark and the others on that flight we called you in here as soon as we heard.'

I nodded vaguely, tears quivering in my eyes. Sir Fergus Marsh, the founder and majority owner of MarshJet, was sitting across his vast teak desk from me. His shirtsleeves were rolled up on his forearms, his tie loosened off. It was quarter to nine in the morning inside the MarshJet headquarters close to Gatwick, but his anguished, red-eyed expression made it look as if it was the middle of the night in a military campaign room.

Mark had been flying home on a late-night flight from New York with five other MarshJet employees. They'd been part of a pitch team sent to make a presentation to an American airline. Three of the team were colleagues of mine from PR.

There was a click to my left and Sir Fergus glanced towards the man who had just set down a phone on a breakout table in the corner of his office. Dominic North, his CFO, was rail-thin and prematurely balding with sunken eyes and a mouth that was pressed into a thin line. He was a withdrawn, taciturn figure, known for watching from the wings while Sir Fergus took the spotlight, but his presence told me how serious things were. In my time at the company, I'd learned that Sir Fergus never made any major decisions without Dominic's backing – or, as Mark sometimes cynically suggested, his say-so. The expectation among most of us was that when Sir Fergus eventually retired, Dominic would take over.

'They're checking radar again,' he said crisply. 'Still no contact from the flight deck.'

'Oh God.'

I crumpled, my body trembling uncontrollably.

Three minutes ago everything had been normal. I'd been sitting at my desk, drinking my first coffee of the day, checking my emails. Then I'd looked up to see Sir Fergus's assistant, Angela, rushing across the office floor towards me, her face blanched white. She'd handed me a piece of paper that told me Sir Fergus needed to see me. Now.

'Kate, if you need to go home, we understand,' he said, smiling his kind, grandfather smile. 'We can arrange a car. Angela can go with you.'

I blinked. Squeezed my hands tighter.

'Is there anything we can do? I don't know, a search operation, or, or . . .'

'These are all the things we're looking into. We'll do everything we can. Dominic has an inside line to the airline and the authorities. We're going to do our best to keep you up to date with what we find out.'

I unfurled my hand and checked my phone for messages again, for missed calls from Mark. My thumb shook as I tried calling him once more, swiping at my nose, tears streaking down my face.

I looked up, lost, pressing the heel of my hand to the side of my head, my phone diverting hopelessly to voicemail. In the corners of my mind, other images were pressing in. The plane roaring downwards in a fireball, spearing into the ocean, breaking apart.

'Am I going to see him again?'

'Kate. This could be nothing. An anomaly. We have to hope for the best.'

'I can't . . . I don't want to go home. Please. I want to stay here. If there's going to be information coming in, if there's anything you know, I want to hear it. I have to know.'

Sir Fergus paused and looked with concern towards his CFO. I saw Dominic hold his look, measure it, then nod back.

'OK, Kate. Stay. But if that's your decision, and only if you feel capable of helping us, then I'm afraid there's something I may need to ask from you in return. Right now, you're the only person in communications we have on site.'

17

Friday 6.11 p.m.

The soft shunt of the door closing behind Joel snapped me out my reverie, bringing me back to myself. I was sitting alone inside the cube, stunned.

It didn't feel real. None of this felt real.

Joel had to know he'd crossed a line. Forget Edge's mantra about breaking rules. I'd spent enough time on their company website to know it was impossible to miss their employee charter. They trumpeted their credentials as an ethical employer. They talked about valuing the needs of their staff. My experience today totally contradicted that. Maybe Joel was only now realizing how much trouble he could be in.

Good.

I was breathing too fast, trying to stop the tears from gushing out. I cradled my forehead. Took some deep breaths.

Control yourself.

The tumbler of water was in front of me. I reached for it shakily, raising it to my lips.

As I stared down into the trembling liquid, I allowed another vision to fill my mind. It was my favourite memory from our honeymoon: Mark cradling me in his arms on a pristine white beach. We were barefoot. Mark's white linen shirt and tightly curled hair were shifting slightly in the soft

73

sea breeze, his eyes happily crinkled against the sunlight. And the way he stroked my face – always with his thumb, always while cupping my cheek in his palm – soothed me even now.

I should get up. I should walk out of here.

What was stopping me?

Embarrassment, mostly.

In my mind's eye, I was thinking of all the young staff on the main office floor. I could picture them watching me as I tried to keep it together on my way to the exit, knowing I wasn't fooling anyone.

I flinched at a sudden, jangling noise inside the room.

The desk telephone had started ringing.

I stared at it, setting my glass down on the desk with a thump, a sudden flare of irritation burning inside me, a hot coal pressing against my breastbone.

He hasn't even diverted the phone.

Had I ever been a serious candidate?

I glanced quickly at my surroundings. The slatted blinds were still closed. The track lights shone brightly. Nobody was coming in through the door.

The phone continued to ring, and as it did, a new thought struck me, bringing with it a deep tremor of unease.

Sometimes when we're hiring, we like to use psychometric tests. Other similar techniques.

Maggie had mentioned dummy exercises to me. Hayley had dismissed that on our way up here, but was *that* what this was? I supposed it was possible this was some crazy, out-there stunt. Perhaps it was designed to break me down and build me back up again. Test my initiative.

Or it could be Joel calling to see if I was OK with him coming back in. But that didn't really seem to fit with his attitude and demeanour when he'd left me.

Answer it, or don't answer it?

My breathing was still funny. My throat felt raw and choked. I doubted I would be able to keep my voice steady if I did answer.

The phone rang on.

Then a truly nasty thought occurred to me.

Was it possible Joel had known about Mark all along? Had he been leading me to this point deliberately?

Think about it.

I knew it was standard practice for prospective employers to scan the social media feeds of job candidates. And even a cursory look at my Facebook page would reveal my posts about Mark and my membership of the support group that had been formed by the relatives of those who perished in the Global Air tragedy. I didn't update my personal feed often. There really wasn't much about my life nowadays that seemed worth sharing. I visited the Facebook memorial group even less because it hurt too much. But scroll back fifteen months and anyone could see my first, tortured posts after the plane crash, or the handful of maudlin posts on the difficult birthdays and anniversaries that had come since.

I felt wounded. Sickened.

They're a really great company to work for and we have so much fun.

But this wasn't fun.

It was cruel and exploitative.

Or perhaps the ringing phone was just a coincidence. Bad timing.

It stopped.

The silence that followed was as thin and whispery as the blood through my veins.

I was finding it difficult to think straight. If this was a test, had I failed it? Did I care?

I bit my lip and thought about Mark again, standing on that perfect white beach. The gentle caress of his thumb on my cheek. What would he say if he really could be here with me now?

And there it was. Simple as anything.

Get up and go.

Walk out with your head held high. Without looking back.

I didn't need this. Nobody needed this.

There would be other jobs and opportunities.

I rolled back my chair, got to my feet. My hands and feet were buzzing with an excess of adrenaline and nerves. All the blood seemed to have drained out of my head, leaving me weightless, giddy.

I turned and faced the door, then paused.

There was no noise at all from the other side. It was almost *too* silent.

In a flash of paranoia I pictured Joel sitting on the edge of a workstation facing the door, kicking his legs to and fro, smirking as the team surrounding him started a slow clap when I emerged.

Ridiculous.

Open the door and see for yourself.

But before I could move, the telephone started ringing again.

I tensed.

I *could* pick it up. If this was some crass, insensitive challenge, I could face it down, tell them just what I thought of their company and *then* walk out.

But a small voice of doubt murmured inside my head. If this was a test, then maybe I *shouldn't* answer the phone. Joel had talked about the leading clients and brands Edge represented. As a company, they'd value discretion and confidentiality. Would answering the phone be perceived as a misstep?

No way to tell.

And no way to win.

So I compromised.

I didn't answer the phone, but I didn't open the door to the cube, either.

Instead I raised my hand up beside my face, speared two fingers between the slatted blinds and separated them.

But Joel wasn't sitting there, waiting for me.

There was nobody out there at all.

18

Friday 6.16 p.m.

There was no movement. No noise. The ceiling lights were dimmed all across the office floor.

On the workstations in front of me, I could see that most of the desktop computers had been shut down, their monitors greyed out. A few others had the Edge logo displayed.

If I didn't know better, I could have believed that I'd somehow imagined all the people who'd been here when I'd arrived, the energy and commotion I'd seen. It was gone six now, but it still struck me as odd that the office could have emptied so quickly and so completely.

The desk phone continued ringing behind me. A jagged bleat.

Had everyone left or were they – what? Hiding?

I released the blind and stepped backwards into the cube. I didn't like this. I definitely didn't want to be alone in this office with Joel, not after the way he'd treated me.

The phone stopped ringing again but somehow the jangle seemed to echo on inside my heart.

I was going to leave now. I would grab my bag, cross the office floor with my head down and . . .

I stopped.

A groan escaped my lips.

My bag was gone. It wasn't on the floor next to my chair. Where I'd put it was now just empty space.

I whirled around, but it hadn't been moved anywhere else. It was definitely missing.

I spun back and snatched at the door handle.

In that split-second, the temperature inside the cube seemed to plunge about ten degrees.

I was staring at my hand. At the door handle that hadn't moved.

I knew what it meant, of course. I understood right away. There was no way I *couldn't* know. But somehow, my brain refused to accept it.

I pulled on the door.

I pushed on it.

It made no difference.

It was locked.

I hadn't heard a lock engage. There wasn't even a keyhole. *Why* was it locked?

I didn't let go of the handle yet. Something wouldn't allow me to let go.

I looked up, then. On instinct. My dimmed reflection stared back at me from the glazed ceiling overhead.

Turning, I gazed over my shoulder towards the soundless telephone, a slow creeping in the base of my skull – a powerful, almost primordial sense of how messed up this all was.

The call must have been intended for me. I didn't have any doubt about that now.

At last, I released the door handle. I was shaken and I

hated how the blinds were closed all around me. I didn't just feel shut in, I felt hemmed in, blinded.

Crossing to the opposite side of the cube, I parted the blinds and looked out, but all I saw were the same things I'd seen before, more or less. The dimmed ceiling lights. The abandoned workstations. Even the arcade dance machine had been unplugged and was unlit.

Again, I allowed the blinds to close and then I stepped back into the middle of the cube. My fingers brushed up against the edge of the glass desk and I withdrew them as if I'd been scalded.

Now what?

I nudged the chair I'd been sitting on to one side. It rolled on its plastic castors and bumped up against the blinds, making them shiver.

There was a plastic rod next to each blind. A pull cord beside that. Lunging forwards, I yanked on a pull cord and kept pulling, hand over hand as the blind zipped upwards. When it was secure, I opened the next blind along and the next after that.

The three blinds I had opened gave me a view towards the refectory. Again, there was nobody there. The lights above the kitchen units were similarly dimmed. The counter surfaces were clear and wiped down.

Hayley had told me they were all heading out for a birthday celebration. Perhaps they'd left and forgotten about me.

A scratch of trepidation in the middle of my spine – like a match being struck.

Easy, Kate.

On the desk behind me, the phone began to ring again.

A strange kind of foreboding descended on me. A hot, kinetic tremor radiating out from the base of my spine.

I reached my hand out very slowly. The downy hairs on the back of my wrist were raised. When I touched the receiver my hand felt oddly deadened, almost as if it belonged to somebody else.

Answer it quickly. Like ripping off a plaster.

I lifted the receiver from the cradle and raised the receiver to my ear.

There was a small, febrile click.

'You took your time, Kate.'

It was Joel.

'What's happening?' I asked. 'Where is everyone?'

'They've left. It's the weekend.'

I reached out for the chair next to me for support. My fingers dug into the leather upholstery, compressing the spongy foam beneath.

'I want to leave now,' I said, in a voice that seemed to be coming from a very long way off – a place where reasonable, normal requests like mine could be made and granted. 'I'm not interested in this job any more.'

'Ah, well that's a problem, Kate. Because I can't let you go. Not yet.'

'Listen, I . . .' My voice wavered. *Control it.* 'Look, I'm telling you I want to leave and you have to let me out. I want my handbag back, too.'

'Why don't you sit down, Kate? You look a little shaky. I'm worried that chair is going to roll away from under you.'

He can see me.

I turned, horrified.

But he wasn't standing behind me on the other side of the glass. He wasn't anywhere.

There was just the cube I was standing in and the empty office floor that surrounded it.

A click.

Dead air.

I dropped the phone.

19

Three miles away, inside St Thomas' Hospital, close to Waterloo Station and Westminster Bridge, Kate's brother, Luke, was thinking about his sister, wondering how her interview had been, if it was over yet, hoping like crazy it had gone OK. She hadn't texted him and that worried him. It was difficult to shake his lingering doubts that going for this job had been too big a step, too soon.

Not that he'd said anything to Kate. At least not directly. He hadn't wanted to upset her or jinx the opportunity. It had been much too long since he'd glimpsed even a flicker of excitement in his little sister's eyes.

He felt a pang, the same way he always did whenever he thought of how vulnerable Kate had become since Mark had been taken from her. Like many of his patients on the cardiac ward where he'd worked for the past eight years, his sister's whole life had been ripped apart by one dreadful jolt. Before losing Mark, she'd been so confident. So *together*. Their parents' deaths had been a blow, no question, but it had forced them to grow up fast, become self-reliant. It had toughened Kate. Hardened her resolve. Luke had envied her for the way she'd struck out for what she'd really wanted in life, right from the very beginning, as soon as she could.

He'd kept every postcard she'd ever sent him from her time as cabin crew, from locations all over the world. He'd taken pride in her career in PR, her promotions and campaign successes. Her life had always seemed so big and colourful to him. It had been painful to watch it become so dreary and small.

He was snapped out of his thoughts by a listless groan from the elderly man lying in the hospital bed in front of him.

'Mr Pinner?' Luke placed his hand gently on the man's arm. 'Mr Pinner, it's Luke again. I'm just checking your levels.'

The man in the hospital bed was gaunt and slack-faced. For seventy-six years old, he was in relatively good shape. Except that his heart had abruptly stopped beating the previous day when he'd been coming down his attic stairs.

Afterwards, there was always the delayed shock. The shattering disbelief that something inside you could have failed so suddenly and so completely, mixed in with the haunting memory of the paralysing pain.

'How are you feeling?'

The rheumy eyes completed a slow creep around Luke's face without focusing. The mouth gaped but no words came out.

'The doctor says you can have something to eat now. I'm going to see if I can rustle you up some soup. Rest up, OK? I'll be back in a little while.'

Luke hung the chart on the end of the bed and wheeled his equipment trolley towards the nurses' station. There were six patients in the bay behind him, ranging from a coronary angioplasty and a stent insertion in bed one to heart failure in bed five and a post-op bypass in bed six.

A typical Friday.

He sneaked his phone out of the pocket of his scrubs and checked for messages. Still no word from Kate. He felt another low rumble of apprehension, storm clouds massing in his mind. Surely her interview was over by now?

'Pizza or Chinese?'

The question came from Barbara Okafor, the Deputy Ward Sister. Dressed in pale pink scrubs, she was sitting behind the cluttered counter with a phone hooked over her shoulder. Luke took a moment to consult the ward chart on the whiteboard in front of him before answering.

'What did Rosa say?' he asked.

'Pizza.'

'Sam?'

'Pizza.'

'Dr Summerhayes?'

'Pizza.'

'So my chances of getting Chinese are . . . ?'

'Not good.'

Luke nodded. It had become a tradition for the tightly knit team to order in food at the end of the week. If it was quiet, they'd find a private room together and hunker down for five or ten minutes. Catch up with one another. Try to blow off some steam.

Who knew? Maybe this evening there'd be a few slices left over that he could take over to Kate's place. She'd see what he was really doing, of course – checking up on her – but it would give him some cover.

'How is Anna this evening?'

He tried to keep his tone neutral but Barbara still showed him the full whites of her eyes by way of response.

'Something on your mind?' he asked her, innocently.

'If you are telling me you haven't checked on her yet, I am going to bend you over that counter and tan your backside. Don't think I won't.'

'Tempting.'

'I'm serious.'

'And I'm getting to it.'

'That girl is in love with you,' Barbara said, as if it was one of the foremost mysteries of the universe.

Luke smiled, despite himself. 'I'll look in on her.'

'Oh, I bet you will.' She reached into the mound of paperwork in front of her and handed him a chart. 'Room six is due an assessment.'

Luke feigned surprise. 'And you don't want to look into those dreamy blue eyes of his? I've seen you laughing with him, Barbara. I think you may have a crush of your own.'

'Do not make me beat you around the head with this phone.'

'I'm going, I'm going.'

Luke back-pedalled, showing her his palms.

'You didn't tell me what you wanted on your pizza,' Barbara called after him.

'Chow mein,' he called back with a wave.

Room six was one of their private rooms. Luke pushed his way inside and glanced at the middle-aged man sitting up in the bed in front of him. He was lean and athletic-looking. A reminder that appearances could be deceiving where coronary care was concerned.

Luke clicked his pen and pointed to the textbook the man had flipped closed and set down on his lap when he'd entered the room. 'How's your Portuguese coming, Mr Nicholls?'

'Better than the Norwegian I tried to teach myself last year.'

'I can imagine. You saw Dr Summerhayes this afternoon. How'd that go?'

'You tell me.'

Luke hooked his foot around a wheeled stool and rolled it closer to the bed before sitting down.

'Your figures don't look half bad.'

'For someone waiting on open-heart surgery, or a regular human being?'

'You mind if I run through a few things with you?'

'Be my guest.'

It took close to fifteen minutes to get through everything and Luke was distracted throughout. The phone in his pocket still hadn't buzzed with a message from Kate. It made him wonder if maybe he should have practised some more interview questions with her. Or perhaps the problem was that she'd been overly rehearsed.

He shook his head, tightening his grip on his pen. Applying for this fancy new job had always been a risk. A pivot point, he suspected. And if the interview had gone badly . . . Well, he feared how she might take another loss.

'Am I keeping you from something?' Mr Nicholls asked him.

'You're keeping me from a hundred things. But that's OK. We're done.'

Luke clicked his pen, stood up from his stool.

'Who's next on your hit list?'

'Pretty girl. Room four.'

'Tell her I said *olá*.'

'I will not, Mr Nicholls.' On his way out the door, Luke gestured to the call button on the side of the bed. 'If you need anything, hit that. Nurse Barbara could use the exercise.'

'I'll tell her you said that.'

'You do, and there'll be two of us needing surgery. Get some rest. It'll be a while before any of us are back with you now.'

In the corridor, Luke pulled his phone out and felt another twinge of disquiet as he stared at the empty screen. For just a second he thought about calling Kate, raising her spirits if needs be, but then it occurred to him that perhaps her interview had been delayed or it had run longer than anticipated. It would be a mistake to interrupt her. Better to give it a little while and hold off for now, he decided. Trust in his sister. In karma, too, for that matter. She deserved only good things.

20

Friday 6.21 p.m.

I ran back to the door. I rattled the handle. It was still locked. I banged on the glass with my fist. I shouted and yelled. I kicked the door with my foot.

'HELLO! IS ANYBODY THERE?'

No answer.

I banged again, louder this time.

My heart was pumping hard. Anger coursing through me.

'HELLO! ANYONE?'

Nothing.

The only sound I could hear was my own ragged breathing.

Was this a stunt – an outrageous, amped-up psychometric test – or was it something worse? Was Joel an unhinged maniac who, for whatever reason, had decided to torment me? But why *me*? I was ordinary. My life was ordinary. I think that's what I was struggling with most of all: the certainty that there had been some kind of mistake here, but that I had been caught up in it all the same.

I turned from the door. The telephone handset was dangling over the edge of the desk, swinging from its cord.

I picked it up.

On the phone, a series of printed labels had been fitted

next to the speed dial buttons. One of the labels was marked BLDG SECURITY.

I waited a looming moment, staring sightlessly through the panels of glass in front of me, my finger hovering over the button. Joel had to be watching me from somewhere out there with my bag. Would he try to stop me? After a few seconds, when he still didn't show himself, I went ahead and prodded the button.

Nothing happened.

It jolted me for a second before I realized I hadn't hung up the phone from the previous call. Quickly now, I tapped down on the cradle and pressed the button for building security again.

It made no difference.

No.

I tried the button marked RECEPTION and got the same result.

I hit 0 and that didn't work, either.

My blood ran cold. There was a metallic taste in my mouth.

It wasn't simply that there was no connection, I realized. There was no dial tone either. Just dry silence from the earpiece.

Try an outside line.

I pressed 9 and got nowhere. I jabbed it a second time. I hung up properly and waited a beat and repeated the process all over again. When *that* didn't work, I plucked the phone jack out of the base of the phone and replaced it, then ducked down and followed the cable to a socket in the floor, took it out and reconnected it.

The phone remained dead.

This is why he took your handbag. He doesn't want you to have your phone.

Something skittered across my heart – some portend of a terror I wasn't ready to face just yet. It took me a long moment to set the receiver down into its cradle again, and when I did I felt like I was dropping a pebble into the dark pit of my own deepest fear.

My skin felt suddenly waxy and numb. Something was amiss with my vision, too. My sight was vaguely blurred at the edges, as if I was watching events unfold from behind a fogged pane of glass.

Stress. Fear.

Do something. Act.

I rushed across the room and traced my fingers over the aluminium door plate, then crammed my fingertips into the gap where the latch was engaged. I couldn't reach it. It was fitted flush into the metal frame. The door unit looked solid and expensive. The hinges were on the outside of the door. There was no keyhole to pick and I didn't have any kind of tools with me inside the cube. I didn't even have the propeller pencil Joel had given me to fill in the questionnaire with. There was just the glass desk, the two chairs, the carafe and the cut-glass tumblers, the desk telephone and the track lighting above.

I spun and braced my hands on my hips, staring forwards, trying to clamp down on my fright.

I'm not claustrophobic. Normally. But I was starting to feel suffocated.

I glanced at the remaining blinds which were still closed and then I darted around the room, raising them one after the other. When every blind was up, I turned on the spot, scanning the empty office that surrounded me, searching for movement, for Joel, asking myself what my next move should be.

21

Friday 6.26 p.m.

I began feeling around the glass panels. Each one was taller and wider than I was. The panes of glass were several centimetres thick. I was pretty sure they were made of toughened safety glass.

The panels were fixed and solid. There was a sturdy black girder at each corner of the cube, and there were wide strips of colour-matched metal in between the intervening sheets of glass. The floor was polished concrete.

I completed a fast circuit of the space, running my hands over every nook and cranny, top to bottom, side to side, my breath juddering, my eyes feeling hot and swollen in my head.

I didn't find any weaknesses.

Where was Joel?

I still didn't know. I still couldn't see him. I knew it was possible he could be hiding, perhaps spying on me from behind a pillar or a desk, but deep inside, a much more disturbing explanation had occurred to me. I think the truth is I just didn't want to confront it yet.

Was he watching me remotely? Were there *cameras*?

I thought of how he'd been able to see me when I'd answered his phone call. At that stage, I'd only opened three of the blinds. And yes, he could have had a line of sight into the cube from some secret vantage point, but my guess was I would have spotted him by now.

I glanced up. The track lights glimmered above me. If there was a camera lens hidden somewhere, I couldn't see it.

The idea made my skin crawl.

It also pushed me towards a decision.

Grabbing the chair I'd been sitting in earlier, I wheeled it forwards into the corner of the cube. That placed it a metre or so away from the desk – near enough for the phone cable to stretch to when I took the phone from the desk and placed it on the chair. I then reached out and steadied the chair by the arms to stop it from swivelling, and I climbed up onto it. When I straightened carefully with the chair twisting beneath me, the top of my head was only a short distance shy of the glass ceiling.

I braced one hand on the thick metal girder nearest to me – it was braided with rivets – and reached down to slip off one of my shoes. I switched the shoe to my other hand and ducked down a second time for the phone, picking it up with the receiver still attached. The base of the phone was made of sturdy plastic. I thought it would make a reasonable hammer.

The chair squeaked and rotated under me again. I was afraid it might roll back and I could fall, but I managed to keep it steady as I placed the heel of my shoe towards the top-right corner of the pane – as close as the phone cable would allow me to stretch.

I took a breath and lined everything up.

One sharp blow.

In my mind's eye, if I got it right, the sheet of glass would drop away in one complete piece like a curtain falling from a rail.

The chair fidgeted under me. My knees were quaking.

I checked my aim again and angled my face away, hunching my shoulders.

Then I drew back the phone, squinted at my shoe one last time and—

There was a soft, metallic *click* from behind.

I spun, almost falling.

The door to the cube had popped open.

22

Friday 6.32 p.m.

I stepped down off the chair, returned the phone to the desk and slipped my shoe back on.

I looked at the door for a long moment. It was hanging ajar.

Really?

There was no way the door could have sprung open on its own. It had definitely been locked. But at the same time I hadn't seen anybody approach the cube and I couldn't see anybody close by now.

A strange thing.

Just seconds ago, I'd been desperate to break out of the cube, but now that *he* wanted me to leave, I wasn't sure that was a good idea.

My body felt locked. Stiff.

But then something else struck me.

If he could somehow open the door remotely, then could he shut it remotely, too?

I darted forwards and placed my foot into the gap between the door and the jamb. My breaths came fast and shallow.

Placing my hand against the door frame, I took a small step outside. Absolute quiet surrounded me. Eerie would be an understatement. The office floor wasn't simply empty

96

and silent. It felt desolate. When I glanced towards the floor-to-ceiling windows to my left, all I could see outside was the pale evening sky.

Out of nowhere, there came a sudden, rumbling burble to my right.

I jerked around fast, my heart slamming into my throat.

But it was only a water cooler burping up an air bubble.

Keep it together, Kate.

I was obviously going to have to do *something* here. What was it Joel expected me to do?

I didn't care.

I just wanted to leave.

I set off across the office floor in the direction of reception, threading my way between abandoned desks and filing cabinets, looking side to side, glancing backwards over my shoulder.

I almost stumbled but I didn't see anybody, and when I reached the reception area there was no sign of anybody there, either.

The neon pink sign had been turned off. The desktop computers on the reception counter were powered down. Two desk chairs had been rolled neatly against the countertop.

Standing still, listening closely, all I could hear was the drumming of my own blood in my ears.

I wanted my handbag back. I wanted to take it with me.

Forget it. Get downstairs. Get to security. Get help and come back for your bag later.

I hurried towards the industrial-style metal doors, wrapped my fingers around the handle of the door on the left, and for the briefest fraction of a second before I pulled I felt a flutter against my ribs.

The door didn't shift.

I tried the one on the right but both doors were locked fast.

I bowed my head, acutely aware in that moment of the absolute silence and enormity of the office space behind me. Of how alone I felt.

Stepping back, looking side to side, I searched for a button to press, a door release of some kind.

The only thing I could see was on my left. It was a flat metal sensor plate that looked exactly like the one on the other side of the doors I'd watched Hayley waft her key card in front of earlier.

OK, so perhaps there was a door release behind the reception counter. A button or switch of some kind for Hayley or Justin to press. That would make sense.

I ran back and looked. When I didn't see anything immediately, I shoved papers and blotters out of the way. I wheeled both desk chairs aside and ran my fingers along under the front lip of the countertop. I got down on my knees and craned my neck and looked beneath it.

No button. No switch.

I could see power cables and a printer set on a low drawer unit.

I raised my head. There were two desk phones on the reception counter. I lifted the receiver on the first phone and all I heard was dead air. No dial tone. I tried the second phone and got the same result. I punched buttons and hung up and tried again. Nothing.

The Interview

I set down the receiver, got slowly to my feet and stared at the locked doors ahead of me.

That was when the phones starting ringing. *All* of them this time. Every single phone in the office.

23

Joel watched Kate on the laptop screen in front of him.
He saw her step back from the reception counter and raise
her hand to her mouth.

He had multiple angles on her. There were cameras and
speakers wired throughout the office. Some were concealed
in ceiling panels. Others were in desk tidies, in plant pots.
Several were inside the glass cube. He could also watch
through the webcams on the computer desktops that had
been left on.

She was scared, and it didn't give him any pleasure to see
it, other than a craftsman's appreciation for a task well done.

Strange how life could turn out. There was a time – long
ago now – when Joel had been on the side of the angels. Or
so he'd believed. That was the problem with intelligence
work. You never knew exactly who was playing whom.

Eight years in, his career in the ascendancy, he'd been
pulled aside and commended on his interviewing technique.
Everyone got taught the basics. How to interpret physical
responses, ask open questions, draw out a lie. But Joel had
an innate talent for the work. He believed in his ability to
drill down to the truth absolutely. You had to, in order to
be the best.

Which is why he'd been selected for a delicate assignment. In the back halls of Whitehall, on the extreme down low, a senior civil servant had accused the Home Secretary of leaking government secrets and Joel was tasked with interviewing the government minister late at night, in her apartment, without anybody – including the Home Secretary herself – knowing he'd be there.

And what did he conclude?

She was guilty, no question. Not a shred of doubt in his mind. And that was exactly what he reported back to the boss of his boss, second-in-charge of the Service. And it was also why he was so puzzled, three days later, when the senior civil servant who'd blown the whistle was forced to quit in disgrace amid whispers of sexual harassment, while the Home Secretary had kept her job without the slightest blip to her career.

Wheels within wheels. Circles within circles. It was way above Joel's pay grade to know what kind of a deal had been struck, what leverage had been secured, but that didn't mean he had to like it. It wasn't what he'd signed up for.

He quit six months later, leaving long enough before handing in his resignation to allay any direct fears about what his exact motivations might have been. And, in the habitual way of the Service, his unspoken discretion was rewarded.

The first approach came within weeks. A friend of a friend had recommended him. How would he feel about assisting the Head of Security at one of the world's leading petrochemical companies with the task of vetting their proposed new CFO?

Joel took the job. It was what he knew, what he *excelled* at, and the pay was, frankly, obscene. Just as appealing, it was crucial to his client that Joel's role was strictly temporary and very hush-hush. No one need know who he really was, where he'd come from or what his past had been. It also offered him a way to flesh out some of his more, well, outré, untested methods and theories. No questions asked. No red lines of morality or legality to be troubled by. He had absolute freedom and control.

As it happened, the CFO didn't raise any serious concerns. There were skeletons in his closet, things he'd never told anyone before except Joel – a young man whose apartment he paid rent on (a son his wife knew nothing about) – but far from being alarmed, the company leadership tucked these nuggets away, primed for future use.

Following this success, word got around. The assignments kept coming. All of them were from private companies or wealthy individuals looking for an off-the-books solution to a particular problem – and if sometimes his old employers were pulling the strings behind the scenes, it wasn't anything Joel needed or cared to know. His focus was the UK and Europe to begin with. Later the States and Canada, and then most recently – and most lucratively – the Far East.

Until this particular task had crossed his radar, and he'd pitched for it, and been hired.

And so now here he was, *in the moment*, watching Kate debating whether or not to answer his call.

As he waited for her to make up her mind, Joel slipped on a pair of thin disposable plastic gloves and picked up the acetate folder containing the psychometric questionnaire she'd completed. Her answers were useful to him. Definitely enlightening. But then, so was the folder itself.

He angled it towards the light. And yes, there they were: several viable fingerprints and a solid, greasy thumbprint towards the bottom.

Using a length of clear plastic tape, he carefully lifted the print, then placed the tape over the home button on her mobile, pressed his own thumb down on top and unlocked her screen.

24

Friday 6.36 p.m.

I stepped out from behind the counter and moved sideways until I could look out across the office floor towards the cube. Every phone I could see was ringing simultaneously. They were maddeningly loud. Tiny lights were blinking on and off on every base station, as if I was staring at a demented mission control.

I could have ignored it. I told myself that. But the last time I'd ignored a ringing phone I'd got locked inside the cube.

I moved to the nearest workstation, flattened my palm on the desk and snatched up the phone I found there.

Silence swept in around me. I didn't say a word when I pressed the receiver to my ear.

'Kate, let me save you some time here,' Joel said. 'The phones work when I want them to work. That's all.'

My hand curled into a fist. 'Are you out of your mind? You can't do this.'

'Kate, please. Right now all I need for you to do is take a breath and calm down so we can talk.'

'You're watching me?'

'Yes.'

I turned around, the phone cable twisting with me. I was

staring so hard at my surroundings that my vision shook, but all I could see was the empty office floor and reception.

'Really, Kate. There's no need to be rude.'

My knees flexed.

I'd been holding my hand up with my middle finger extended.

Felt foolish, now.

I lowered my arm in jerking increments, aware of a puckered, tightening sensation at the back of my neck, as if some unseen person had reached out and pinched me there.

'You're going to let me out of here,' I said. 'Right now. Let me out or I'm calling the police.'

'How? You're not paying attention to me, Kate. I control the phones. You know I have your bag with me. And your mobile.'

I stilled.

My breath stopped.

Again, I didn't say anything.

Don't let him see your fear.

'That's a nice photo you have on your lock screen, Kate. I like the sweater Mark has on.'

A vague whistling inside my head.

I was gazing towards the exit doors as he said it but I was no longer really seeing them. Instead, I was picturing the image he was talking about. It was a shot I'd taken of Mark lying on the sofa in our old apartment. It had been a Sunday in November. Mark had been lazily reading the papers, wrapped up warm in a thick knitted jumper I'd bought him for his birthday. It wasn't often he allowed himself to relax like that. His hair was mussed because we'd just been for a walk to get pastries and coffee from a local bakery and it had been stormy outside. I could remember how he'd held me close to keep me warm as we'd strolled along the street.

No.

The intrusion was too much. I tightened my grip on the phone.

'You listen to me,' I told him. 'If you don't let me out of this office right now, I'm going to start screaming.'

'Then scream, Kate. Go ahead. No one will hear you. The floor above you is unoccupied. The floor below you is the machine floor. That's where all the service equipment for the building is kept. Back-up turbines. Air conditioning units. All sorts of raucous machinery. Obviously the windows in this building are reflective on the outside, which means you can't signal out. They don't open and you can't break them, either. They're designed to be shatterproof. Think about it: it's Friday evening, Kate. Most people who work in this building will be out of here soon if they haven't left already. Why do you think we got you here when we did?'

No.

Don't listen to it.

Don't get stuck on it.

But . . . who was 'we'?

Was he talking about Edge? About him and – who? Hayley? Maggie?

That didn't make sense. None of this made any sense.

What did he think this was, a fucking escape room?

'You listen to me, you freak. When this is over, I'm going to report you and Edge to every professional body I can. I'm going to use all my press contacts to get this story out far and wide.'

'Kate. Please. You're shrieking. And this isn't about your interview. It's not about a job. There is no job. This is about you.'

I swayed.

Hold on.

My ears whooshed.

He's just messing with you. He wants you to react.

I blinked tears from my eyes and looked up at the ceiling, catching my breath. It took me a few seconds to acknowledge that what I was actually doing was looking for any trace of cameras or microphones.

I couldn't see anything but that didn't mean they weren't there.

I pressed a hand to my forehead, fighting another spell of wooziness. I tried to ward off my panic. To *think*.

Was it still possible this was an exercise of some kind? I'd been clinging to that idea, but my grip on it was slipping. The thing was, if this *wasn't* real, then the whole thing was a sham. He was lying. And if he could sell me a big lie like this, then he could lie about anything.

I wondered. Was the floor above me *really* unoccupied? I knew it was possible. The press reports about the building had told me that. But I didn't know for sure *which* floors were occupied or not.

Shout. Do it now.

'HELLO! HELLO, IS ANYBODY THERE? CAN ANYBODY HEAR ME?'

I waited, then shouted again, louder this time.

'HELLO! SOMEBODY!'

My heart pounded erratically. I pressed my closed fist to my chest. Held on. It was what I did when I was running flat out in the mornings. Pushing myself harder, faster. Making myself stronger. Riding out my pain. When I'd told my grief counsellor about it, she'd hoisted an eyebrow and told me that a compulsion to run was a better coping mechanism than most of the addictions she'd seen. 'Think of it this way,' she'd told me. 'You're probably in the best shape of your life even while, mentally, you've been at your lowest ebb.'

'HELLO!'

There was still no response from above me or below me, or anywhere else for that matter.

There was no indication that anybody could hear me.

Except Joel.

'Kate, save your energy. Here is what I need you to do for me. I need you to go back inside the cube and sit down and wait for me. When you've done that, I'll join you and we can talk.'

25

Friday 6.40 p.m.

No. Not happening. No way. I wasn't going to go back inside that cube. Not after Joel had locked me in there before. I wasn't going to do *anything* Joel told me to do.

I set the phone down and turned to the exit doors again. I moved towards them and barged them with my shoulder. Pain lit up across my side. I kicked at them. I drummed on the wired safety glass with my fist. The doors were surrounded by metal panels. No way through.

I stopped.

OK. Just supposing for a second there was no release button – or at least not one I could easily find – I knew for a fact there was a sensor plate. So to get out all I needed to do was find a key card.

One key card.

I jogged back behind reception and swept my eyes over the counter. I lifted the computer keyboards. I upended the pencil pots. I ducked and checked the drawers in the unit under the printer, but there were only reams of printer paper inside.

I straightened, fighting a sudden head rush, and turned to face the quartet of thin metal lockers behind me. I opened them one after the other, the metal hinges squeaking and clicking.

I saw typical office detritus. More printer paper. Headed paper. Comp slips. Envelopes of all dimensions and sizes. Pens. Paperclips. Ink cartridges.

No key cards.

OK, that was weird, but perhaps Joel had already checked these places, too. But even supposing that was the case, he couldn't have checked *everywhere*. There had to be a stock of key cards around somewhere. It wasn't as if the people who worked here wouldn't mislay or forget their access cards from time to time.

Unless . . .

Was it possible that everything had been planned in such exacting detail because they'd done this before? Because it *was* a recruitment exercise?

There had to be a way to open the exit doors.

It wasn't possible there was no way to open them.

I returned to them and studied them again for a long moment, then cupped my hands against the narrow panel of wired safety glass in the left-hand door. I peered out. The lights in the vestibule were dimmed in the same way as the lights across the main office floor, casting the vestibule in a swampy green hue. I could still make out the topiary plants and the trio of elevators with their burnished steel doors, looking as if they were sunk inside an aquarium. All three of the elevators were closed. I could also see a plain fire exit door to the right.

I took a step back and glanced at the sensor plate again, my eyes tracking left until I glimpsed something fitted to the bare brick wall. A fire extinguisher. It was painted a bright, glossy red.

I kept staring at it, imagining Joel monitoring my progress from his stupid cameras, and then I strode towards it. A plastic tether held it in place. I loosened the strap and heaved the extinguisher clear in both hands. It was so heavy that I immediately dropped it to the floor with a *thunk*. The base was solid metal. It looked capable of causing serious damage.

Cupping my palm under the handle, I dragged it behind me back to the doors. The base scraped and knocked across the concrete flooring. Once I had it where I wanted it, I puffed air and pushed my hair clear of my face, then planted my feet shoulder-width apart, bent my knees and hoisted the extinguisher up by my shoulder.

My body shook as I bore its weight and then I took a short, truncated test swing, lining the base of the extinguisher up with the panel of safety glass in the left-hand door.

I pulled the extinguisher back again, arms cocked.

Joel had unlocked the doors to the cube when it became obvious I was about to smash the glass. I waited for him to do the same thing now.

And waited.

The extinguisher was getting heavier. My arms quivered.

I bit down on my lip, contemplating the ceiling for a long moment, imagining the cameras I felt sure were pointed at me, focused in on my expression. I arched an eyebrow, as if I was asking him: *Do you really want me to do this?*

For a second, it was as if a part of my mind split off to an alternate reality. I could almost imagine a noisy klaxon sounding, followed by Joel and his team of back-up staff emerging from the wings, clapping their hands, telling me

I could put the fire extinguisher down now because the test was over.

But none of that happened.

There was no response of any kind.

There was just me, holding the fire extinguisher, gradually realizing Joel was calling my bluff.

OK, if that's really how you want to play it.

I faced forwards, stretched my neck to one side, then the other, and lashed out with the extinguisher.

26

Friday 6.45 p.m.

I closed my eyes at the last moment. The impact jarred me. The doors boomed and juddered.

But when I cracked my eyes open again, the glass panel had only just splintered and held.

I tried again. And again. I watched, grimacing, as the panel flexed and splintered. Tiny splits and chips appeared. But the sheet of glass wouldn't give out completely. It wouldn't collapse.

My fingers ached and there was a dull buzzing in my hands – as if I'd been operating a power tool.

I exhaled and lowered the extinguisher down by my side, pushing at the splintered, wired glass with the spread fingers of my hand. Again, there was the slightest flex but I couldn't push the glass fully out.

In any case, the glass panel was so tall and narrow there was no way I could reach more than my arm through the gap even if I broke it. I definitely couldn't climb through to the other side, and I couldn't remember seeing a release on the reverse of the doors that I could make a grasp for. Without a key card I'd still be stuck.

I swiped the back of my hand across my mouth. The doors were thick metal, but maybe the lock that secured them was vulnerable. There was a glint of polished steel in the seam between both doors at about waist height. A bolt of some kind.

I looked up at the ceiling once more, my jaw fixed. This time, I didn't expect Joel to intervene. I think I just wanted him to see the disgust on my face.

Turning sideways on, I gripped the extinguisher by my hip, let out a scream and rammed it forwards at the middle of the doors.

The force of the blow lifted me off my feet.

And achieved almost nothing. It was like hitting a wall.

'Shit.'

My shoulders fell and I dropped the extinguisher onto the ground with a clang. There was a sweaty film on my face now. Strands of hair were adhered to my brow and cheeks. My jacket was rucked up and the tails of my blouse were hanging out.

All right then.

I spun and stumbled around behind the nearest set of workstations. I shoved chairs aside, grabbed up phones and tried for an outside line. I opened and shut drawers and cupboards, searching for a key card. I pushed clutter out of the way.

And all the while, one thing Joel had said to me repeated in my mind.

This is about you.

I didn't believe it. There was nothing about me that could lead anyone to treat me this way. There was nothing I had done.

I thought back over our interview, in case there could

be anything in my application or something I'd said that could have triggered Joel to behave in this way. He'd mentioned the MarshJet court case a couple of times, but that was hardly surprising given my background with the company. And while I got that it was an emotive issue, particularly for the crew who claimed to have suffered serious ill-health from flying on MarshJet planes, my connection to it was tenuous, at best. I wasn't on any witness list. I hadn't been contacted about the case by the defence or the prosecution.

Was there anything else? I couldn't think of anything. Nothing that could have caused offence.

Which just left me again. And Edge.

The idea that this was personal . . . That it was targeted . . .

I couldn't see it.

And then there were the cameras and the elaborately rigged phones. There was the way everyone else had left the office as if on cue after my interview had commenced. It certainly felt as if the entire thing had been orchestrated ahead of time. Faked?

I stopped and looked at the mess I'd created. I hadn't found a key card anywhere. Hadn't found anything even *resembling* a key card. And didn't that seem really odd?

In front of me, the Edge logo was displayed on a nearby computer monitor.

'OK,' I muttered to myself. 'OK.'

I leaned forwards over the keyboard and nudged the mouse. If I could just message someone, access the web . . .

But the moment the screensaver disappeared, a prompt for a username and password appeared in its place.

I growled and shook my head, typed in some random letters and used the mouse to click on the login icon.

The hard drive hummed and churned, then the screen blinked and redrew itself and an error message appeared along with a fresh login prompt.

I cursed and flipped up the keyboard. I checked behind the monitor. If only I could find a Post-it note or a scrap of paper with a username and password scrawled on it . . .

That's when I remembered the clean desk policy Hayley had mentioned. She'd told me that any confidential notes had to be shredded. It was company policy and I didn't doubt that they were equally hot on computer security.

I rifled back through the drawers and papers I'd previously searched anyway. I even checked the bins.

Nothing.

I slammed a drawer closed, then stood with my hand pressed to my forehead, frustration gnawing at my insides. Slowly, I turned my head and looked towards the glass cube again.

What if I did what Joel wanted? What if I went in there and sat down?

And let him trap you inside.

A whole combination of factors wouldn't allow me to do that. Pride. Anger. Fear. Distrust. I thought about how unpleasant Joel's behaviour had been when I'd told him about Mark and my anger bubbled up again, filling my throat.

I didn't want to be in a confined space with Joel. I didn't want to concede *anything* to him. And besides, even supposing he kept his word and came to talk to me, there was no way of telling if he'd let me out of this office. I definitely wouldn't feel safe.

I turned back and looked around me, thinking, searching, and my eyes drifted back to the Edge mantra that I'd first seen when I'd entered reception: *Break your own rules.*

OK, Joel, I thought, *what if I break something else?*

27

Friday 6.49 p.m.

I stopped what I was doing, turned my back on the exit doors and strode towards the full-height windows in front of me, on the north side of the building. I knew they overlooked the main entrance. I also remembered there was a cantilevered glass canopy extending out over the revolving glass doors.

I got faster, madder, jogging and then running until the office became a blur at my sides.

On my way past the final group of workstations I reached out for the backrest of a stray chair. I didn't slow or break my stride. I dragged it behind me, the chair trundling and banging against the floor. When I reached the wall of glass I set my feet and swung hard.

The chair swept through the air, arcing wildly. The base was solid metal and hard plastic. It struck the window with a mighty *whump*.

I don't know what I expected, exactly. I knew the windows were hi-tech. Joel had told me they were shatterproof.

I suppose what I *thought* would happen was the glass would at least splinter and crack, not unlike the wired glass panel in the door I'd attacked with the fire extinguisher. Because shatterproof, to me, suggested that the window *would* break but the fragments would be contained by some kind of – I don't know – film or clever chemical property in the glass. Held in place, yes. But weakened, potentially.

Wrong.

The chair bounced off the glass as if I'd swung it at a transparent rubber wall. My arms juddered. The panel deflected and shivered but that was all.

I lowered the chair and stared at the glass. I touched it with my fingertips. It wasn't cracked or splintered from within. It wasn't even chipped. When I looked down below, there was nothing to suggest that anyone on the street had seen or heard anything.

Maybe if I hit it harder . . .

With both hands, I picked up the chair again and swung it behind me to my left, taking an even bigger, even more exaggerated wind-up. I swivelled at the waist and wrenched my spine around fast, like a tennis player ripping a backhand cross court.

I yelped.

The chair bounced back off the glass so hard it hit me square in the chest. I gasped and clutched my hands to my breastbone. I doubled up and wheezed.

My chest hurt when I inhaled. My skin burned and tingled under my blouse. Very slowly, I uncurled my body and raised my head.

The chair was down on the ground. Two of the castors were broken. One of the plastic armrests had split and come loose.

The glass panel appeared completely untouched.

28

Fifteen months ago

A glass door slid open in front of me. The press briefing room at Gatwick Airport was jammed. Every seat was occupied. There were reporters standing in the aisles and leaning against the walls with notebooks in their hands. Television cameras, camera flashes and a gaggle of microphones obscured my view of the dais at the front of the room, where Sir Fergus was sitting to the far left of a quintet of senior figures from Global Air and Gatwick. Dominic North was some distance away to my right, close to another door, his spindly arms folded, head raised, eyes scowling and watchful as he listened to every word that was being said.

At the forefront of the dais, Global Air's CEO, a harried-looking woman in a dramatic red trouser suit, was standing in front of a television that featured a map of Flight GA1501's last-known location. The tiny white plane icon hovering over the vast blue expanse of the Atlantic flashed like the world's most forlorn beacon. Staring at it, I felt for a moment as if it was the only thing that tethered me to Mark right now. The panic and the fear were rising up in me, choking me. Every time I inhaled, it was as if there was no air in the room. Sweat trickled down my spine.

I should never have come here, I realized. I must have

been out of my mind to say yes. They should never have asked.

'. . . And that is all the information we have for you now. Please understand that this situation is fluid and it is fast-moving.'

I had to get out of here. I had to go.

I glanced towards Dominic but he didn't see me – or chose not to. His gaze was locked on the dais. He'd dedicated his entire life to MarshJet and Sir Fergus, and right now, despite the cool composure he was trying to project, I sensed he was afraid he was watching everything they'd built together fall apart.

That was when the woman in the red power suit cast her hand towards the back of the room where I was attempting to push my way between people, a clutch of hastily compiled documents wilting in the sweat from my hands.

'If you have follow-up questions, we have representatives from Global Air and MarshJet here to assist you. They can advise you on technical matters and any other details you may need, but for now, please, we have work to do and we thank you for your understanding.'

The figures on the dais stood up, chairs scraping, micro-phones crackling. Sir Fergus followed the others out of the room without looking back.

'Dominic!'

He didn't hear me. And before I could reach him, the pack of journalists were on me, pressing in, talking over one another, shouting questions, snatching print-outs. I went up on my toes, but all I could see was the back of Dominic's balding head as he strode out of the room, checking his phone.

'A number of pilots have raised previous concerns about the software systems on the CruiseFlyer, in particular the . . .'

'Can you tell us how the black box recorders are designed to work, what depths they'll function to . . .'

'In the case of an accident like this, the chances of survival are close to zero, but do you have any data to suggest . . .'

'I'm sorry,' I mumbled. 'I can't . . . I just have to . . .'

I dropped my papers, spun around, burst out through the door.

But the corridor was empty. There was no sign of Dominic or anybody who could help me.

The air was even thinner out here. It was as though I'd passed through a space lock into a vacuum.

Black dots swarmed before my eyes. The pressure built inside my lungs. I flattened my hand against the wall in front of me and bent at the waist, the panic suffocating me, the commotion from the press room roaring and blurring like signal interference from a mistuned radio as I raised my hand to my chest and closed it over my heart.

29

Friday 6:51 p.m.

I put my fingers to the window I'd attacked with the chair, physically jolting myself out of my memories, and looked down past the toes of my shoes towards the glass canopy above the main entrance to the building.

Thirteen storeys up.

A flutter of vertigo. My breath condensed on the pane.

I'd felt abandoned and alone on that day fifteen months ago – I'd quit without ever returning to the MarshJet head office – and I felt the same way again now.

People were moving around below me. Distant and ant-like. I could see black cabs and red London buses speeding up and down Ludgate Hill. There were cars and motorbike couriers and cyclists, some of them sweeping up the street opposite.

Nobody looked up at me. And if they did look up, they wouldn't see me. All they'd see was the golden gleam of the evening sun reflecting in the glass.

I shut my eyes for a second, then turned and looked to my right, at the Victorian pub across the street with its stained-glass windows and vintage sign. My insides shrank. Maggie was in there waiting for me, I told myself. She knew what time my interview had started and she had to be wondering where I was.

She can help you.

Because Maggie wasn't the type to just hang around, I didn't think. She'd told me she was driving out of London tonight. And she was pushy – the kind of person who would phone Edge and ask if I was still in my interview. Or maybe she'd leave the pub and return to 55 Ludgate Hill, ask the security team on duty if I'd come back down and signed out of the building.

I didn't think she'd go without me. I'd been flaky in the run-up to this interview and she'd stuck by me. I could rely on her, I thought. *Hoped.* But how much longer would it be until she got impatient enough to check? I didn't want to be on my own here with Joel for even a second longer than I had to be.

Raising my hand to my chest, I rubbed at the spot where the chair had struck me, my chest aching with a sensation not unlike the punch of grief that had felled me that day Mark's plane had gone down.

Just along from the pub, a line of people were queueing at a bus stop. I stared closer. Most of them looked like workers from the nearby offices or the small retail shops, coffee outlets and restaurants that serviced them.

I lowered my hand, then spun away from the window. After looking around me for a couple of seconds, I moved towards the nearest workstation, opened a drawer, searched inside.

My hand settled on a black marker pen. I yanked off the lid. The chemical scent was strong and heady. The pen had a thick, blunt nib, saturated with ink.

Turning back to the window, I drew a giant capital H on

it, from about head-height down to my knees, the nib squeaking against the glass. Stepping over the broken chair, I then drew a huge backwards E in the next window to my left. I added a large backwards L and a P in the next two windows along.

I stopped and stared down at the queue of people, holding my breath.

Nobody was looking up at me.

Nobody noticed.

I bounced on my toes, impatient, dropping the pen and looking around me again. There were two plug outlets sunk into the floor by my feet, and there were desk lamps on every workstation I could see. I ran back and collected two lamps, unplugging them and then plugging them into the floor sockets, switching them on and angling the bulbs at the glass.

I stood there, waiting some more, the glare of the bulbs warming my skin. Most of the people in the bus stop queue were staring down at their phones. They looked stoop-shouldered, exhausted, bored. None of them cast even a cursory glance my way.

I banged my fist on the glass.

'Come on, someone. Please.'

I checked anxiously behind me for Joel, then stared at the front door of the pub again for any sign of Maggie, and when I still didn't spot her, I stepped over the chair to my right, looking off towards the ancient dome of St Paul's and the crucifix atop it. Beyond St Paul's was a sprawling cityscape of office blocks and construction cranes, distant skyscrapers, ancient buildings, roads and railway lines, patches of greenery. Another time, in different circumstances, I might have enjoyed this view. It was supposed to have been one of the perks of working here.

Not now.

Ducking low, I adjusted the angles of the desk lamps again. I checked my message, checked the street.

A man who had been walking away from St Paul's had stopped and was gaping up towards the peak of The Mirror, shielding his eyes with his hand.

He was standing on the opposite pavement, dressed in a garish shirt, cargo shorts and white training shoes. There was a camera looped around his neck and what looked like a pamphlet or guidebook in his other hand. As I watched him, he raised the camera and aimed it upwards.

I stilled, waiting for him to see my message, pause, lower his camera, peer closer, signal to somebody, point or shout.

But he just snapped his photograph, then lowered his camera, consulted his map for a second and walked on again.

I stared after him, feeling something drain out of me, disbelief percolating through my veins.

My message hadn't worked. It couldn't be seen.

Maybe later, when it gets darker . . .

But I didn't want to be here when it got darker. I didn't want to be here, full stop.

Fighting against a clutch of panic, I allowed myself one last lingering look at the pub, hoping, I suppose, that Maggie might somehow sense me watching for her, cross the street, come to my aid – but when that didn't happen I finally abandoned the window and hurried on around the perimeter of the office.

I paced by the fake hot-air balloon basket and the shell of the campervan with its padded vinyl seating inside. I brushed my fingers across the crackled surface of the old carousel horses. I passed the swing and the gazebo entwined with its fake plastic flowers.

Outside, I now had a line of sight down over Fleet Street towards Trafalgar Square and the people and traffic darting this way and that. The view rotated away from me as I cut away to my left, passing between the arcade dance machine and the ping pong table towards the climbing wall. Two inert, brightly speckled climbing ropes were threaded through a pulley system in the ceiling. Both ropes were fastened to webbed climbing harnesses at the other end. I touched one of the ropes and moved on, then pulled up short.

I was staring into an area of mostly empty office space that extended back behind the brick partition wall running behind the refectory. A handful of empty workstations had been pushed to one side. Some spare chairs had been stacked one on top of the other. In the middle of the space, next to one of the exposed metal pillars supporting the ceiling, I could see a large beige photocopying machine. At the far end of the room was the area where the new gym was being installed.

There were glass privacy screens with a temporary blue protective film applied to them and behind those were dust sheets and step ladders, paint tins and rollers. The air was perfumed with the smell of emulsion paint, and drops of thick blue plastic sheeting had been taped up to protect the windows and walls from paint spatter and dust. A number of sealed cardboard boxes were stacked behind the glass screens. They had graphics of fitness equipment on the outside.

A distant streak of movement from beyond the window next to me caught my eye. When I looked properly, I saw that it was a passenger plane, banking high above Battersea Power Station, its metal fuselage glinting in the sunlight, a milky contrail spooling out from its exhausts. The pilot would be circling in a holding pattern, I knew, waiting for a landing slot to become available at Heathrow. I'd flown the same spirals countless times myself in the past.

A queasy unease rippled through me as I lowered my gaze and took in the view towards the London Eye, Westminster Bridge, Parliament and Waterloo. The murky trench of the Thames gleamed in the evening light like molten lead.

Close to Waterloo Station was St Thomas' Hospital. Luke would be in there now. Like Maggie, my brother knew about my interview. He was probably wondering why I hadn't been in touch to tell him how it had gone.

I turned back to the room again, peering towards the gym area and the empty floor in between. And that was when I noticed the two doors a short way down the partition wall to my left. The door nearest to me was blank and unmarked. The second door had a metal push bar fitted horizontally across it and a green sign above. On the sign, two words were picked out in white font: EMERGENCY EXIT.

30

Inside St Thomas' Hospital, Luke looked up from Anna's medical notes as he entered the private room she was in. He tried not to react physically to the sight that confronted him. It was a blow to see how visibly she'd deteriorated in the past twenty-four hours.

'How's my favourite patient doing this evening?'

The inside of Anna's oxygen mask misted with condensation as she exhaled a weak laugh, then tugged it aside.

'Haven't you heard?' Her speech was slow and faint. 'They found me a new heart. My transplant went . . . swimmingly.'

'We'll get you there, Anna. We're doing everything we can.'

'You'd better.'

Her face was grey. There were tubes snaking in and out of her arms, and her brown hair was mussed and fanned out around her pillow. Twenty-six years old and every day, she seemed to sink deeper into her mattress.

'Are your parents in the canteen?'

Anna's parents had been keeping vigil at her bedside since she'd been admitted more than a fortnight ago. They were a kind, sweet couple, painfully courteous to all the doctors and nurses, utterly wrecked by the cruel medical misfortune their daughter faced.

'Not tonight. I sent them home.'

Luke tipped his head to one side. 'Must have taken some persuading.'

'I told them they needed a break. We still have a few days left until, you know. They need to save their strength.'

'Anna . . .'

'*I* needed a break. Is that bad? Just . . . it's really hard dealing with their worry all the time, you know?'

'Yeah.' Luke eyed the read-out from her EKG and flipped over the top sheet on her chart. 'Actually, I think I do.'

'Your parents were the same, then?'

He shook his head. '*I'm* the same. With my sister. She had her job interview today.'

'Oh yeah!' She pushed up from the bed a little on her elbows. 'How did it go?'

He shrugged. 'She hasn't texted me to say yet.'

'You didn't text her?'

'Did you text your parents this evening?'

'Maybe later.'

'Exactly.'

'You think your sister needs some space?'

'I think maybe we both do.'

He let that settle as Anna dropped back down onto her mattress. He wasn't sure what it was about her, but he'd shared more with Anna than he'd shared with anyone in a long time. There were people who claimed that confronting your own mortality equipped you with a particular kind of wisdom. Normally, Luke would have dismissed that out of hand, but with Anna, talking with her – well, there was *something*. A connection.

It helped.

Then again, perhaps it had more to do with him – with the lens he was viewing her situation through and the way he was responding to her prognosis. Life – as the cliché went – could be so unfair.

'It's Friday night,' she told him.

'It is.'

Her eyes sparkled and she smiled mischievously. 'Do you know what I would do if I wasn't stuck in here?'

'I have a feeling you're going to tell me.'

'I would find a boy I liked and I would make him ask me out on a date. I'd get all dressed up. Do my make-up and hair. We'd go drinking. Dancing.'

'Sounds like a good time.'

'Oh, it would be.'

Now her smile became more than a little wistful, and Luke felt bad for her all over again.

'I'm done here, Anna. I have to go and finish up. My shift is over soon.'

She mock-pouted. 'Already?'

'I'll check in on you tomorrow, OK? First thing, I promise.'

He tapped the frame at the end of her bed, crossed towards the door.

'Luke?'

He spun back.

'You need to stop worrying about your sister so much. Trust me. She just wants you to treat her like everything is normal. That's all any of us really want.'

'Yeah, maybe you're right.'

But it was hard. Harder than she knew. Because as much as Luke had confided in Anna, it was difficult to explain the depths of trauma his sister had really been through.

In the corridor, on his way back to the nurses' station, he glanced in through the porthole of glass in the next room at Mr Nicholls, who appeared to be talking to himself, enunciating deliberately, apparently repeating a Portuguese phrase. As he watched him, Luke pulled his mobile out of his back pocket and checked the screen.

Still no word from Kate.

His unease dangled inside him, a heavy weight suspended from a fraying thread.

Rationally, he understood that what Anna had said was right. He got that the healthy thing would be to give his sister some space.

But when it came down to it he was her big brother, and with their parents gone, it was on him to look out for her. A quick hello and a check-in couldn't be so bad.

He brought up her number, thought for a moment, placed the call.

The phone took several seconds to connect and after that it rang several times before diverting to voicemail.

Again, that wasn't like Kate, and he felt another stab of worry before reminding himself that it didn't necessarily mean she was in a bad place. Perhaps she hadn't heard her phone. Or it could be she'd gone for a run to clear her head. Luke was the one who'd persuaded her to join him for a jog in the first place. He'd argued it would be good for her mental health to get some exercise and fresh air, although if he was honest, he'd been surprised and a bit alarmed by how fully she'd committed to running as an outlet, how dedicated, almost obsessed she'd become.

He thought about leaving her a message, then decided not to. She'd see that he'd called when she checked her phone. She could call him back or not, depending on how she was feeling. He'd leave that up to her.

31

Friday 6.58 p.m.

I felt stupid.

This was a state-of-the-art high-rise. And yes, I'd seen a fire door out in the vestibule, but obviously there had to be more than one emergency stairwell.

I glanced up at the ceiling, thinking of the possible cameras that were concealed there, anxiety crackling through me as I sprinted forwards.

It was a large, empty space. Hurrying across it, I kept expecting Joel to appear and yell at me. Try to stop me in some way. But he didn't show himself and when I reached the door, I immediately grabbed the release bar and pushed down. The bar hinged and rotated and I shoved with the heels of both hands.

No.

The door didn't open.

I reared back and tried again. I shoved down hard on the bar. My skin tightened and flushed. My head felt light. I scrunched up my toes and dug in with the balls of my feet, grunting and struggling, and when the door still didn't move I hit it with the flat of my hand and yelled out.

Lurching sideways, I snatched wildly at the handle of the door to my left, expecting it to be locked or barred in some way, too, but to my surprise it flapped downwards and the door opened right up.

Sketchy dimness on the other side.

I ventured closer, afraid Joel could be hiding there, or some other trick might be awaiting me. I prodded at the door.

No resistance.

It swung fully open.

I reached in carefully and flipped on a light switch. A small cupboard materialized from the gloom. The cramped space was lined with fitted metal shelving. Most of the shelves were stocked with office equipment. It looked like a back-up for the stash of supplies I'd found in the metal lockers behind the reception counter.

I checked behind me again in case Joel was creeping up on me, then edged inside and took a closer look, going shelf by shelf. Everything was neatly organized and arranged. There were boxes and boxes of copier paper, all of them banded with plastic packaging straps. There were supplies of envelopes and padded delivery bags. There were hole punches and paperclips and boxes of elastic bands and several spare desk lamps.

There were no key cards. There was nothing I could use to help me get out of here.

A trickle of acid in the pit of my stomach.

I left the light on and stepped dazedly out of the cupboard, staring forwards.

It was staggering that this could happen to me. Utterly incomprehensible.

After a few seconds, I realized I was looking at the

photocopying machine in the middle of the floor space. There was a tickling sensation on the inside of my skull.

I darted forwards.

The photocopier was a mighty thing. Tall and wide and beige, roughly the same size as the abandoned workstations that had been shoved together nearby. An electrical plug was fitted into a socket on the floor. There were plastic wheels on the bottom of the machine.

It was whirring softly in sleep mode. I yanked the plug out of the floor and the machine quietened with a sound like a vacuum cleaner powering down.

Laying the plug and cable on top of the document feeder, I kicked the brakes on the plastic wheels free before twisting and heaving the machine away from the pillar, as if I was manhandling a loaded shopping trolley.

It was heavy.

I moved around behind it, flattened my hands on the sides and heaved.

The machine clattered and lurched. The metal casing wobbled and deflected. The wheels trundled and rolled, flapping around crazily, then gained momentum and juddered on.

The machine zigzagged. Shimmied. A paper drawer flew out and flew back in again.

I didn't stop. I kept pushing. Faster. Harder. Digging in with my legs. Speeding across the concrete floor. Zeroing in on the fire door. Getting closer now. Lowering my head.

At the very last moment, I bared my teeth and shouted as I rammed the machine the final few metres into the door.

The corner of the machine struck first with a mighty *crack*.

But the door didn't give way.

The machine simply hoisted up into the air for a fraction of a second before I collided with the reverse of it, the edge of the metal casing driving deep into my stomach.

I folded forwards, sprawling over the lid, banging my knees.

'Shit.'

I staggered away, clutching my stomach, fighting a rising surge of fury and nausea. When I tugged my blouse out of the waistband of my skirt and lifted it, I could see a red band carving across my flank. My skin was roughed up and sore to the touch.

The photocopy machine clicked and ticked, like the cooling engine on a car.

The fire door was dented but the lock, hinges and frame remained intact. I stared ruefully at the frame, then pushed off from the machine and marched stubbornly away across the office floor.

32

Friday 7.03 p.m.

I entered the gym area that was under construction. I was holding my hand against my side. Pressing down on my pain.

The walls and windows surrounding me were protected by plastic decorating sheets. More plastic sheeting crinkled beneath my feet. When I glanced to my right through the glass privacy screens, the blue plastic protective film still attached to the panels made the rest of the office appear watery and diffuse.

I scanned the work area in front of me for tools, but all I could see were paintbrushes, rollers and tins. A pair of grubby overalls were draped over a step ladder.

To the right of the ladder, the large cardboard boxes of gym equipment were stacked in a haphazard row. From the illustrations on the sides of the boxes I could see that they contained treadmills and exercise bikes. Another box had been opened already and some of its component parts had been unpacked and laid out on the floor. The image on the side of the box was for a cross trainer.

I padded closer and surveyed the items down on the ground. There was a large flywheel and two plastic foot pads. There was a pair of long, curiously shaped handles that

138

looked a bit like ski poles. And there were two metal bars that looked as if they would connect the ski poles to the flywheel. The bars were about the length of my arm, with screw holes bored through flattened flanges on the end.

I snatched one of the bars up, testing its weight in my hand. It was lighter than I expected, hollow, but I thought it might work as a makeshift pry bar.

Turning, I tramped back to the fire door, barged the photocopying machine aside with my hip, then raised the bar over my shoulder and jabbed the flattened end at the centre of the door.

Another small dent. Another low thud.

The pole snagged at the skin of my hands.

I adjusted my grip and punched the bar into the same spot several more times, working it side to side without making much headway, and then I used my backside to shunt the photocopier sideways even further before trying to wedge the bar into the gap between the door and the frame.

The gap was tiny. The flattened end of the bar was a couple of centimetres too thick. It wouldn't fit and it kept skidding clear.

I hit out at the frame sideways in frustration. There was a small, audible *crack* but I couldn't tell where it had come from. The frame didn't appear damaged in any way.

Stepping to my right, I attacked the door frame from the other side. A fragment of timber flew off. I jabbed at the frame again. Another chunk spat free. I attacked the same spot, over and over, faster and faster, until a crack appeared and spread, and I managed to blast a portion of the door frame about the size of my hand away from the brick wall underneath.

I then attacked the frame on either side of the gap with the bar. The frame was screwed securely to the wall. I guessed I could knock it free eventually, but one look at the area I'd removed showed me there was no real way for me to force the end of the pole into any kind of gap between the brick and the door.

I stopped and glanced up for a second.

And got that same tickling sensation inside my skull again.

It took a few moments for my conscious brain to catch up to what my subconscious mind was telling me, and then I lowered the bar and just stared.

The sign hanging above the door didn't just read EMERGENCY EXIT. It also had an image on it of a small white stick man fleeing from some cartoon flames.

33

Friday 7.07 p.m.

I kicked off my shoes, tossed them aside and ran back to reception in my stockinged feet with the metal pole in my fist. When I got close to the double exit doors, I pulled up sharply, looking to my left and right.

Just along from where the fire extinguisher had been fitted to the wall there was a fire alarm panel. Behind a square of safety glass was a bright red handle. Etched across the glass were the words: BREAK GLASS IN CASE OF EMERGENCY.

I squared up to it and raised the metal bar in the air.

I didn't pause and look up at the ceiling this time. I didn't want to give Joel any opportunity to stop me.

Turning my face away, I punched the bar through the glass panel. The glass cracked and sprinkled downwards. Pulling the sleeve of my jacket down over my hand, I brushed the remaining fragments clear and grasped hold of the alarm handle.

At that point I *did* pause.

Not for long, but it was long enough for the doubts to set in.

I wasn't sure exactly what would happen next but I was afraid it might be nothing. If Joel had been brazen enough to lock the emergency exit, perhaps he'd disconnected the alarm system, too. Or, I don't know, maybe I'd pull the lever and a ridiculous explosion would go off, showering confetti in the air, signalling the end of my ordeal.

A silly thought, but on some level it seemed credible to me. I suppose that's as good a sign as any other of just how off-kilter this entire situation had made me.

I tugged down on the handle.

And again, absolutely nothing happened.

For a fraction of a second.

Until the most enormous din started up.

The noise was everywhere. All at once. It was frenzied. Shrill. So loud, in fact, that in those first few seconds it felt to me like a physical force, pushing me down.

I squinted forwards. White emergency lights flashed and strobed overhead. One lamp rotated wildly above the reception counter. Other bulbs twitched across the office floor behind me. A single light was flashing out in the vestibule, its glare flickering through the wired panels of safety glass.

I wondered if the doors would be unlocked now. Perhaps there was an emergency release.

I moved towards them at a crouch, but no, when I tried them they remained secure.

I backed away and turned once more. The alarm shrieked on. Joel could call me now – on every phone again if he wanted to – and I wouldn't hear at all.

For a second, looking out across the flickering office floor, I felt as if I was watching the scene unfold on an old-fashioned zoetrope. I think that contributed to the weird sense of unreality that was tugging at me. Or maybe it was just simple confusion – sensory overload. The alarm was so loud and raucous it seemed to be yammering inside my head.

I couldn't see Joel. I raised a hand to shield my eyes and squinted out, moving forwards, bumping into a desk.

I tripped on something. No idea what. I kept going until I emerged from between the workstations and neared the giant windows overlooking the entrance to the building, my backlit SOS scrawled on the glass. I swung at the glass with the bar. Again, it didn't break. I struck it a second time, the bar vibrating in my hands, and then I leaned forwards and looked down.

Men and women in business clothing were streaming into the street from the front of the building, clutching bags and clasping phones to their ears, like in a scene from a disaster movie. Still others were gazing up over their shoulders at the uppermost floors of the building.

I was having trouble adjusting to what I was seeing. The alarm hadn't just been triggered on this floor, I realized, but throughout the entire structure.

A deep, powerful twist of anxiety and apprehension corkscrewed inside me.

Reality slammed in.

There was no longer any way this could be a stunt or an exercise. This was much too big for that. It had gone too far. But if the evacuation I'd set in motion was real, then the response to it had to be real, too. Somebody would have to come up here to check why the alarm had been triggered. And Maggie would be looking for me, wanting to know I was OK. All I needed to do now was keep away from Joel and stay safe until help arrived.

34
Friday 7.11 p.m.

Hide. That was the first thought that struck me. My second thought was: *Protect yourself.*

The metal bar was hollow and lightweight. If Joel came at me, I could swing at him with it, but if he grabbed it and ripped it away from me, I'd be defenceless.

The alarm shrieked in my ears. The emergency lighting pulsed and flashed.

My heart was pounding, my breathing accelerating. Every second I hesitated seemed endless – time slowing down.

Move, I told myself. *Do something.*

Through all the light, scatter and noise, I locked onto the refectory. Then I ran.

You know those nightmares you have where you're running to escape some terrible danger but you don't seem to be getting anywhere at all? This was like that, only worse, because I had no clue where the danger was coming from. I didn't know where Joel was right now.

Maybe he was in the toilets?

I almost stopped as I passed the cube. I hadn't thought to check them before now. Hayley had told me they were behind reception. If Joel was in there and heading my way, he could be rushing towards me any second.

144

The instinct to turn around and run in the opposite direction was strong, but I fought against it. I veered around the long meeting table, catching my foot on a chair, sprawling forwards, pushing up from the table, loping on.

I faced up to the kitchen, flung open cupboard doors and drawers.

I found something in the third drawer I opened.

A kitchen knife.

It had a long triangular blade. A green rubberized handle. Perhaps earlier today someone had used it to cut birthday cake for Justin.

Now it was a weapon.

Maybe. If I was prepared to use it.

I wrapped my fingers around the handle and squeezed. The blade quivered alarmingly. Weirdly, I seemed to have no strength in my arm at all.

The idea of stabbing somebody with it . . . Cutting them . . .

I pushed it away.

Deal with it when you have to.

Again, I turned and contemplated the office, casting quick, darting looks around, the knife in one hand, the metal bar in the other. The open-plan layout didn't offer many hiding places. I discounted the glass cube right away. Not only because it unnerved me but also because I'd left all the blinds up on the inside.

Joel had been watching me before and I knew it was possible he was watching me now.

I considered the gazebo to the left of the cube but a bulb was popping and rotating above it. It would illuminate me too brightly.

Make a decision. Quick. I whined to myself, shaking uncontrollably, and that's when I felt it for sure.

A shifting of the air.

A stirring in my blood.

A cold breath against the nape of my neck.

A whole crescendo of primitive, instinctive responses that screamed one urgent message to me: *He can see you.*

I spun.

But I couldn't see him. Not yet.

35

It had taken her long enough to trigger the alarm, Joel thought to himself. He'd expected her to get to it sooner.

That was disappointing, but not a major hurdle. Long experience had taught him that you had to be adaptable, where human nature was concerned.

He got up off the floor with his laptop open and balanced on the flat of his palm. The screen of his laptop was divided into a grid of several smaller windows. Each window displayed an image from a different camera that he could zoom in on or switch between if he so chose.

True, the flashing lights had whited out some of the windows on his screen, but even so, he'd seen enough to know that she'd grabbed a knife from the kitchen to go along with the metal pole she'd taken earlier. He'd watched her debate what to do next and he'd seen her run towards a workstation to scramble beneath it.

Joel was the only one who could see any of this because he'd placed the security cameras on this floor on a loop ever since the last of the staff had left, when it was only him and Kate in the cube.

After closing his laptop, Joel zipped it inside his black nylon backpack and tightened the straps over his shoulders.

He was standing in the back-up emergency stairwell. He'd been sitting right behind the fire door when Kate had attempted to force it open.

The space reeked of new paint. It was an easy guess that the stairs had barely been used since the building had opened and not a single person had passed him on their way out since the alarm had been triggered. Because of the unoccupied floors, the number of people currently working here was already low, and of those who'd still been in the building this evening, his hunch was that most of them had used the main stairwell to get out or even the elevators in contravention of the building's evacuation protocols. It didn't surprise him. Joel had witnessed the same phenomenon in office blocks all over the world many times before. Once the alarms began to screech, people lost all sense of reason and logic. Panic took over. They fled.

Not him.

After releasing the heavy bolts he'd fitted to secure the fire door, he pulled it open, shunted the photocopier aside and stepped into the office. The alarm was riotous, the lights blinding. He checked his watch and saw that he would have to move fast.

36
Friday 7.14 p.m.

I crouched under the kneehole of the desk I'd chosen. It was a tight fit. The alarm shrieked above me. The emergency lights cast flickering shadows on the floor. The knife was in my fist down on the ground, the metal pole next to me.

The desk I was cowering under was on the far side of a horseshoe with a partial view towards reception. I kept my eyes trained on the exit doors and tried to make myself as small and still as possible.

My back and legs ached. My knees trembled against the ground.

I couldn't tell if Joel was close. There was no way I could hear him over the commotion of the alarm. From the angle I was on, I knew I wouldn't see him coming unless he approached me from reception. And if he *did* come that way, he'd be able to see me.

You chose a bad hiding place. Move.

But my body wouldn't obey my brain. My fear was too paralysing.

A hot, tingling second of anticipation. All my nerve endings seemed to be alight.

Was he here already?

I thought about easing my head out and taking a look but

149

then I decided against it. If he was standing near to me I'd give myself away.

Jaw clenched, knife trembling, I blinked the sweat from my eyes and retreated even further into my crawlspace.

37

Joel felt an added kick of adrenaline as he rounded the partition wall. The office space was alive with noise and light. Chaos all around him.

He jogged past the gaming area and the glass cube, then cut left, striding by the gazebo and the carousel horses. When he reached the windows Kate had written on, he stepped in between the lamps she'd placed on the ground, craned his neck and looked down.

He could see a modest crowd of onlookers in business clothing gathered on the opposite pavement. A few stragglers were exiting the building to join them. Several of the workers had on lightweight jackets or were carrying briefcases and laptop bags. Already, lots of them were peeling away and leaving the area to begin their weekends. He didn't anticipate that many of them would come back inside.

After switching off the lamps and turning from the window, Joel zeroed in on the desk he'd seen Kate dive under. Just in front of it, a desk chair had been rolled clear.

With a series of fast, purposeful strides, he was upon it.

The lights flickering in his vision. The alarm screaming in his ears.

A duck and a lunge and he reached out for Kate, snatching for her arm, her hair, anything.

He grasped only air.

What the—?

The crawlspace was empty.

His head snapped up.

She must have moved after he'd closed the laptop. He must have just missed her.

He was still puzzling it out when he glimpsed a hint of movement just off to his right. Something other than the flashing lights.

There.

A desk lamp rocked and teetered. It was on the very edge of one of the desks in the next horseshoe of workstations along.

The lamp teetered some more.

Then it toppled off the desk onto the floor.

Oops.

Kate must have bumped it.

Joel vaulted the desk and sprinted after her.

38

Friday 7.17 p.m.

The noise of the lamp hitting the ground struck me like a fist to the throat.

I heard a scuffle of footfall behind me.

Now.

I sprang up from underneath the desk I'd moved to, on the *opposite* side of the desk to Joel. The plug socket for the lamp was in my fist. I'd tugged on the cable to create a diversion after I'd seen him move away from the window.

My breath juddered.

Joel was still rising from a stooped position, the confusion only slowly leaving his face when he saw me.

'Don't move!' I yelled.

My words came out louder than I'd intended. A sudden venting of all my terror and nerves. I let go of the plug and took hold of the kitchen knife in both hands in front of me but I couldn't keep it steady. The blade caught the flash and flicker of the emergency lights. The metal pole was on the ground by my feet.

'Stay back! I have a knife!'

'I can see that, Kate.' He raised his hands, gently patting the air. 'Kate, it's OK. You can relax now. It's over.'

I stared at him, not quite shaking my head. He had a black

backpack slung over his shoulders and I watched as, very slowly, he slipped his arms free of it and placed it down on the ground.

'You passed the test, Kate. You did well.'

Still I didn't say anything.

'Kate, please. What I need for you to do now is trust me and put the knife down, OK?'

Not OK. Not in a million years.

The shrill alarm drilled into my chest. My tongue felt dry and bloated in my mouth. I glanced fitfully towards reception. Why was nobody coming yet? Where were they?

'Kate. Look at me. *Kate.*' When I jerked back around, he raised his hands a little higher and spread his fingers up by his shoulders. He looked calm, reasonable. 'We don't want anyone getting hurt here.'

'Then don't come any closer to me.'

He hesitated.

Good.

I glanced down at the pole by my foot. The desk was still between us but it didn't feel like enough of a barrier.

I held my ground, swaying. Pressure behind my eyes. Pressure in my sinuses. The lights stuttering like camera flashes and the din of the alarm making it hard to hear my own thoughts.

'Kate, it's OK. You triggered the alarm. But it's not a big deal. You've seen the reaction from everyone in the building, right? That's because there are safety protocols in place.'

I wet my upper lip. I was shaking uncontrollably. I knew I couldn't say anything just then. I had no idea what I would say.

'You remember Tony? He's the security guard you met on the front desk when you came in.'

My breath snagged. The way he said it suggested he was certain of that. Had he been watching me?

'Relax, Kate. We've done this before. Tony knows the kind of scenario we like to run here at Edge. He'll be here any second now. It's his responsibility to cancel the alarm you set off and tell the alarm monitoring service that it's a false alarm. But first you have to put down the knife for me, OK?'

The crazy thing is, I almost did. I think part of me simply *wanted* this to be over. I wanted to be able to accept it was just some wildly improbable exercise that had got out of hand.

But that was the problem. It was just *too* wildly improbable. Even in the midst of my panic, I could tell that no self-respecting company could possibly allow a hoax fire alarm evacuation to be carried out as part of a recruitment process – especially in a building that was occupied by other firms and businesses. No company – not even Edge – could condone what Joel had done to me. And that was why, even as he was attempting to convince me this had happened before, I didn't believe him.

I *couldn't* believe him.

I think he sensed that. I saw something change in his eyes. A tremor of doubt or uncertainty. And when I saw it, he saw me see it, and in that instant, everything turned.

'OK, Kate, if that's how you want this to go . . .'

I didn't wait for the rest. I was already spinning away, pushing off from my leading foot, breaking into a run.

I managed two steps. Three.

It was as if I was trudging through sand.

Then my head was wrenched violently backwards and pain ripped across my scalp.

I screamed.

He must have leapt over the desk to get at me. Snatched for my hair.

My upper body pivoted backwards from my hips after my head, like I'd run into a horizontal beam. I screamed again and tried to lash out with the knife, but by then he'd gathered me into his arms and he was bundling me forwards. I tripped and fell. He pushed me face down over a desk.

My elbows struck first. Then my chin. Breath exploded from my lungs.

His weight crashed down on top of me, pinning me.

I twisted and writhed. I jabbed at him with the point of the knife. His fist circled my wrist. He crushed my bones. Then he slammed the back of my hand down against the desk until the knife fell out of my grasp.

No.

I scrambled for it with my other hand but he got to me before I could grab it, knotting his fist in the hair at the base of my neck, twisting it, tearing it, yanking my head upwards and away.

A bolus of phlegm in my throat.

Fear like firecrackers going off inside my skull.

I kicked out at his shins, his knees.

He bent my arm back behind me, jamming it upwards. A shard of agony in my shoulder joint, streaking down to my elbow. For a horrifying second, I felt sure my arm would break.

I stilled.

And that was when the alarm stopped on a fractured note.

The silence that followed seemed strangely unnatural and forced.

My hearing was still recovering from the onslaught of the siren, not to mention the urgent pounding of my blood, but I *thought* I caught a muffled sucking sound that could have been the doors into reception closing, followed by cautious footsteps.

'Hello?' The voice was male, uncertain. 'What's happening here?'

I would have screamed if I could but Joel exerted more pressure on my elbow joint, and for a sickening second there was only the red-hot pain inside my head and the terror of worse to come. His lips grazed my ear, his breath on my face.

'He's sixty-four, Kate. He has a wife. A daughter. Did he tell you he was retiring soon? Do this right and he lives. But make trouble for me and I'll kill him. And then I'll kill you.'

39

Joel palmed the knife as he pushed off me. I could still feel the weight and crush of his body as he stepped clear.

I stayed where I was for a trembling second. When I turned, cradling my elbow, I looked at the guard and it was all I could do not to shake my head and beg for help.

He was standing in the threshold of the reception area, staring back at me, clearly troubled by my appearance and uneasy about the scene he'd walked in on. His eyes kept darting to Joel and darting back to me again, his lips moving slowly, as if he wanted to be able to tell himself this was something other than what it appeared to be.

'Miss? Is everything all right?'

The note of concern in his voice almost undid me. He was shorter than Joel and when I didn't respond right away, he went up on his toes to look past Joel to get a clearer sight of me. There was a mobile phone clutched in his right hand, a computer tablet in his left. He was wearing a luminous safety vest over his blazer and his face was damp and flushed – from getting up here in a hurry, I supposed.

He was overweight and out of condition. If Joel attacked him, there would only be one outcome. He could kill him. I believed that.

'She's fine,' Joel said. 'We just got a little carried away, is all.'

A shudder of revulsion passed through me.

Even as he said it I could see the picture he was attempting to paint and how things between us might appear. My skirt was rucked up. My blouse was rumpled and untucked. My skin was glowing. I was breathing hard. My hair was loosened and in disarray.

And then there was Joel. Handsome. Confident. Together.

He cupped a hand to the back of his neck and worked a rakish grin. The knife was in his other hand, concealed behind his thigh. My eyes were drawn to it like a magnet and he must have known that because he tapped it with his index finger twice like an improvised Morse code. A warning and a reminder: *Don't make me hurt him.*

The guard was still peering at me, his mouth squirming beneath his moustache. I could tell he was looking to me for confirmation of what Joel was saying to him but I couldn't help him with that.

In my scrambling mind, a part of me was still sprawled over that table. Joel's body pressing into me. His breath in my ear.

I remained sickly still as Joel moved forwards, taking several steps closer to the guard, silently rolling the metal pole under a desk with his foot, blocking the guard's view of me and the wider office floor. With his hand behind his thigh, he double-tapped the knife blade again. I took the signal to mean: *Back me up here or else.*

'Did you mute the alarm on this floor with that tablet or cancel it altogether?' Joel asked him.

The guard didn't answer. He was too distracted, too unnerved. He glanced to his side, at the cracked glass panel in the door and the extinguisher down on the ground. Then he took several steps sideways until he could see the office layout more fully. His eyes widened as he read the message I'd scrawled on the windows.

'Miss, I didn't . . .' He shook his head and stared at Joel, lowering his hands. 'You didn't tell me there'd be anything like this going on. You never said . . .'

A long, see-sawing moment.

It was as if all the air had been sucked out of the room.

Everything seemed to be spiralling.

Everything spinning out of control.

'Is the building empty?' Joel demanded.

The guard was flailing. He didn't respond. For a moment, he seemed to be as lost and trapped as I was.

'I'm sorry,' he blurted. 'I had no choice. My daughter, she's—'

'Hey!' Joel snapped his fingers. 'I told you. Let me worry about your daughter. Now focus. Is everybody out?'

His daughter. What was he about to say about his daughter?

The guard seemed to brace himself against something – a suppressed inner pain or fear – and then he nodded, and sagged and looked down at his tablet.

I felt something inside me tear and give way.

'The system says everyone who works here has checked out, yes.'

'What about the rest of the security team?'

'They clocked off at six-thirty. It's just me now.'

I leaned back against the desk behind me. My body had gone limp and puppet-like. It was a struggle to breathe.

He has a wife. A daughter.

What had Joel done? What was he prepared to do?

Why?

'And the emergency response?'

No answer.

I was still reeling, so it took me a second until I noticed that Joel had snatched for the guard's wrist, lifting his hand with the tablet in it until he could check the screen. Again, I stared at the knife Joel was concealing behind him. I was terrified he'd lash out any second.

'The monitoring service has called me once already,' the guard replied woodenly. 'They're waiting on my report.'

'Call them now,' Joel told him. 'Tell them you've checked and everything is fine. There's no need for any fire crews to respond.'

I watched them, unmoving. Staring at the guard, I realized that our roles had been reversed because now I was the one trying to catch up to what was unfolding before me. I also suspected that I'd misinterpreted the way the guard had been looking at me when he'd first come in. What I had read as uncertainty and concern might just as easily have been a mixture of shame and fear.

'No,' I said. 'No, please. You have to—'

I took a step forwards but Joel thrust his hand towards me, palm out, signalling for me to stop. Again, the finger of his other hand tapped the knife blade. Again, I thought of how easily he could strike.

'Make the call,' he told the guard. 'Do it now.'

The guard delayed for a moment more, giving me a pained and conflicted look, then he shook his head miserably and raised the phone.

'This is Tony Johnson,' he said in a hurried tone, when his call was answered. 'I'm the fire safety officer at 55 Ludgate Hill, EC4M 7JW. The building passcode is Zulu Bravo Whiskey. I'm confirming a false alarm on floor thirteen. We had some people moving furniture up here. They accidentally knocked the alarm.'

He listened.

'That's right. All is clear. We're sorry if we wasted anybody's time.'

He listened a moment more and then ended the call.

I stared at him. I couldn't move.

'Good,' Joel told him. 'Now reset the alarm and disconnect it from this floor.'

The guard lowered his gaze to his feet and trudged towards the panel on the wall. I watched him reach out, pause for a moment and then push the alarm lever back up. He bowed his head and tapped several times at the screen of his tablet. When he was finished, his entire body seemed to slump.

'Is it done?' Joel asked him.

'Yes.'

'Then go downstairs and wait for me. I won't be long. In the meantime, I want to know if anybody comes back in. Anyone at all.'

'And my daughter? When will you—?'

'When we're finished. Like you were told.'

The guard gave me another anguished look, then shook

his head in a harried apology, dropped his eyes to the floor and crossed back to the doors.

'No, wait!' I shouted after him. 'Please! Come back!'

He fumbled his security pass over the reader on the door, as if he was terrified somebody or something was pursuing him.

'You can call the police. You can ask for help.'

'No,' he muttered, shaking his head. 'No, I can't.'

And with that he hauled the door back in a hurry and squirmed through and away.

I darted after him but Joel reached out and snatched for my wrist, yanking me back. Our eyes met and held. Then I looked down at the knife at his side. I made a grab for it with my free hand as, behind me, I heard the muffled clunk of the doors sealing and locking again.

40

Friday 7.27 p.m.

I didn't let go of the knife.

Joel just looked at me. I didn't like being this close to him, especially after the fear and discomfort I'd seen in the eyes of the security guard. But I still didn't pull my hand away.

Blame it on my stubborn streak. If I'd been honest in my interview, I would have told Joel that was my biggest weakness. I've always had a problem letting things go.

'What have you done to his daughter?'

'Nothing. Yet. If he does what he's told, she'll be fine.'

That shook me. I wondered where she was and what threat could be hanging over her, if it was real or not. The guard clearly believed it was genuine, though, and that made me even more afraid. Why was Joel doing this? What did he want from me?

The silence between us was interrupted by the muted *ding* of an elevator arriving out in the vestibule. My heart plunged as I thought of the guard stepping into a carriage and pressing a button to take him to the foyer. I pictured the elevator descending, taking my hopes of being rescued away with it.

That was when I finally released the knife and slapped Joel across the face.

I did it before I'd even really processed what was happening. Before I'd thought through the consequences. I just lashed out.

Afterwards, the crisp sound of the impact hung in the air between us.

He remained horribly still, his face averted. I could see the marks my fingers had left behind. White to begin with, then flushing red. It must have hurt him. My hand was stinging badly.

I stumbled backwards, raising my arms to cover my face. I was afraid he would strike me back, beat me. It was there in the bunching of his shoulders, the darkening of his eyes. I saw his fingers tighten into a fist as he ducked to pick up the metal bar but then, equally quickly, he flung the bar away to his right, towards the climbing wall.

He's waiting for something.

I was horrified to think what that something might be.

He straightened and reached around behind his back, lifted up his shirt, slipped the knife down under his waistband. He then strode past me, walking beyond the desk he'd pinned me against, towards the windows overlooking the entrance of the building.

I waited a few seconds before spinning away and bolting for reception.

'The doors are locked, Kate,' he called back calmly. 'You're wasting your time.'

I tried them anyway. I pushed and I pulled on them. I rattled them. They wouldn't open.

There was nobody out in the vestibule. The guard was definitely gone. I could see a down arrow illuminated in a digital panel above the elevator carriage on the left. He had to be going down to the lobby, like he'd been told.

'Why don't you come and join me over here, Kate?'

I swung away from the doors. I was feeling light-headed, dizzy, and the ground seemed to be slipping away from under my feet, like sand being dragged by an outgoing tide.

I raised a hand to my temple. My head buzzed. There was a mild ache behind my eyes.

Joel was framed in the middle of one of the tinted glass panels – the one I'd written the backwards L on – with his hands in his pockets. The metal strap of his wristwatch glinted in the light from the desk lamps. The sun outside was bronzed. His head was down and he was looking at the street, like a stock photo of a businessman deep in thought.

Inside, I felt a hot spike of anger and hurt. My elbow was still sore, the joint unsteady. I touched a hand to it and flinched, thinking again of how the tentacles of pain had skittered through my body. Thinking of how close he'd come to breaking my arm.

'Everyone's leaving, Kate. I don't see anyone coming back in.'

A hollow sensation inside my chest. Cold pimples across my skin.

I found myself walking towards him even as I wanted to stay back. I think perhaps I needed to see it for myself. When I neared the windows, I kept my distance and craned my neck to peer down. It was true. Small groups of office workers were walking away along Ludgate Hill in both directions. More of them were disappearing along the road opposite.

'I couldn't have emptied the building better myself, Kate.'

My breathing hurt.

He wanted this.

You've done everything he expected you to do.

'Friday night, Kate. You're thirteen storeys up. You're all alone. Trapped in a box in the sky.'

'You listen to me.' I swallowed. 'This is a mistake. I don't know who you think I am, or what you want with me, but you have the *wrong person.*'

He considered me with his hands in his pockets, then shrugged casually and slowly removed one hand to show me what he was holding.

My phone.

There was a swatch of clear plastic tape on the home button and when he pressed it the screen bloomed with light. I saw the photo of Mark in his autumn sweater and felt the press of more tears against the backs of my eyes.

'Please,' I said. 'Don't.'

He contemplated me, intrigued.

'It's important,' I told him. 'There's . . .'

But I didn't know how to explain. I didn't want him to know.

'Kate, it's almost time for your interview. Your *real* interview this time. There's just one more thing before we begin.' He tapped at the phone with his thumb, rolled out his bottom lip. 'Tell me about Maggie.'

41

Friday 7.32 p.m.

'**She's my recruitment agent,**' I said.

'I know that, Kate. What else is there I should know about her?'

'She's—'

I didn't finish. I was too distracted, still struggling to get my head around what Joel had just said to me. I didn't understand what he'd meant when he'd said it was almost time for my 'real' interview to begin.

His mind games were becoming exhausting. I couldn't tell how afraid I should be. Tony had been afraid. That was obvious.

'Kate, she's been sending you texts.' Joel cleared his throat and started to read. 'Hi? I'm in the pub. Where are you?'

Oh God.

I resisted the instinct to look down at the street and search for Maggie. He couldn't know she was here. I couldn't tell him. She was the only one now who might come looking for me soon.

During my interview, Joel had asked me who knew I was here today. I'd thought it was a strange question at the time but perhaps it was worse than I realized. Perhaps he wasn't intending to let me go. Was he hoping he could make me just . . . *vanish?*

'Kate? Look at me. Where is she meeting you?'

'She's—'

But I couldn't complete the thought. I was sinking. Drowning.

'Kate, focus. Don't make me hurt you again.'

I rubbed my elbow, holding it against my body.

'Answer the question, Kate. Where is Maggie right now?'

'Balham.'

A quick response. Simple. Clear.

'Close to your place?' he asked me.

I hated that he knew that. But then I remembered that my address had been top and centre on my CV.

'Yes.'

'Are you lying to me, Kate?'

Don't look down at the street. And don't think about the knife. You don't want him thinking about either of those things.

'No. I'm not lying.'

'Huh.' He worked a puzzled expression and used his thumb to scroll up on the phone screen. 'Well, that *is* weird.'

I didn't respond. I didn't trust myself to. I was afraid I'd just blundered into another trap.

Joel cleared his throat and started to read again – slower this time. 'I came out of the pub when I heard the alarm. Couldn't see you leaving the building. Everything OK?'

My grip tightened on my elbow.

'Keep lying to me, Kate. I really don't mind. Every time you do, I learn from it. You're just making it easier for me and worse on yourself.'

My legs almost gave out. With anyone else, I would have taken it for bravado. But with Joel, I wasn't so sure. He sounded so confident. So composed.

I thought about my interview again. About his strange, intrusive questions and all those intense, probing looks he'd given me. All that *watching*. Then there was the psychometric test he'd made me fill out.

From what he'd said, it was almost as if he wanted me to believe that every move I'd made since he'd left me on my own and the phones had started ringing was a move he'd anticipated. *But what if he actually had?*

For a dizzying second, I had the weirdest, most unsettling sensation of another psyche loose inside my brain – as if Joel had been fumbling around in there, upsetting and re-ordering my thoughts.

You're just imagining it.

But I wasn't.

Something about his attitude, the way he was studying me, told me that. As I stared up at him, I felt myself physically recoil.

'I just wanted to protect her,' I whispered. 'She's not important to you. You don't have to worry about her. I only said I might meet her for a quick drink.'

He looked at me for another long, careful moment, then nodded towards the view of the road below.

'Do you see her, Kate? Which one is she?'

'I don't—'

'At least look before you lie to me.'

I closed my eyes for a moment. *Stupid.* Then I turned and gazed down.

A heady swirl of vertigo.

The drop seemed to yo-yo beneath me.

A constant stream of cars, buses and taxis slipped by.

Small knots of people were still gathered on the opposite pavement, but none of them were onlookers from the building any more. They were drinkers from the pub, perhaps fifteen or twenty in all.

Most of them were smoking cigarettes and holding glasses of beer and wine. They were dressed in office clothing, nodding their heads to one another and talking animatedly. A regular get-together at the end of the working week.

I couldn't see Maggie.

Not to begin with.

Until I did.

Stay still. Don't give anything away.

Even from up high, I recognized her dark green jacket and work trousers. Her mop of strawberry blonde hair. Her oversized handbag.

She was standing off to one side, not far from the bus stop, close to the edge of the pavement. It looked as if she was waiting for a break in the traffic to cross the road and come over to the building looking for me.

'Well?' Joel asked.

'I don't see her. She's not there.'

Again, he watched me. I turned to him and stared back as plainly as I could, wanting him to keep his eyes on me, not wanting him to watch the street. I tried to keep my expression as neutral as possible. If it was true that he could somehow read my responses, my best defence had to be giving him nothing at all to read.

But then he broke away and sighed, returning his attention to my mobile, typing a fast message with both thumbs.

'Hey, Maggie,' he dictated. 'Really sorry. The alarm held us up just as we were finishing. Can you wait a bit longer?'

He hoisted an eyebrow, his thumb poised over the 'Send' icon. I didn't look away from him. I didn't dare to.

Please tell me you've crossed the road already, Maggie. Please tell me you're out of sight, that he can't see you . . .

'OK,' I told him quickly. 'Maybe I did see her. But if I tell you who she is, you have to promise me you won't do anything to hurt her.'

'That's not how this works, Kate.'

'Promise me.'

'Really, Kate? You want me to start lying to *you* now?'

I stared at him. I knew I needed to delay for as long as I possibly could but again, I couldn't see that I had much choice. If he sent the message pretending to be me, he could go on to say anything he wanted to Maggie. He could convince her I'd changed my mind and headed home. He could make it so there was no chance she'd come inside and speak to Tony the security guard, get suspicious, fetch help.

If I was lucky, she was across the road already.

'Fine,' I told him. 'There she is.'

I put my finger to the glass and pointed. Joel considered me closely before turning his head and gazing down at the street.

'Which one?'

'The small blonde one? With the cigarette? In the group?'

Even as I said it, my attention was elsewhere. I was glancing sideways to where Maggie was taking a step off the kerb, then hesitating and moving backwards as a taxi roared close.

Move, Maggie.

'Grey suit?'

Forgive me.

'Yes.'

Joel fell silent as he took in the scene. In the intense hush that followed, all my senses and nerve endings seemed to be stripped back and exposed. I tried not to fidget. Tried not to react in any way. I also tried to convince myself it was going to be OK. That Maggie would hurry forwards any second, kick up a fuss with Tony, demand to know where I was. That I hadn't just placed a random stranger in peril.

The woman I'd identified was thin and willowy with long blonde hair. One of her arms was draped across her stomach, the other holding a cigarette to her lips. She seemed to be laughing at something one of the men in her group had said to her.

'Just for the record, Kate, I want you to know that I know you're lying to me right now.'

'I'm not.'

'Really? Well, let's see, shall we?'

My phone emitted a whooshing noise as he dispatched the text.

I swallowed painfully, staring at the street, flattening both hands against the glass. I looked first at the random blonde woman I'd identified, then to where Maggie was getting ready to dart out after a bus blasted by her.

Hurry. Please.

I glanced at Joel. His brow had furrowed. For a half-second, what might have been a troubled expression crossed his face. At first, I didn't understand quite why, but then I noticed that the blonde smoker had reached into the inside pocket of her jacket.

For a phone?

Everything seemed to slow down in the seconds that followed. The blonde's hand seemed to somehow get caught inside her jacket. The bus that was passing Maggie blocked my view of her momentarily.

I stared at the random blonde woman as she snatched her hand free.

But she wasn't holding a phone.

She'd removed a packet of cigarettes and now she flipped back the lid, offering them to one of her companions.

And meanwhile the bus had sped on and Maggie had stepped back from the kerb. She was looking down at her side, delving around in her handbag. I saw her remove her phone, glance at the screen, then gaze for a long, perplexed moment towards the entrance to 55 Ludgate Hill.

'Well, what do you know?' Joel said. '*There* she is.'

42

Joel felt a chill engulf him as he stared out of the window.
Outwardly, he had to appear in control. Inwardly, he was
rocked.

For a second there, he'd doubted himself. For a second
there, when the blonde woman had reached inside her jacket
he'd wondered if he'd misread Kate. That *never* happened.
And with Kate, well, there were complications. He'd prepared
himself for that. But still. Troubling.

Then there was the recruitment agent. He'd been briefed
on how she'd been teed up, of course; how she'd been
approached on behalf of Edge and pointed towards Kate as
the kind of candidate they were looking for. But he'd had
no idea what she looked like because he'd had no reason to.
He hadn't expected her to be here right now. That wasn't
any part of the plan.

He recognized her, now that he knew who she was. He'd
seen her loitering in the atrium when he'd been waiting for
Kate to arrive. Back then, she'd been irrelevant to him. Just
another worker-drone killing time by scrolling through her
phone. Part of the backdrop.

Not any more.

She could place Kate in the building after it was evacuated.

His own text had told her Kate was still here. There was no telling what complications she might trigger when she didn't see Kate soon. And that meant he would have to deal with her, somehow.

He glanced sideways at Kate, the tension straining inside him like a worn rubber band. For the moment, she seemed too distressed to pick up on his own unease, flattening her hands against the glass as if she wished she could somehow reach through it to Maggie, who was waddling back towards the pub on the corner of the street, tapping at her mobile. Seconds later, Kate's phone buzzed in his hand.

No problem. Sounds promising!

'Well, looks like it's time for me to go and introduce myself to Maggie, Kate.'

She whirled around, her face looking hard and scraped.

'What do you mean? What are you going to do?'

The fine veins throbbed in her temple, quicker than before. Joel wasn't a superstitious person, but he had a bad feeling. Not a premonition, exactly, but the chill that had started in his chest was getting worse, spreading out from the centre of his body, tiny fissures of ice running down his arms and legs. For someone who was always in control – who prided himself on controlling his emotions – it was a new and unwelcome sensation.

He held Kate's stare for a few more seconds, then reached out for her arm, grabbing the back of her neck.

'Hey! Get off me!'

He squeezed her skin, pushing her face down, spinning her sideways and marching her towards the cube.

'Stop! You're hurting me!'

She braced her hands out on either side of the doorway, resisting him, but he pushed her harder, forcing her on. With a final violent shove, he flung her into the far corner of the cube. By the time she'd stopped herself and turned back, her body coiled and primed to lash out, he'd pulled the kitchen knife from the waistband of his trousers.

'Steady, Kate. Don't do anything we'll both regret.'

He crabbed sideways, keeping his eyes and the blade held on her as he reached for the chair Kate had moved away from the desk into the corner. He dragged the chair clumsily towards him by its backrest, pushing it behind him, rolling it out of the room.

'Send the other one over to me,' he said, gesturing to the chair that was still behind the desk.

She ignored him.

'I don't want you breaking any more chairs, Kate. I want you to wait here calmly until I get back and we can talk.'

'Tell me what you're going to do to Maggie.'

'That's not your concern.'

'Tell me.'

'The other chair, Kate. Now. I won't ask you again.'

She scowled at him, furious, but then she relented and moved towards the chair in a huff, seizing it violently and shoving it towards him.

He caught it before it hit his leg.

'Better.' Stepping backwards with the chair, he reversed out of the cube and reached for the door. 'Don't go anywhere while I'm gone, Kate.'

The door closed and locked.

She glowered out at him, her hair hanging across her eyes

and mouth as he crossed to where he'd dropped his backpack on the floor. He scooped it up and zipped the knife inside. He then slipped the bag on over his shoulders, tightened the straps and stared at Kate, held securely inside the cube.

'Promise me you won't hurt her,' she shouted.

He didn't reply. He simply turned and strode away. Past the refectory and the games area, pausing only to pick up the metal bar, then moving on beyond the climbing wall. When he reached the far side of the office, beyond the partition wall and out of sight of Kate, he hustled towards the gym area that was under construction, then veered sideways and blasted through the fire exit door.

The moment he was on the other side, he dropped the metal bar and closed and locked the door behind him, then bent forwards at the waist, balled his hands into fists, leaned against the wall. His heart was pounding. He was sweating under his shirt.

This shouldn't be so difficult.

He couldn't allow it to be.

Thirteen floors.

He lurched towards the staircase, grabbing the banister, threading his way down. Three breathless minutes later he reached the ground floor. The fire door ahead of him opened onto the atrium, and he cracked it open and peeked out.

At first, the space appeared deserted. A stark mausoleum of limestone and glass. He experienced a fresh stab of panic until his eyes swept to the left and he saw the security guard.

Tony had his back to him, standing with his hands on his swollen waist, his feet spread, shoulders slumped, looking out at the street.

Joel guessed he was watching after the last of the employees who'd left the building, perhaps trying to reconcile himself to the scene he'd walked in on upstairs, maybe only now beginning to reckon with how much danger his daughter might really be in.

Things had changed for Tony now, too. Thanks to Kate. Thanks to *Maggie*. It was another complication Joel was going to have to address, and not in the way he'd intended or hoped.

First things first.

Backing off, he eased the door closed in front of him and raced down another four flights of stairs before stepping out into the parking level two storeys below. The bare ceilings were low. The lighting was yellow. The air smelled of cold diesel and concrete.

There was no sign of anybody here and only a few vehicles remained. One of them was the black Audi that had been parked at Gatwick for him when he'd flown into London the previous afternoon. Joel moved towards it, opened the boot and stashed his backpack inside.

Yellow arrows on the floor directed him to the exit ramps. He slammed the Audi's boot closed and locked it, then followed the arrows at a jog, running upwards and upwards again until he saw sunlight ahead. He ducked under one of the striped parking barriers. Stepped out onto the street.

And paused.

To his left he could see the front entrance of the building and across from it the pub Maggie was in. The temperature was warm, the evening air gritty, the road traffic noisy and abrupt. There were relatively few pedestrians around. It helped that Ludgate Hill wasn't a residential area. Now that the working week was over, there was little reason for most office workers to linger here. Come the morning, tourists would be visiting St Paul's and the Millennium Bridge, but none of them would have any clue about what was happening thirteen floors above them.

Especially if it was over by then.

Wiping the sweat from his face, Joel flattened his hair, tucked in his shirt and paced across the road.

43

Friday 7.44 p.m.

I slammed my hands against the glass cube. Spun away.
Clutched my head.

I didn't know if Joel really only planned to talk to Maggie,
but I knew I couldn't trust him. I also knew he had the
knife. And even if he *did* just talk to her, it was a worry. He
could tell her anything at all.

I swore and tugged at my hair, then turned and looked
at the office surrounding me again. At the jumbled sprawl
of empty workstations outside the cube. The useless
computers.

My head was ringing. My pulse felt so erratic it was as if
my blood was jumping under my skin.

Use it.

I spun and snatched up the phone from the glass desk.
And got no dial tone at all. I slammed the receiver back
down, braced my palms on the edge of the desk and shoved
hard.

It didn't move.

I stared down at the metal legs of the desk, tracing along
them to the ground with my eyes. The horror hit me anew.
The legs were bolted to the floor.

Like in a prison cell.

Dropping to my knees, I quickly felt around the bolts that had been used. I couldn't turn them. They were set fast. And I had nothing to loosen them with except my fingers. If I couldn't move the desk, then I couldn't use it to ram my way out of here.

It's Friday night, Kate. You're thirteen storeys up. You're all alone. Trapped in a box in the sky.

'Fuck this.'

I pulled my skirt up past my knees and clambered onto the desk, almost upsetting the carafe and the tumblers. The glass surface of the desk seemed relatively solid underneath me as I eased up into a crouch. It didn't give out. Just to be safe, I placed my feet over the metal framing at either side of the desk and then I straightened fully and looked up.

The nearest track lights were warm against my face and the glass ceiling of the cube was only a foot or so above me. I could touch it with my hands.

I pressed against it. I pushed. My feet slipped on the desk. The panel didn't flex or move. It didn't creak. All I succeeded in doing was leaving a series of sticky handprints on the glass.

Pausing for a moment, I gazed around the top of the cube close to me. There was a metal crossbeam to my right. I went up on my toes and studied it, seeing how the glass was bonded to the metal with black resin.

I scraped at it with my nail. A tiny fleck of resin came free but most of it was on top of the glass where I couldn't get at it.

I flicked it away and felt along the crossbeam, thinking

that maybe I could find something, a loose bolt or a metal shard of some kind. All I found was dust and grit.

And a thin, coppery cable, almost as fine as a human hair.

I tugged on it. It plucked free of the beam. I tugged some more. The wire glimmered like fishing twine. Looking down at where my feet were placed, I took a careful step forwards, went up on my tiptoes and pulled again.

A small object popped free and dangled from the cable.

It was cylindrical in shape, about the size of a pen lid, with a tiny glass bead on one end.

A camera.

I pulled it towards me, ripping more of the wiring free from the crossbeam. Eventually the wire pulled taut and then disappeared through a tiny hole that had been drilled in the top of the beam. I traced the wiring back the other way and found a second camera and a second tiny hole.

I stared at the cameras for a second, thinking, and then I took them in my hand and yanked the wiring out of them, shoving everything back onto the crossbeam, wiping the dirt from my palms.

44

The atmosphere inside the pub was muted, the lighting meagre, the air smelling of spilled beer. Some of the smokers Joel had seen from the office window were gathered around a small round table to his right. Among them was the blonde woman Kate had tried to misdirect him to. Ahead and to the left a bar stretched along the length of the room, with a bar-back mirror positioned behind shelves of colourful spirits and cans of alcopops stacked in pyramid displays. Two floppy-haired, boorish City types in salmon-pink shirts were braying and laughing in a doomed attempt to impress the girl behind the bar.

Joel spotted Maggie sitting alone in a booth towards the rear, her big handbag on the table in front of her next to a large glass of white wine. There was a bulging Filofax open in her hands; the lid of the Sharpie she was writing with was wedged in the corner of her mouth.

He walked towards her, cautious, the worn floorboards tacky beneath his feet. 'Excuse me? Are you Maggie?'

She looked up at him, eyes wide, not bothering to take the pen lid from her lips just yet.

'I'm Joel White. From Edge.'

Now she nodded, an appreciative smile forming on her

lips as she removed the pen and shook hands with him. 'You want Kate,' she said.

'We do, yes.'

'Where is she?'

If she had suspicions, she didn't show them. She was all business. Eager to cut a deal, clearly, but also, he suspected, doubting that he had the seniority to make it happen.

'She's upstairs with Amanda. Talking through some of the details of the role. Can I join you?'

He slid into the booth seat opposite her, not waiting for an answer, watching as Maggie flicked the Sharpie repeatedly against her Filofax, leaning back to assess him in turn.

'We'll need a starting salary of forty-five thousand a year,' she told him.

'You know we're offering forty.'

'But you'll pay forty-five.'

He spread his hands, as though he might be inclined to concede the point. In reality, he was monitoring her, scanning her for any signs that he should be concerned.

'And salary bumps for the first three years, on a schedule to be agreed between us in writing. Plus performance bonuses.'

'We should be able to accommodate that.'

'Just like that?'

'It'll need Amanda's sign-off.'

'And you're telling me Kate wants to accept the position?'

It was the opening he'd been waiting for.

'Come and ask her for yourself. We have office drinks on Fridays. You're here right now, Kate's here, we're here. If you come up with me, we can get the details worked out together and have a drink to celebrate. Why wait until Monday?'

He let it dangle, eyeing her cautiously. There was no sign of any reticence, though he did detect an attempt to conceal her own eagerness. Probably she was running the sums on how much she stood to make if Kate signed on the dotted line.

After pursing her lips, she made a pretence of glancing at her mobile before nodding in a casual way. 'I can do that. But I'll need to speak with Kate in private first.'

'Not a problem. Shall we go?'

He stood and waited at the end of the table as she closed her Filofax, securing it with a grubby elastic band. She necked a mouthful of her wine, dumped her belongings into her handbag and shuffled out of the booth in front of him. She was short with a generous waistline but she moved with the rushed efficiency of a veteran City worker.

'What happened with the building evacuation?' she asked him from over her shoulder as she pushed through the pub door and emerged onto the street outside.

'False alarm.' He kept close to her side as she spotted a break in the traffic and set off across the road.

'You didn't evacuate?'

His antenna tingled. Was she making conversation, or was there something behind the question?

'It's the third false alarm this week. They're still having teething problems with the system. And we were just finishing up anyway. But yes, strictly speaking we should have come down. You can take that as a measure of how much we want Kate.' Ahead of them, the revolving glass doors were stationary. Joel made an effort not to look at her as he took a key card from his wallet and waved it over a sensor, opening a swing door to the side. Tony was monitoring them with a stern, watchful expression from a stool behind the security desk. 'That's actually something I need to smooth over a second. Do you mind waiting by the waterfall for me? I'll get you signed in, join you there.'

'Whatever you need.'

He watched her bustle on across the atrium, reaching into her bag for her phone without looking back. Her footsteps echoed. The lobby was otherwise silent and empty. There was nobody else around. Only when he was sure she was out of earshot did he approach the front desk.

'What's she doing here?' Tony's face was tight and strained above his moustache.

'Not your concern.' Joel leaned closer. 'And lower your voice, will you?'

'You didn't mention anyone else. You never said—'

'I'm mentioning it now,' Joel said, with finality.

He nodded towards the plain door set into the wall behind the counter. The door opened onto a private office where earlier Joel had shown Tony the photographs they had of his daughter, Sophie. There were shots taken from inside Sophie's home in Harpenden. Shots taken from the man stationed outside in her street. There was also her iPad. They'd collected it from her bedside table. Joel had shown Tony how her calendar app told them where she would be on any given day for the upcoming year. He'd demonstrated how it allowed them to track her phone and pinpoint her location. Afterwards, Tony had raised a liver-spotted hand to his scalp, running it down over his slackened face to his mouth, shaking his head, too astonished and afraid to speak.

'Time to make the call,' Joel said now. 'You held up your end of the bargain. Your daughter is going to be OK.'

Tony eyed him suspiciously. 'That's it?'

'I told you. We have what we want.'

The guard leaned sideways and contemplated Maggie again. She was tapping at her phone with both thumbs, her huge handbag suspended from her wrist. Joel could tell Tony was uneasy about what he was seeing. And that was the problem now. That was what had changed fundamentally and had to be fixed.

Until Maggie was on the scene, it was only ever going to be Kate they needed to worry about. If people came along afterwards – the police, say – asking questions, Tony could be made to tell them whatever Joel's clients wanted him to tell them, or risk having his daughter put in danger again. But add Maggie into the mix, add a bunch of questions about how *two* women could possibly go missing with links to the same building at broadly the same time, and – well, it didn't add up to a sum Joel could easily square.

'You can make the call yourself,' Joel told him. 'But not out here. We do it back there where no one else can hear.'

Tony's tongue flicked over his lips. 'And then it's over?'

'Yes. Then it's over.'

Joel moved around behind the counter and waited until Tony climbed down off his stool, the brass buttons on his blazer catching the light overhead. He looked at him for a wary second before scowling and leading him through the doorway into the narrow, cramped room beyond. A line of grey metal filing cabinets were butted up against the wall to the left. A bank of surveillance monitors were positioned behind a workbench to the right alongside a pegboard of keys.

Tony reached out towards the phone on the workbench but his hand never got there. The dimensions were so tight they didn't allow him any space to react as Joel surged forwards, wrapped an arm around his chest from behind and yanked him backwards off his feet.

Joel held on grimly, clamping his hand over the man's mouth.

Tony was bulky and surprisingly strong for his age, and they bumped into the filing cabinets as he moaned and tried to throw Joel off. He kicked and grappled for a handhold. A pen pot got knocked off the counter and struck the floor, biros spreading everywhere.

Joel glanced back, nervous of any noise. But by then he had Tony where he needed him. On the ground with both hands pressing down hard on his mouth and nose.

Two minutes later, he sprang up and away, swiping his shirtsleeve across his face. Tony was staring blankly upwards but it still seemed to Joel as if there was something accusing in his stare.

He shied from it, plucking an elevator key from the pegboard, then stepped out of the room, swung the door closed behind him and sent a quick wave to Maggie when she glanced up from her phone.

His shirt collar felt too tight against his neck. He ran a finger around it, swallowing with difficulty.

The visitor book was on top of the counter and he dragged

it towards him, willing himself to focus, to block out the physical memory of the moment when Tony's body had fidgeted once, twice, then finally gone limp in his arms.

Kate's name was two lines up from the bottom of the ledger. Once he found it, he swept his eyes along the row to the right and saw that Tony had done as he'd been told, and had filled in a time shortly after six o'clock in the column marked Time Out. There was no need to worry about a signature because Kate had signed the book earlier. He also didn't need to worry about the cameras inside the atrium, or anywhere else for that matter. In five or ten minutes from now, he would be back inside the security office and he could wipe all records for the past twenty-four hours.

He made no new entry in the ledger for Maggie. She'd signed herself out shortly after Kate had arrived. As far as the paperwork was concerned, it would be as if she'd never returned.

'All set.' He fixed a smile to his face as he paced across the lobby, closing in on Maggie as she popped her phone into her bag. She still conveyed no trace of any misgivings or doubts. 'Thanks again for sending Kate to us, Maggie. We think she's special.'

'I think so, too.'

Behind Maggie the waterfall splashed and chattered. Otherwise there was just the towering silence of the lobby and the furious pounding of the blood in his head, the shaky energy in the tips of his fingers. He stood close to her and leaned forwards to press the call button for the elevators.

'Please,' he said, when the doors parted on the middle carriage. 'After you.'

45

Friday 8.02 p.m.

I searched around me for other cameras and wires. I managed to stretch up to feel along two more crossbeams from my position on top of the desk. I also inspected the track lights I could reach. Then I clambered down off the desk and searched the rest of the cube, pushing my face close to the glass, studying every indent and possible hiding spot, prodding around in the seams between the metal beams and the glass panels. I pulled back the blinds and checked behind each of them, too.

I didn't find any other devices. It made me wonder if the cameras I'd found were actually just dummies or decoys of some kind. I wouldn't put it past Joel, but I had no way of telling for sure.

As I searched, my mind looped on thoughts of Maggie and how Joel had gone to meet her, what he might say to her, what he might do. At the same time, I couldn't help thinking this was all my fault. I knew it wasn't a rational thing to think. I was also aware that it was definitely self-pitying. But ever since Mark's death, I'd had this sense that I was somehow tainted. Damaged. Perhaps even cursed. Deep down, it was hard to escape the notion that my whole life now existed in the shadow of a dark star and that by connecting with Maggie, I'd somehow dragged her under its influence, into the gloom.

I tried to shake the thought from my mind as I pushed up off the floor and rattled the handle on the door to the cube again. When it still didn't open, I got down on the ground on my backside and kicked in frustration at the glass with my heels.

The glass thudded. The impact jolted me backwards.

I kicked out some more, cursing Joel and the situation I was in with each impact. I was still kicking and cursing when I heard someone shouting my name and I looked up to see Joel pacing across the office floor towards me.

He was alone, no sign of Maggie. The leather folio case he'd had earlier was tucked under his arm. He also had a woman's handbag scrunched up in his left hand.

No.

I shuddered. The bag was big and functional. It definitely looked like Maggie's handbag. There was no way she'd just give it to him.

In the seconds that followed, a horrid, intense chill spread out through my trunk, like in those moments when you're swimming in open water and you get the instinctive, irrational sense that there's some unseen creature beneath you – that at any second it might snatch for your legs, drag you down.

'Move back, Kate,' he called through the glass.

I didn't. I stayed where I was on the ground.

'Don't make this harder than it needs to be. We both know I'm coming in there. I don't want to have to hurt you to do it.'

I stared at him. He cocked his head to one side, waiting for me to move, pressing the handbag against the glass door.

'You know who this belongs to, don't you?'

I broke eye contact, my eyes scanning his shirt where it was tucked into the waistband of his trousers. Did he still have the knife?

'Move back, Kate.'

'What did you do to her?' I shouted.

He motioned for me to move without answering my question.

'If you've hurt her . . .'

Again, he said nothing. He simply watched me and waited until I finally got to my feet and stumbled backwards, my heels aching, feeling behind me for the glass wall I was about to bump up against.

As I watched him, he slipped one hand into his pocket and a second later there was a small *click* as the door unlocked. He opened it and I immediately bolted forwards, trying to push past him.

I didn't get very far before he grabbed me around my waist and lifted me up off my feet.

My legs windmilled. I screamed and beat his shoulders and upper back with my fists. He squeezed my waist, crushing me, the edge of the leather folio digging into my flesh, and then he drove me backwards, slamming me and holding me against the glass.

The panel clattered behind us. I winced at the bright pain that ignited across my shoulder blades and down my spine.

As he pinned me there, he kept his face close to mine.

I spat at him.

He flinched and blinked, lowering his head, gathering himself. Then he went very still for a long, long moment before finally releasing me and stepping clear. He blocked my route out of the cube as he reached into his pocket for a handkerchief that he used to wipe his face.

That's when I noticed the spots of blood on the sleeve of his shirt. The reddish-brown flickers around his pen pocket.

No.

The numbing chill in my torso became more intense.

'You hurt her, didn't you? Why did you hurt her?'

Joel lifted his head and stared at me. If he was sorry or ashamed he didn't show it. He just watched me, and then, quite suddenly, he moved to his side and placed Maggie's handbag down on the glass desk, setting the folio down next to it. His back was to me. I watched his shoulders rise and bunch beneath his shirt.

I stared at the door. I thought of running.

'You're not fast enough,' he told me, shaking his head. 'Neither was she.'

A violent tremor ripped through me, as if that unseen creature I'd been afraid of had set its teeth around my ankles, pulling me under.

I felt sick, limp, and by the time he turned around and walked out of the door to fetch the two leather chairs from our interview and carry them back inside the cube, I was shaking perceptibly, as if I'd been plucked out of the ocean, wrapped in a foil blanket, stupefied by the horror I'd experienced.

My core temperature seemed to drop as he positioned the chairs on either side of the desk, then sat down in the same chair he'd been sitting in earlier, pushed Maggie's handbag aside and opened the leather folio in front of him.

'Kate?' He nodded towards the chair opposite him. 'It's time.'

I didn't move.

'Sit down, Kate.'

I remained standing.

'If Maggie could talk to you now, she'd tell you to sit down. She'd insist on it. Trust me.'

Finally, I edged forwards. My steps were clumsy and unsure, the concrete floor hard and cold beneath my stockinged feet.

I swallowed as I reached out to my chair and eased myself down in slow increments, the chair creaking and settling under my weight.

'Let's start again, shall we? We're going to talk now, Kate, and you're going to answer my questions, and you're going to do it truthfully this time or Maggie will suffer more than she has to.'

I held myself steady – as steady as I could – and stared at her handbag. All I could think of right then was the blood on his shirt.

'I want you to tell me what you've done to her.'

'Do you know what amazes me, Kate? It's almost like you need a refresher on how an interview works. So here's the thing: I ask you my questions, and you answer them, and at the end you'll have an opportunity to ask some questions of your own. Got it?'

I dug my nails into my palms, thinking of how Maggie had seized hold of my hands down in the lobby, telling me how I was perfect for this role and how everything was going to be OK.

'Are you ready, Kate?'

'Just tell me what it is that you want.'

'OK, good. Then here's my first and most important question: Where's your husband, Kate? Where is Mark right now?'

46
Friday 8.07 p.m.

An acid churning in my stomach, creeping up into my throat. A feeling like hot needles piercing my flesh.

'Why are you doing this to me?'

I was trembling. Hurting.

'Just answer the question, Kate.'

'It's cruel.'

'Answer me. The truth this time.'

'You know the truth. Mark is dead. I told you he died in the Global Air disaster.'

'Funny, isn't it, how we call it that? Have you ever noticed how it's nearly always the airline, not the aircraft manufacturer, that gets associated with a plane crash, Kate? Pan Am over Lockerbie. Malaysian Airlines Flight MH370. The Global Air disaster. Why do you think that is? Good PR?'

My hands gripped the armrests of my chair as a vision flashed in my mind. It was the same horrific vision that haunted me in my very worst dreams.

The plane breaking up. The plane going down. And Mark, knowing what was happening, terrified, clinging on.

I knew too much about air travel to kid myself about how awful it would have been for him. I knew how the oxygen masks would have deployed and been swinging around. I knew how the pilots would have waited until the very last moment to shout, 'Brace, Brace.' I knew how the passengers would have been screaming and crying and worst of all, how Mark would have known there wasn't any hope.

He was an aeronautical engineer. He had experience as a pilot. They were at thirty-eight thousand feet when the rapid descent started. Mid-Atlantic.

'Kate.'

In my nightmares, I was on board with Mark when the plane tore downwards but I was never able to touch him or talk to him, tell him how much I loved him. All I could do was stare helplessly as the night-time cabin rocked and clattered, and the screaming descent continued until the black ocean rushed towards us and the world tumbled away from us both.

'Kate, look at me.'

I didn't look. I couldn't. I squeezed my eyes tight shut, winded, as if I'd been strapped into my chair and beaten, the vision flaring like a bright, painful spotlight in my mind.

'Kate.'

'*How dare you.*'

'Kate—'

'Two hundred and ten people died.'

My chest hurt. I felt hollowed out. The back of my throat was stinging, raw. At the same time, a hot, shaking fury was building inside me. If I hadn't been gripping on to my chair I would have lashed out.

'Two hundred and ten. Do you understand what that means? Do you have *any* idea?'

Now I did look up at him. Slowly. I could feel my emotions contorting my face into something savage and ugly.

'Are you sick?' I said. 'Is that what this is? Do you get off on tormenting other people? Does this make you feel good about yourself?'

He didn't answer me. He just stared back neutrally, as though he was maintaining a watchful distance. After a short while, he seemed to exhale, as if I'd disappointed him, then he reached out for the telephone receiver and punched a long series of digits into the keypad.

The sequence was much too extensive for a telephone number. I guessed it was a code to unlock the phone system.

Finally he paused and pressed a button for the speaker.

The purr of the dial tone hummed loudly inside the cube.

He held my eyes and dialled again. An outside line this time.

I heard a series of burrs and clicks followed by a sonorous ringing tone.

The phone rang just twice before it was answered.

There was a knocking, fumbling noise, then a short pause followed by some laboured breathing on the end of the line.

'Talk,' a rasping voice said.

47

Friday 8.11 p.m.

Joel gauged me carefully from across the desk before lowering his mouth to the speaker.

'She says she doesn't know anything. She says he's dead.'

Dead.

The word seemed to ricochet inside my chest – the same way it had ricocheted, over and over, for fifteen months now. The word never settled. All it did was cause me more pain.

The wheezing grew more pronounced on the other end of the line. 'Is she telling the truth?'

My eyes watered. I bit the insides of my cheeks and shook my head at Joel. Keeping me prisoner was one thing. But this. This was twisted.

'Too early to say.'

'We have time.'

'Should I continue?'

As Joel waited for a reply, he studied my responses as if I were a specimen on the other side of a thick glass screen.

'Call me when you have an update,' the voice wheezed.

The call disconnected and Joel leaned back in his chair.

48

The moment the call was finished, the man with the wheezing breath picked up a different phone and dialled a different number.

'Give me an update,' he said.

There was a pause on the end of the line. 'I know for certain they've been talking to someone today.'

'When?'

'Morning and afternoon. It's the same person who first made contact three weeks ago.'

'Tell me what else you know.'

'They're nervy but increasingly excited. They're sure they're onto something big. They've ordered food and they're working late. I heard one of them say it's going to change everything.'

'By when?'

'By Monday, definitely.'

'Anything else?'

'Yes. They're paranoid about leaks. But don't worry about me. I can handle it.'

49

'Who was that on the phone?' I asked Joel.

His face shaded with regret. 'That was my client.'

'I don't understand.'

'I told you, Kate. I work in crisis management. My job takes me all over the world. Right now, you're the crisis I'm managing.'

'But . . .'

My words trailed away to nothing. I had no idea what I was trying to say. None of this made sense to me. It couldn't make sense.

I pushed back my chair, got to my feet.

I hadn't planned on making the move. Instinct had driven me to it. But now I found that I didn't know what to do next.

'Sit down, Kate. You don't have anywhere to go. And right now I need you to look at these pictures.'

He opened the leather folio towards the middle, waited a moment as if running through some internal debate with himself, then turned it towards me and slid it across the desk.

I didn't want to look at what he was showing me – I knew it couldn't be anything good – but I also knew I was going to have to look eventually, and so I steeled myself and glanced down.

I saw two plastic pockets containing two colour photographs. The photographs appeared to have been blown up and printed on A4 sheets. The quality wasn't great. The images were grainy, blurred.

I tried to keep control of myself. I was trembling again.

Both photographs were of me.

Both had been taken, when? A fortnight ago?

I could remember the Saturday morning now. After another sleepless night, I'd risen early and ridden my bicycle to Camden Market. I'd bought soda bread, a scarf, flowers.

And, apparently, someone had photographed me.

But not just that.

From the way Joel was watching me, I sensed there was something more I was supposed to be seeing, and when I looked again at the photographs a trapdoor swung open beneath my feet.

I crashed back down into my chair.

There. Among the strangers in the backgrounds of both photographs. Was that supposed to be . . . *Mark?*

I let go of a sharp breath.

The figure was indistinct. The focus not quite sharp.

It looked like Mark, but different.

Him, but older.

His hair was longer around the ears and neck, greyer at the temples. He had a thick lumberjack beard. A flat cap. He was wearing a wax jacket.

A sob funnelled up inside me but I didn't let it out because my fist was jammed in my mouth. I bit down on my knuckles. Tears welled in my eyes.

I'd sometimes wondered what Mark would have looked like as he'd grown older, and here somebody had done the work for me. I knew the technology existed. Photoshop. Age progression software. But for what? Why?

I looked up. The tears blurred my sight. There was a scalpel-sharp precision to Joel's gaze as he monitored my responses.

'The man who was hired before me to find Mark lost him shortly after these photographs were taken.' He was speaking calmly, almost gently, as if to soften the blow. 'Best guess, he spooked him. Your husband realized that someone was following you and he got away.'

'That's a lie. You're lying.'

I reached a hand out to the photographs, then immediately pulled back. I didn't want to touch them. I didn't want to be contaminated by them.

It was bad enough that I'd been followed and photographed, but it was even worse to think that this whole thing hadn't just been about today. There had been a build-up to it. A *plan.*

'It's OK, Kate. We know he's been with you.'

'No.'

'The man who took these photographs also spoke to your neighbours. The woman downstairs? He showed her these photographs and she confirmed she'd seen Mark at your apartment.'

The woman downstairs was a bitter old spinster called Faye. She spent most of her time in her overgrown back garden, fussing over her plants and her cat. Her garden apartment had a separate entrance to my ground-floor flat and I rarely bumped into her or spoke to her when I did. Partly it was out of embarrassment. The floors weren't so thick that Faye wouldn't have heard me crying in the middle of the night.

But she would have told me if someone had been asking about me, I thought. I hoped so, anyway.

'He also gained access to your place. When you were out. What would you say if I told you we have forensic evidence that proves Mark has been there, Kate? Fingerprints. Hairs. All of them a match for Mark.'

'I'd say you were lying.'

'It's science.'

'It's bullshit. All of this is bullshit. Every last part.'

I flung my arms around, feeling the hard certainty of it growing inside me like a tumour.

After Mark's death, I hadn't been able to face staying at our place in Highbury. Too many memories. Too much hurt. To begin with, I'd moved in with Luke for a short time. Then I'd rented my current flat close to Luke's place in Balham.

But supposing someone had been inside my flat, was it possible they could have found traces of Mark? I imagined so. There were so many of his things I still hadn't been able to bring myself to get rid of. I had boxes in my bedroom that contained some of Mark's most cherished items. Books. CDs. Papers. Sometimes I took out old clothes that smelled of him and pressed them to my face, slept with them next to my pillow. It didn't help. Nothing did. It just made the longing worse. But I did it anyway.

In that sense, I suppose I *had* brought Mark with me to my new place. The spectre of him, anyway. But all things considered, it seemed much more likely that Joel was simply trying to unbalance me for reasons I still didn't fully understand.

'This man was sent back to your flat again, Kate. Yesterday? When you were at work. Before my flight landed.'

My scalp tightened. I didn't know why he was telling me this. I knew he could just be trying to unsettle me further but again, there was that odd note of sympathy in his voice, as if he was genuinely sorry to have put me in this position. I wrapped my arms around my torso, holding myself close.

That was when I remembered something, my mind hurtling backwards to when I'd got home the previous night. I'd come in with a bag of groceries from the mini supermarket near my Tube stop. I'd dumped them on the table. Opened the fridge.

And then I'd had this feeling. This odd, creeping sensation. *Like I wasn't alone.*

I'd silently closed the fridge and crept through my apartment. It didn't take me long to check the place. There was only one bedroom, the living room and the bathroom to search. And there was nobody there. Nothing amiss.

But even so, my discomfort had persisted. I could remember now that I'd put the chain on the front door because I'd been so unnerved. It wasn't something I normally did.

'No,' I told him. 'No, I don't believe you.'

'Kate, please. Listen to me. I'm trying to help you. Look at where you are right now. Look at everything I have control of here. Do you really think the people who hired me had any difficulty hiring someone else who could get inside your apartment?'

Without breaking eye contact, he reached forwards and took hold of the folio, dragging it back to him, spinning it around. He flipped forwards to the next plastic pocket, eyed me for a cautious moment, then removed an item from inside, which he placed face down on the glass desk in front of me.

I looked down at it.

The item was a flimsy, rubberized sheet, about the size of a small envelope. The surface was black with gritty accretions stuck to it.

I loosened my arms from around my body and slowly reached out to it. I gulped air and flipped it over.

My world flipped over with it.

Another photograph.

This one was sealed behind a clear plastic film with a cheap, sea-blue frame surrounding it. The frame was decorated with motifs of sea shells and dolphins. The words ST LUCIA were printed along the top in a gaudy yellow script. The rubberized backing was actually a magnet.

It was my favourite photograph of Mark and me together. The image I returned to in my mind over and over. Just the two of us on honeymoon on the perfect Caribbean beach, Mark standing behind me in a linen shirt with his arms wrapped around me, eyes crinkled against the sun.

I kept it stuck to the fridge in my flat.

50

'Can I ask you something, Kate?'

I didn't reply. If he really was working with other people, then they hadn't just invaded my home. They'd trespassed on my heart.

Joel had no idea how much this photograph meant to me, or how it had sustained me in the months since I'd lost Mark.

I should have noticed it was gone last night. But then, I suppose, on some level, I had. I'd been putting my groceries away in the fridge when I'd first sensed something was wrong, even if I hadn't made the connection. I'd been in too much of a rush, too preoccupied with thoughts of my job interview and all the prep I needed to get through. And now it turned out the entire thing had been – what? A scam just to get me here so I could be confronted with how easily they'd broken into my home? I'd like to be able to tell you I faced down the threat the photograph represented to me without letting it get to me. But that would be a lie.

I was shaken.

'Why did you even want this job, Kate? My personal opinion? It doesn't seem like you.'

I touched my hand to the photograph and looked at the

version of myself in the image. The past me was smiling freely. A sense of rightness and contentment seemed to ooze from my every pore. I hadn't known it then, of course, but looking back now, I could say without doubt that it had been the happiest day of my life.

'You don't know me,' I whispered. 'You don't know anything about me.'

'Don't I? Look around you, Kate. This place is all surface, no substance. You're better than this. You know you are. Was it the money? I guess I can understand that. It must have really burned you when you didn't get anything from Mark's life assurance payout.'

For the first time in a while, it felt like one of Joel's barbs had missed its mark. The truth is I didn't care about the money. I never had. Mark was twelve years older than me. And while it was true that he had a generous company life assurance policy from MarshJet, I'd always known upfront that nothing would be coming my way in the event of his death. We'd discussed it before we got married. The arrangement had suited us both.

So no, Joel was wrong. The only thing that burned me was losing Mark.

'The money went to his daughter,' I said.

'Rosie. What is she now? Nineteen?'

Again, I didn't respond. Rosie was twenty and I was sure he knew that. The part I didn't like was that he was mentioning Rosie at all. I thought of how he'd threatened Tony's daughter and I felt my anxiety coalesce and intensify, a cloying mass in the middle of my chest.

'Do you talk to her much, Kate?'

'Not as often as I'd like to,' I said carefully. 'But then I guess you know that, if you're really as informed as you claim to be.'

'Second marriages. They can be tough. Am I right?'

For a brief moment, I wondered if he was speaking from experience, but then the thought came crashing in that I had no reason to care. I didn't want to know or understand Joel or what was driving him to do this. I just wanted to get away from him. And if that meant keeping him talking until someone could find me, or find Maggie – assuming she was really still OK – then I was willing to go along with that.

I gazed at the photograph again. Since I'd lost Mark, I'd spent so many hours staring at it, wishing I could somehow follow a path back through my memories of our honeymoon to a secret place out of space and time where we could be together again.

'What was it?' Joel asked me. 'Daddy's little girl didn't like the idea of you giving it to her old man?'

'No. That wasn't it. Rosie and I got along.'

'His first wife, then.'

'Paula.'

'Paula. Right. Did she drip poison in Rosie's ear?'

I didn't give him the satisfaction of saying yes, although as it happened, that was more or less it. Mark's marriage to Paula hadn't been a happy one but Mark had loved his daughter, Rosie, with everything he had. He'd tried hard to make it work. He and Paula had been split up for more than a year before I joined MarshJet and we first met. We'd both been part of the team launching the new CruiseFlyer jumbo. It had been an intense, exciting time. A lot of late nights in the office. A lot of opportunities to talk and flirt. There'd been a spark between us right from the very beginning, but we'd taken it slowly because of Rosie. She was twelve when we met. Mark didn't ever want to do anything to cause his daughter pain.

Now, almost nine years later, one of the hardest parts for me about losing Mark had been losing my link to Rosie, too. And not simply because we'd been close – although I liked to believe we had been – but because I knew Mark would have wanted me to watch over Rosie for him. Paula, though, had done everything in her power to make that close to impossible. At the start of the previous summer, the two of them had moved to San Francisco, where Paula was from originally.

'Then again,' Joel said, 'I can understand why you wanted out of the airline industry. First, you know, because of how Mark exploited the Global Air disaster.'

'Mark didn't exploit anything. He died in that crash.'

'And second because of the cabin air scandal.'

I stilled.

'Yeah.' He fixed on me. 'Now we're getting to it.'

51

Joel studied Kate's responses. Her pupil dilation. The tiny movements of her lips. All this toing and froing. And now that they were here, what did he know?

Nothing, for certain.

And that was a problem. He'd never experienced anything quite like this before. She was giving him so many mixed signals.

Or perhaps it was him this time. Maybe his judgement was impaired. Perhaps he wanted this one too much.

'Why are you doing this to me?' she asked him.

'You know why, Kate. Mark told you why, didn't he?'

Again, she shook her head, but there was less certainty in it now and he wondered if her defences were finally slipping.

'Then how do you explain the photographs I showed you?'

'You faked them.'

'And the forensics?'

'They don't exist.'

She was leaning back from him, her complexion pallid, her nostrils pinched. He could tell she was scared and in deep distress. Her eyes looked reddened and hollowed out, somehow dimmed.

Under the surface, he felt a tug of sympathy. But he also knew her emotional turmoil was necessary to him. Keeping her unbalanced was part of his process. In his experience, it was only when someone was really pushed that they'd let the unvarnished truth slip out.

'And what about all this?' he continued. 'The interview? You. Me. My client?'

She couldn't hold his stare. Her eyes drifted away to the tumbler of water.

'I don't understand why you're doing this to me.'

'But you do, Kate. Think about it. Did you tell yourself Mark knew nothing? Did that help?'

She shut her eyes. Scrunched up her face. She seemed to have gone inwards again.

He waited a long time for her to come back to him and return to the room. When she did, there was no expression of renewed determination on her features. There was no sense that whatever calculus she had been running in her mind had led to a decision being reached. Her gaze returned to the glass of water and that was all.

'Drink if you want to, Kate. I'm in no hurry.'

She didn't. She wouldn't allow him even that win.

He moved his chair closer to the desk. One of the castors squeaked. When he reached towards her she flinched and pulled back, but he was only stretching to touch the photograph he'd laid down in front of her.

'Come on, Kate. Mark knew there was a problem with those planes. He *knew*. Don't sit there and tell me you didn't at least *suspect* what was going on. Let me tell you how his behaviour would have been in the weeks before the crash. He would have been agitated, withdrawn, irritable. He would have had trouble sleeping. Trouble concentrating. He would have found it difficult to be around you or be intimate with you. He would have made excuses to go off on his own, get some space. I bet you tried to talk to him about it and he told you there was nothing to worry about. Just work stress. Nothing for you to concern yourself with. But you kept on at him, didn't you, and he confided in you, finally. Is that why you quit? I can tell you have integrity, Kate. It would have been hard for you to look your colleagues in the eye. That's why you haven't been at the protests, isn't it?'

He watched her lift her hands and clench them together, as if her emotions were a rubber ball she was squeezing tight. But then she shut her eyes and stilled, and he sensed her go inwards again.

What demons was she battling with? he wondered. What wouldn't she allow him to see?

52

Seventeen months ago

'Mark? It's late. What are you doing up? Come back to bed.'

'In a minute.'

'Mark.'

I crept across our living room barefoot, the hem of the old T-shirt I had on grazing my thighs. Mark was sitting at the small fold-out table by the window, a floor lamp casting him in a halo of light. His briefcase was open, multiple papers spilling out.

'Whatever it is can wait until morning,' I told him.

I placed a hand on his shoulders, felt the knotted muscles under his skin. He was dressed in an old vest and a pair of boxer shorts, his bed hair clasped in one hand. I noticed him try to slip one of the documents away, but I reached for it before he could.

'Mark, please. Don't do this.'

I picked up the report. I could still remember helping to put it together. It had been my task to disseminate the technical data into a usable format. I'd used subheadings, pie charts, graphs.

Three months before, Mark had burst into my office at MarshJet's HQ waving an inch-thick report in his hand. It had

215

been put together by a team of independent experts and approved by the aviation regulators.

'It's here,' he'd told me, and there was no hiding the relief on his face. 'It's the confirmation we've been waiting for.'

'It's good?'

'Better than good.' He'd flipped to a page towards the front of the report, stabbing it with his finger. 'Average findings across two years of flights show the cabin air quality on MarshJet planes was as good or better than normal indoor environments.'

'All of them?'

'There was one flight where we neared the red line but we never exceeded it. It's proof, Kate. Undeniable.'

I'd stood up and hugged him. More than anyone else, I had some inkling of the terrible pressure Mark had been under at work. As the Head of Research and Design for MarshJet, he'd tortured himself with the idea that the designs and schematics he'd approved and signed off on could have somehow endangered the lives of pilots and cabin crew.

I'd squeezed him. 'Can I tell people now?'

'You can tell everyone. Shout it from the rooftops. Get it out far and wide.'

So I had. We'd gone to the press. We'd shared the findings with the unions representing pilots and cabin crew. We'd made sure that MarshJet's legal team were armed with all the data they could possibly need.

But the allegations kept coming. The media featured haunting stories of cabin crew and pilots suffering terrible illnesses. And the unions had carried out research of their own. They cited studies showing that instances of chronic *neurological decline and other severe and debilitating illnesses were significantly higher among flight crew and pilots who had flown mostly or exclusively on MarshJet planes.*

Which had led Mark back to his paperwork and his designs. Back to this report. As if by poring over it, he could somehow block out his deepest, most secret fears.

'Please, Mark. Come back to bed.'

'In a bit.'

'You can't keep doing this to yourself.'

'Can't I?'

And with that he'd reached into his briefcase and thrust another document at me. It was a handwritten letter that was fitted into the top of his briefcase. The paper was thin and fragile. The handwriting was in a looping blue script. When I opened it, I found that held within the delicate pages was a photograph of a woman in her mid-to-late fifties with hollowed-out eyes and a paisley headscarf covering her scalp. She was being helped to blow out a birthday candle by what was probably a grandchild.

'The letter is from her daughter,' Mark told me, his voice broken and distant. 'Her name was Melanie Turner. She was a flight attendant who flew on MarshJet planes for twenty years. She died last week.'

53

Friday 8.28 p.m.

'You think he gave something to me, don't you?' I said.

'Do I?'

'Before he died. You think Mark gave me some – I don't know – proof of the allegations against MarshJet. Some way of showing that the cabin air was toxic. That it really did make crew ill. Documents. A confession. That's why someone was in my flat. That's what they were searching for.'

'Go on.'

'And that's why you've made up all this stuff about Mark. To mess with my head. Unbalance me.'

'And what about you, Kate? What are you trying to hide? You didn't tell me I was wrong about Mark. About how he was *before* the accident.'

I hadn't denied it because I couldn't. Because what Joel had said and implied had come too dizzyingly close to the truth.

That was one of the hardest parts about losing Mark: the secret knowledge that I'd already lost him little by little before his death.

And of course I'd asked him about it. I'd tried to get him to open up to me. But Mark had only shaken his head and told me he couldn't explain it – nobody could.

I should have pushed him harder on it. I knew that now. Though in truth, a part of me had been thinking it ever since the crash.

Sometimes I wondered: Was there more to the claims MarshJet faced than Mark had told me? I'd flown on MarshJet planes when I was cabin crew. So had lots of my friends. As a member of the MarshJet board, had Mark knowingly endangered my life, and the lives of thousands of others?

And what about the role I'd played as a publicist, re-assuring people it was safe to fly? Had I been duped? *Used?*

I didn't know the answers to those questions. They were lost somewhere in the depths of the mid-Atlantic, along with the bodies of my husband and most of the other passengers, and the souls of all who perished.

For me, it was just another element of the tragedy I tried never to think about. It was one thing to know and live with the knowledge that Mark was dead, and that he'd been taken from me in such a harrowing way. The last thing I needed to dwell on was whether he'd also been part of a cover-up that I'd been unwittingly drawn into as well.

But even if I'd got him to confide in me, it wouldn't have changed things. The disaster would still have been the disaster. The plane he was on would still have gone down. Maybe the only difference was there wouldn't have been that lingering snag in my conscience. The restless unease that came from knowing Mark hadn't been fully at peace when he'd died. That he hadn't, truly, been the Mark I'd fallen in love with.

That was why I'd tried to cut myself off from the media circus surrounding the MarshJet trial. It was why I'd shied away from the TV news coverage as much as possible. And yes, Joel was right, it was why I hadn't gone anywhere near the pilots and cabin crew who were protesting outside the High Court, demanding restitution and a public inquiry.

But now here I was, sitting across from a man who was confronting me with the very questions I'd tried so hard to avoid. A man whose role I was suddenly terrified I was beginning to fully understand.

'Is that who your *client* is?' I asked. 'MarshJet? Do Edge represent them?'

'In a manner of speaking.'

A hot crackling under my skin. I shouldn't have asked him that, I realized. Because knowing the answer to that question could only increase the danger I was in. But I'd asked anyway. I needed to know.

'And on the phone just now?'

'Careful, Kate.'

'Tell me.'

'Are you sure you want to hear this?'

No.

'Yes.'

'OK. Then that was the man himself.'

I swallowed, thinking about how Sir Fergus Marsh had called me into his office to tell me about Mark's plane going down. At the time, I'd been struck by his kindness and compassion. But he'd sent me into that press briefing room. I'd been abandoned there, fed to the wolves when I was at my most vulnerable. So who was to say he wasn't capable of being behind something like this?

Sir Fergus had been keeping a low profile in the media

for the past year or so – at least until the trial had begun, at which point I had heard that he'd flown into London ahead of giving evidence in person, releasing a press statement that he had absolute confidence MarshJet would be exonerated. Normally, the tabloids couldn't run enough stories about his glamorous lifestyle with his young wife in Monaco. Over the years there had been countless paparazzi shots of him lounging on the deck of his latest mega-yacht, chomping on cigars, surrounded by the rich and famous. There were rumours he'd been ill. Whispers he'd been receiving treatment at a private clinic in Switzerland for an undisclosed illness. I supposed that might explain why I hadn't recognized his voice on the phone just now.

'You're saying that was Fergus Marsh?' I asked.

'You want me to call him back for you?'

54

Joel motioned to the phone, though he had no intention of making the call. He sensed Kate understood that but he waited for her answer anyway.

She shook her head weakly.

'No?'

'I think you should let me go.'

'Can't do that, Kate. The trial resumes Monday morning. They're saying there could be a verdict by as early as next Friday, if things go badly for my client. And they will if Mark testifies. Word is the prosecution team have a secret witness.'

Kate's eyes were fixed on his but he saw her hand stray towards the photograph of her husband again.

'If what you're saying is really true and Mark is alive – if he's been inside my flat – it stands to reason you should let me go.'

'Oh? How so?'

'Because if he's followed me once he'll follow me again. If he's come to my flat once he'll come to it again.'

'And then what? You'll call me if you see him?'

He stared at her, shook his head.

But then he saw the flicker of a smile on Kate's lips. It was a broken, painful smile.

'You won't let me go because you know you're lying,' she told him. 'You won't let me go because you know Mark is dead.' She paused and looked up towards the corner of the ceiling, tears in her eyes. 'I want to see Maggie now.'

'No.'

'I have to know she's OK.'

'I can't help you, Kate.'

'This is crazy.'

'Is it?'

She nodded, and this time her face began to crumple. 'Mark is dead.'

He waited. Again, that burning in his bloodstream. And a tick-tick-tick like a clock running too fast inside his head.

In all the interviews he'd conducted over the years, all the quests for the truth he'd been tasked with, he'd always prided himself on his self-discipline. His patience and objectivity.

It was a shock to find how easily it could all slip.

'He should be, Kate. I'll give you that. He should have gone down with the rest of that plane.'

55

Friday 8.34 p.m.

There was something in the way he said it. Something in the force and the unsteadiness of his voice.

He should have gone down with the rest of that plane.

Emphasis on that word 'should'.

It was as if he was implying that the disaster hadn't been an accident.

For just a second, I thought of everything I knew about the tragedy – all the information I'd been forced to confront, the details I'd gleaned by calling in favours from former colleagues at MarshJet. It all amounted to the same thing. The investigation into the crash was still ongoing. An intermediate report had found that the plane did not break up before it hit the Atlantic. That meant there was no explosion. No bomb. And still very few answers.

Officially, an international team were still searching for the plane's black box flight recorders. Unofficially, most newspaper articles seemed to have concluded the black boxes were lost for good somewhere down on the ocean floor in an area of deep and rugged terrain.

Of the 197 passengers, 3 air crew and 10 cabin crew on board, only the bodies of 58 passengers had been found floating among the wreckage on the surface of the ocean.

224

One of them was a friend of mine from the PR team at MarshJet. Mark was not among them.

In the press, there had been speculation that a new computerized stall-safe system on the plane and the pilot's misunderstanding of how it functioned could have contributed to the tragedy. In the weeks and months after I'd left the company, MarshJet had put out several statements insisting their avionics were not at fault. And even though some senior pilots had come out and argued against the idea that pilot error could be to blame, the absence of any similar problems with other MarshJet planes seemed to discredit that defence.

Unless MarshJet had lied.

That was the problem with the black box recorders being unaccounted for. All kinds of conspiracy theories could spring up.

'Two hundred and ten people died,' I said again.

I kept circling back to it. Because it was confirmation to me of something monumental and tragic and impossible to ignore.

Because one of them was Mark.

56
Friday 8.35 p.m.

Hey, it's me. We boarded on time. I just wanted to call to say I love you and I'll see you when I land. Hope you're sleeping well.

They were the last words Mark ever spoke to me. Actually, he spoke them to my voicemail. My phone had been on silent while I was sleeping and I hadn't woken. I'd kept the message stored on my phone ever since. I still listened to it most days. And yes, it devastated me, but it also brought me an odd kind of comfort. It was one more reason why I wanted my phone back from Joel.

I liked hearing Mark's voice and the tenderness wrapped inside it. I liked the way he told me he loved me. The way he'd told me he'd hoped I was sleeping well.

In the message, he was almost whispering. My guess was he'd been sitting next to another passenger he hadn't wanted to disturb. Or perhaps he was embarrassed about being overheard by one of our colleagues.

His message was the kind of thing he'd said to me or texted me countless times before when he was boarding a flight. I'd said and texted similar things to him. *We've boarded. See you soon. I love you.* Words to say in case the worst should happen. Words to ward off a disaster.

Except the disaster had come anyway and there was nothing anyone could do to reverse it now.

I'd had dreams that turned out otherwise, of course. Dreams where I'd answered Mark's call in the small hours of the night and begged him to get off the plane. Where I told him I'd had a premonition. Anything. Where I'd pleaded with him and he'd listened to me and I'd saved him.

But of course I hadn't. I couldn't. And that crushing reality wrecked me anew whenever I woke to find that I was alone in bed, or when I listened to his message late at night with tears streaming down my face.

Back when we were together, before his death, in the tender moments after we'd made love, I used to place my hand on Mark's chest to feel the runaway beating of his heart. I liked to keep my hand there, close my eyes and really concentrate until gradually, it would start to feel as if the beating of Mark's heart was inside my palm, as if I could hold it with me the same way you might hold a butterfly in your hand. Gradually, I'd take my hand away and place it over my own heart, and it would seem for a short while as if I could feel the two rhythms merging and entwining. As though my heart and his heart were combined.

I'd tried the same thing many times since Mark's plane had gone down. I'd placed my hand over my heart on count-less occasions. I'd felt the beating of my own heart under my skin and I'd closed my eyes and longed to feel the faint echo of Mark's heartbeat in my palm, but I could no longer conjure up the background rhythm. I think, more than anything else, that's what convinced me he was really gone. Each time I did it, I was reminded again that I was alone and that something had been taken from me that could never be replaced.

You didn't fake a connection like the one Mark and I had had. I'd loved him with every part of me. Still did. Always would.

And because of that, I also knew that Joel was lying to me. Certainly about Mark. Possibly about other things, too.

It's not as if I didn't *want* to believe him. In many ways, Mark's loss felt so total to me that it also seemed wholly inconceivable. Even now, I knew I would give anything, do anything, to place my hand on his chest and feel the beating of his heart inside my palm one more time.

It's just that I also knew it wasn't possible.

'Fuck you,' I told Joel now. 'I grieved for my husband. I'm *still* grieving for him. You should be ashamed of yourself.'

57

Joel watched Kate for a long moment after she'd spoken.
He concentrated on keeping his responses in check while
he waited for the tide of emotion inside him to subside,
knowing that he needed a sense of clarity now more than
ever.

Focus on why you're here.

He considered the raw emotion in Kate's voice, her barely
suppressed rage. He could tell she resented being studied so
openly, especially when she was so angry and exposed. But
just as he was studying her, he became aware that she was
studying him, too. A tangle of unease clogged his lungs.
What did she see? What did she *think* she saw?

'OK, Kate. I apologize.'

She relaxed by a fraction.

Odd.

Did she think that was it?

'But Kate, I have to explain something to you now that
might surprise you. The fact is there are plenty of people
who do the kind of work that I do. More than you would
imagine. You've heard the expression "information is key",
haven't you?'

She didn't respond. She just glared.

'Well, information is key for you, Kate. It's the key that can open the doors to this office for you. I want you to think about that. But I also need for you to understand that this information is also of crucial importance to my employer. They want to know something from you and they hired me to uncover that something. That's my expertise. Identifying the truth. Making a judgement on it. Knowing when someone is lying to me or not. Trust me when I tell you that I'm the very best there is, and my point is that I can't go back to them with nothing. I just can't. That would be bad for you and even worse for me. They're expecting results, Kate. *They're relying on me.* So if I go back to them with nothing, I might as well put a gun against my head. And I really don't want to put a gun against my head. Understand?'

Yet again she didn't respond.

'My point being, Kate, the reality we both have to confront here is that they will have hired other people. As a back-up. My clients want guarantees. They can't afford for anything to go wrong. You can see that, can't you? And I can guarantee to you that if it comes down to it, anyone who comes in here and replaces me will take a very different approach to my approach. There wouldn't be the same kind of . . . discussion. Do you understand what I'm saying?'

'You're threatening me.'

'No, Kate. See, that's my point: these *other* people would be threatening you. If it comes to it. I'm trying to help you.'

A flicker in her cheek. A stray look at the door.

He'd got through to her, he thought.

'Now, if you want my personal opinion that would be a foolish strategy. Why? Because it leads to questionable results. Every time. Believe me. In my experience, if someone starts hurting you, you'll do or say anything you can to make it stop. And then it gets tricky, if you're in my shoes, to sift the truth from the lies. How much of what you're hearing can be relied on? How much should be disregarded? Do you see?'

Nothing.

'Kate? Do you see?'

'Yes,' she muttered.

'Good. Because what sets me apart – and the reason I'm here now and not one of these other people – is that I do everything I can to provide reliable information to my clients. How do I do that? It really only takes three things. Number one, I watch someone, very closely, the same way I've been watching you. Number two, I talk, one-on-one, like we're doing right now. I set everything out. I try to be as transparent and as fair as possible, and I pay attention to what I'm told and not told. But it's not always as simple as that. Which brings me to my third tool.

'My third tool is time, Kate. It works because it's so versatile. It can stretch forwards to create space.' At this, he pulled his hands apart to demonstrate, as though he was stretching an invisible strand of elastic – the same way he'd demonstrated the same thing so many times before. 'But time can also count down.'

And now he clapped his hands together, hard.

She flinched.

'That can really help focus the mind, Kate.'

A long beat.

Her lips parted. They were dry and cracked.

Instinctively, she glanced down at her glass of water again.

'Go ahead, Kate. Take a sip. I don't mind.' When she shook her head, he said, 'No? You're sure?'

It didn't surprise him that she refused. Not when the offer was on his terms. The part she didn't understand quite yet was that *everything* was on his terms. It had been from the start.

'Well . . . That's probably wise, Kate, because it might reduce the time we have together more than I anticipated.' He reached out to the folio, flicking idly through the pages. 'I have all kinds of information about you in here, Kate. Including your medical history. Your heart op when you were little? You don't have any long-lasting effects from that, am I right? I hope not. Because if you're on any kind of heart medication that we missed, that could seriously reduce the time we have left to figure this thing out.'

He paused and watched her eyes widen and darken, the doubt begin to penetrate and spread.

'Can you feel it already? I wonder. It starts as a tingle, usually. Some people mention a slight metallic taste. Others say there's a bitter sensation at the back of your tongue. You get dizziness. Blurred vision. Then your throat gets parched. Are you burning up? It's probably too early for that but most people burn up. Sort of like a fever. Some people experience tremors or hallucinations.' A small shrug. 'Then, finally, cardiac arrest.'

58

Luke's shift finished late, as it usually did, and he was on his way out of the front exit of the hospital when he saw the woman closing up the florist's shop. The metal shutters at the front of her concession were halfway down and the woman was ducking under them to shift the last of her stock back inside.

'How much for that pink balloon?' Luke asked.

He'd changed his plastic clogs for yellow training shoes and they squeaked against the pimpled rubber flooring as he moved closer and pointed. The woman lifted her head and considered him. She took in his scrubs and laminated ID, the backpack he had slung over one shoulder, his worn and tired face.

'Half price to you, if you have cash.'

'Deal.'

She took a pair of scissors from her apron and separated the helium balloon from the pack floating by the till. Luke counted out the money and she studied him as he put his wallet away, the balloon bobbing next to him.

'Trouble with your girlfriend?'

'No,' he told her. 'It's for someone else.'

Back upstairs on the ward, only Barbara remained from

his shift. She had her coat on in front of the nurses' station and was gossiping with the new team. They all watched him approach. There were knowing smiles and cat calls. He waved them off, hurried on by.

Outside Anna's room he peered in through the glass porthole in the door. For a second, he thought that she was sleeping and he felt a small twinge of disappointment, but then she rocked her head his way, a faint smile lit up her face and she lifted a hand to beckon him in.

He pushed through the door, the balloon bumping against the wall as he entered. In the muffled hospital quiet, all of a sudden he felt self-conscious, silly. 'I guess I just thought . . .' He shuffled. 'You said you wanted a date and I know this isn't that, but there are roses on the balloon and since we're not allowed flowers on the ward I figured . . .'

She pulled her oxygen mask down. 'This is how you dress for a date?'

He gaped at his scrubs. 'Oh, I—'

'I'm joking.' She patted the space on the bed next to her. 'Sit.'

'I really don't have to. I mean, if you're tired, or if you were about to sleep. It's important you get your rest, Anna.'

'All I do is rest. Sit.'

He did, handing the balloon to her, watching the delight in her eyes as she allowed the ribbon to slip through her fingers, the balloon rising towards the ceiling.

'You're sweet,' she told him.

'You think maybe I should put that somewhere else?' He began to stand. 'I can tie it to the end of your bed, or in the corner, maybe?'

'No.' She grabbed his wrist with surprising strength and pulled him back down. She didn't let go and for a second, he got the feeling that she was holding on to more than just him. As though she was clinging to an idea, maybe. A possibility.

Her hand was cool. Her grip steadily weakened. Luke looked down at her face and then away, feeling everything knotting and twisting inside. During his nursing career he'd seen more than his fair share of heartbreak and tragedy, and yes, he'd also witnessed moments of genuine, life-affirming joy. But this was something he could never reconcile himself to. A young woman who should have had her whole life ahead of her, barely clinging on, ebbing away.

'I've been thinking about my sister,' he told her. 'About what you said to me earlier.'

'I didn't mean to interfere, Luke. Ignore me. I—'

'No, that's OK. Really. It's just, what I was saying before, me worrying about her, it's not only that she's had a tough time lately, although she has, it's that . . .' He stopped. Thought about how best to put it. How he could possibly explain everything that bound him to Kate. 'My sister was born with a hole in her heart. They found it when she was little. I was little, too, obviously. Older than her but still only a kid. She was five for the first operation. I was eight. So I remember. My aunt and uncle looked after me but I remember how my parents spent all their time at the hospital with her. Just like your parents have been spending all their time with you. And I remember coming to visit her. And the thing is, the operation went really well, and so did the next one. Looking back, it was almost routine. She's been fine ever since. Much fitter than me. But afterwards. I don't know.'

'You worried about her.'

'Yeah. I mean, on the outside, she was so strong. She did all these amazing things. She grew up and travelled the world.'

'But let me guess – you still see the little girl in the hospital bed?'

'Sometimes. I guess I do.'

'I mean, it's not so hard to figure out. It's why you work here, isn't it?'

'No. No, that doesn't have anything to do with—'

But he stopped. Because maybe it did. Maybe it always had and he just hadn't faced it until now.

'It's OK.' She squeezed his fingers. 'You don't have to explain. She hasn't been in touch with you about her interview yet?'

'No, not yet.'

'Do you want to check on her?'

'Part of me does. It's what I've always done. But another part of me thinks maybe I shouldn't this time. Maybe I should let her deal with whatever happened to her today by herself. And I don't want to make it seem like I'm smothering her either, so . . .'

'So?'

He sighed. 'My washing machine is broken.'

'I don't—'

'My washing machine is broken, and usually when I'm concerned about Kate I tell her I need to do laundry at her place. I go over there and I put a load on and then I have to wait for the washing machine to finish, which means we'll start talking.'

'And you'll get to help her.'

'Not always.'

'But sometimes.'

'Yeah.'

'Is that what you're going to do tonight?'

He thought about it, looking up at the balloon skimming the ceiling tiles, as if it was trying to find a way out of the room. 'I don't know, Anna. Really, I don't.'

59

Friday 8.39 p.m.

My heart thumped.

It hurt.

I wanted to believe it was another lie. I wanted to convince myself of it.

But then, with a flush of panic, I thought of the sour taste in my mouth. The chalky sensation on the back of my tongue. When I swallowed, my throat felt hot and sore, but now I was beginning to wonder if there wasn't some kind of swelling back there, too. Then there was the wooziness I'd been experiencing. The hazy vision.

Oh God.

I raised a hand to my chest. Felt the runaway beating of my heart. Joel was right that I wasn't on any medication. I hadn't needed any cardiac check-ups since my teenage years. As far as my GP was concerned, my heart was just as healthy as a regular person's. Probably stronger, with the challenging runs I'd been putting myself through during much of the past year.

But was the rhythm becoming erratic or was I imagining it?

'You drank the water, Kate. You think maybe you should have stuck with coffee after all?'

I stared at my tumbler, then the carafe. Joel had poured himself a glass, too. I could remember that. But his glass still appeared full. I hadn't seen him raise it to his lips.

The water looked perfectly clear. There was no powdery residue. No oily translucence.

But still.

There *was* a sort of tingling on the back of my tongue.

'Are you . . . Are you saying you've poisoned me?'

'Well, technically speaking you poisoned yourself, Kate.'

Everything that happened next happened in a rush.

I bolted from my chair, out of the cube. I ran for the kitchen and snatched open a cupboard that was stocked with supplies and condiments. I saw paper plates, plastic cups, disposable cutlery. And something else I'd noticed before.

A cardboard dispenser filled with individual sachets of salt.

I grabbed a handful, took down a glass from a high shelf and ran water from the sink. I tore the salt sachets open. Dumped their contents into the glass. Then I swirled the mixture around. A whirling vortex. I raised the glass to my lips and swallowed.

'Kate? Kate, it's much too late for that.'

My throat opened up. I gagged.

I threw back another mouthful and then I bent forwards over the sink as everything gushed up out of me. I clung on to the taps as my stomach heaved and clenched. I stayed that way for what felt like a long time, until, weak and shivery, I slid to the ground.

My skin was clammy. My hair was pasted to my forehead. My eyes felt too big and hot inside my head.

I didn't move as Joel walked closer and squatted in front of me with the folio case in his hands.

'I'm sorry, Kate, but it's already in your system. It only takes a tiny dose.'

Again, I wondered if he was lying. I hadn't tasted anything amiss when I'd drunk from the tumbler of water earlier. But then, I hadn't been suspicious.

I was under an enormous amount of stress right now. I'd just been sick. But even so, this felt *different*. Wrong. I could sense it the same way you can recognize the early symptoms of a cold or the flu. The slight fever. My upset balance. The soreness in my throat and the tingling on my tongue, as if I'd been injected in my gum with a local anaesthetic.

'Kate.' He reached for my face. I pulled away but not by enough. He peeled a strand of hair from my brow. 'Talk to me and I can help you, Kate. We can get you to a hospital so you have the care you need when you need it. And you are going to need it.'

He cupped my cheek in his palm. He stroked me with his thumb.

The same way Mark used to.

I slapped his hand away.

'You have a few hours still before it really kicks in, Kate. You need to think carefully about what you're willing to share with me. But first I'm going to give you some space and time to think. I have to go and check on Maggie.'

He straightened and looked down at me. His face was cast in shadow, the outline of his body rimmed orange by the glow of the sun dipping low outside the windows behind him.

He turned and walked away. Moments later I heard the doors in reception unlock, open and seal behind him again.

60

Out in the vestibule, Joel let go of a breath and clamped a hand to the back of his neck. He was on edge. Restless. Equal parts exhilarated and appalled by what he'd done to Kate. What he'd *had* to do.

But still.

He'd hoped for a clearer outcome by now. Instead all he had were the same questions he'd started with, added to a nervy awareness of time running out.

Kate's stubbornness didn't surprise him. One look at the background information he had on her had told him she would be no pushover. She was a fighter. It was probably something she'd learned from a young age when she'd been sick. And it was clear to him that she loved her husband deeply. Now the question became how much did she love him. How much did she know.

Moving to his side, he reached his arm in behind the tall planter to his right and removed the two mobile phones he'd stashed there.

The first mobile was Kate's. He accessed it as before using the taped thumbprint, checking for any new messages or missed calls and finding there were none.

The second phone was a cheap burner. There were no

messages or missed calls on it. There was only one number he would ever dial.

A twinge of discomfort as he placed the call.

While he waited for the connection, he turned and peered through the glass panel in the door to see Kate hurrying past him with her head down, clutching her stomach, on her way to the bathroom. That was OK, he told himself. He'd checked the bathroom earlier. There was nothing in there that could pose a risk.

He was still looking in through the doors when the phone was answered. He heard the rasp and crackle of throaty breathing on the end of the line.

'I have a progress report,' he told Fergus Marsh.

'Go on,' Marsh wheezed.

'She says she doesn't know anything. At all.'

A long pause.

His temples ached and throbbed.

For a strange moment, as Joel listened to the constricted breathing on the other end of the line, it was as if the office in front of him was breathing – like a giant organism that was gently expanding and receding before his eyes.

'Do you believe her?'

There it was. The question he was required to answer. The question he was being paid to answer. The question he had to handle particularly carefully right now.

'It's possible she's telling the truth.'

'Your job is not to tell me what's possible.' The voice rasped and snapped like a rusted saw blade. 'Your job is to give me an answer.'

As if he didn't know that.

The throbbing in his temple intensified and he pressed against the area with his fingertips, sending a jolt of pain crackling across his brow. He'd suffered from migraines since he was an adolescent. He couldn't afford to get one now.

How to navigate the right response?

Normally, Joel had a much clearer sense by this point. Normally he could feel himself edging towards a verdict even before his head had settled on a definitive answer.

Except not today.

Not so far.

That had to change, eventually. One way or another.

But no client wanted to hear that. And especially not a client for whom everything was on the line.

'This is a process. We're still talking. We have time.'

'Your *time* is running out.'

Another blinding thump from his forehead. It was like he'd told Kate. There would be a back-up of one kind or another. He suspected it was the man they'd had watching Tony's daughter – the one who'd broken into Kate's flat. Not that it made any difference who it was, really. The only thing that mattered now was how long Marsh would wait before sending them in.

A streak of something close to panic forked downwards from his brain stem, branching out. Synapses flashed. Muscles cramped.

Trust your process.

Trust yourself.

'That's what I'm relying on,' he said, and ended the call.

61

Sir Fergus Marsh wheezed and grimaced in the aftermath of the call, gripping hold of the richly lacquered desk in front of him until his knuckles whitened. The ceaseless pain was like thousands of tiny paper cuts at the back of his throat. It never went away, though usually the morphine masked it better than this.

He rode out the latest wave of agony. A few more seconds of torture, followed by one more phone call and then he could rest for a spell. Using his other phone, he dialled on speaker and waited. He waited an irritatingly long time.

'I need another update,' he rasped.

'They're strategizing,' his source whispered back. 'But they're being more cautious. They're starting to get doubts.'

'Tell me about their strategy.'

'They're developing two approaches. One if they have the testimony they want for Monday. Another if they don't.'

'Why the doubts?'

'They don't have any control over the person they've been talking to. They expected to hear from them again this evening but they haven't been in touch.'

For several seconds, the only sound was his haggard

breathing. In moments like this, the ceaseless noise was somehow worse than the pain and physical discomfort. More than anything, he craved the mental silence he used to take for granted. It was so much more difficult now to hear himself think.

Had they underestimated Kate Harding? Could *she* be the witness?

Three weeks ago, their source inside the prosecution team had alerted them to a transformation in the prosecution's case. They'd received a call from someone using voice-distortion equipment. The caller had tantalized them with a sample of data from a cache of information that only Mark Harding had ever accessed or collated – unless he'd passed it on to his wife or somebody else. The revelation had forced them to confront a previously inconceivable question. Was Mark really dead? And if he wasn't, how could they find him before it was too late?

But if the team were expecting to be contacted this evening, while Kate was contained . . .

'You didn't tell me that before.'

'I tell you what I know when I know it.'

Sir Fergus hung up without another word and stared forwards for a long, harrowing moment, then turned towards the corner of the room, where Dominic North watched him from the shadows, one half of his face bleached white by the slanted light from a standing lamp. Dominic's narrow fingers were steepled, pressed to the underside of his chin. Sir Fergus had seen him adopt the same thinking pose many times before when they'd made crucial decisions together in the past.

'This is why we arranged a back-up,' Dominic said now, as if it was the most reasonable observation in the world.

Sir Fergus screwed his eyes shut against a fresh resurgence of pain. 'It's too early for that,' he murmured.

'Is it?' Dominic angled his head fully into the light, his features gleaming like a skull. 'Sometimes, I find myself wondering if it's not only your health that's started to fade.'

It was an amazing thing, Sir Fergus reflected to himself, how the loyalty and fealty of one man could curdle over the years into something so insidious.

'We can't be hasty.' He shook his head. 'I won't be boxed in like that again.'

'Is that how you see it now? I call it conviction, Fergus. The courage to do what has to be done when it needs to be done. You know how this has to end.'

'If the board ever find out . . .'

'The board. You hired paper people for paper positions. What have your precious board ever done for this company when it really counts?'

Sir Fergus closed his mouth, fighting against the instinct to swallow, knowing that it would only heighten his agony. He was in league with a viper, and while he knew it was far too late to defang Dominic now, he was also conscious that tonight, more than ever, he couldn't afford to be rushed.

'We hired an expert to give us a professional analysis.' Something scraped inside his windpipe as if a strip of sandpaper was lodged in it. 'If Mark Harding is a threat, we need to know it. If he's not, we may know who is.'

'*You* hired an expert, Fergus. I hired an exterminator.' He gestured to the phone. 'Make the call.'

The great weight that had been pressing down on his shoulders seemed to drain through him and settle in his lungs. Slowly, he steeled himself for one more effort and punched in another number which automatically diverted to an anonymous voicemail service. It was a precaution, among others, they'd been told to expect.

No names. No details. Keep everything vague.

'Be primed and ready to step in,' he croaked, after the beep had sounded. 'But wait for my go-ahead.'

62

Friday 8.52 p.m.

Automatic lights blinked on as I entered the bathroom.
There were cubicles on my left. A row of sinks to my right.
I tore off my jacket, dumped it on the floor, reached out for
one of the sinks. I ran cold water from the tap and let it
flush over my wrists. I splashed my face. Then I looked at
myself in the mirror. It was a shock to see my reflection. I
was gaunt and hollow-eyed. My lips had a bluish tinge.

I leaned closer and pulled down my eyelids. I opened my
mouth, stuck out my tongue.

My stomach rumbled. I had cramps.

I snatched some paper towels from the dispenser, patted
my face dry, rolled up the sleeves of my blouse.

Think.

For just a second, my mind turned to the photographs
Joel had shown me from my trip to Camden Market. The
saddest part wasn't how cruelly the image had been manipulated. It was that I actually wanted to believe Mark had
been there. I wished so badly it was true.

I bit my lip and looked at myself in the mirror, then slowly
raised my hands to my blouse and undid the top two buttons.
I eased my right hand beneath the fine material, my fingers
finding their way to the familiar, notched scar running down

over my chest. It was white and raised. A little bumpy. I took a deep breath and pressed my hand down over my heart.

I could feel it beating. A frenzied rat-tat-tat-tat.

I tuned it out, searching for a pure, clear space in the centre of my mind, waiting for the long-remembered echo of Mark's heart to come through to me.

But there was nothing there. There was just utter stillness and absence in my palm. Only my own heart banging away in my chest and the hard, sterile silence of the bathroom that surrounded me.

I swallowed dryly and withdrew my hand. I refastened the buttons on my blouse.

'You have to be strong now,' I told myself. 'You are strong.'

It was something I used to tell myself after I'd lost Mum and Dad. A mantra I conjured up to drive myself forwards, make myself go on. I was alone right now but that was OK. I'd been alone before. I could get myself out of this situation. I *would* get myself out of it.

It was just me.

Only me.

And Maggie, a voice whispered inside my head.

I spun and looked towards the closed door to the bathroom.

Why hadn't I thought of it before?

63

Friday 8.58 p.m.

The silence was unnerving when I stepped out from the
bathroom. But it wasn't a complete silence. I was growing
more attuned to my surroundings now. As I stalked along
the corridor and ventured out into the reception area, I
was able to pick up the smallest nuances in the sound-
scape.

There was the background hum of the few computers that
were still working. The low-level shudder of the fridge in
the refectory. The whirr and bluster of the air conditioning
system funnelling through the ceiling ducts and vents. The
buzzing of the lights overhead.

Goosebumps on my skin.

The double doors to the office remained closed. I stepped
towards them and pushed and pulled. Still locked.

I spun around. There was no hint of any movement across
the office floor. Outside, twilight had fallen, casting the tinted
windows in a darker hue.

Everywhere *looked* abandoned. I didn't think Joel was here
but I knew he could be watching me remotely. I also knew
he could be back any second.

I moved forwards, fast.

Rushing would make my heart beat faster and I guessed

it might increase the spread of any poison in my body, put me at more risk.

It was a strange thing, thinking of my heart being vulnerable suddenly. Ever since the operations, my parents and doctors had been at pains to tell me everything was healthy, that I could live my life without fear. And in that respect, I had. But now, to think that I was just one skipped heartbeat away from everything simply . . . stopping.

I ran, the muscles of my legs taut and straining.

The glass cube was ahead of me.

I swerved in through the doorway.

It was still there.

Maggie's handbag.

I lunged inside and grabbed it from the desk, then backed out of the cube and looked around for somewhere to hide with it.

I wasn't going to scurry under a desk this time. Not again. I saw the carousel horses and the campervan. I saw the gazebo and the swing. Then I saw the basket for the hot-air balloon and rushed for it, tightening my grip on the bag.

I jumped inside, crouched low. The basket was woven from abrasive wicker. It scratched my skin through my blouse as I rocked backwards on my heels and raised my head to scan the office floor towards reception.

There was still no movement.

Still no sign of Joel.

I parted the bag and thrust my hand inside.

I was hoping for a phone but I didn't find one in the main compartment or the zipped side compartment. Joel must have taken it.

The Interview

Upending the bag, I dumped its contents out in front of me.

A Filofax the size and consistency of a house brick. A rolled-up shopping bag. A compact umbrella. Two tampons, a deodorant stick and a page torn from a magazine. I unfolded the page. It was an article with a banana bread recipe.

I sorted through the rest of the things that had fallen out. There was a laminated badge with Maggie's name on it that looked like it had come from a recruitment networking event. I also found a set of car keys and house keys.

Nothing else. No purse. Joel must have taken that as well.

I snatched at the bag and pulled it inside out. There had to be something that could help me. But all that emerged was a sprinkle of dust, fine grit and lint.

I set the bag to one side and picked up the Filofax. Undoing the rubber band that was holding it together, I turned to today's date and saw the time and location of my interview jotted down. Flicking back I could see my name scrawled and circled on several other days, including the morning two weeks ago when Maggie had first contacted me and, to my surprise, I'd found myself talking to her while Simon and Rebecca were out. Beneath my name and number were a few short notes about our discussion. *Needs confidence. Great experience. Wants excitement. Edge?*

I quickly flicked through the rest of the Filofax, fanning the pages, then dropped it to one side, pushing up from my knees. Stepping out of the basket, I moved towards the sheet of glass I'd attacked with the office chair. The chair was still there on the floor, broken and inert. The panel of glass remained stubbornly intact.

I ducked and switched both desk lamps back on to

illuminate my SOS message again, but even though it was darker outside, I saw nothing to indicate my plea for help was visible when I looked down at the street.

There were a few pedestrians hurrying along with their heads down, none of them looking up at me. There were no clusters of smokers outside the pub. Vehicles were passing below, though not as many as before. To my right, lights were shining in some of the windows of the office blocks in Paternoster Square.

People would be working late, I thought. Lawyers and accountants. Management consultants. Financial advisers. They would be at their desks, tapping at computer keyboards, and perhaps every now and again one of them would look up and glance my way.

And all they'd see was one more gleaming, mirrored window amid hundreds of others.

I closed my eyes, spread my fingertips against the glass and listened to the ambient noises of the office floor that surrounded me.

I listened to the computers and the fridge and the air ducts and the electric lights.

That was when I noticed it.

A new sound.

A low, bass thrumming.

I turned, squinting, trying to understand what I was hearing.

It was definitely there – *something* – beyond the noise of the office environment and the whooshing of the blood in my ears.

My head snapped left and I zeroed in on it.

The noise wasn't coming from *inside* the office.

It was coming from outside the double doors.

64

One floor down, there were no double doors. There was no smart vestibule outside the trio of elevators. None of the elevators ordinarily stopped at the twelfth floor. Joel had needed the maintenance key he'd taken from the security room to gain special access via the lifts.

He stepped out of the elevator into a thrum of noise and heat. The air was hot and gritty, the lighting dim. There were no picture windows at all. Instead, the perimeter of floor twelve consisted of a complex system of vents and louvres.

55 Ludgate Hill contained two mechanical floors. One was located just above the penthouse. The other was in front of Joel now.

He moved forwards quickly, past pipework and plumbing systems. He saw water tanks and boilers. He saw pumps to circulate hot water and other pumps to distribute air. There were chillers for the air conditioning system. There was an electrical switchboard. Further back he could see a telecoms master board and multiple computer servers.

He kept going until he reached Maggie. She was sitting on the dusty floor with her chin on her chest and her legs out in front of her. Her upper back was resting against a hot-water pipe. Her arms were secured around the pipe behind her, bound knuckle to knuckle with duct tape. More of the tape had been secured over her mouth.

Joel stepped closer, the chalky fragments of a migraine pill dissolving on his tongue, the unfamiliar angst he'd been fighting for most of the evening reaching a new and fluctuating pitch.

Her head jerked up and she whimpered from behind her gag, her nostrils flaring. Her grubby face and clothing were damp with sweat.

From the fear that burst behind her eyes, it was clear she thought he was here to attack her, perhaps worse.

It made him feel . . . strange. Joel had more than enough self-awareness to know that he was a very long way now from the essentially good person he'd once believed himself to be. His actions over the years – the interviews he'd carried out, the pressure he'd applied to people who were not equipped to withstand it – had changed him, no question. But he was no mindless thug. He took zero pleasure from killing for killing's sake. What had happened with Tony, for instance, weighed on him more than he wanted to admit. He'd rushed things, probably. Perhaps, with more time to think, there might have been another way.

Perhaps there could be with Maggie.

He had no idea what story she'd been spun. When Sir Fergus had first contacted him through a mutual intermediary he'd simply explained the set-up he preferred and how a recruitment agent would be necessary. But he did know Maggie had come here today. He knew she'd arranged to meet Kate for a drink following her interview. And it was clear from the records in her Filofax that they'd been in regular contact.

Two things sprang from that.

One, keeping her alive – for now – offered him leverage over Kate. If it came to it, he could threaten Maggie in front of her.

And two, it was possible that Kate had shared something with Maggie – something seemingly innocuous – that might just give him the answer he needed, if he failed to get it from Kate.

'Maggie.'

Her breathing rate accelerated, her cheeks bulging around her taped mouth as he dropped to his haunches in front of her, watching her shrink back, noting her natural responses, studying her mannerisms and behaviour, logging it all for possible later use.

'It's OK, Maggie. Try to relax. I just want to look at you.'

65

Friday 9.04 p.m.

I ran back past the hot-air balloon basket and streaked between desks with my gaze locked on the doors leading out from reception.

I couldn't see who or what was out there.

The noise I could hear was hard to place. It was a kind of percussive, scuffed droning, not unlike the old and sometimes cranky washing machine in my flat.

I was afraid it was Joel. Afraid he was doing something destructive to the doors. He could be barricading them in some way. Making doubly certain I couldn't get out.

A kick of panic.

Perhaps his intention had always been to leave me locked in here until whatever toxin he'd introduced to my body had completed its work. Maybe there was never any possibility I was getting to a hospital.

Or maybe he was coming in here with whatever was making that noise.

I glanced down at the workstation I was passing. It was mostly empty. But there was a desktop computer. A keyboard.

The keyboard was wireless. I snatched it up and raised it over my shoulder. My arms shook so badly the keys rattled.

I stalked forwards.

Closer.

Closer.

The noise coming from outside the doors was far louder now, droning at a relentless, vibrating pitch.

I turned sideways-on and edged nearer. I moved past the reception counter.

I wet my lips. Blinked the perspiration from my eyelids.

From the angle I was on, I couldn't see clearly through the glass panels in the doors. And because of the dim lighting on the other side, most of what I could see was the milky reflection of the office and the reception counter behind me. Then I saw the shimmer of my own reflection as I stepped closer. My face ballooned and distorted until my nose was almost touching the glass and then, finally, my reflection faded away and I was staring into the vestibule.

At Raul.

He was facing away from me in his cleaning overalls, operating his floor-polishing machine. It was vibrating and shuddering incredibly fast. The bristled discs underneath flailed around. He had his feet braced shoulder-width apart but his hips and upper body were juddering as he swept the machine from side to side.

His headphones were on.

I dropped the keyboard and banged on the door with my fists. I yelled.

He didn't hear me.

I grabbed for the door handles. I yanked on them hard.

The doors rattled and shook but it wasn't enough to get his attention.

I kicked the door and waved both hands, hoping he might

catch a glimmer of my movement reflecting from the metal casing of the elevators.

'Raul! Raul, look at me!'

I shouted so loudly it seemed impossible he couldn't hear me. Impossible that Joel wouldn't hear me, too.

'Raul, please!'

My throat ached but Raul's steady progress continued undisturbed. He was in no rush at all. If he was listening to music through his headphones – and I guessed that he was – then he probably had the volume cranked up very loud to compensate for the racket of the machine.

'Raul!'

I stepped back.

I braced my hands on my hips.

Turn! I willed him. *Look at me!*

But Raul didn't turn and the desperation sapped at me.

Joel had told me he was going to check on Maggie, but how long would that take? How long until he returned?

I looked around, thinking of what to do, my eyes passing over the fire alarm that Tony had deactivated. After the alarm had sounded, Raul must have evacuated the building along with everybody else before coming back inside to continue his shift.

Wait.

Next to the alarm panel was a collection of light switches. Eight of them altogether.

I stretched for them and flicked them all up and down with both hands.

The light fittings above my head blinked on and off.

So did the lights out in the vestibule.

66

Friday 9.07 p.m.

I leaned to my right and stared wildly through the cracked panel of glass at Raul. He tipped his head back and glanced up towards the ceiling at the flickering lights. He released the handles of his machine. Gradually, he removed his headphones from his ears.

The machine slowed and whirred into silence as Raul looked to his left and right.

'Raul! Raul, over here!'

I continued to flick the lights on and off as Raul turned and ducked and peered in confusion through the glass.

He flinched and did a double-take when he saw me.

'I don't have a key card.' I pointed to the sensor. 'You have to let me out.'

A broad smile of sudden understanding split his face. He nodded energetically and held up a finger, then dipped his hand into a pocket on his jumpsuit and removed a key card that was attached to a rubber tether. He wafted his key card over the sensor and I stared intently at the steel plate on my side of the doors.

I rocked forwards on my toes. Flexed the fingers of my hands.

For a split-second, I was terrified the door wouldn't unlock. I feared that Joel had disconnected the sensor somehow.

But then a tiny green light illuminated and the lock unlatched.

I felt a flush of relief as I grasped at the door handle, yanking the door open, stepping out.

'Oh my God, Raul, thank you. Thank you. You have no idea . . .'

But my words trailed away as the fire exit door swung open to my right.

My heart slammed into my throat.

Joel stepped through.

At first, his face was angled downwards and he didn't see us. Then his chin jerked up and he froze.

'Run!' I yelled.

It happened too fast for Raul. It was too confusing. He didn't move right away and he was blocking me with his bulk, and all I really succeeded in doing was triggering Joel to respond.

He sprang forwards from his toes, launching himself at Raul with a grunt, grabbing hold of the lapels of his overalls and spinning him around and around. As Raul yelped and shouted, Joel drove him hard into the wall across from me.

'No!' I screamed. 'Stop it!'

I clutched at Joel's shirt, his arms. A startled groan escaped Raul's lips.

'Get off him!'

I hooked a finger into Joel's shirt collar and jerked him backwards. He gagged and reached out for me with one arm, using his other forearm to pin Raul against the wall. Raul was squirming, scrabbling, looking at me in stunned and desperate alarm.

Joel patted my arm, then my shoulder. He felt my face, cupped his hand beneath my jaw and shoved me violently to one side.

I collided with an elevator door.

My shoulder and head struck steel.

I saw stars.

It took me a second or so to recover. I put a hand to my temple. Pushed off from the elevator. Swayed.

That was when Raul let go of a winded groan and doubled up from the waist.

Joel had punched him in the stomach.

Raul dropped to his knees.

Joel took a handful of Raul's hair. He yanked his head back, exposing his throat. With his other hand he groped down towards the plug socket behind him. He was reaching for the electric cable for the floor-polishing machine.

With an intense, crackling horror, I realized that if he could pick up the cable he could coil it around Raul's neck. He could—

I dived for the cable, banging my elbows, my chin. I snatched at it with both hands and twisted and yanked on it hard. The plug sprang out of the wall, barely evading Joel's grasp.

Raul looked at me in a daze, his head held in Joel's grip.

Joel stared back at me with his shirt bloodied and askew, an expression of grim defiance on his face.

I dragged the cable towards me, hand over hand. I got to my feet.

The cable was looped over my right hand. The plug was at my side.

'Kate,' Joel warned. 'Don't do—'

I lashed out, flicking my wrist. The cable cracked the air. The plug struck Joel's face. He swore and turned his head away.

I dragged the plug back towards me. I was still pulling it in when I heard Joel let go of an anguished howl before snatching Raul's head violently to one side, then the other, very, very fast.

He yelled and dashed Raul's skull against the wall.

The sound of the impact was so awful – so shocking – that I immediately let go of the cable.

It just dropped from my hands.

Then I shuddered, powerless, as Joel growled, and whined, and did it again.

67

Friday 9.11 p.m.

When he was finished – when it was over – Joel turned
and stared at me. His face was puce. His hair glistened. His
neck and shirt and hand were speckled red.

'It wasn't supposed to be like this,' he panted. 'Nobody
else was meant to get hurt.'

I shook my head repeatedly, stepping backwards.

Raul was lying motionless on the floor. I didn't dare look
at him.

The call buttons for the elevators were behind me. I felt
for them, fumbled them. I pressed them again and again.

'You see what happens when you get other people
involved, Kate? First Maggie. Now this guy.'

His shoulders sagged and he wiped his mouth with the
back of his hand. The vivid red mark from where I'd caught
him with the plug gleamed on his cheek like a wet scar.

Maggie . . . What had he done to her?

A *bing* behind me.

The doors to the furthest elevator parted.

I backed up into the carriage, jabbing at the button for
the ground floor.

My knees flexed. I cried.

All I wanted was to huddle up in a ball as the doors closed, but they hadn't even moved before Joel appeared in the gap in front of me, bracing the doors open with his elbow and foot.

I could feel the heat radiating out from his body. The anger and frustration.

There was a red emergency call button on the other side of the carriage. I lunged for it but he grabbed my arm, yanking me around.

I screamed and lunged again.

My fingers didn't quite touch the button.

He held me back, his other hand coming towards my head.

He was going for my neck. He was going to attack me the same way he'd attacked Raul.

He snatched for my hair. He tugged on it hard. I screamed again as he forced my head forwards, jamming me into a crouch, spinning me around and leading me out of the carriage ahead of him.

I cried out in pain, trying to resist him, but he tightened his grip on my hair and pushed me roughly towards the double doors to the office.

I almost fell as he reached into his pocket and removed his key card, then whirled me around and held me down at arm's length as he stepped over Raul to stretch towards the sensor plate on the wall.

This time I had no choice but to look. Raul was lying on his front. He wasn't moving. His head was a terrible mess. Joel was forcing me down so close to him that I could hear the tinny reverb playing through the headphones that were still fitted around his neck.

I pulled my eyes away from his face, lowering them to his chest and torso as the doors unlocked. There was no sign that he was breathing. The white cable from his headphones snaked towards a pocket on his overalls.

I thought about that, my mind scrambling to latch onto something.

My vision stuttered and then I moved, my hair ripping as I dived for the ground.

A flash of brilliant pain lit up my scalp. Joel still had a hold of a hank of my hair. But by now I was twisting, swinging up with my arm, not unlike the way Joel had punched Raul in the stomach. But my hand wasn't closed in a fist. It was spread wide open. And I aimed lower than his stomach, making a grab, squeezing hard.

Joel roared and let go of my hair. He jumped out of the way. Clutched at his groin.

I turned back and felt for Raul's pocket, my hand finding his phone inside. I ripped it free, yanked the headphone jack clear and sprang for the office doors.

They were still unlocked.

They crashed open.

I stumbled.

'Kate!'

I ran without looking back.

The phone was up in front of my face. The screen jolted and shook. The office floor bounced and tilted in my vision.

I heard a door thump open behind me. Footfall.

I jabbed the home button on Raul's phone with my thumb. His lock-screen picture appeared. A different shot of his young wife and baby girl. His wife was in hospital scrubs.

267

She was holding the baby with a cannula leading out from her wrist.

I didn't know Raul's passcode. I couldn't access his phone in the normal way. But down in the bottom left-hand corner of the screen I could see the word EMERGENCY. I jabbed it and the phone screen opened up. Two bars of signal.

'Kate, you call *anyone* and I will have to kill you.'

I glanced up. Desks in front of me, blocking my way. The backlit, backwards HELP on the windows ahead of me.

I veered left.

My thumb struck 9.

'Kate. Think about what you're doing.'

Another 9.

More desks lay ahead of me. The hot-air balloon beyond that.

I split right this time.

Hit the third 9.

As I angled my thumb down over the green 'call' icon, something slammed into me from behind, taking me out at the knees.

My legs went sideways. I flailed forwards, falling just shy of the hot-air balloon.

The phone bounced out of my grip.

I couldn't tell if my call had connected or not. I had no idea if there was somebody on the end of the line.

'Help me!' I screamed. 'Help!'

Joel jumped onto my lower back. He pressed me down into the floor, reached up past my head.

I struggled to push up into a crawl. I fought to reach for the phone. It was just ahead of me. I could see the lit screen.

'Hello! If you can hear me, I'm at—'

Joel's palm was on my mouth, squeezing hard. His skin was hot and oily. He flattened my lips. Crushed my gums.

I couldn't get the words out.

I bit him.

He swore and snatched his hand away.

I stretched again for the phone.

He grabbed hold of my wrist and wrenched my arm behind me, hauling me around so that I was lying on my back, looking up at him, pinned.

Then his fist came at me, fast, and I braced myself for a blow that never came.

When I opened my eyes I could see that he'd made a grab for the phone, and as he lifted it past me I noticed the seconds of a call counting upwards.

. . . 8 seconds . . . 9 . . .

I *thought* I heard a distant voice on the end of the line, but it was cut off when Joel pressed his thumb down on the red phone icon and disconnected the call.

68
Friday 9.14 p.m.

'Kate, please. I'm trying to help you here. If you listen to me, I can keep you alive.'

'By poisoning me? By holding me prisoner?'

He pushed me down as he got to his feet with Raul's phone in his hand. He shook his head in disgust and pinched the bridge of his nose between his finger and thumb, as if he was having to mine reserves of patience that were running dangerously low.

'They won't trace your call, Kate. Even if they did, it would take them too long. And it doesn't matter anyway. As far as anybody knows, you're not here. You were signed out from the visitor book. You left hours ago.'

My heart was pumping furiously in my chest. My stomach hurt. I felt dizzy, short of breath.

Could that be true? Yes, I realized. Easily. Tony could have fixed it for him with a simple pen stroke. And now if anyone came here looking for me – Luke, say – they could be shown the ledger and turned away.

'They could try calling you back, I suppose.'

Before I could stop him he dropped Raul's phone on the floor, raised his foot and stomped down.

I rolled sideways. Fragments of plastic showered my body,

catching in my hair. He raised his foot to stomp a second time, and this time I scooted backwards until my tailbone bumped up against the base of the hot-air balloon.

There was a brittle, hard crunch as Joel ground the heel of his patent leather brogue from side to side. His shirt was stained and ripped and his tie was loose. Right now he looked a million miles away from the well-groomed professional who'd introduced himself to me just a few hours ago.

I was trembling badly. My fingers clawed into the ground.

When he lifted his shoe, Raul's phone was a shattered mess. Completely obliterated.

I shook my head.

'He just had a baby,' I told him. 'His name was Raul. He had a wife. A new daughter.'

Joel looked at me flatly and for a few short seconds, it was as if I saw another side to him, as if a part of him had split off in some way. His gaze became distant. He sighed and looked up at the ceiling. It seemed as though the consequences of what he'd done really were weighing on him. But then the moment passed and his expression hardened again.

'Get up, Kate.'

I shrank back.

'Seriously?'

I didn't move. I couldn't. I thought about Tony and the threats that had been made against his daughter. I thought about Maggie and the blood I'd seen on Joel's shirt when he'd returned after intercepting her.

Behind me, my hands were tangled up with the items I'd dumped out of Maggie's handbag. The sleeve of my blouse snagged on a stray shred of wicker from the hot-air balloon basket.

The terror was swelling in my throat, choking me. My heart was thumping so hard it seemed to be beating on the outside of my chest.

'I'm not going to ask you again, Kate.'

I moved back another inch.

It was too much for Joel.

He stepped forwards and grabbed hold of my arm. My leg. I kicked and I screamed. Didn't matter. He dragged me across the scuffed concrete floor towards the glass cube, scraping my skin, pulling me in through the door. I bucked up off the ground and tried to run past him but he slammed me back down again, getting two hands around my lower legs and flipping me backwards over my head. I pinwheeled and crashed against the glass. I was tangled up on the floor. In the corner of the cube.

From my slanted viewpoint, I watched as Joel grabbed hold of both chairs and dragged them angrily out of the cube. Once he had them outside, he turned and looked down at me on the floor.

'You're making this harder than it needs to be,' he told me. 'For both of us.'

'You killed him,' I spat back. 'You didn't have to kill him.'

'As if I don't know that,' he said, and then he stepped outside and pushed the door closed behind him with the flat of his hand.

69

Friday 9.18 p.m.

I saw how he locked the door this time. He did it with a small gadget that he took from his pocket. Again, I didn't hear a door lock engage but when he tested the handle it didn't turn.

I watched as he swivelled away from me, then walked across the office floor with one hand stuffed in his pocket, the other rubbing at his face.

I wondered if he'd meant what he'd said. I wondered if it would change anything, if he'd relent and let me go. Perhaps things had got so far out of hand that he'd cut his losses and leave. Maybe he'd just abandon me here alone.

As he neared reception, he took a chair from behind a workstation and wheeled it ahead of himself, moving beyond the partition wall until I couldn't see him any longer.

I got to my feet, swaying. I was shivering so hard I wrapped my arms around myself. I was drained, scared. My scalp itched and ached from where my hair had been pulled. My elbow was tender and so was my stomach from where I'd crashed against the photocopying machine. There were bruises across my legs, knees and hips.

The sour taste at the back of my tongue was still there. And I was getting this weird, out-of-sync effect with my eyes, as though the vision in my peripheries was moving faster than the rest of my sight every now and again. A kind of spatial vertigo.

It could all be shock. I knew that. It could also be down to adrenaline, physical exertion, stress, despair.

But I believed he'd poisoned me. He could have given me a sedative, or a slow-acting hallucinogen, or . . .

Anything.

I pushed the thought away and focused on the call I'd managed to make on Raul's phone instead. The nine seconds I'd spent on the line. If my call had been answered right away, the operator would have heard my shouts. They'd know I was in trouble.

And they can't find you.

My heart clenched.

I reached out and tried the door handle. I rattled it. Slapped both hands on the glass.

If Joel came back in here. If he cornered me . . .

I startled when he reappeared. Whatever strength I had left seemed to drain out of my body.

He was backing up around the partition wall, dragging the office chair behind him. Raul was slumped on the chair, his arms out by his sides, his legs splayed, his heels juddering lifelessly across the ground. Joel was holding him in position with one hand placed across his chest.

I clamped both my hands over my mouth.

Any faint hope I might have had that Raul was still conscious, that he could be saved, vanished in that moment.

I moved past the desk, watching as Joel manoeuvred Raul beyond the games area, between more pillars. He held him upright and trundled him on into the far side of the office behind the refectory wall and out of sight.

I stayed dead still as I waited for Joel to emerge again.

The wait seemed to take a very long time.

Standing in the ringing silence of the cube, barely daring to breathe, I began to feel as if all the air had been sucked out of the room and I was suffocating. It was a sensation that only grew worse when Joel returned, alone this time, and strode directly towards me.

70

Friday 9.25 p.m.

He didn't come inside the cube.

He stopped on the other side of the glass and just stared at me. There was a kind of resignation about the way he was looking at me. In a curious way, it made me think that perhaps he was as boxed in as I was.

Then he broke the spell between us by tilting his body to his left, my right, and reaching around behind him to remove my phone from the back pocket of his trousers.

He contemplated the screen for a moment, pressed the unlock button with his thumb. Afterwards, he held the screen up against the glass and watched me with that same odd mixture of remorse and conviction again.

I glanced at my phone and immediately wished that I hadn't. I shook my head. The dread rose up in my throat.

Hey Sis, how did the interview go? I'm on my way over to yours with some laundry. Wine and a debrief?

Luke's text had been sent two minutes ago.

'Why are you showing me this?'

He didn't answer me but I got a terrible feeling that I knew why. He'd told me that I was endangering other people by involving them in what was happening to me. And if Luke went to my flat and found I wasn't there, he might begin to ask questions. He might start searching for me. He'd know how unusual it was for me not to be home at this time of night.

Then I thought about the man Joel had watching Tony's daughter. What was to stop him sending him after Luke?

'No,' I said. I pulled my hands inwards and cradled them to my chest. 'You don't have to do anything to him. Just text him back. Tell him I don't want to see him. He'll understand.'

But even as I said it, I knew it wouldn't work out that way. I knew Luke. I knew he'd come around to my place regardless.

My guess was Joel suspected the same thing. Or more likely he could tell I was lying to him.

'I can call him,' I pleaded. 'You can stand right next to me. I'll say anything you want me to say.'

Again, Joel didn't move, although his pupils contracted by a fraction.

He seemed to be considering it.

But then the moment passed and I saw him reach a new kind of decision. I watched it form on his face. A taciturn hardening of his features. The way his brow knitted and his eyebrows forked downwards. The slight hook at the side of his mouth.

I watched as he pulled my phone away from the glass, turned it off, returned it to his pocket.

'Please,' I shouted. 'Leave Luke out of this. I'll talk to you now. I'll tell you anything you want to hear. Anything.'

He stopped me by raising his hand and shaking his head.

A single drop of fear hit my stomach and rippled outwards.

And that was when he finally began to speak. I couldn't

hear him through the glass. I had no way of telling if he was talking aloud or if he was simply mouthing the words to me but he did it so slowly, so deliberately, that it really didn't matter either way.

I watched his lips moving. I saw his breath fog on the glass. And then I felt the words get their hooks inside me, tear at me, shred my insides.

Three words in total.

Three words, but that was enough.

'It's. Too. Late.'

71

Friday 9.28 p.m.

Joel turned and walked away from me.

I shouted after him. I yelled his name. I banged on the glass. He didn't slow.

I watched him move behind the wall that shielded me from the reception area and I waited for him to return. I went up on my toes. I craned my neck.

This time, he didn't come back.

'No,' I whispered.

I waited another minute.

'Please don't do this. Please.'

But the only response was the silence that surrounded me and the stillness from outside the cube.

I lost it then. A full-on raging fit. I hammered on the glass. I threw myself against it. I kicked it and I shouted and I yelled and screamed. After a minute or so, I stopped and braced the heels of my hands against the desk behind me, lowering my head, closing my eyes. All of London surrounded me and nobody except Joel knew I was stuck in here.

I whined to myself, thinking about Luke. I didn't want him to get caught up in this. I wanted to believe he would get to my flat and leave again before anything could happen to him. But I didn't believe it. I was terrified.

Luke rode his bike to work every day. It was a twenty-five-minute cycle ride from St Thomas' to the street he lived on. If he was grabbing his washing, he'd need to go inside his flat first, then make his way to mine. Call it thirty, thirty-five minutes.

If Joel was planning to leave me here and confront Luke himself, he had ample time to do it. I didn't know if he had access to a car, but if he didn't he could order an Uber or flag down a cab and get there ahead of Luke. So could the other man he had working with him. They could watch for Luke from the street or, worse, from inside my flat. Joel had my handbag. My keys.

Or maybe the man who broke into my home before is in there already.

I rose up from the desk and stared at the phone. I snatched up the receiver but there was no dial tone at all.

I slammed it back down, crossed to the door, shook the handle. I put my shoulder to the glass. Then I unfurled my fist and looked down at my hand.

I could see the indent from Maggie's keys in the flesh of my palm. I'd gathered them up when I'd backed away from Joel and bumped into the hot-air balloon basket.

There were five keys altogether on a key fob for a Mini car. One was a car ignition key. I selected the longest house key instead. The brass was worn and oxidized. The teeth were dulled from use.

I gripped the key between my finger and thumb and used it to score a long, diagonal line across the glass door in front of me.

The key squeaked and slipped.

It left barely a scratch.

I pushed on the panel but it didn't appear to have been weakened at all.

Turning around, I contemplated the glazed panel immediately opposite the door and, moving towards it, I tried the same thing. The key slipped and screeched and left only a faint trace of its path behind.

Try something else.

I got down on my knees. I spread my fingers against the bottom corner of the panel. Then I gripped the key harder, drew back my hand and stabbed forwards hard.

The tip of the key punched right through to the other side.

I was so surprised that I let out a gasp, pressing my forehead to the panel. Looking down, I could see the very front of the key poking out. I twisted it and turned it. The key crunched and then stuck. I reversed it and tugged it back out.

The tiny hole was rounded and precise. It looked like a small pellet had been fired at the glass panel from a gun at very close range. The damage that surrounded the hole was minimal. Fractional splinters radiated out, then stopped.

I pushed at where the hole had been formed but the glass wouldn't give or flex. If anything, the hole only served to show me how thick the panel of safety glass actually was.

I stabbed it again. A centimetre to the left of the first hole this time. A fresh hole appeared, the same as before. I turned the key and it crunched and scraped, then I tugged it back out again.

The glass was now weaker between the two holes but it still wouldn't push through.

I stabbed above and below and to the side of it, again and again.

In a little over two minutes, I created a whole network of holes.

Then I stabbed *between* the holes, merging them together, forming the beginnings of a larger opening about the size of a tennis ball.

My knuckles were getting bloodied. My grip on the key was beginning to slip. I wiped my fingers against my blouse and stabbed some more, gradually widening the hole, sniffing against the tears that were threatening to come, focusing on the task in front of me, trying to keep my fears about Luke at bay.

My hand was really starting to hurt now.

I didn't slow.

Another ten holes.

Twenty.

The opening was now a little bigger than my fist.

I pushed at the glass surrounding it with my fingertips. Tiny fragments sprinkled onto the floor.

I switched keys and carried on. The bleeding got worse. I wiped my hand on my blouse again.

The hole was getting steadily bigger.

After several more minutes, it was about the same size as the span of my hand. Soon afterwards, it was a little more than double that.

I rocked back on my heels and took a ragged breath, checking behind me, making sure I was alone, that Joel wasn't back. When I put the keys on the floor and stretched out my fingers, the cuts and scrapes made me grimace.

The blood was running down over my wrist towards my elbow.

Ignore it.

I pushed at the remainder of the glass panel. It still felt solid. I shifted around and kicked it with my heel. Twice.

It remained stubbornly in place.

Gripping hold of the key again, I went back to stabbing and stabbing and stabbing, making the hole wider.

My mind kept circling back to Luke. I kept picturing him entering my flat, calling my name. Something about the way Joel had looked at me through the glass – the way he'd told me it was too late – convinced me Luke was in serious danger. I couldn't stand the thought of Joel unleashing the same kind of brutal, violent attack on my brother that I'd watched him launch against Raul.

I cried out. Fresh nicks and cuts criss-crossed my knuckles. By now, I'd forced out a jagged, triangular gap in the bottom right-hand corner of the panel. I thought it might just be big enough for me to squeeze through.

Rising up on my knees, I flattened both hands against the panel again. When I pushed, it creaked and clunked but it wouldn't give out.

I looked at the ground. It was dusted with glass, inside and outside the cube.

Reaching up under my skirt, I pulled down my tights. I stepped out of them, balled them up in my bloodied hand and used them like a cloth to clear the glass.

A few fragments remained by the opening, glittering under the track lighting.

Close enough.

Keeping my tights wrapped around my hand, I lay down on the ground on my back with my head next to the hole. Then I shuffled backwards, carefully feeding my hands and then my arms through the hole to the other side, lifting my buttocks from the ground, pushing off from the concrete with my shoulders and bare heels.

I got my elbows through, followed by my head. The glass scratched at me. A sharp point jabbed into my arm, popping my skin. I felt a cut open up as I squirmed and pushed some more. A small corner of glass snapped free to give me more space.

I paused, my breath hitching in my throat.

The rest of the panel was now suspended immediately above me. If it gave way – if it dropped and collapsed – it would shuttle downwards like a guillotine blade.

Move.

I wriggled and grunted, flinching and baring my teeth as more nuggets of glass dug into my shoulder blades and lower back.

I got my hips free, my knees, my feet.

I pulled myself up and dusted myself down with my tights. Then I stood there, holding my bloodied hand by the wrist, looking out at the silent office.

72
Friday 9.44 p.m.

It was full dark outside now. I picked my way between the drifts of glass on the floor and crossed to the window where the desk lamps were shining. Gripping one of Maggie's keys, I stabbed at the glass.

'Fuck!'

The key stopped dead, my bloodied fingers sliding over the serrated teeth. I winced and changed my grip, grabbing the key overhand, ramming it against the panel up by my shoulder. Same result. I moved left, right, higher, lower, but I found no weak points. All I succeeded in doing was opening the cuts to my hand.

'Crap.'

My bleeding was getting worse, blood dripping onto the floor. I jammed the keys into the chest pocket of my blouse and ran to reception, trying the exit doors for what felt like the hundredth time, finding they were still locked, and then moving around behind the counter.

I'd spotted a first aid kit in one of the metal lockers earlier and I tore it open, using some antiseptic swabs to swipe at the cuts on my hand. Several of the cuts looked worse than superficial and probably needed stitches. The rest stung and wept and that was it. I packed a padded dressing around the back of my hand and secured it with a bandage, tying it off with my teeth.

Do something. Help Luke.

I ran back through the office, veering around the partition wall. I saw Raul slumped on the chair at the far side of the room, close to the floor-to-ceiling windows.

Pinpricks of electric light shone all across the city vista beyond him, shimmering and smearing off the Thames. A lone red beacon pulsed at the top of Battersea Power Station.

I stared at Raul's reflection in the glass. His eyes were dark holes. His head was slackened and tilted to one side.

I took a breath and looked down at him.

I'd never seen a dead body before. When Mum and then later Dad passed away, Luke and I had agreed that we wouldn't view either of their bodies. And of course, Mark had been taken from me in a way that made it impossible for me to say goodbye.

I was almost glad of that now.

There was a greyish pallor to Raul's skin. An odd translucence to his lips. The damage to his head was . . . horrible.

'I'm sorry,' I told him. 'I am so, so sorry.'

His right arm was extended towards me over the arm of the chair, the fingers of his hand unfurled, almost as if he was reaching for something just beyond his grasp. It made me wonder if in his final moments he had reached out for his wife and daughter – if he had been thinking of them both.

I crouched by his side. I could smell the wax he'd applied to his hair. One of the laces of his work boots had come undone.

'Forgive me, Raul.'

I started by searching his chest pocket. He had his name embroidered on an oval badge that was stitched to it. My fingers bumped on something and I scooped out a twist of paper, furred and crushed with age. It was nothing of consequence, just an old, faded receipt for something that had been laundered countless times.

Next I tried his trouser pockets. The pocket on the left had a handkerchief in it. The pocket on the right was trickier to access and when I eased my fingers inside, grimacing at the invasion I was responsible for, I found that it contained his wallet.

I gently removed it. His wallet was made from scuffed olive fabric with a Velcro seal. I glanced at his face again – as if I was asking for permission – and then I separated the Velcro fastener and unfolded it.

There was another photograph of his wife behind a plastic window. That stopped me. This time it was just her and Raul, and from the creased lines in the surface of the photograph and their much younger appearances, it was clear to me that it had been taken many years ago, maybe in the early stages of their romance. She had her lips pressed against his cheek. He was grinning toothily. Her hair was longer. His face was thinner. It looked like a shot that had been taken in a photo booth.

I moved on.

Behind the wallet was a donor card. That affected me, too. I knew from what Luke had told me that many of his patients had died over the years waiting for organs that wouldn't come. There was one patient, Anna, who he'd talked a lot about lately because he was worried the same thing would happen to her.

Perhaps it was a holdover from the heart defect I'd had fixed as a child, but being willing to help other people – complete strangers who are facing the most dire of medical struggles – was about the most noble act I could imagine. Raul had taken that decision. He'd put the necessary arrangements in place. But also I knew from my conversations with Luke that unless I found some way out of here soon, it was unlikely I could get help to him in time for any of his organs to be harvested.

I gently squeezed the pad of his hand – already it felt like squeezing damp clay – and looked through the rest of his wallet. I found banking cards and store discount cards, an expired gym membership card, an out-of-date train ticket. I found a twenty-pound note and a scattering of coins.

I didn't find a key card. I didn't find anything that could get me out of the office or that might enable me to summon help.

I stood and placed my arms around him, easing him gently forwards and feeling inside his rear pockets, finding nothing at all. It was as I rocked him backwards into his chair that I felt the elasticated rubber tether secured to his belt loop. I remembered that I'd seen it before. When he'd let me out into the vestibule, his key card had been attached to it.

But there was nothing attached to it now. The tether had been severed a short distance from his belt loop. It looked as if it had been cut with a knife.

73

Friday 9.50 p.m.

I moved clear of Raul's body, cradling my bandaged hand.
My skin was itching like a rash. All down my legs. All along
my arms. It felt like my tongue and throat were swelling.
Was my chest tightening, or was I imagining it?

I panicked about the poison again. I was afraid I was
running out of time.

So concentrate. Fix this.

I looked all around me. At Raul, and the view outside. At the
area where the gym was being installed, and the fire exit door,
and the photocopying machine I'd used as a battering ram.

I set off towards the fire exit. My balance betrayed me.
For a fumbling second, it was as if the floor had flipped
upwards on a crazy angle and I was trudging up an incline.
Then the floor slammed back down again and I stayed still
for several seconds, regaining my bearings, scared.

Take it easy. Focus. You're going to be OK.

I steadied myself, then fixed my gaze onto the fire door
and paced towards it without the floor falling away from
me again. I pushed down on the horizontal bar fitted across
the middle of the door. It still didn't open. Whatever had
been blocking the door on the other side was still there. It
was still unmoveable.

Turning around, I banged my fist off the photocopying machine in frustration.

Then I stared at the photocopier. The electric cable and plug were curled loosely on the ground by my feet. I grabbed the plug and slammed it into a socket on the wall. When I straightened, my vision tunnelled once more. My ears were ringing.

Hold on.

The photocopier emitted a cheery, two-tone note. I roused myself, my vision clearing, the ringing in my ears subsiding. The touchscreen control panel was illuminated a watery blue. From somewhere deep inside, the machine hummed and whirred. A menu of options were running along the bottom of the panel screen:

Copy.

Scan.

Photos.

Fax.

I hadn't sent a fax in years. Who has? But I knew that some businesses still maintained a fax line as a back-up.

Did Edge?

I wondered.

Sending a fax required a working phone line. Joel had rigged the office phone system in such a way that I couldn't dial out without an access code. But if the fax system was operational, it would work via a secondary phone line.

Perhaps Joel had overlooked it.

My hands buzzed with a dose of nervous energy. There were multiple paper trays under the lid of the machine. I yanked the uppermost tray open and found that it contained a stack of A4 sheets of paper. I took a sheet out, slammed the tray shut. Then I stepped around behind the machine, shoved it aside and entered the stationery cupboard. There was a bunch of Sharpie pens in a box on one of the metal shelves. I took one and made my way back out again.

With the sheet of paper laid flat on the lid of the photocopier, I pulled the lid off the Sharpie with my teeth and scribbled a message.

My name is Kate Harding. I've been taken hostage and held captive by a man called Joel White at the offices of Edge Communications, 13th Floor, 55 Ludgate Hill. I was here for a job interview. The phones don't work. This man has threatened to kill me. He's murdered a cleaner called Raul. He's also threatened the family of the security guard on duty here. His name is Tony. I think he has hurt or restrained my recruitment agent, Maggie Thomas. Maggie works for Abacus Recruitment Services. They can verify I had an interview with Edge this afternoon. Please send the police. This is an EMERGENCY!!!

I looked at the message for a second, then added something further.

My brother, Luke Harding, is also in danger at 17b Beaumont St, Balham. His life is under immediate threat from the same man.

I added Luke's mobile number and my home telephone number, then placed the sheet face down in the document feeder on top of the machine.

'Come on, come on.'

The control panel had dimmed. I tapped it to wake it up. I then tapped the icon marked 'Fax' followed by 'Send To'.

The control panel invited me to insert a fax number to send the message to using a numerical keypad. I input the number 9 for an outside line and then I added three more 9s. Finally, I hit 'Send'.

The machine paused for a long, long second – long enough for me to think nothing at all would happen – but then it buzzed and chattered and sucked up the sheet of paper.

I gripped hold of the machine. Beneath the lid, a bar of bright light swept forwards and back. There was a deeper, grinding hum, as if the internal processors were slowly sparking to life, followed by four sharp, electronic notes imitating the dialling of a four-digit number. After that came a succession of laboured, droning, chirping noises before the machine paused a second time, then shuddered and quaked and spat out a fresh sheet of paper into the outlet tray.

I picked it up. It was warm and curled. In the middle of the page was a blurred and compressed copy of my hand-written message. Above it was a printed report.

**** THE FOLLOWING FAX HAS FAILED TO SEND TO THE RECIPIENT 9999 ****

FAX SENT: 1 MINUTE AGO.

REASON: CALLS TO 9999 ARE NOT PERMITTED.

74

Joel stood in the humming silence of Kate's hallway with the front door closed behind him.

He raised a gloved hand and flipped on the lights.

The property was a drab Victorian conversion. Water stains marked the ceiling overhead. To his left was a cramped galley kitchen. He passed through it to the window at the far end and peered out.

Streetlights illuminated the rows of plane trees and parked cars lining the road. A man and woman walked a dog. There was no other movement. No sign, yet, of Kate's brother.

Joel wondered how much Luke knew and what Kate might have told him. He himself didn't have any siblings. Most of his life, he'd been a loner. But Kate and her brother were obviously close and he knew it was possible she might have confided in him.

Backing away from the window, he took in his surroundings. The kitchen was cheaply furnished with dated cabinetry, chipped laminate countertops and a small, fold-out side table. There was a fridge with leaflets and notes tacked to it. He flicked through them quickly, moved on.

Start with her bedroom.

He found it at the end of the hallway on the left and was

not surprised when he turned on the ceiling light to see that it had such a sad and transitory feel. The walls were yellow chipboard. The single curtain drawn back from the window was in a neutral shade of linen. There were no pictures on the walls. Only a simple duvet and pillows on the bed. An open rack of clothes off to one side.

It was an echo of his own lifestyle, in a way. The nature of his profession meant that he was always moving on, always seeking out new assignments. He had hoped to change that once, build a real future, but that was all in the past.

He thought of Kate now, locked in the cube, compared to the Kate she'd tried to present herself as at the beginning of her interview. The snapshot of her life he was getting from her bedroom could not have been less like the confident and immaculately styled woman she'd attempted to portray.

Beneath the window was a stack of document boxes, bellied with age. Next to them was an old and worn dressing table scattered with make-up products.

He started with the dressing table.

The flat had been searched. He hadn't lied about that. But it hadn't been searched by him, or by anyone with his level of motivation. And since Kate hadn't told him nearly as much as he'd hoped, it could be that her bedroom might tell him more. If there were answers here, he would find them.

He had to.

But he didn't find them in the dressing-table drawer or amongst her make-up. He crouched and looked under the dressing table, behind it. He upended her chair, all to no avail.

That was when his phone started vibrating. His burner. He unzipped a pocket on the lightweight jacket he was wearing and removed it. *Unknown Caller.*

75

Sir Fergus could hear nothing at all on the end of the line.
He waited, not foolish enough to speak until he knew who
he was speaking to, and watched as Dominic levered himself
out of his chair and stalked towards him across the room.
He flattened his hands on the surface of the desk, lowered
his balding head to the speaker, his movements twitchy,
irritated. Several more seconds passed. Then:

'I told you not to call me. I told you I would call you.'

Sir Fergus remained motionless. He was not used to being
spoken to so abruptly. He was insulted and embarrassed,
and one look at Dominic told him he'd taken it even worse.

You hired him, Dominic's glare seemed to be saying. *Control
him.*

'It's been over an hour since your last update,' Sir Fergus
croaked.

'I'm a professional. I call you when I have information to
share.'

'You're an employee,' Dominic snapped. '*Our* employee.'

There was no immediate response, but if Joel was surprised
or concerned to discover that Sir Fergus had someone with
him he rapidly adjusted.

'The situation is delicate right now. I need more time.'

'And we need your decision,' Dominic told him.

'You have until Monday.'

'To neutralize the threat. But first we need to know where the threat is coming from. You'll get us an answer by midnight. No later. Do not disappoint us again.'

76

The call ended and Joel stared at the time on the phone screen. Midnight gave him just over two hours. Enough time to wait for Luke, if he showed soon. And if he didn't, he would return to The Mirror. Tackle Maggie. Speak to Kate.

In the meantime, he could conclude his search. He could . . .

He stopped.

Was that a noise from the hallway? A creak?

Slipping his phone away, he crept back across the room, pausing by the doorway. But when he eased his head out, everything was as it had been.

The noise was probably a water pipe or a settling floorboard. Or perhaps it was a tenant in one of the other flats.

Ducking back into the bedroom, Joel tackled the document boxes, lifting them one after the other onto the bed. A puff of stale air wafted out of the first box when he removed the lid. It was filled with photograph albums and old CDs. He rifled through them quickly, dumped everything on the floor.

The next box held banking records, paperback books, an old picture calendar. The final box contained a few pieces of men's clothing. A faded pair of jeans, plaid shirts, knitted jumpers.

He delved his hands under them. Turned them inside out. Felt the seams.

There were no hidden slips of paper. No data sticks. Nothing.

He didn't bother tidying the items away or returning the boxes to where he had found them. Kate wouldn't be coming back here, ever, and he had no reason to conceal his search. He no longer had time.

Next he went through her clothes, ripping them down off the rail, turning them inside out, emptying the pockets.

After that came the mattress and the pillows, followed last of all by the bed frame. He felt around the legs for hidden cavities, of which there were none. He dragged the bed away from the wall and uncovered nothing but dust bunnies.

Who was it who had spoken on the phone after Sir Fergus? How many others had been in the room?

That was when he heard another noise from out in the hallway. Louder this time. Clumsy. The scratch of a key in the lock. The click of a latch releasing.

In one fluid movement, Joel unzipped another pocket on his jacket, took out his pistol and swept into the hall.

77

Calls to 9999 are not permitted.

I slammed the side of my good hand against the photo-copying machine. The bitter, smoky taste was intensifying at the back of my tongue. The itching on my arms and legs was getting worse and I couldn't resist scratching at it. I knew it could just be my fear getting away from me, but my heart seemed saturated and too heavy in my chest.

Calls to 9999 are not permitted.

But that didn't necessarily mean I couldn't send a fax. I had heard the machine dial out. It had *tried* to connect. Perhaps all it meant was that it wasn't possible to contact the emergency services by fax on the 999 number. Maybe all I needed was a number I *could* fax.

I stopped scratching and tapped the control panel again. 'Fax'. 'Send To'.

For a second, I closed my eyes and clenched my fists. A tumbling sensation. As though I was falling backwards into myself and my memories.

Every day for the past nine months I'd sent emails from my Simple PR account. And every email I sent contained a footer that included my name, my role at Simple and the contact details for the company. I'd told Simon and Rebecca endless times that nobody included fax numbers any more. I'd tried to explain, as subtly as I could, that the fax number they listed was an indicator of some of the ways in which their business was out of touch.

I hadn't got anywhere with it. They'd had the fax number for years. They also had boxes and boxes of headed paper with the fax number listed on them, and Simon didn't see the point in getting new paper printed when they could just hold on to the existing fax number instead.

In the nine months I'd worked there, I'd never once seen Simon's ancient fax machine functioning. It was positioned on a bookshelf by the door to the office. A dusty grey box of a machine. The office equivalent of a Betamax player.

I conjured up the number in my mind. There was just one digit that was different from the main telephone number.

I hit 9 on the control panel and tapped in the number, then returned my handwritten message to the document feeder and listened to the machine dial out, hum and chatter until it spat out a fresh report.

I snatched the sheet from the tray and looked at it.

My body sagged and I let go of a cry of relief.

**** THE FOLLOWING FAX WAS SUCCESSFULLY TRANSMITTED ****

FAX SENT: 1 MINUTE AGO.

78

In the front room of an unlit and empty house in Clapham,
south London, the blue light on an ancient fax machine
blinked to life and the machine began to chatter and whirr.
It sucked in a single, yellowed sheet of A4 paper and rattled
and hummed as a dried-out printer ribbon whipped from
side to side. Thirty seconds later, the barely printed paper
looped out of the front of the machine, hung precariously
for a moment, then dropped, swaying like a feather, until it
curled inwards and slipped under the bottom of the bookcase
with just a corner sticking out.

Nobody was in the house to witness it. Simon and Rebecca
were several streets away, sitting around a sturdy kitchen
table with six of their closest friends, drinking wine and
chatting companionably, in no hurry to go home.

79

Friday 10.01 p.m.

In the seconds after I sent the fax, a rush of heat pulsed upwards from my toes to my head. A vague and whispery energy fizzed under my skin.

Maybe it was simple relief. Maybe I just . . . let go. But I suddenly felt much worse.

Leaning against the photocopying machine, I squinted forwards. My eyes were playing tricks on me again. The empty office looked blurred and indistinct, as if a fine mist was spiralling in from the corners of the room, descending from the ceiling.

I was bone tired. Breathing hurt. I felt totally wiped.

I almost slumped down to the ground and rested for a while but I didn't. I stayed upright, refusing to give in, even as the air around me dragged at my arms and legs like a riptide.

A phone started ringing.

It seemed to be coming from the other side of the office, just one phone this time.

I took three steps forwards.

Mistake.

The world pirouetted. The floor canted up wildly to my left and then my right, a rolling wave.

I put my arms out and steadied myself against the wall, but even the wall seemed to be slanting.

The phone's shrill clamour continued.

Get to it. Hurry.

I pitched myself forwards, veering sideways unintentionally, stumbling towards the climbing wall. I snatched at a rope. Twisted around. Stumbled on.

My footsteps were so heavy it felt like the soles of my feet had been coated in sticky glue.

The fuggy air felt hot as shower steam against my skin.

The phone continued to ring.

It's the desk phone in the glass cube.

I blundered forwards, crashing into something. It spun me around. My leg hurt. I kept going, my heart pounding, the ground rotating under me like an out-of-control treadmill.

Eyes open. Mouth open. Gasping air.

Sweat stung my eyes.

I clasped a hand to my heart. It was rebounding violently against my ribs.

I had to get to that phone.

Ahead of me, the outline of the cube smudged and doubled. The office furniture threw monstrous shadows across the floor. The shadows morphed and merged like Rorschach ink blots. I splashed through them. Waded on.

And struck glass.

The cube.

The phone was ringing just a few metres away from me, but the sound seemed to be coming from far away and deep underground. I peered through the glass at the base unit. A light on the front of it flickered and pulsed.

Answer it. Move.

I felt along the glass with my hands, crouching low until I located the shattered hole. When I got down on my knees, it felt as if a mattress had fallen on me.

I crawled slowly forwards.

My chest skimmed the ground. My head was heavy as a boulder. Almost too heavy to lift.

When I emerged through the hole, I looked up at the phone on the glass desk. It was miles away. I crawled closer.

Get up.

Nothing.

Get up and get to the phone.

My arms trembled. I pawed at the edge of the desk.

The phone rang again.

I grabbed for it and missed, then tried once more, heaving myself up on the edge of the desk, refusing to quit. This time my fingers tangled in the spiral cord. I tugged it towards me as I fell backwards. The cord stretched and then the receiver hopped free of the cradle and sprang across the desk towards me.

The ringing stopped.

I clutched the receiver and pressed the damp plastic to my ear.

80
Friday 10.04 p.m.

'Kate?'

I cried, clamping my free hand over my eyes.

'Kate, it's me. It's Luke. I'm at your place.'

'I know.' My voice sounded warped and distorted, as if it was being played back to me at the wrong speed. 'I know, how did you—'

'I'm not alone, Kate. There's a man here with me. He has a gun.'

In my life, I'd only experienced the power of words to stop me like that once before. It was when Sir Fergus Marsh had looked at me from across his desk and told me about Mark's plane disappearing from radar.

This time, everything stopped.

My breathing.

My mind.

Time.

I'd gone from a shimmer of overwhelming relief to absolute terror in seconds. Mental whiplash.

'Get out of there,' I told him.

'I can't.'

'You have to, Luke. You have to go right now. You have to—'

'He can hear you, Kate. He's listening to us. We're on speakerphone.'

I didn't say anything. I couldn't.

Fear encased my lungs.

I thought about Joel pointing a gun at my brother. I thought about how quickly and savagely he'd beaten Raul.

I felt sick.

'He's asking me about Mark, Kate. He wants to know where he is.'

'Mark's dead,' I whined.

'I know. I told him already.'

More silence. It seemed to stretch and fray.

I was holding the receiver so tightly my knuckles cracked.

'I love you,' I told my brother.

Luke didn't answer.

That terrified me.

I pushed myself up into a sitting position, clinging to the table leg.

'You listen to me,' I said, much louder this time. I wanted Joel to understand that I was talking to him now. 'You listen to me and leave my brother alone. He has nothing to do with this.'

Silence.

'DO YOU HEAR ME? Leave him alone and come back here and I'll talk to you. I'll tell you anything. Whatever you want to hear.'

More silence. Thin and twisting.

Then Joel said, 'The truth this time?'

He sounded so calm. So contained.

I trembled.

'Yes.'

'All of it?'

'Yes.'

Another long, long second of silence followed.

Then a bang exploded from the receiver and I screamed and threw away the phone.

81

Friday 10.07 p.m.

I stared blindly forwards. Pressed my hands against the sides of my head.

I rocked, tucking myself into a ball.

But no matter what I did, I couldn't block out that bang or what it meant for me. It kept repeating inside my head.

I reached for the phone but when I lifted it again the line was dead.

First came the gush of emotions. Fear and horror and the awful, crippling need to get to Luke, help him, all the while knowing I couldn't.

Next came the stab of pain. It was sudden and paralysing and startlingly intense.

It began in my chest. A fierce acid sting. Then a violent cramping, as though someone had reached both hands in through my ribs, gripped hold of my heart and squeezed.

I threw back my head. The acid radiated outwards into my trunk, arms and legs. It soaked into my muscles.

I couldn't breathe.

Couldn't move.

I hung suspended, waiting for my heart to beat again, terrified by what Joel had done to me.

I knew I couldn't get to a hospital. There was no one here who could help.

My heart didn't beat. It had seized.

My entire body cramped. My fingers and toes curled. I went cold even as I sweated from every pore.

Then I toppled forwards, staring sideways at the telephone receiver, a feeble croak escaping my lips and a corona of dimness moving in from the peripheries of my vision towards absolutely nothing at all.

*

I don't know how long afterwards it was that Mark came to me. Time, like everything else, became a blur.

He opened the door to the cube and walked inside, standing looking down at me with his hands in his pockets. He got on the floor beside me. He stroked my hair. He kissed my hand. He told me he loved me. He told me he'd been waiting for me. He pressed his forehead against my forehead and he stroked my cheek with his thumb.

I let go, then.

It was easy. I knew and understood that my whole life had been building towards this moment. It felt right.

Mark's love filled me up. It poured out of me like a bright white light that carried us both away to a place where we could be together again.

*

I came to with my face pressed against the bare concrete floor. The phone was in front of me. The track lighting burned down on me from above.

I was alone.

Lonely night was creeping in through the glass windows that ringed the office floor towards my lighted cocoon. Only the desk lamps shining on my emergency message contrasted with the dark.

I pushed up from the ground.

My chest ached as though it had been stamped on.

My mouth was so dry my tongue felt like carpet.

I wanted Mark to come back and take me away from all this.

But Mark was gone and I was terrified that Luke was gone now, too. Before my interview, my life had become a mess. I'd been locked in a spiral of grief and self-pity for so long that the spiral had become an endless loop I couldn't break free of.

I missed Mark with every atom of my being. I missed everything about him and the life we'd shared together. I missed our nights on the sofa, cuddled up watching reruns of old US sitcoms. I missed having him read other people's tweets out to me and laugh at lame jokes I didn't get. I missed lazy Sunday morning sex, and breakfast in bed, and how safe he made me feel when he draped his arm over my shoulders, kissed my head, smelled my hair.

For the past fifteen months I hadn't been able to move on from him. I understood how other people who'd been widowed were able to pick themselves up again, rebuild. I knew it was what Mark would have wanted for me. But all I'd wanted was to go backwards. Rewind.

Until now.

Because somehow, this wasn't over for me yet.

Whatever had happened to me – whatever pain or paralysis had gripped hold of my heart – had released me again. I wondered if it was a precursor of something much worse to come, a tentative seizure before a full-blown heart attack. Or maybe Joel had got his dosing wrong and I'd survived.

I didn't know.

All I knew for certain was that when Joel came back I was going to be here waiting for him.

I wouldn't let him win.

82
Friday 11.19 p.m.

I was sitting with my back against the glass, hugging my knees with my arms, when I first glimpsed movement outside the cube.

It looked as if two figures were moving through the dimness beyond reception. To begin with, I wasn't convinced that what I was seeing was real. I was afraid it was another hallucination.

Then the figures moved into the haze of light shining out from the cube and I saw the blood on the side of Luke's face, his grossly swollen eye, his hobbled walk and harrowed expression. I saw how his hands were bound together in front of him with duct tape. And I saw Joel following him from behind with a gun pointed at his spine.

I hugged my knees tighter. I swallowed against a sob. I didn't stand up quite yet. I was afraid of moving too quickly, petrified of my chest pain returning. My entire body felt like one giant trigger point. I was haunted by the idea that the slightest exertion would cause my heart to stop beating again.

There was a discreet *click*, the door unlocked, and Joel motioned for Luke to open it with his bound hands. It took him a moment to bend and manipulate the handle and limp backwards out of the way. Then he sidestepped and shuffled forwards through the door to stand in front of me.

I shook my head.

Tears stung my eyes.

Finally, I couldn't hold back any longer, and I surged up and wrapped my arms around my brother's neck.

I hugged him.

Neither one of us spoke.

I leaned back and touched a finger to Luke's eye. He winced and pulled away. The skin was badly bruised and puckered. I was pretty certain he couldn't see out of it. His other eye was flitting rapidly side to side, reading me intently. There was blood in his hair and on the back of his neck, leaking into the neckline of his blue hospital scrubs. I didn't think he'd been shot. Joel must have faked it. But perhaps he'd struck him with his gun.

I wondered if Luke had struggled and tried to get away from Joel, or if his injuries were a sign of how desperate Joel had become – if he'd beaten him to try and get information out of him.

'What has he done to you?' Luke asked me.

That jarred me. I realized how awful I must look.

Luke raised his bound hands and gently pulled down the skin under my eyes with his thumb. He touched the back of his hand to my forehead. Felt the pulse in my neck.

'You're burning up.'

'Don't.' I pulled his hands down, wincing at the damage to his face. 'I'm sorry. I didn't want for you to get involved in this.'

'Sit down,' Joel said, from behind.

There was a clatter as he kicked one of the interview chairs in through the door behind Luke, then sent the second chair rolling in after it. He motioned with his gun to the chairs and the desk.

'One on each side.' He sounded tense, under pressure. 'Like before.'

I stared at him. His face shone wan and ghost-like against the darkness coming through the office windows. I waited for him to show some semblance of remorse or shame but he seemed to be in a different mindset, focused on whatever misguided mission he hoped to accomplish. He was obviously in a hurry.

'Do it now.'

He swung his gun until it was pointed at my body.

A shudder coursed through me.

'I'm not going to ask you again, Kate. We both know you don't have time to waste here.'

I glanced at Luke as a question flitted across his face. It wasn't a question I wanted to answer right now, even as I hoped that Joel was wrong – that the poison had done its worst already. I was drained and achy, but I wasn't in any immediate pain.

I lowered my head and reached for the nearest chair, rolling it over behind the desk without looking back at my brother. Then I stretched for the second chair as Joel's gun hovered over me.

'Sit down,' I told Luke, guiding him to the side of the desk where I'd been sitting during my interview with Joel. I took the chair on what had been Joel's side of the desk.

Joel waited until we were both seated before stepping

further into the cube, glancing for a long moment at the hole I'd punched in the glass.

'Put your hands on the desk,' Joel said. 'Let me see them.'

I raised my arms slowly. They felt as heavy as lead pipes.

Luke took hold of my fingers and rubbed at the blood-spotted bandage on my hand. The duct tape was digging into the skin of his wrists. His bad eye was weeping and his good eye was fixed on me, but there was nothing there for me in it. Just an odd kind of distance, as if he couldn't bring himself to look at me directly. I think we both understood at that moment that neither one of us was getting out of here alive.

'I'm so sorry,' I said again.

'Don't,' he whispered.

He hung his head. I guessed it was because his face was about to crumple and he didn't want me to see. For fifteen months, he'd held me up. He'd been so strong.

'I've got to be honest with you, Kate,' Joel told me. 'You gave me mixed signals earlier. Sometimes I believed you, even when I didn't want to. Other times, not so much.'

'If Mark was alive, don't you think I would have told you by now?'

'Actually, no.' He waved his gun between us. 'That's what made things tricky for me. I like you, Kate. We have more in common than you know.'

'The feeling's not mutual.'

'Yeah.' He nodded. 'Yeah, I get that. But let me lay it out for you again in really simple terms. We have the photographs of Mark following you. We have the reports from your downstairs neighbour of Mark being spotted around your apartment. We have the forensic report identifying Mark's hairs and fingerprints in your flat. We have a source inside the prosecution team for the Melanie Turner trial and we know that somebody has been talking to them. For almost three weeks now, they've been teasing them with information that would be devastating to my client. Things that only Mark, or somebody Mark confided in, could possibly know.'

'I told you already, that's—'

'Bullshit? Right. But here's the thing, Kate. Here's the difference between you and me. I know when I'm telling you the truth. And you want to know who else does? Let me give you a clue.'

He raised his left hand in the air, as if he was trying to shield Luke from seeing. Then he pressed the muzzle of the gun against his palm in my brother's direction.

I faltered.

It was only the tiniest thing, but I felt Luke pull back from me by the smallest amount.

He dropped his gaze.

'What's he talking about?' I asked him.

Luke shook his head.

I squeezed his fingers. He caught his breath. Then he raised his face and looked up at me with a harrowed expression, and I felt something inside me crumple and turn to dust.

Joel might have had all the techniques in the world to assess if somebody was lying to him but I didn't need them with Luke. I knew him too well.

I could see the truth on his face.

The hurt.

The shame.

'No,' I said. I let go of his hands. 'You . . . No . . .'

And then my brother said something to me. Something that stopped my heart more completely than any poison ever could.

'I'm sorry, Kate. Please don't hate me. This is all my fault.'

83

Friday 11.27 p.m.

The ground was collapsing under me. I was falling.
Tumbling.

Everything I knew. Everything I was certain of. All of it
gone in an instant.

Luke stared back at me from across the table. He might
as well have been on the other side of the city from me. I
could see the sorrow and the anguish in his expression but
there was a gulf between us now. It wasn't one I knew how
to cross.

'He's . . . alive?'

'Yes,' he said quietly.

I released his hands. I stared at him, shaking my head.
Mark is alive.

I kept repeating the words in my head but somehow they
wouldn't stick. I should have been elated but instead it felt
as if my insides were disintegrating.

Mark is alive.

And then, of course, the kicker: *And he didn't tell me.*

Hot tears scorched my cheeks. I had so many questions
I didn't know where to begin.

'When did you . . . ? How . . . ?'

Luke shot a sideways look at Joel, as if he needed to be

319

careful about how much he said. I didn't care about any of that.

'Tell me, Luke.'

'It happened about two weeks ago,' my brother whispered.

Two weeks ago. That was around the time I'd been to Camden Market. Around the time the photographs of me had been taken with Mark in the background.

Did that mean they were real?

He'd been so close to me. Only metres away.

I should have seen him, I thought.

Then: *No. He should have come to me.*

My husband had never done anything to hurt me. That was what I'd always believed. We'd rarely argued. If we did, it was only ever about something minor, and it was always Mark who took the first step to make up. He never cheated. He never lied.

Or so I'd thought.

Now, I didn't know what to think. The totality of his deception left me stunned.

'Why did he tell you? Why didn't he tell me?'

'He said he was protecting you.' Luke nodded at Joel. 'He said it could be dangerous.'

'Have to give him credit for that one, Kate,' Joel said.

A ball of hot energy exploded inside me. Joel must have sensed it because he took a step backwards, raising his palm in the air.

'Take it easy, Kate. I did try to tell you.'

I was having difficulty with that. The man who'd held me captive. The man who'd murdered Raul, taken Maggie, blackmailed Tony – the man who'd terrorized me, poisoned me and invaded my home to attack my brother – had been more honest with me than my husband.

Mark is alive.

'How . . . ?' I shook my head. 'He was on that plane. He had to be because he was on the passenger manifest and that can't be faked. I know it can't be faked. It would have been checked by the airline staff. Verified by computer and two flight attendants. It would have been run by the pilot and the co-pilot before take-off.'

'You mean the same crew who died when the plane went down, Kate?'

I stared forwards sightlessly. A cold horror wrapped itself around my heart and lungs, coiling tighter and tighter. He was telling me Mark hadn't been on board. He was telling me that the final message Mark had left on my voicemail had been a lie.

'He should have gone down with the rest of that plane,' I muttered.

Joel cocked his head to one side.

'That's what you said to me. He should have gone down with the rest of that plane. Are you telling me Mark was a target? That the plane was, what, sabotaged because of him? By MarshJet?'

Neither one of them answered.

I felt like I'd been punched. My mind immediately turned to my colleagues who'd been killed in the disaster, especially my three friends from the MarshJet PR team. Two of them had been married. One of them had left behind twin girls. The company had set up a charitable foundation in their memories. Everyone had been devastated by their loss.

'Did Mark know? Please tell me he didn't know.'

I sat there, winded. I didn't understand much of what I was hearing. But there was one thing that did penetrate. If it was truly possible that MarshJet had done something so horrific – if they'd brought down one of their own planes with hundreds of people on board – then the stakes would be enormous.

Forget about the trial in the High Court. Forget about bankrupting the company. Everybody involved in this would go to prison. They'd be reviled around the world.

I looked at Joel. He'd told me his client was Sir Fergus Marsh. If he was involved in this, then he had everything to lose. Enough to do whatever it took to find Mark. Enough to have Joel do what he'd done to me.

'Mark told me he had to stay hidden until the right moment to come forwards,' Luke said. 'He's been waiting for this trial, Kate. He thinks if there's enough media attention, if he's in the spotlight . . . He's paranoid. He doesn't trust anyone.'

'He trusted you.'

'Not how you think. I only saw him because I went to your flat to use your washing machine. I got the shock of my life when I saw him. I wanted him to call you. I was begging him to do that. I told him how bad it had been for you. But he pleaded with me. He made me promise to wait until after the trial. He said he had to keep you safe, but if anything went wrong, at least I could tell you the truth.'

The truth. I shook my head. I could have seen Mark. I could have touched him, held him. Didn't Luke understand that I would give everything up just for that?

'You're my brother,' I told him.

'I did what I thought was best. I didn't—'

'Are you finished?' Joel cut in. 'Because if you're finished I have one more question for you, Luke. I'd like for you to tell me where Mark is right now.'

84

Friday 11.33 p.m.

'I don't know,' Luke said. 'Honestly.'

Joel sucked air through his teeth. 'Please think carefully before you lie to me again.'

'I'm serious. I don't—'

Joel stepped forwards and drilled the muzzle of his gun into Luke's skull, on the opposite side to his injuries. Luke cried out as the bloodied side of his face was driven towards the surface of the glass desk. He lifted his bound hands in a gesture of surrender, straining to look up at me with his good eye. Beads of sweat popped on his forehead.

I stared at Joel, shaking my head. 'Don't! Please!'

His expression was grim, determined. 'I thought I'd already made it clear that I'm not screwing around here, Luke. Now, can you call him or not?'

'No, I can't. I—'

He said it too fast, with too much tension in his voice. It was obvious he was lying.

My blood ran cold.

'So you can call him. Good.' Joel moderated his voice and eased back slightly on the pressure he was applying through the gun. He seemed to take a moment to process what Luke had told him and collect himself before speaking again. 'I'm

324

going to need for you to do that now, Luke. I want you to tell him he needs to come here.'

'You'll kill him,' I said.

He swung to me, looking genuinely perplexed. 'What do you care? You already thought he was dead once.'

Keeping his gun held on Luke, Joel ducked in slow increments to pick up the base unit of the phone from the floor where I'd dropped it before. He then ducked a second time for the receiver.

As Luke straightened up from the table, I could see a sticky red smear left behind on the glass. Part of me was scared he would be tempted to try something – some desperate, last-ditch effort – but he seemed to understand as well as I did that that would be a mistake. Instead, he watched me, his face arranging itself into a pained apology.

I looked back at him and tried to wrap my head around everything I had heard. If you had told me just a day ago that my husband was alive, I would have dropped to my knees, praised God and the heavens, wept uncontrollably. I wondered if there was something wrong with me to explain why I wasn't feeling that way now. Perhaps it was shock.

'One other thing you should know, Luke.' Joel was tapping the long code to unlock the office phone lines into the keypad. 'Your sister needs to get to a hospital and she needs to get there soon. Think about that before you try anything stupid.'

'What does he mean?' Luke asked me.

I swallowed hard and reached up slowly to tap two fingers against my heart. My chest still ached but my heart wasn't cantering wildly right now. If anything, it felt oddly desensitized.

I tried not to let my emotions overwhelm me as I watched the horror spread across Luke's face.

'I don't understand.'

'You don't need to, Luke. You just need to call Mark.' Joel checked the time on his wristwatch, frowned, then prodded a final button and the brash dial tone purred through the phone's speaker. 'Better tell him to hurry.'

Luke stared at me, his good eye bulging. I could tell he wanted to doubt that things were as serious as Joel was suggesting, but I was pretty sure my sickly appearance told him otherwise. As a cardiac nurse, he knew the warning signs to look for, even if he hadn't been told about the poison in my system. He'd felt my pulse, noted my fever.

Maybe you're not through the worst of it. Maybe the attack you had before was just the start.

I clenched my hands, fighting against the fear. I didn't want the pain to come back again. I never wanted to feel that way again.

Luke swallowed audibly, then reached out for the phone, blinking at the keypad for a long, spiralling second. I got the impression he was recalling the number he needed to dial. Mark must have made him memorize it.

Again, that stunned me. For the past fortnight, my brother could have dialled my phone and connected me with my dead husband, but he hadn't.

The choices we make.

Luke lowered his hand to the keypad and began inputting a number. Joel watched him closely.

My mind shifted course again, jarring me as if I was on a commuter train that had changed tracks.

Mark had been in my apartment. Luke had surprised him there.

What was Mark doing in my apartment?

I supposed it was possible he'd been looking for something among his belongings that he'd left behind. Or perhaps he'd been leaving something for me as Joel had suggested. If he had left something, why hadn't I seen it? How had Joel missed it?

The phone continued to ring. It seemed to ring for a very long time.

That worried me.

If Mark was lying low, I didn't think he would stray very far from whatever phone number he'd given to Luke. He had to be somewhere near to London, surely, if his intention was to appear as a witness at the court trial.

I was suddenly scared something had happened to him. Maybe the man who had taken his picture had got to him. Or perhaps one of the other back-up options Joel had mentioned had become involved.

Or worse, perhaps Mark had simply run again. He could have decided the risks were too high. If he had run, then everything Joel had done was for nothing. He would kill us. I was certain of that.

'What's the hold-up?' Joel snapped.

'Just wait a second.'

'If you're trying to mess with me . . .' He took a step forwards, jabbing the gun at Luke again, an unexpected kind of desperation modulating his voice.

'I'm not. I'm—'

There was a click.

327

A pause.

Some low-level background noise. Indistinct murmurs and chatter.

For a second I thought that perhaps the call had been answered in a busy street. Maybe in a restaurant or a hotel foyer.

Then a male voice came on the line.

'Stephen Ward.'

85

Friday 11.37 p.m.

Stephen Ward sounded like a pretty unremarkable name.
Joel probably thought it was an alias Mark had been using.

I knew differently.

For one thing, it wasn't Mark who answered the phone.
Even after all this time, I believed I would recognize his
voice when I heard it. And for another thing, Stephen Ward
wasn't a name but a place.

'Dwayne, is that you?' Luke said.

'Luke?'

My brother closed his eyes for a second. 'Yeah. Listen, I
need for you to patch me through to room six. I have to
speak to Mr Nicholls.'

Joel leaned back, exhaling, shaking his head. I could see
a sense of release flooding through him.

Stephen Ward was the general cardiac care ward that Luke
worked on at St Thomas' hospital.

'Come on, man,' the staff member called Dwayne said.
'You know what time it is? He's sleeping. Did you forget
something earlier? Do you want me to give him a message
for you?'

'He won't be sleeping. Trust me. I have to talk to him,
Dwayne. It's important. Just patch me through.'

'OK,' the man said dubiously. 'I'll try. But this is on you.'

The phone switched to hold music. Something classical. It felt both too familiar and too innocuous for the moment we were in.

'You hid him at your hospital,' Joel said.

Luke winced at me. He lowered his voice, as if he was trying to keep this part just between us.

'We made a deal. I promised I wouldn't tell you I'd seen him as long as I knew where he was at all times. He said he couldn't do that because he had to move around. He couldn't stay in one place. That's when I had the idea. I talked with one of the doctors I trust, called in all my favours. We have a little more latitude with some of the private rooms. We checked him in under a made-up name. Worked up some medical records. We've been keeping him under observation. Nobody else knows.'

A low thud from my heart. Again, it hurt. I had a feeling like the muscles around my chest wall were cramping. But not from any poison this time.

I was shaking my head, fighting back the tears. Luke had been going to work and seeing Mark every day. He'd been talking to him and all the time he'd said nothing to me.

There was a whole series of questions I wanted to yell at him: Where had Mark been? How had he coped? Had he asked about me, and what had Luke told him about my life now?

But before I could get to any of those, the hold music ended and I could hear the prolonged hiss of dead air on the end of the line, as if the person who'd answered was being extremely cautious.

'It's Luke,' my brother said.

The wait for a response seemed to last decades. I saw Joel lean closer to the phone.

'You're not calling to check on my Portuguese, are you?'

'We have a problem,' Luke said.

'What kind of a problem?'

It still hit me.

Even after everything Luke had already told me. Even after I'd mentally prepared myself for it.

This was the voice I still heard in my dreams, in videos on my phone, on that voicemail he'd left me. The voice I missed so much.

Mark.

Have you ever had one of those moments when something so significant happens to you that you feel as if you're floating up out of yourself, monitoring your reactions from above, as if you're watching a play from a seat in a theatre? This was like that, only about a hundred times more intense.

I saw myself shaking my head and clutching hold of the arms of my chair. I could feel how wide my eyes had grown. My mouth. The rest of the room, however, seemed to disappear entirely. For a second it was just me, on my own, with my dead husband on the end of the phone.

He'd only said a handful of words and I still felt as though a building had collapsed on top of me.

Luke gave me a pensive, searching look that seemed to ask if I wanted to say something. But I couldn't. Not yet. It was too much.

'Listen, I'm not alone here.' Luke was speaking carefully, trying, I guess, to reckon with how best to explain the situation he was in, looking between me and Joel. 'You're on speaker. Kate is with me.'

The silence became a vacuum that sucked all the air out of my lungs.

I heard Mark draw breath.

'Kate?'

I cried then. A kind of gasping half-sob. I couldn't breathe.

I'd wanted for so long, so badly, to be able to hear Mark say my name again. I'd never dared to believe I really would.

'I've missed you.'

I rocked forwards in my chair. I pressed my hands to my mouth.

'I can hear you, baby. I can hear you. I'm here.'

I nodded, even though he couldn't see me.

'I can hear you, too,' I whispered.

Even then, it was hard to believe I was speaking those words. It was difficult to accept this could really be happening. And of course, it couldn't last. Reality had to come crashing in again.

'Who else is with you?' Mark asked.

'That would be me,' Joel told him. He braced the flat of his hand down next to the phone, as if he was holding himself up against an unbearable weight. He looked at the time on his wristwatch again. 'Mark, I want you to know that I'm holding a gun on your wife and brother-in-law right now. It's starting to get heavy and my patience is running low. I'm going to give you an office address and I need you to get here inside twenty minutes, or so help me, I'm going to start pulling the trigger.'

86

Mark had always known it would come to this. On some level, anyway. And yes, he'd buried it deep down. Obviously he'd hoped it would work out otherwise. It was why he'd been so cagey when he'd contacted the prosecution team, even going so far as to use a phone app to disguise his voice and gender in the calls he made. All of his approaches had been tentative, steadily testing the water, carefully trying to establish if the murky pool he was dipping his toes into was safe before he waded all the way in. He'd planned on appearing at the trial on Monday as a surprise witness, giving his testimony, saying what had to be said and then dealing with the fallout.

What was that saying? Men plan, God laughs.

All of his running. All of his hiding.

It had all come down to this.

He sprang out of bed in his hospital gown, knocking his language textbook to the floor, ripping the cannula out of his wrist. He had a polo shirt, trousers and shoes stashed in a cupboard in the corner of the room and he hurriedly pulled them on. He didn't have time for socks and he was still jamming his wallet into his pocket and buttoning his fly as he burst out of the hospital room and sprinted along the ward.

He'd told Luke this wouldn't work. He'd explained why he had to do things his way – why he couldn't risk involving the police or any other government agencies because he had no idea how far the corruption spread. He'd given him chapter and verse on his experiences of life on the run.

But in the face of all that, Luke had said one thing he couldn't counter.

'I can't tell my sister I saw you and let you walk out of here without stopping you. I can't do it. There are some things she can live with. Just barely. She won't be able to live with that.'

And wasn't that, he thought now, the real reason why he'd gone to Kate's flat? He'd known it was a risk. Secretly, he suspected he'd wanted a reason to reveal himself. Running for this long, and this hard, had been beyond lonely and tough. He'd had to fight the urge to contact Kate every minute of every day.

Now, late at night, the ward was still lit in that all-encompassing, greenish hospital hue. It smelled of whatever antiseptic cleaner had been used on the linoleum flooring mixed with a background note of boiled vegetables. He tore past a zone of occupied beds to his left. The nurses' station was ahead on his right.

There was a large male nurse sitting behind the counter. A junior doctor and a female nurse were talking in front of a whiteboard. All three of them were dressed in varying shades of blue scrubs. Their jaws dropped as they watched him approach.

'Mr Nicholls?' the doctor asked. 'Mr Nicholls, what are you doing?'

He didn't answer. He just ran. This wasn't the doctor Luke had squared things away with. She must have thought he was out of his mind.

Perhaps he was.

He was breathing too fast. His lungs were already stinging. The muscles in his legs were stiff and tight. He'd been lying in bed too long.

'Mr Nicholls!'

Mark turned and looked back. Almost fell. The female nurse and the doctor had darted out from behind the counter after him. The doctor was holding her stethoscope against her chest.

Mark burst through a pair of double doors into the corridor. He looked to his left and right. One good thing about hospitals: they had signs everywhere. He saw an arrow pointing towards the exit.

'Mr Nicholls, come back!'

He accelerated.

The exit sign pointed to some elevators and stairs to Mark's right. He picked the stairs. Three flights. It would be faster than waiting for the elevator.

He crashed through the door to the stairwell and jumped down the first flight of stairs, colliding with the wall ahead of him.

He had no idea what the doctor and nurse might do. Would they take the elevator down and try to intercept him? Return to the ward?

Twenty minutes.

He must have used two of them already.

When he got outside, he'd flag down a taxi. Steal a car. Whatever it took.

Fear spread through his body. There was no doubt in his mind that the man who'd spoken on the phone would carry out his threat to shoot Kate and Luke. He was sure he had a gun. When you were dealing with an organization that was prepared to target one of its own passenger planes to wipe out a whistle-blower, you immediately understood that anything was possible.

He landed hard at the foot of the next flight of stairs. Pushed off and continued on.

He was getting light-headed. There was a painful stitch in his side. He'd lost weight during his travels. Not deliberately. It was just that an existence where you spent every waking moment checking over your shoulder wasn't conducive to a good diet. And the weight loss was deceptive anyway. He wasn't nearly as fit as he'd been fifteen months ago, when he'd been able to keep regular appointments at the gym. The rush of blood in his ears became a deafening roar.

He blocked out his discomfort and focused on Kate. He thought of how she'd looked at the market that day. The moment he'd seen her up close, it had taken all his willpower not to approach her, touch her. He recognized his own weaknesses well enough to know that if he hadn't spotted the man taking photographs of her, his resolve would have cracked.

But he'd had to back off. Flee. He'd changed Tube trains three times, resolved never to return to the hostel where he'd been staying, and still he'd been terrified it wasn't enough.

The next day he'd let himself into her flat. Picking a snap lock was another skill he'd learned during his new life. He'd told himself he had to make sure she was safe.

And look how well that had turned out.

Exploding through another set of doors onto a corridor lined with textured rubber flooring, he streaked onwards, faster than his body could handle. Never as fast as he wanted to go.

He swung left, right. He passed a porter wheeling an empty bed along and a woman and a man crying silently on plastic waiting chairs.

His route took him to the hospital's main entrance. A cafe area to his left. A newsagent's and florist's on his right. All of the businesses were shuttered and closed up for the evening. An automatic glass exit door hissed closed up ahead.

Mark clamped a hand to the ache in his side and laboured towards it.

A man in a security uniform stepped out to block his way.

The man was short and fat with a domed head and a goatee beard. A two-way radio was gripped in his hand. From the look on his face, Mark could tell he'd been told to expect him. One of the medics on the ward must have called ahead.

The security guard adjusted the waistband of his trousers and held up a hand. Mark understood in that moment that he had a choice to make. He could slow down and try to explain something of his situation. This was a hospital, after all. It wasn't a prison or a police station. He was checked in on a voluntary (albeit fabricated) basis. He could discharge himself any time he cared.

But all of that would take time. He'd be expected to speak with a doctor. Sign some paperwork.

It was time he didn't have.

A sudden wariness flashed in the security guard's eyes as he signalled again for Mark to halt and he didn't slow.

Mark lowered his head and charged.

The security guard took a half-step backwards. He glanced over his shoulder as the automatic door registered his movement and slid open.

In his mind, Mark readied himself for a tussle. He'd played rugby in school a couple of lifetimes ago. He could drive the man out of the way. Hand him off.

But as he drew closer and dropped his shoulder, the guard surprised him by stepping sideways and sucking in his gut.

And then Mark was past him, bursting out into the cool night air, looking all around him for where to go next.

87

Friday 11.42 p.m.

I had spoken with my husband. I'd just talked to Mark.

That should have been such an ordinary statement to make but of course it wasn't.

A sense of unreality gripped me. I felt like I'd fallen into a parallel dimension, one where the most remarkable and most terrible things were capable of happening at the exact same moment in time.

I thought about the timescale Joel had given Mark. Twenty minutes wasn't long for him to get from close to Westminster Bridge to Ludgate Hill, but I guessed it was possible. Just. I didn't think from the way Joel had spoken and acted that he would allow any leeway. Perhaps he couldn't take the risk that Mark would call the police.

I doubted Mark would do that. Not when he'd been hiding on his own terms for so long. He obviously didn't trust the authorities. And he knew my life and Luke's life were on the line.

But then a small voice whispered inside my head: *He let you believe he was dead. He left you behind once already.*

I forced the thought away. There was too much I didn't know to make a judgement on that.

Twenty minutes until I saw Mark again.

Less now.

I looked up at Joel, the hurt burning inside me like a furnace.

He would kill Mark, I thought. He would do it himself or hand Mark to other people to do the actual killing.

I couldn't – *wouldn't* – allow that to happen. Not after everything he'd put me through. Not when I had the chance to save Mark.

Joel stared back at me questioningly, an unspoken thought or doubt pulling at his features, tweaking and distorting them in ways I was struggling to understand. He seemed at once sympathetic to my situation but also absolutely ruthless. I sensed there were two Joels I could appeal to. I just didn't know if I could get through to the one who might understand.

'I'm sorry you had to find out like this, Kate,' he told me. 'Truly.'

'You don't have to hurt him. You don't have to do anything to him, or to us.'

'If I don't, somebody else will. I told you already.'

'That's no excuse.'

His brow furrowed. I got the impression he really did want to explain himself to me; as if, for some reason, he felt he owed me that much.

'What about the people who got ill flying on MarshJet planes?' he asked me. 'Or what about all the people who died on that flight? Do you think they'd want me to give Mark a free pass?'

He searched me. I got the impression he was hunting again for a truth he seemed to think I had hidden, perhaps even from myself.

'I think they'd want to know more,' I said carefully. 'I think they'd want to hear from Mark, listen to him, understand what happened.'

'And if he couldn't explain it? Or what if his explanation wasn't good enough for just one of them?'

'There's no way Mark would have wanted for anyone to get sick or die.'

'You still can't accept it, can you? You still can't see him for what he really is.'

'And what's that?'

'He's like me, Kate.'

'Mark is no killer.'

'No? Then maybe we're all just caught in the same web, doing what we have to do. Is that it?'

'Mark is a good person. I know he is.'

'I used to say the same thing about myself.'

'It's true about Mark.'

'Are you sure, Kate? Face it. You don't know anything about him. Not really. You couldn't help me here at all.'

He cast his gun around the office, scrunching his face up in a dismissive way, taking a fast moment to consult his wristwatch again. I wondered if it was his own timescale he was working towards or somebody else's. I wondered what his rush was.

I leaned forwards, gripping hold of the desk.

'I want to,' I told him. 'Help you, I mean.'

'And how would you do that?'

'I don't know. Yet. But there has to be something inside you, somewhere, that knows this is wrong.'

His eyes flashed, becoming hard again. I'd said the wrong

thing. Set him off on the wrong path. He disengaged from me, turning towards Luke.

'There's something you're not sure of,' I said quickly. 'Something about all of this that doesn't sit right with you. I can tell. You're not the only one who can read people. This is about something else for you.'

He stilled for a second. 'You deserve better, Kate,' he said quietly. 'I can see that now. I'm sorry this happened to you. I wish I could give you what you want – truly – but I can't.'

I deserved better than *what*? I wanted to ask him. Better than being held against my will and tormented in an office building after hours? Better than finding out my deepest, most secret fantasy had been true all along, only to have it ripped away from me?

'You disgust me,' I told him.

'Kate.' Luke shook his head in warning.

'What?' I asked. 'Do you really think he could do anything worse to me, or to you for that matter?'

The panicked look Luke gave me told me that was exactly what he thought. Here we were, sitting across from one another, beaten and bruised, under guard. I'd been poisoned. I was feeling spent and tingly, like I sometimes did after one of my runs, my limbs weary, my blood sugar low. My symptoms weren't anything like as pronounced as they'd been earlier and I was grateful for that. But I couldn't shake the worry that my heart would stop beating again any second. There was a gun pointed at my brother's head. Joel planned to kill Mark.

And it could still get worse.

'This conversation is over now, Kate.'

Joel surged forwards and snatched at Luke's bound arms, lifting him roughly from his chair, jamming his gun into Luke's spine. Luke sucked in a draught of air and arched his back, hopping forwards.

'No. Wait.'

'Luke and I have to go downstairs now. To meet Mark.'

'Take me instead.'

I stood up so rapidly the ground see-sawed beneath me. I clung to the desk and my chair as Joel gave me a pitying look.

'That's not going to happen, Kate. I need a hostage who isn't going to collapse on me.'

He shoved Luke ahead of him out of the cube, hustling him on towards reception. He was clenching Luke's shoulder in one fist, holding him upright, the gun drilling into the bloodied area behind Luke's ear.

I pitched myself forwards in pursuit. Joel hadn't shut the door to the cube. He must have realized there was no point with the hole I'd created in the glass. But my wooziness hadn't quite passed. I slalomed through the doorway, banging off the frame, blundering into a desk.

'Wait!'

Joel forced Luke further ahead of me. I levered myself up off the desk and followed.

I had to see Mark again. I wanted him to see me. I wanted us to share that connection, however fleeting, even if it was only for a second. Even if Joel snatched it away from us both.

They reached the exit doors.

'Joel, please! Listen to me.'

He whirled around, pressing his gun against Luke's head so hard that Luke stooped forwards, almost crashing to the ground.

'I did listen to you, Kate. I heard you. More than you know.'

He waved a key card in front of the sensor plate, opening the doors and manhandling Luke through before pausing one last time. Something that might have passed for real sympathy tightened his brow.

'It's better you stay here, Kate. For your sake. You don't need to see this.'

'I need to see my husband.'

'Rest up, Kate. This will all be over soon.'

He stepped through the door, closing it after him. I ran forwards and grabbed for the handle.

It was already locked.

I banged my fist on the door, pressing my face against the cracked panel of wired glass. An elevator carriage opened up and Joel manoeuvred Luke inside, then turned back to face me, standing behind him. Luke's head was canted to one side by the gun pressing into his scalp.

'Stop this! Please!'

The last thing I saw as the doors slid closed was my brother raising his good eye and looking back at me. The conflicted expression on his ruined face was one I'd seen before – it was the same look he'd given me when he'd been sitting next to me at Mark's memorial service. It was a look that seemed to say *I'm here for you* and *I've lost you* all at the same time.

88

Luke's temples throbbed as the elevator plummeted downwards. There was a screeching white ache inside his head as though a spike had been driven through his skull. His puckered eye felt as big as a dinner plate.

An awful hollowness sucked at his insides.

He hated leaving Kate behind. He'd never seen her looking so sickly. And he was scared for himself.

Deep in his cerebrum, his primal instincts screamed at him to do something. Now. Sooner rather than later. Make a move for the gun. Be bold.

But he was paralysed by fear. His hands were bound. And he couldn't see Joel clearly. He was standing behind him, just outside his peripheral vision. It was disorientating only being able to see out of his good eye.

The elevator panel was off to his right, a desperate lunge away. There was a red emergency stop button.

'Don't.' Joel stepped sideways and straightened his arm, extending the gun towards Luke's face. 'I don't want to have to shoot you in here. Too messy.'

Luke recoiled.

'You must really love your sister, Luke.'

He didn't reply.

'Maybe she can't see it right now, but I get how hard it must have been for you. You did a difficult thing. We make the greatest sacrifices for those we love the most.'

He had no idea.

Kate had moved in with Luke the day after the plane crash. She'd stayed in his spare room for weeks before she was even close to being capable of moving into her own place. Some nights, she'd scream in her sleep and he'd hurry to her bedside, ready to tell her she was safe and he was there for her when she woke. But there were other nights – shameful nights – when he'd heard her and he *hadn't* gone. Nights when he'd stayed in his own bed and pretended, in the morning, that he hadn't heard her at all. His sister's trauma had been so intense it was like staring at the sun. He'd had to shield himself from its glare.

It was his deepest, most terrible secret.

Had been, anyway.

'I should have told her sooner,' he said.

'You were protecting her.'

'She deserved to know.'

The elevator tore downwards. Floor 8 . . . Floor 7 . . . Floor 6 . . .

Luke's good eye burned and stung as he looked up at the numbers. Inside he was raging. At himself. At the thug standing next to him. At Mark, for the position he'd put them all in.

'What have you done to her?' he asked. 'Why was she looking so ill?'

There was a moment of buoyancy as the elevator slowed and came to a halt on the ground floor. Joel waited, then motioned with his gun for Luke to go first when the doors parted.

'The thing is, Luke, sometimes the truth can be overrated. Believe me when I tell you that you really don't want to know.'

89

Friday 11.47 p.m.

I had only one purpose now.

Get out.

I turned from the doors and rushed back to the cube, picking up the phone from the desk. I'd seen Joel enter the unlock code before Luke had dialled the hospital. I hadn't seen him enter another code since. But when I pressed the receiver to my ear, the phone wasn't working. There was no outside line.

How?

I threw the phone aside and stepped out of the cube, staring at the desks in front of me. I tried another phone and another. Same result.

My gaze tracked left and right. Over other workstations. Over the meeting pods and the reception area and the refectory. Towards the lighted windows with my message scrawled on it.

Think.

There had to be something I hadn't tried before. Something that would help. I had this nagging feeling that I'd overlooked something. As if the answer was staring me in the face.

I moved closer to the windows, but all that was staring

me in the face was my own reflection, hovering outside in the dark.

I put my hands to the glass and looked down at the street outside. The pavements were empty. There was no sign of Mark.

My heart ached for him.

He'd said something to me once. It was when I was working on a weekend, trying and failing for what felt like the hundredth time to revise a pitch for some media coverage I couldn't get quite right. We were in our living room, cuddled up on the sofa. 'You only get frustrated because you never give up,' he'd told me. 'You don't quit.'

'You never give up,' I repeated to myself now. 'You don't quit.'

I gazed at the buckled chair down on the floor for a moment, then pushed off from the windows and dashed by the cube. I raced on towards the partition wall running along behind the refectory and closed in on the photocopying machine.

I checked the outlet tray. There was no new print-out waiting for me. No return fax from Simon and Rebecca.

Snapping my head up, fighting against the sense of hopelessness and desperation that was pressing in on me, I looked across the darkened space towards Raul. His body hadn't moved but something drew me to him, a kind of magnetic pull. I ran closer.

Late-night London was lit up outside, a greenish smear of the city's sodium lighting washing across Raul's face and hands. And there it was again. That feeling that I was missing something. It felt as if my mind was circling around it, skirting close to it, like water funnelling down a drain.

I glanced off to one side, towards the ghostly outline of the gym area and the decorating equipment inside it.

'Help me, Raul,' I whispered. 'What is it I'm missing?'

For a moment, I thought again of the photograph he'd shown me of his wife and daughter. I thought of how happy he'd been, how much he had to live for and how guilty I felt that all of that had been taken from him. It was clear from the way Hayley had interacted with him and talked about him afterwards that he was popular around the building and she was genuinely fond of him.

And then it struck me. The thought I'd been circling. The way out from here that I'd overlooked.

How could I have missed it before now?

90

The black cab Mark had hailed rocked along Fleet Street.
He didn't speak with the driver, a heavyset man in a West
Ham shirt who kept sneaking glances at him in the rearview
mirror as if he was afraid Mark was going to attempt to run
off without paying.

Mark could understand why. He'd been out of breath when
he'd flagged down the cab. He was hastily dressed. Now he
was sitting forwards gripping the door handle next to him,
staring out of the window he'd cracked with the intensity
of a prisoner on day release.

He'd been inside the hospital for just over a week since
Luke had put in place the necessary arrangements, but it
felt like so much longer. There was a freshness to the night
air streaming through his window. And there was an undeniable novelty to seeing people passing by on buses or
walking along with phones pressed to their ears. Ordinary
life. He'd been cut off from it for so long. Oddly, it was the
smallest things he pined for most of all. The regular things.
The simple routines of washing up after a meal, watching
TV, even paying the household bills.

For all Mark's endless running, lying in the hospital
had been the hardest thing of all. He'd almost walked out

countless times. Exhausting as it had been, there was a sense of reassurance in constantly moving on. On the ward, when he wasn't putting on a show of confidence for Luke's benefit, or for the doctors and nurses who checked on him without knowing the real reason he was there, he'd spent most of his time wondering if the door to his room would fly open any second and a thuggish hospital-orderly-who-wasn't-really-a-hospital-orderly would come sweeping inside to kill him.

Obviously he knew he was heading into a trap right now. He also understood that he didn't have a choice. From the moment he'd made that first tentative approach to the prosecution team, he'd been aware that he risked laying a trail that could lead back to him. Or maybe not a trail so much as a fuse – one that, if ignited, would blow apart everything he loved so much.

For the past year and a bit he'd been living by his instincts. Doing the prudent things. The safe things. He'd spent time in Canada. Newfoundland, mostly. Then a spell in Eastern Europe. Budapest. Krakow. And finally a few months in Bergen.

Midway through his time in Norway he'd returned to America briefly. Using the new identity papers he'd acquired in Poland, he'd flown international into Miami followed by a domestic flight on to California. On his second day in San Francisco, he'd driven to Stanford and sneaked into the back of a packed lecture on the history and structure of Western movies.

Rosie was there.

It had been his daughter's dream to study film and it

helped to know she was fulfilling her wish. Rosie was sitting many rows ahead of him towards the front of the theatre. Her hair was no longer dyed purple. She'd cut her naturally brown locks short in a bob. At one point, the young, handsome guy sitting next to her slipped her a note. She read it. Smiled. After the lecture, Mark had found a secluded spot under an oak tree in the quad and had watched his daughter sitting unawares with the guy on the grass, their legs entangled, surrounded by their bags and textbooks. They'd kissed, and Rosie had smiled, and the guy (dressed preppy with a crew-cut – far more conventional, Mark noted, than any of the boys Rosie had dated in her rebellious teen years when she'd seemed determined to make an art out of driving her father mad) had taken her hand and whispered something to her, making her laugh.

That laugh. It shattered him.

He'd wanted to go to her, of course. The big reveal. *Ta da! Surprise! I'm still alive!* But that wasn't why he'd come. He'd come to check she was doing OK. That she'd been able to move forwards with her life. To know she'd cope if the plan he'd set in motion went wrong.

It was different with Kate.

The moment he'd entered her flat he could tell she was in a very bad place. Everything about her new life had felt wrong.

Then he'd seen the picture on her fridge of the two of them together on their honeymoon and it had brought it all back. Everything he'd attempted to push deep down inside.

He knew Kate. He loved her. She was a fighter, but perhaps losing him had been one blow too many. The Kate he'd known had always been house-proud, but the dismal, blank state of her flat spoke of something else.

And now he'd made it so much worse.

It had been foolish and vain of him to follow her. Stupid to go to her place. Cowardly to lie low in the hospital instead of disappearing for good.

He'd been weak and selfish. He knew the stakes and he'd still placed her in peril. He'd wanted so much to find a way back to her that he'd risked everything, and now look what had happened.

So yes, he was going to follow the instructions he'd been given. Perhaps if he did, they would let Kate go. He knew the odds were not good but he had to try.

And, fine, he could tell himself he owed Kate the truth. He could tell himself he wanted to say sorry to her face to face, beg her forgiveness. Even if it cost him his life. Even if, after everything he had sacrificed and all they had been through, he didn't make it to court on Monday.

But the simple truth was, he wanted to let Kate know how completely he loved her. He needed to say it one more time.

'Here we go, mate.' The cabbie swung to the kerb in front of a pub that had closed up for the night. He nodded across the street towards a high-rise office building, most of it in darkness. 'My wife says it looks like someone screwed up the window order. They got a load of bathroom mirrors by mistake.'

Mark ducked and stared towards the lighted entrance to the towering building. The revolving glass doors were motionless. He couldn't see anyone at all inside.

'Here.'

He passed the driver some wadded notes and stepped out of the cab into the quiet street, crossed the road. There was no need for any subterfuge. The caller had said twenty minutes. His time was almost gone.

For just a second, Mark wondered how he would get inside, but then he saw Luke emerge from behind a reception counter and make his way towards a small steel pillar just inside the entrance. He was in his hospital scrubs and training shoes. Blood on his face. His wrists looked to have been bound together somehow.

Mark watched as Luke pressed a key card against the pillar and a side door opened.

He stepped through.

It wasn't until he was inside and the door had swung closed behind him that the man in the ripped and bloodied work shirt stepped out from his hiding place with the gun in his hand.

91

Friday 11.53 p.m.

I moved out from behind Raul and strode forwards across the office floor.

My heart was beating crazily fast but I didn't slow.

Another substance was coursing through my body now, competing with whatever contaminant Joel had slipped into my water.

Adrenaline, yes. And something else.

Hope. I had hope now.

If I could get out of here and get downstairs, if I hurried, if I got there in time . . .

If. If. If.

I had no idea if I could make it or what I might be confronted with if I did. I had no idea if I could help Luke, save Mark. But one thing was different. I thought I had a chance now where previously there was none.

The screened-off gym area was ahead of me. I could see the dust sheets and painting gear, the boxes of gym equipment behind the panels of smoked privacy glass.

I padded forwards onto the plastic sheets laid over the floor, facing up to the blue plastic sheeting tacked to the windows and walls. My body tensed. I lifted both hands. For

356

a second, my arms were so heavy with dread it felt like I was lifting kettlebells. I tore the sheeting down.

And there it was, staring back at me.

The stray thought my mind had been groping for. The misfire in my brain whenever I thought of Raul.

It all went back to something Hayley had said to me after Raul had wheeled his cleaning trolley out of our elevator carriage.

Raul's a total sweetheart. He's supposed to use the service elevator, but everybody here knows him and he's so nice he totally gets away with it.

There was a service elevator.

I was looking at it.

My skin fizzed with a hot static charge. The elevator seemed to throb before me. A tiny part of me was afraid it was another hallucination, but when I reached out and pressed both palms to the metal, it was hard and cold to the touch.

Joel must have known about the elevator, too. It wasn't something he would have overlooked. Had he just assumed I wouldn't find it?

I took a step back. The elevator was fitted in the middle of the end wall and it was very wide – about double the width of the passenger elevators out in the vestibule. The doors were painted a pale cream. They were mighty things that opened and closed vertically with a horizontal seam in the middle. There was a strap hanging from the uppermost door.

As I grabbed for it, I realized something else. The builder-decorators Hayley had said goodbye to had passed us in the atrium carrying their tool boxes. But they hadn't come down in the trio of passenger elevators we'd been waiting for. And they wouldn't have tramped down thirteen storeys of stairs with their tools. They must have used this elevator.

My heart lifted as I pulled down on the strap.

The doors creaked and clunked but didn't separate. They were secured somehow.

No.

There was a call button to the left of the elevator doors. Beneath it was a keyhole.

I groaned.

The slit for the keyhole was rotated sideways. Underneath it were printed the words CALL ELEVATOR.

So that was why Joel hadn't been concerned that I might find it.

If I had no key, I couldn't call the elevator.

If I couldn't call it, I couldn't get out.

Shit.

I thought of the rubber tether that was attached to Raul's coveralls. Maybe there had been an elevator key secured to it as well as a key card. Joel must have taken them both.

I traced my finger over the keyhole.

If this is all that's in my way . . .

I reached up to the pocket of my blouse, removing Maggie's keys and weighing them in my palm. I selected the smallest key and tried it in the keyhole. The key went partway in and then stopped. I pushed on it, hitting it with the padded bandage on my hand. I twisted it. It wouldn't turn.

I yanked it out and tried the other keys, ramming them forwards, one after the other.

They didn't fit at all.

'Please not this. Please.'

I was so close.

I put the keys back in my pocket and heaved on the elevator strap again, twisting around.

Something jabbed into my hip. It was the small ledge between the doors, where the lower door protruded slightly. I put my elbow on it and pushed downwards. There was a tiny shift of movement. A gap appeared.

Enough to slip a wedge into?

'Come on, Kate.'

I spun around, scanning the area behind me for the parts of the cross trainer. I stepped towards them and picked up another one of the metal bars with the flattened end. I then moved out from behind the glass privacy screen and rushed across the office floor towards the stationery cupboard. I swept inside. Looked around me. Made a grab for one of the desk lamps I'd seen earlier.

Emerging from the cupboard, I carried the lamp and the pole to the service elevator, the lamp's plug and flex dragging and skipping across the ground.

There was an electrical socket beneath the elevator control panel. I plugged the desk lamp in and switched it on. The glare slashed at my eyes.

I angled the lamp downwards with my toe and seized the canvas strap, tugging on it and placing my knee on the ledge formed by the lower door. Once the gap appeared again, I stabbed the flattened end of the metal pole into it.

It fitted.

I rocked back, stretching out a hand for the lamp, aiming

the beam into the gap and peering closely until I saw a glint of metal near to where I'd wedged the pole. It looked like a catch of some kind.

'You can do this.'

Dropping the lamp, I gripped hold of the pole and wrenched it sideways. I clenched my teeth. My biceps strained. There was an abrasive screeching followed by a metallic *clink*.

I stopped.

My head lolled as a fresh dose of wooziness assailed me.

I blinked and shook it away, then tightened my grip on the pole and pulled one more time.

It slid sideways fast.

Too fast.

The metal catch flipped out of the way all too easily; the paired elevator doors separated immediately and yawned open on a counterweight system.

I wasn't prepared for it.

I fell forwards.

The pole dropped down into the shaft ahead of me.

I grabbed for the side of the elevator. Kicked the lamp with my foot. It tumbled into the void, the cable tangling around my ankle.

My stomach lurched.

My bandaged fingers slipped.

The pole banged and clunked endlessly below me.

I felt gravity pulling me after it but I dived sideways, slamming down onto my elbow and hip, scrabbling at the floor.

Too close.

Sitting upright gingerly, I eased back towards the opening, holding fast to the side of the shaft and gazing down over the ledge.

A smell of cold cement wafted up at me. The lamp swung side to side, bouncing fissures of light around. In the flashes, I could glimpse the smooth cement walls of the elevator cavity and thick metal cables the size of my wrist stretching down through the middle of the chasm. And down below me – way down towards the very bottom of the shaft – I could just see the mechanisms on the roof of an elevator carriage.

92

Joel studied Mark Harding without speaking as he stood before him in the late-night foyer. A dead man. A ghost.

'What now?' Mark gestured to the gun Joel was holding. 'Are you going to shoot me?'

He said it simply, clearly, his voice oddly accepting in the stillness of the lobby.

'Now we talk, Mark.'

'You're not going to talk to me. That's not your role here.'

'We have to talk a little first. You need to convince me there are no documents or materials hidden anywhere else. No recorded confessions that are primed to be sent to the prosecution team or a newspaper if you disappear.'

He watched Mark glance over at Luke. He saw him take in the injuries to Luke's head and face, the way he was leaning to the left, his breathing laboured.

'I want to see Kate first. I have to know that she's OK.'

'Once we've talked. After you've convinced me.'

'No, I want to see her now.'

Joel shook his head. 'That's not going to happen.'

'I could run out into the street. I could start yelling for help.'

'And I could shoot you and Luke before you get out of

that door. But I'm not going to do that because you're not going to run. We're going to talk, Mark. You know how this has to go.'

He seemed to consider it for a brief moment before nodding cautiously. There were no dramatics. There was no attempt to bargain or plead. Joel had seen it before. When someone reached the end of the line, they generally understood there were no more choices to be made.

He could relate.

Somewhere in his pocket, his burner phone was vibrating. Midnight. The deadline Fergus Marsh had imposed. Joel elected not to answer. The phone was set to silent. The buzzing didn't carry, even in the silence of the foyer.

'Where are we going?' Mark asked him.

'I have a place in mind.'

93

Fergus Marsh listened to the phone ring out. There was no answer. No response of any kind.

In the brittle stillness that followed, a sense of disbelief and futility washed over him. It was hard to believe the man he'd hired had failed. His references had been exemplary.

'Send the contingency option in,' Dominic told him. 'Do it now.'

'No,' he croaked. 'We wait.'

'That's a mistake. We have to close this thing down.'

He held Dominic's stare, a wordless tussle taking place between them.

You told me that once before.

He'd known it was a terrible decision at the time, of course. A gross and irredeemably evil act. But Dominic had insisted there was no time for other options. They were in so deep, their denials so public, the truth would have doomed them.

He'd been weak, then. He'd allowed himself to be persuaded. Mark Harding had to be stopped. Irreversibly. Unquestionably. One murder concealed and distorted by the magnitude of a far more terrible crime.

Was he being equally weak now? he wondered. He was aware that his own obstinacy was, at least in part, born out

364

of denial. And wasn't there also a part of him that simply wanted to prove Dominic wrong, reassert his authority?

'All you're doing is delaying the inevitable, Fergus. I was right the last time. I'm right this time, too.'

'We wait,' he rasped.

Though already, he understood the waiting would be torture. With every second that passed, his doubts would multiply. He knew it wouldn't be long until they reached a critical mass.

94

Saturday 12.01 a.m.

Kneeling in the opening, I raised my head and looked upwards. The shaft climbed so high that the light didn't penetrate all the way to the top. Above me there was almost nothing but a vast, gloomy emptiness.

I *could* see the elevator doors one floor up. I could also spy a luminous plastic handle on the reverse of the doors. It was glowing green. A quick glance at the door I had opened revealed a similar handle. I guessed it was attached to the catch that had prevented me from separating the doors to begin with. It had to be a safety release.

I rocked back from the opening, sucking in a breath of stale air, peering at the steel cables hanging down in the middle of the shaft. There were four of them but they were too far away for me to reach. My eyes scanned the flat cement slabs lining the cavity walls. There was no maintenance ladder or any other kind of access system I could see.

I leaned out over the opening again. My stomach contracted. Dread bulged at the back of my throat. There was another luminous handle on the reverse of the doors one floor below me.

I rocked back.

A hard awareness settled in the pit of my stomach.

I couldn't just stay here. My symptoms might have abated but they hadn't gone entirely and there were signs they might come back. Joel had told me I would die if I didn't get to a hospital. And Mark's twenty minutes were already up. If he'd come for me, he'd be with Joel now. Joel already had Luke held at gunpoint.

Turning, I gazed back across the office floor, a prisoner contemplating my own personal gallows. In the distance I could just make out the ropes hanging in front of the climbing wall.

95

Police Sergeant Christine Harris of the City of London Police Force had a stab vest on over her dark blue, short-sleeved uniform shirt, beneath a police cap that featured the force's distinctive red and white chequered band. Her vest was equipped with multiple pockets and pouches, as was her equipment belt. Between them they contained, among other items, her speed cuffs, her extendable baton, her incapacitant spray, Taser and police radio. Her colleagues in the armed response unit of the Force were equipped with firearms, primarily for terrorist incidents. Harris was not.

It was her police radio that burst into life now.

'Control.'

'Harris. Go ahead.'

'Christine, I need a favour.'

Harris cursed. Her partner on patrol, Constable Terry – a tall, gangling black man with an infuriating grin – chuckled next to her. They both recognized the dispatcher on the other end of the radio as Alan Potts. At a never-to-be-repeated Christmas party where Harris had drunk too much vodka and danced on too many tables, she had, for reasons that still escaped her, rounded off her night by taking Potts home for some (she assumed, because she couldn't, truthfully, remember) seriously underwhelming sex. Ever since, Potts had talked to her this way. Always Christine, not Harris. Always with the timid, slightly embarrassed voice of a shy, possibly infatuated man who had seen her naked.

'What kind of a favour, Potts?'

'Are you close to Ludgate Hill?'

Harris could have snapped at him that of course she was. The beat for all City of London police officers was tightly focused on the relatively small area of the so-called Square Mile – the historic heart and traditional business centre of London.

'We're on New Change now.'

Actually, she was standing just along from the entrance to a high-end mall that doubled as a bar and restaurant complex. Harris had been on the Force long enough to remember when the site had been occupied by the stately offices of a law firm.

'Right. This is, um. I don't know how to explain it really.'

Harris clicked off her radio and rocked back on her heels. Her feet were too warm inside her steel-capped dress shoes. It had been a hot day and even this late at night she could feel the day's warmth rising up from the pavement, bathing her hands. Seven hours until her shift was over. She wanted to get home, get showered, eat breakfast and sleep.

Terry nudged her arm. 'Is he asking you on a date, do you think?'

'Shut it.'

'Christine?' came the voice on the radio.

She clicked the button to transmit. '*Sergeant* Harris.'

'Right. The thing is—'

'Oh, Christ. Just hurry up and get to it, Potts.'

Bad mistake. She immediately glared at Terry before he could work up some dumb crack about *that*. His eyes lit brightly all the same. She knew now what she'd hear from the others when she got back to the station later.

Just hurry up and get to it, Potts. Give it to me, Potts.

'A rather curious thing happened earlier, Christine. I took a call from a fax machine.'

Give me strength.

'What did you say?'

'A fax machine. The call came through on an emergency code. When I took it all I could hear was the . . . gobbledegook. You know, the electronic sounds.'

'We take calls from faxes now?'

'No. That's the point. We never have.'

'It was probably a mistake of some kind.'

'That's what I thought, too.' A pause. 'But it bothered me. I checked our system and it has the number listed as coming from an Edge Communications. I tried calling them back.'

'And?'

'No answer. The phone wouldn't connect.'

'There you go then. Their phone system is down or screwed up in some way.'

'There's something else. I just checked our centralized records and we received an automatic signal from a fire alarm at the building where this company is located earlier this evening. Call monitoring was informed it was a false alarm that originated from the thirteenth floor. That's where this Edge Communications is based. I know it doesn't sound like much but it feels a little odd to me and I thought, if you're not in the middle of something else . . .'

Harris glanced at Terry. She groaned. 'You want us to check it out?'

'If you could. Just quickly. For—'

She cut him off before he could say *me*.

'Where exactly is this Edge Communications?'

'Close to you now. In The Mirror.'

Harris twisted at the waist and looked up past the rounded dome of St Paul's Cathedral. She could see the feathered tip of the reflective office tower Potts was referring to soaring skywards. There didn't appear to be any lights on inside the uppermost floors, but Harris knew that was deceptive. It was characteristic of the specialist glass windows installed in the building and one, as a police officer, that bugged her. What was the point of having a window if you couldn't see both ways?

'Christine?'

She thought about it as Terry rolled his eyes in front of her. She shared his scepticism, but then again, there was no denying their shift had been quiet so far, and it wasn't as if they had anything pressing to respond to right now. Besides, as irritating as Potts could be, he was an experienced dispatcher with form for following up on interrupted or non-responsive calls that had led to important saves in the past. Last autumn, it was his quick thinking that had enabled Harris to respond to a silent phone call from a waitress who had been cornered in the back of the restaurant where she worked by her abusive boss. Now that she thought about it, it was that incident that had led her to seek out Potts to buy him a drink at that ill-fated Christmas get-together.

'Fine,' she said, raising a hand to ward off Terry's inevitable griping. 'We'll take a look. But stop calling me Christine.'

96

Joel made Mark and Luke take the stairs, not the elevator.
A precaution on his part. Gun or not, he didn't want to be
locked in a steel box with two men who had to know they
were shortly about to die.

'Keep moving.'

Luke was leading, his hands secured in front of him. Joel
had his pistol aimed at the back of Mark's head.

A hot quiver rushed through him and for a second he was
tempted to pull the trigger, get it over with, be done. But he
resisted the impulse. There were other factors to consider.
Kate had been right about one thing – almost. *This is about
something else for you.* Except it wasn't about him. It was
bigger than that.

Why had Mark come back? *Trying to do the right thing.*
Could he really be so naive? Didn't he understand it was
much too late for that?

They reached the bottom of the stairwell and Luke hesitated before the fire door ahead of them. His head and
shoulders plummeted. He began to tremble in his thin cotton
scrubs.

'Open that door and go through,' Joel said. 'Take ten paces
and then stop.'

97

Saturday 12.07 a.m.

There were two harnesses suspended from the brightly patterned ropes hanging in front of the climbing wall, each equipped with a jangling collection of karabiners and belay devices. I tugged down on the rope attached to the harness closest to me and the other end of the rope whipped through the pulley system overhead.

There was a muffled clunk and my head jerked up. *Shit.* A karabiner was clipped to the end of the rope. I hadn't taken it off and now it was gummed up in the pulley embedded in the ceiling.

As I gaped up at it, a sudden sharp pain ignited in my sinuses. My vision blurred and doubled. I froze. For a moment, I allowed my eyes to shut. I could feel the runaway tempo of my pulse in my eyelids. I pinched the bridge of my nose, holding my breath, trying to maintain a degree of control. Gradually, the pain dissipated. It didn't spread. But it was one more warning I didn't need.

Snapping my eyes open, I reached for the second rope, bringing it towards me, my hands fumbling with the karabiner attached to the end. It took me several attempts to get it unscrewed and unclipped. As soon as I had it removed, I pulled sharply down on the rope and watched it spiral upwards, shuttle through the pulley and then clatter down next to me in a loose and heavy pile.

I grabbed an armful of rope along with the harness and the karabiner and returned to the elevator shaft with the rest of the rope trailing behind.

At the opening of the shaft I gave myself a second to breathe. Then I stepped into the harness, heaving it up over my skirt, which bunched around my thighs and waist. It restricted my movement so I unzipped my skirt a little, then secured the buckles on the harness, tightening any loose straps I could see.

A short distance behind me was one of the exposed metal girders. I hurried towards it, adrenaline pushing me faster than I knew I should probably be going. But I couldn't think about my heart or how vulnerable it might be right now, I just needed to get to Luke and Mark.

My mouth was tacky. Blood swarmed in my ears. I cast the end of the rope around the girder, gathering it clumsily from the other side.

My vision blurred again. I stilled until it slid back into focus. There was a loop formed by a complicated knot at the end of the rope. I gripped it in my quaking palm and clipped the loose karabiner to it. With a halting breath, I then secured the karabiner to the rest of the rope and pulled it taut. It seemed like a relatively secure anchor – as secure as I could make it anyway – and I carried the rest of the rope back to the opening of the elevator shaft, unclipped it from one of the karabiners attached to my climbing harness, and tossed it over the side.

I shuffled closer to the drop, clutching the lip of the

opening and gazing down. In the angled slash of light from the suspended desk lamp, I could see the rope dangling a few metres below the luminous safety release handle on the elevator doors one floor down.

Picking up a fistful of the rope from the floor, I formed a loop in it and jammed it through the belay device, attaching the belay and the rope to the karabiner I'd just released, then securing everything to my harness and tightening the screw on the karabiner.

Was that right?

Maybe. I could just about remember how we'd been taught to do it for the MarshJet charity abseil. Back then, we'd had instructors with us. I'd had Mark next to me. Everything had been checked and double checked. And it had still been nerve-racking.

Tears flooded my eyes. If I got this wrong . . .

'Enough,' I murmured. 'Stop.'

Before the doubts and the terror could fully clamp down on me, I sat on the edge of the cavity, my bare feet hanging over the abyss. A swirl of vertigo taunted me. Cool air swirled up from below, lifting my hair. I placed my palms flat on either side of me.

I was shaking all over as I shifted around onto my belly and grasped the rope above and below the belay. With tears streaming down my face, I began to lower myself.

98

'Shouldn't there be someone on duty behind the front desk?'

Police Sergeant Christine Harris leaned back from the sleek wall of glass in front of her as she considered her partner's question. She rattled the locked door to the side of the revolving glass entranceway. She didn't know why. Frustration, mostly. She hadn't truly expected to find anything untoward here when Potts had asked them to take a look. Now? It was hard to know what to make of what she was seeing.

Inside, concealed lighting illuminated the luxurious lobby. Harris could see acres of polished stone flooring and what appeared to be an indoor waterfall. Overhead, glass mezzanine walkways bisected the atrium. She knew it was supposed to be impressive, and in a way it was, but it also struck her as a bit, well, crass. Which was not to say Terry didn't have a point.

'Seriously,' he said. 'A building this size, this prominent. No way do they leave it unattended overnight.'

'A security guard could be doing a sweep of the floors. They probably have a set schedule.'

'What if a courier arrives? Or someone orders a takeaway food delivery?'

'Then the delivery rider would have an order number to call. Same thing with the courier.'

'So how do you want to play it?'

Harris stepped back further, her hand alighting on her baton. They could wait, she supposed. Odds were Terry was right. This late on a work day, even a Friday, there were takeaway food deliveries all over the City. And Harris had seen enough of life in the Square Mile to know that an office worker might come down in the elevators to leave, or arrive outside the building at any moment.

'Try the intercom again,' she said.

'Seriously?'

'Humour me.'

Terry sighed and pressed the steel-plated button set into the granite wall next to him, triggering a loud rasping noise. He arched an eyebrow and stared back at her as he held the button down. But there was nobody behind the front desk to answer the call. And OK, maybe it was possible some work-shy security guard was taking a nap behind the closed door around the back of the front desk, but nobody could ignore the intercom for this long if they were close by. And they'd already tried phoning the main number for the building twice.

'Do you want to check the rear entrance?' Terry asked.

Again, Harris didn't think it would lead to anything, but she was about to tell him maybe they should take a quick look when she got another burst of static on her radio.

'Control.' It was a woman's voice this time. 'We have reports of a suspicious vehicle parked on Cheapside, close to St Paul's Station.'

Harris pressed her thumb down on the button to transmit and shared a pensive look with Terry. They took calls to investigate suspicious vehicles every shift. It was nearly always nothing. But Harris, like every officer on the Force, worked and lived with the awareness that another terrorist attack on the city could come at any moment, in any way. Weekend nights were as dangerous a time as any other.

'On it.'

She turned and began jogging across the street, holding her radio steady against her vest. They could cut through Paternoster Square, be on the scene in under five minutes.

But that didn't mean she'd forgotten about 55 Ludgate Hill. It was like Terry had said. There really should have been someone on duty behind the front desk.

'Control, can you transfer me to Potts?' she asked as she ran.

'Negative. He's on another call.'

'Then give him a message for me. Tell him I need a number for 55 Ludgate Hill. And I don't mean the number for the front desk. We've been trying that. I want to speak to the owners of the building.'

99
Saturday 12.13 a.m.

Panic hit me one metre down the shaft. My arms felt deadened and weak. The bandage on my hand allowed the rope to slip too quickly through the belay device.

I slammed against the cement lining of the cavity. My feet flailed for grip. I somehow managed to stop myself from tumbling further, clinging to the rope, my toes crunched against the interior wall.

I pressed my forehead against the rope. I could see the whites of my knuckles in the dim.

My fingers burned. The rope slipped some more.

I shrieked and looked down, my feet fluttering beneath me.

Mistake.

The end of the rope dangled precariously below me and after that there was nothing for hundreds of metres.

A *creeeeeak* from above.

I glanced up. My heart pounded. Was the rope chafing against the ledge? Maybe the karabiner was about to fail.

I had to keep going. There was no way I could pull myself back up now. I didn't have the grip, or the strength.

Or the time.

'Move, Kate,' I hissed to myself.

I trembled violently as I resumed my awkward walk down the wall, the rope chafing the skin of my hands. My knees quaked. My toes curled into claws. I steadied myself. Swallowed. And repeated.

I thought about Mark to try to block out the terror. I thought of his voice on the phone and how amazing it was that he was alive. Then I thought about the lies he'd told, how he'd let me think he was dead for fifteen months. A hot anger surfaced. I loved him but in that moment I hated him, too. And then I thought of Luke, the blank fear in his face when he'd looked out at me from the elevator, and the bile rose into my mouth.

'Move,' I repeated. 'Keep moving.'

My foot slipped again.

I screamed and clung desperately to the rope. I kicked out with my legs. I spun and twisted. I got myself under control.

I continued on.

Inch by awful inch, the rope scuffing through the belay device, until I neared the opening just above the reverse of the metal doors below me. My toes were skimming the edge of the cavity. The luminous release catch was another metre or so down.

Tiny tremors passed through the rope.

Whining with the exertion, I lowered myself further.

Now my body was about halfway down the uppermost elevator door. Tightening my grip on the lower part of the rope, I snatched my other hand away and grasped for the luminous handle.

I missed.

Twisted.

My hip and upper body banged against the elevator doors.

I tried again, missed again.

Panic beat like a drum inside my head.

I regripped the rope with both hands, the harness digging into my hips and thighs.

I glanced down.

Dread choked me. I was afraid to remove both hands from the rope again. But my right foot was close to the release catch. If I could just reach it, then maybe I could knock it to one side.

I stretched. I kicked out.

Nothing.

I was still a few centimetres shy.

I clenched my teeth and fed a little more rope through the belay. My body twisted around to face the wrong way.

A weightlessness formed in my stomach.

My arms shook and almost gave out. My elbow was still weak and unstable from the way Joel had bent it earlier. The joint screamed.

I kicked and flailed and turned myself back around until I was facing the elevator doors again. Then I tightened my stomach muscles, thrust out with my legs and swung myself like a pendulum.

I stretched out my toes. I kicked at the safety catch. It flicked to one side.

The doors parted slightly. A gap of light bloomed between them. I shrieked and forced my toes into the crack, then my feet, separating my legs in a scissor movement.

The doors opened further. Not all the way. But perhaps *just* enough.

My upper body was twisting again, tipping backwards. I struggled against gravity, writhing in the opposite direction while I squeezed my legs even further over the lower elevator door. I could only keep one leg all the way through. My other leg flapped clear until I was straddling the door as if I was riding a horse.

'No!'

My strength went. My hands slipped. The rope whipped through the belay. I flung myself forwards, ducking my head. My forehead glanced off the upper elevator door as my weight bore down on the lower door, shunting it downwards.

I slammed forwards onto unfinished cement. Bashing my chin and hands and knees, scrabbling for grip.

I lay there, hardly daring to move, as if I was stranded and spread-eagled in the middle of a frozen lake.

I was trembling all over. Bucking with spasms of disbelief and fear. My heart was beating so wildly that it kept pushing me up off the ground. All around me I could hear a deep, machine-like whirring. The air was as warm as the womb.

I raised my head.

I saw metal ducting and electricity panels. I saw curved aluminium panelling and giant, humming machines.

And further back I saw something else.

'Maggie?'

100

Joel stood in the taut silence of the parking garage with his eyes on Luke, his gun on Mark. Both men were kneeling on the ground a short distance in front of him, a safe distance from each another. Luke had his head down and his wrists secured in front of him, almost as if he was praying. Joel had told Mark to sit on his hands.

'You don't have to do this,' Luke said to him.

Joel hated when people said that. As if anything in life was really, when it came down to it, a choice. That was the great fallacy of lying. Eventually every truth – even the hardest or the most unpalatable – would be exposed. And this time, they were going to be punished, too.

He clenched his gun tighter, watching now as Mark glanced nervously across at his brother-in-law, then looked slowly back at Joel, squaring his shoulders, lifting his chin. Perhaps, being older, he felt an onus to step up. More likely he was aware that his own actions were what had got them both into this situation. Or maybe he sensed how much this mattered to Joel.

'You said you wanted to talk,' Mark said to him. 'Let's talk.'

'OK, Mark.' Joel's lip curled as he adjusted the aim of his gun to the centre mass of Mark's body. 'Let's.'

101

Saturday 12.18 a.m.

After loosening the harness and untangling it from my
legs, I hurried forwards and took Maggie's face in my hands.
Her skin was hot and damp. She was slumped on the floor.

'Oh God, Maggie, are you OK?'

She moaned at me. The silver duct tape that was preventing
her from talking was glistening wet. I picked desperately at
the end with my nail.

'This is going to hurt.'

She nodded, her eyes pleading with me to hurry. I felt
weak all over, shivery with exhaustion. My grip was strangely
numb as I ripped the tape free.

Maggie inhaled in a gasping gulp.

'My hands.' She grimaced. 'Please. I can't feel them.'

I leaned sideways, looked behind her. Her wrists had been
bound together behind a pipe. Joel had used the same silver
duct tape that he'd applied across her mouth, wrapping it
over and over. Her fingers were pale and bloated. The flesh
on her lower arms was engorged, almost purple. It would
take me too long to unpeel the tape.

'I'm going to need a knife, or—'

'Over there.'

Maggie motioned with her chin to a scrap of metal that

was protruding from under the base of what appeared to be an industrial-sized cooling unit. There was a motor or a fan rumbling inside. Hot air was wafting from the exhaust, bathing Maggie's body in the cloying heat.

I crawled forwards, stretched for the piece of metal, lifted it in my hands. I was sweating so profusely I nearly dropped it.

'Hurry, Kate.'

'Let me try.'

I crawled back behind her, wiping clammy perspiration from my face and then picking and sawing at the tape. Beads of sweat formed on my brow and dropped and splashed on the ground. I was aware that time was running short so I started hacking at the tape, heedless, nicking Maggie's skin.

She winced. 'What happened to you?'

'Same thing as you. Joel.'

'Why?'

I shook my head. 'We don't have time for that.'

The tape began to loosen. I scrabbled at it with my nails. Maggie groaned in pain as the tape suddenly released. She tried to pull her arms forwards but shouted in agony instead.

'It's OK,' I said. 'Here.' I gently lifted her arms onto her lap, then looked all around me, scouting out which way we should go, shying from looking back at the elevator shaft. I wanted to move as soon as possible but I couldn't just leave Maggie here alone.

She bared her teeth and swore as she flexed her fingers in tiny degrees.

'Hurts,' she told me.

'I'm sorry.'

'I didn't think anyone was coming.'

'We need to move you, get away from here. Do you know where he is?'

Her eyes widened in panic. 'No. Do you?'

'He has my brother. My husband, I think.'

'What?'

I went to help her to her feet and my eyesight blurred again. Tiny fissures of pain crackled through my chest.

No. Not now.

I released her, wrapping my arms around myself. My hearing grew muffled. My temperature soared, my scalp prickling with heat. I rocked, stamping my feet.

'Kate? What is it?'

Maggie levered herself up from her knees with a grunt of exertion.

'Kate?'

'I'm OK,' I told her.

I squeezed myself tighter, willing it to be true, urging the pain not to spread and paralyse me again.

'Have you called the police?' Maggie asked me.

I shook my head, screwed my eyes tightly shut. 'No. We need to find a working phone.'

'He took mine away from me.'

I nodded, then opened my eyes carefully. I hoped if I didn't make any sudden moves I might be OK. 'Can you walk?'

'Can you?'

'I have to get downstairs.'

I took one step forwards. Wavered. In front of me, the wall to my side flipped down towards the floor like the page of a picture book being turned.

Hold on.

Not yet.

I pressed my hand to the side of my head. I was shivering all over, the horrible numbness streaking up and down my arms, an electric current fizzing in my gums.

'What's happening to you?' Maggie asked me.

I shook my head again, fighting to stay upright. 'Did he give you something?'

'How do you mean? You mean like a roofie? Jesus.'

'I mean water. Anything to drink or eat?'

'No. I wouldn't have let him.'

Maggie was standing now, her shoulder braced against the machine opposite me, the familiar bullishness taking hold of her again. We locked eyes for a second. Both of us looked terrible. Both of us were grimly aware of it.

'How did he get you up here?' I asked.

'Main elevators. They're this way.'

She pushed off from the machinery and laboured forwards, cradling her arms across her body. The sweat had stained her blouse all across her back. There were dirty scuff marks on her legs.

I traipsed after her, my ankles tangling. The winding corridors between the humming pieces of equipment were confined and dim. It was as if we were threading our way through the bowels of a battleship.

'There,' Maggie said. 'Just ahead.'

The elevator bank was directly in front of us. The elevators were surrounded by exposed metal beams and loops of electrical wires. When we got closer I could see that there were no call buttons, only a keyhole.

'They won't stop on this floor without an elevator key,' I said, desperately turning in circles. I scanned the ceiling. Were there cameras here, too? Could Joel see us?

'Stairs.' Maggie nudged me towards a fire exit door. 'We can try the elevators from the next floor down.'

102

Sir Fergus could stand the wait no longer. They hadn't heard from Joel. His deadline had more than elapsed.

A steel band of tension coiled around his skull, tightening remorselessly. His throat was aflame.

Pivoting forwards in his chair, he dialled on speakerphone and heard the voicemail service pick up.

'Finally,' Dominic murmured.

Sir Fergus kept his head down as the beep sounded. 'You have my go-ahead,' he wheezed. 'Clear this mess up.'

103

'Tell me about MarshJet,' Joel said.

'What do you want to know?' Mark asked him.

'Start with the toxic cabin air.'

'That's complicated.'

'Simplify it.'

'Is this necessary?' Luke asked.

Joel ignored him, watching Mark closely for any signs he was about to embellish. At the same time, he was aware that Luke was sneaking glances *his* way, but he didn't believe either of them were a threat right now.

He was also confident they wouldn't be disturbed. The parking bays were almost entirely empty. There was what looked like a modified electric golf cart in a corner to his left, close to the service elevator. The only other vehicle was his rental Audi.

'MarshJet's planes are unsafe,' Mark began. 'You must know that by now.'

From his kneeling position he looked up at Joel with a searching intensity. Joel didn't expect him to lie. He knew he had hoped to testify about MarshJet on Monday morning. He was sure Mark understood now there was no way that would happen. This was as close as he would get. As close as Joel could allow him to get. He might as well unburden himself while he could.

'I'm interested in when you knew about it.' Joel was keenly aware of the faint rumble in his voice, a precursor of the storm to come – the one he was doing everything in his power to contain right now, his finger tightening on the trigger as if a part of him was beyond his control.

'Sooner than I was ever meant to. Later than you probably think.'

'Enough with the cryptic answers.'

He could see Mark looking at him curiously as his words faded away across the echoing asphalt. Perhaps he thought he was unbalanced. And maybe he was. He knew for a fact he was wound too tight and that he had been for much too long.

Luke had picked up on it, too. 'Just tell him what he wants to know,' he hissed at Mark.

'OK.' Mark stared at Joel. 'I knew for sure about a week before I ran.'

'Not before?'

'No.'

'How come?'

'Dummy paperwork. Dummy results. The air-monitoring reports from all our planes were rigged with fake data. The regulators signed off on false information.'

There it was. The confirmation he needed. Part of it anyway. But Joel wanted more.

'How did you find out?' he asked.

'All the illnesses that were being reported by pilots and crew . . . it was hard not to be overwhelmed by it. And I was responsible for overseeing a lot of our designs. To begin with I just wanted reassurance, I suppose. So I took a scheduled flight on one of our planes. I had an air-monitoring kit in my hand luggage. The readings I got, they were off the chart.'

'Dangerous?'

'Even with basic equipment I picked up readings of toxic gases that were way above safe levels. When I got back from that flight I spoke to a tech guy on our IT team. I got him to go into our records, pull raw data from a number of different aircraft. We have sophisticated air-monitoring systems installed. When I went through the figures I found multiple instances of toxic fume events.'

'What is that?'

Mark hesitated, a fresh question drifting across his face. 'Why do you want so much detail?'

'Get a gun of your own and you can ask the questions, Mark. Until then, you can answer mine.'

'OK,' Mark said carefully. 'It can happen when what is known as "bleed air" is released from the engines during flight to help maintain cabin pressure. That's normal. What was abnormal was that according to the original data I was seeing, the cabin air was being contaminated with highly toxic levels of hydraulic fluids and engine oils.'

Joel's saliva pooled in his mouth, hot and thick. He swallowed, but afterwards his throat still felt bone dry.

'Did you tell anyone?' he asked.

'Yes.'

'Who?'

Mark shuffled on his knees. A sign that he was about to

deflect in some way, or that he was simply uncomfortable? Luke looked pointedly at him again, urging him on. Joel took a step closer. It would be so easy now to lash out with his gun, rake it across Mark's face. But if he started, then how would he stop?

'I was going to report it to the board.'

The gun trembled in Joel's hand. 'But . . . ?'

'I spoke to the CFO directly first instead.'

'Dominic North.'

'That's right,' Mark said levelly.

He was watching Joel with that penetrating gaze again, like a chess player trying to gauge the moves his opponent had in mind. It was beginning to click together for Joel, now. He had read profile pieces about how closely Sir Fergus worked with his long-time CFO. He suspected it was Dominic North who had spoken to him on the phone earlier.

'He told me I must have made a mistake and not to go searching for issues where there weren't any. I told him that wasn't acceptable to me. Sir Fergus and the rest of the board had to be informed. We'd need to issue a statement while we carried out a full investigation. Ground the planes indefinitely. Upgrade our engine and air-filtering systems. Put everything right.'

Joel's ears popped. His breathing was rapid and shallow. He kept his gaze locked on Mark as he nodded to the Audi. 'Like with a recall on a car.'

'Right.'

'I'm guessing it would have cost a lot of money?'

'Money?' Mark blew air through his lips. 'Millions for the refits, but that wasn't the real issue.'

'What was the real issue?'

'The compensation we'd be liable to pay. First, to the airlines for all the missed flights they'd have to contend with. Second, to their staff whose health had been affected. There was more and more evidence of serious illnesses among crew who flew regularly on our planes. Severe headaches. Chronic vertigo. Nerve trouble. Neurological damage and cognitive degeneration. Loss of sight. Cancer. The company had been arguing there was no connection between the quality of our cabin air and the acute health problems crew were reporting. The regulators and airlines backed us up. I believed that was correct but all of it was built on a lie. The liability would be endless. It would be ruinous.'

Mark fell silent for a moment. He seemed chastened, reflective. When he spoke again, Joel could hear the bitterness in his voice. It made him wary. He knew only too well how easily emotion could colour the truth.

'Dominic asked me to sleep on it first. He said that if I still wanted to go ahead with all this he'd back me up.'

'He was lying to you.'

'When I got to my car that night, there were two men waiting for me. Men not unlike you. They insisted I went for a drive with them. They showed me pictures of my daughter. Pictures of Kate.'

'And you didn't warn them?' Luke said sharply, sounding genuinely shocked.

Mark appeared stung by the question, but Joel moved things along before they could be waylaid.

'That's when you decided to run?' he pressed.

Mark glanced at Luke, but Luke was too busy shaking his

head in disapproval to look back. Joel wondered if he would have been so willing to help his brother-in-law if he'd known the full story, how much danger they were really all in.

'Not right away, no. That wasn't until I was in New York.'

'So what changed?'

Mark looked at him in quiet defiance.

'Something changed,' Joel pressed. 'All I'm asking is for you to tell me what it was.'

'Why do you care?'

'Because I want to know all of it. Because I want to hear it from you.'

'I went back into our computer system.' Mark's voice sounded hoarse, but not because he was whispering. It seemed to Joel as if this was one of the most difficult parts for him to reconcile himself to. 'I had print-offs of the fume data my IT source had recovered for me, downloads of spreadsheets, but what I had was really only a snapshot. There was more. Only, when I went back in, it was all gone. Everything had been wiped. And when I tried to contact my IT guy he was gone, too. He hadn't shown up for work. He hadn't called in sick. When I tried contacting him at home, on his mobile, I couldn't get hold of him. It was like he'd disappeared.'

'You were scared.'

'Very. But more than that, I couldn't live with myself. With knowing what I knew and not doing anything about it. I'd got this letter. I . . .' He looked away. Composed himself. 'You start to think of all the thousands of people who crewed our planes. You start to think of how many of them had got sick and didn't know why. Not for certain. It seemed to me that if I could join the dots then, I don't know, maybe it would help the medical teams treating them, or at least the company could help to fund their care.' He paused. 'My wife used to be a flight attendant. Thanks to me, she helped to tell people our planes were safe. Karma scared me, I suppose. I thought if I said nothing . . .' He shook his head. 'I couldn't shake the idea that Kate might be one of the unlucky ones. My worst nightmare would be if Kate got ill.'

104

Saturday 12.29 a.m.

I almost fell as I stepped out of the elevator into the lobby.
It wasn't a faint. I didn't collapse. It was simply that my legs
went from under me.

I made a grab for Maggie, clinging to her shoulders to
hold myself upright. She was crouched forwards slightly,
holding her arms against her sides.

My vision was a mess. My pulse felt sticky. There was a
raging thirst at the back of my throat.

I couldn't see any sign of Joel, Mark or Luke. I couldn't
hear anything except the feverish backwash in my ears.

'I don't think they're here,' Maggie whispered. 'Let's get
out while we can.'

'No, wait.' I motioned with my chin to the front desk
where the security team had been earlier. It was abandoned.
There was no sign of Tony. 'There are phones over there.
We can call 999. And there's CCTV behind that door. I have
to take a look at it.'

'That's a bad idea.'

'I need you to get me there, Maggie.'

'It's not safe.'

She tried to lead me towards the exit doors but I allowed
my body to go limp, weighing her down.

'Kate!'

'He has my husband. My brother.'

'Then the best thing we can do is get out of here and call the police.'

I looked at her. 'It's your fault I'm here. I wouldn't have come here without you.'

She faltered. 'Kate, I had no way of knowing—'

'I don't care. You owe me. Now help me to get over there.'

Maggie glanced at the front desk, then at the exit doors, as if she was sizing up the distance between them.

'Please, Maggie.'

She huffed. 'This better be quick.'

I leaned on her for support as she moved forwards, the two of us stumbling along together. Outside in the darkness, a black cab was driving by. Maggie saw it, her breath catching. She tried to raise her arms to signal to the driver but then whimpered as the pain hit. We both watched the taxi speed past. There was no one outside on the pavement.

'Keep going,' I urged her.

She led me around behind the front desk and towards the back office.

When we opened the door together, Maggie was the first to scream.

105

Police Sergeant Harris considered the hipster couple in
front of her and tried, not entirely successfully, to conceal
the weariness in her voice.

'You need to find somewhere else to stay tonight. You
can't sleep here.'

'For real?'

This was from the guy with the deep V-neck T-shirt and
the multiple bracelets around his wrists. The lean brunette
pouting next to him looked Insta-ready. Big eyes, trim hips.
She probably existed on a diet of rice crackers and air.

'Seriously, officer. We'll be out of here first thing in the
a.m. As soon as we bag some drone shots for our vlog we'll
be on our way.'

Constable Terry snorted derisively. He was at the back of
the van, shining his torch inside. Harris didn't need him to
tell her what he'd found. They were coming across it more
and more often. Young influencers sleeping in converted
vehicles with the intention of being up at the crack of dawn
to snag the perfect London footage.

'I'm going to pretend I didn't hear that,' Harris said. 'You
can't fly drones in this area.'

'What is this?' the girl muttered. 'Russia?'

'Get your van out of this area. Do it now, before I start asking if you have the right paperwork to be using this vehicle as a camper.'

Harris returned the guy's driving licence to him with a meaningful glare. The couple moaned and bitched as they climbed into the cab. The van's exhaust spewed fumes as they pulled away.

'How long do you think until they're back?' Terry asked as they watched them go.

'Inside an hour.'

'You care?'

'Not if I don't see them again.'

Harris pulled out her phone and checked the text Alan Potts had sent her while she'd been talking to the Insta-couple.

The Registered Owner of 55 Ludgate Hill is down as EFX Holdings. Number follows. Alan.

At least he hadn't called her Christine.

She made the call. It was answered after only three rings. A machine picked up. Harris pulled her mobile away from her ear so that Terry could hear the message. The offices of EFX Holdings were closed for the weekend. Regular office hours were 8 a.m. to 6 p.m. Monday to Friday.

'Figures,' Terry said.

Harris turned to look back beyond St Paul's towards the darkened high-rise.

'You want to go and take another look, don't you?' Terry asked her.

'You know what? I really don't.'

106

Saturday 12.32 a.m.

'**Oh my God, is he . . . ?**' **Maggie didn't complete the** sentence. She didn't have to.

Tony was sprawled on his back on the floor, his limbs splayed at odd angles. A biro was embedded in his neck, his bloated face bruised and mottled around his nostrils and mouth.

I could hear the halting tempo of Maggie's breathing behind me, and from the threshold of the small room I could sense the terrible stillness all around Tony's body.

'Just . . . give me one second,' I said.

'No, Kate. Don't.'

She was shaking her hands out, sucking air through her teeth, partly from horror, I thought, and probably also because she was trying to get her blood moving again.

'I have to see the cameras.'

I moved forwards into the room towards the grid of security monitors. As I stepped closer to Tony, I thought about how scared he'd been for his daughter. Was she OK? I reached out to a filing cabinet for balance and stared at the screens. The bright flickers stung my eyes.

'Kate, we have to go.'

'Just wait.'

I couldn't see them on the monitors and something inside me opened up with a yawning fear. Then I glimpsed movement on the bottom left of the grid.

My heart lurched sickeningly. I let go of a strangled breath. Luke and Mark were kneeling on what looked like bare, unfinished cement. Joel was standing over them with his gun.

No.

The screen flickered again. Mark lifted his face to the camera.

I felt a deep pang.

'I see them,' I said.

'Where?' Maggie checked over her shoulder, terrified.

'I don't know. There's . . . I can see a car behind them.'

'Basement parking.' Maggie said it in a rush, not bothering to conceal the relief in her voice at the realization that Joel wasn't going to jump out at us from anywhere close. 'I parked there earlier.'

'I have to get there.'

'What? No. Are you crazy?'

I pulled my gaze away from the screens and weaved out of the room, tilting sideways, slamming into the front desk. Maggie made a grab for me, then sucked air and pulled back, stamping her foot at the pain in her arms.

'Try the phones,' I told her. It felt like my mouth was coated in treacle. 'Call for help. Tell them it's an emergency. Then get yourself away from here.'

'What are you going to do?'

'I have no idea.'

'You can barely walk, Kate.'

'He's aiming a gun at my husband and my brother.'

I paused at the end of the counter and looked back at her. She held my gaze, looking troubled, but then she nodded, seeming to resolve herself to what I'd asked her to do, staring down at the phones in front of her as if they were a conundrum she didn't know how to solve.

I didn't wait any longer. I pitched myself forwards across the atrium, my legs juddering under me. I was aware that I was walking on a slant but there was nothing I could do about it. The limestone tiling was hard and unforgiving against my bare feet.

I kept fearing I'd hear a gunshot any second, funnelling up from the bowels of the building. Kept imagining how I'd sense deep inside that Mark was really gone.

I swallowed something warm and sickly. Listened to the buzzing and clicking in my ears.

After what felt like an eternity, I made it to the far side of the lobby near the waterfall. Knowing there was no way I could manage the stairs, I jabbed the button for the elevators, and when the doors parted on the middle carriage I pretty much fell inside.

There were buttons marked P1 and P2. I slapped P1, collapsing backwards against the wall of the carriage behind me, peering across the foyer at Maggie.

One of the phones had started ringing. I saw her bare her teeth and use both hands to knock the receiver loose, then duck her head to talk as the elevator doors closed and I began my descent.

107

The moment Kate was gone, Maggie immediately straight-
ened her back, picked up the receiver, cleared her throat and
spoke clearly into the phone.

'55 Ludgate Hill. Front desk. How may I assist you?'

Her expression remained alert as she listened to the police
officer on the end of the line. Her face betrayed no flicker
of doubt or unease as she was told about the strange emergency call from a fax number.

'Officer, I apologize. We have had some issues with our
phone system this evening. But I can assure you that I have
recently been up to the offices of Edge myself and there is
nobody there now.'

She paused and listened, keeping her attention fixed on
the illuminated panel above the elevator Kate had taken.

'You're absolutely right, officer. We're short-staffed tonight.
Normally there would have been somebody on the desk
while I was upstairs. If you'd like to come back now, I'd be
more than happy to talk with you in person . . . No? Well,
I'm here all night if you change your mind. Good night,
officer. Thank you for your concern.'

She hung up, waited a beat, then dialled the number
for the anonymous voicemail system she'd diverted her

phone to before stepping into the elevator with Joel. After inputting her passcode number, she listened to the two messages that were waiting for her before setting down the phone.

108

Saturday 12.38 a.m.

I had no plan. I wasn't armed. I was, at best, barely lucid.
I leaned against the polished sides of the elevator carriage,
staring dazedly ahead. My chest heaved, but my breathing
felt feeble. I was burning up again.

I didn't know how bad it would get or what I was about
to walk into. The only thing I could think was that I had to
somehow stall Joel.

How long would it take for the police to get here after
Maggie called them? Five minutes? More?

The elevator chimed.

The doors parted.

I took a painful breath and stepped out.

They weren't here.

I was alone.

I peered around me in confusion. My head hurt. I had
taken the elevator to parking level one. It was a starkly lit
space. The parking bays were painted green. The rest of
the tarmac was a milky blue that reflected the overhead
lighting. I could see tyre marks smeared on the ground.
They arced towards a down ramp leading to the lower
parking level.

I could hear voices down there, dimly.

I tripped as I moved forwards. The light was a series of thin, stabbing blades, slicing at my eyes. The low ceilings pressed down on me. My toes scuffed the floor.

There was a car to my right. It was the only car parked down here. A red Mini. It was reversed into a space close to the down ramp.

I flapped at the pocket of my blouse and pulled out Maggie's keys with the Mini fob attached to them.

Could I get in the car and drive it down there? Form a distraction?

I padded towards it. I doubted the sound of my bare footsteps would carry, but if I unlocked the car remotely there'd probably be an electronic squawk. Better to slip the key in the driver's door instead. The old-fashioned way. But even the simplest task was beyond me now. My head dropped. I was ham-fisted. I kept missing the keyhole. My vision swarmed. I scratched the paint.

Then I dropped the keys.

I peered at them.

I tried to pick them up once. Twice. I missed both times. The second time, I over-balanced and nearly pitched forwards onto my face. I sensed that if I fell I wouldn't be able to get back up again. I knew that my time was running out.

I stood there, wobbling.

My heart thrashed against my ribs.

A part of me really wanted to slump down and close my eyes. Drift for a while. Let go.

I reached for the metal railings behind the car. I used them to heave myself towards the down ramp. I stumbled and clung on.

The air seemed to clog in my lungs as I tramped downwards, pressing my body into the railings, the voices I could hear gradually growing louder, clearer.

109

The gun was getting heavier at the end of Joel's arm, tiny
spasms working their way down towards his wrist. He adjusted his grip and reached his other hand inside his jacket. He took out a phone.

'Please,' Luke said. 'You don't have to do this.'

Joel ignored him. He kept his attention fixed on Mark.

'Tell me about the plane crash.'

'What's to tell?'

'Was it an accident?'

He stumbled over his words, forcing them out. His throat ached as if he'd regurgitated an egg.

Something seemed to pass between him and Mark, then. Joel couldn't tell for certain what it was, but he wondered, just maybe, if Mark was beginning to understand.

Luke looked between them both, wary. Perhaps he sensed a shift, too.

'No,' Mark said. 'I don't believe it was an accident.'

'Why?'

'Best guess? The flight system was sabotaged.'

'For what purpose?'

'To kill me. To stop me from talking to the right people in the right government positions in London and at the

European regulator. Two days before that flight . . .' He exhaled. Looked up at the ceiling. 'That was the day the data went missing from the computer system and the first time I called someone outside the company. At the regulator. We discussed setting up a face-to-face meeting in London.'

'And?'

'And I don't think they could take any more chances.'

'Who do you mean by "they"?'

'MarshJet. I don't know who, exactly. Dominic North, I'm guessing. Fergus. They must have had my phone bugged. Or it could be that the person I spoke with at the regulator tipped them off. They must have sources in the prosecution team for this trial, too, right? That explains why you're here.'

'Back to the plane crash. Keep talking.'

'I don't know what else you want to hear. I was already booked to fly home with some of the team from MarshJet. I was a threat. They couldn't allow me to land here and speak with the regulator in person, give them what I had, but if they stopped me from getting on that plane their actions would raise questions of their own. Maybe a link would be drawn between our missing IT guy and me. Maybe a hundred other things would come into play. They didn't have long to react. I like to believe that if they had, they would never have done something as terrible as they did.'

Joel grunted. He was tapping at the screen of his phone, pulling his gaze away intermittently. Luke was watching him closely, body tensing, as if he was thinking about making a move.

'You boarded the plane?'

'Yes.'

'Then why weren't you killed?'

Mark shrugged. 'I helped design that jet. I could tell you a dozen ways to get off that plane before it took off.'

Joel's head pulsed. He was processing, one part of his brain continuing to monitor Luke. It wasn't as if Mark had told him anything he hadn't anticipated hearing or suspected, but it was still shocking to hear it for real.

'What did you think when you heard the plane went down?' he asked him.

'I don't . . .' Mark blanched. 'I can't begin to say how awful that was. I had no idea they would do that, go that far. All I wanted was to disappear for a while, cover my tracks. I thought that if I let a few weeks go by, I could get to the regulator then. If I had known . . .' His words trailed away but he didn't look down. He stared back plainly, and Joel saw the pain and the guilt he lived with every day. 'Colleagues of mine, good friends, were on that flight. All those poor people. Kids . . .'

'You didn't say anything,' Joel cut in. 'You didn't come forwards, or talk, or go to the press.'

'Because I was scared. Because I didn't have proof that they sabotaged one of their own planes. I was waiting for the findings of the air accident investigation. And because the stakes were too high and it had to be safe first. I was afraid for Kate, my family.'

'And the court case?'

Luke moved slightly and this time, Joel turned to him and shook his head, swinging his gun towards him by way of warning. He could shoot him right now. Mark was the one he wanted to hear from. But he didn't want to distract him. He needed to complete this.

'Go on,' he told Mark.

'I knew I owed it to the people who died in that disaster to testify. To the crew who flew on our planes and got ill. To myself. My wife. I had to appear in court, raise enough questions so that everything could be looked at in the open, nothing could be concealed, but I didn't know who to trust to get me there safely. I was wary about the prosecution team after what had happened with my approach to the regulator. I was afraid they might be compromised. Same thing with the press, the police. There was no one I could trust.'

Joel stared at him. He was conscious of a deep and penetrating coldness spreading out from within. It seemed to him that Mark had given him everything he needed now. There was really only one last thing to do.

'Two things I need you to know,' he said, pointing his gun back towards Mark, waves of nauseating heat pulsing out from his chest, flushing his neck. 'You were never getting to that court room. Your evidence was never going to be heard. One way or another they would have stopped you. Dominic North. Fergus Marsh. Marsh was here with me earlier, by the way. I'm pretty sure there are witnesses to that. CCTV. He hired me to take your wife prisoner and interrogate her. To kill you. And I took the job gladly. Because if it wasn't me, today, it would have been somebody else. Someone like me was always going to stop you.'

Mark hesitated, clenching his jaw as if to brace himself. 'And the second thing?'

Joel tapped once more at his phone. He swallowed thickly and set the volume up high. When the message began to play, it seemed to tear through him from the insides out, ripping him, shredding him.

It was a message he'd listened to almost daily but it never lost its power to wound him. It had been that way for fifteen long months.

In the background there were screams. A high-pitched engine drone. A sequence of thumping, bumping, clashing sounds. And then a woman's voice, panicked, distressed, saying, '*Joel . . . Joel, honey, I don't know if you can . . . Our plane . . . in trouble. We're . . . wish I could talk to you right now. I love you, Joel. I love you. I'm sorry . . . Oh my God, we're—*'

110

Saturday 12.45 a.m.

I pushed away from the railings, weaved down the ramp. My legs wobbled. I somehow kept myself up.

When I fixed my gaze forwards again, I could see that Joel was staring back at me. There were tears in his eyes. Tears in mine. I saw him, saw *into* him, and I saw that he saw me do it. I knew in that moment we both understood one another. I knew that he had lost someone on that plane and how badly it had broken him, because for a long time I'd believed I'd lost the same thing.

'I'm here for the truth,' he called to me. 'I never lied to you about that. Might have lied to my client . . .'

Mark and Luke turned their heads to face me.

Time stopped.

I stared at my husband.

It was so strange to be able to say that. *I stared at my husband.* Words that shouldn't have made any sense but that somehow didn't feel wrong now. Mark was here with me. I could see him only a few steps away.

He looked just like he had in the photographs Joel had shown me. His hair was longer. There were deep seams in the skin around his eyes. He'd lost weight.

But it was him.

I wish I could explain how I felt in that moment. I can't. Trust me, to have everything you've ever wanted, really deep down wanted, right there in front of you and to know it was about to be ripped away . . .

I shuddered. I was so exhausted.

I needed to go to him. I wanted to touch him.

'Let them go.' My voice was faint and scratchy. It took so much effort to talk. 'Please. Let them go and we can talk about this. I understand. I—'

'No.' Joel lifted his chin. 'It's over, Kate. I'm sorry. I swore to myself I would do this. I made a promise to her. I vowed that I would make sure the people who did this didn't go unpunished.'

My heart beat raggedly in my chest, racing quicker and quicker, out of control.

'You can't blame Mark. You can blame MarshJet, or Fergus Marsh, or Dominic North. You can blame whoever they got to sabotage that plane. You can—'

'Why can't I blame them all?'

I watched him, feeling like I was staring at a man teetering on the edge of a narrow platform hundreds of metres in the air. A man who was steeling himself to jump.

'Then do,' I told him. 'But don't do this. What is this going to achieve?'

'I've spent my life in small rooms, Kate. Rooms like the one you and I were in together. Hunting for the truth. Mining it. But do you know what happens, afterwards? The truth stays locked in those rooms, more or less. It stays with me and with the people who hire me. They make it go away or they manipulate it. You can't rely on the police, on governments. You can't rely on courts or the justice system. All of it can be rigged and bought. You can see that now, can't you? But not this time. This time I'm going to get the truth out. No more secrets in small rooms. No more walls. Because that's the only way there can be consequences. It's the only way to bring these people down.'

'Then let me help you to do that. I can you help you. It's my job. It's what I'm good at.'

'You already did.'

He took a slow step forwards, angling his gun down at Mark's head.

'Don't. Please.'

'Look away, Kate.'

'Even if Mark had been on that plane, I would never do what you're doing here. I don't believe the person you think you're doing this for would want you to do it, either.'

'Well, I guess that's the difference between us, Kate. This is *my* job. My very last one. And I have nothing left to lose.'

His arm was shaking. He bit his lip.

Mark didn't look at him. He looked at me instead. He smiled. I saw the sorrow in his eyes but I saw something else, too. A kind of acceptance. I think it was Mark's way of letting me know that on some level he'd always believed it would end this way, or perhaps he thought it was what he deserved. That he'd made his peace with that.

'I love you,' he told me. 'I will always love you.'

Sobs rose up in me. I felt so tired. So drained. A numbing pain streaked across my ribs. I could feel the distant flicker of my pulse in my fingertips as I began to sink down to one side.

'What have you done to her?' Luke asked. 'Is it your heart, Kate? Please. Let me help her. There's a defibrillator in the lobby. I saw it. I can—'

'Stop talking,' Joel yelled at him.

I raised both my hands and cupped them over my chest. My heart was beating so wildly, so violently, it felt as if it was trying to fight its way out of me.

Tears streamed down my face.

I'm not sure of the exact order of what happened next. I'm not sure if Mark looked up first, or if I did. I'm pretty sure Luke shouted. I know he pushed up to his feet. I saw Joel step backwards. I saw him shift the angle of his gun.

My heart stopped.

It just ceased.

The terrible pain ripped through me again, much worse than before.

My arms flung outwards.

My head tipped back.

I heard the engine noise. I saw the horror in Joel's expression. And I turned just in time to see the Mini bearing down on me.

Maggie was behind the wheel.

She looked different, somehow.

I couldn't breathe. Couldn't move.

Then Luke's hands were on me, grabbing me. Shoving me away. The desperate roar of the engine. The wing mirror clipping my side.

I fell to the floor. I clutched at my chest.

The car sped on. It bottomed out at the base of the ramp. Sparks flew.

I saw Mark leap sideways and I heard the gunshots. Glass exploded. The car shimmied and veered. Then the sound of an impact. A bullet went high. Debris rained down from the ceiling. There was another scream, I think, followed by the screech and stink of brakes, and then the Mini collided with something and stopped in an instant.

I listened in the warped silence that followed.

I could hear a hissing sound. A ticking of metal. The splashing of liquid hitting the floor.

But I couldn't see anything. I was staring upwards. My back was arched. I wanted so badly for my heart to beat one more time. To keep beating. I wanted it even as my vision dimmed.

111

The rest came to me in snatches. Even now, I don't know how much of it is memory and how much is invention. I do know that Mark lifted me in his arms and carried me up two flights of stairs. In my mind, I can still see the jab and slant of the lighting overhead. I can feel Mark's arms cradling me tight. I can feel the coolness of the flooring when he laid me down in the atrium and I can smell the perfumed chlorine of the waterfall nearby.

I *think* I remember the whining of the charged defibrillator by my side. I have no recollection at all of Mark pulling open my blouse, or applying the paddles.

Perhaps you're wondering if the shock from the defibrillator hurt. I sometimes wonder the same thing. I don't recall any pain, or if I do I suppose I've suppressed it. What I do remember is the most amazing feeling of energy surging through my body. A true, life-giving force that seemed to replenish every part of me.

I remember bucking up off the floor. I remember taking the most enormous, cleansing breath. I remember Mark saying my name over and over, holding me, hugging me, leaning back, cupping my face.

That was when we heard footsteps.

They were halting and scuffed. They drew nearer.

Mark's arms tensed around me as Maggie appeared.

Her hair was mussed. There were glass fragments on her shoulders. A line of blood trickled down from the corner of her mouth across her chin.

She had Joel's gun in her hand. I could tell from the assured way she was holding it that it wasn't the first time she had held a gun.

She stared at me flatly for several long seconds, then raised the gun and pointed it at Mark.

In that moment, I knew and understood several things all at once.

I knew that Maggie was not who she'd appeared to be. I remembered what Joel had said to me about how other people would have been hired in case he failed and how merciless they would be in finishing what he'd started. I realized he'd been mistaken about only one thing. The back-up Sir Fergus Marsh had arranged was not some shadowy assassin waiting in the wings to be notified if and when they were needed. It was Maggie, and she'd been part of this from the very beginning. If I'd somehow got away from Joel, if I'd made it out of the building, she would have been there waiting for me. I wouldn't have suspected a thing.

She didn't move closer. She was close enough already. Any nearer and she must have known that Mark would try to stop her.

She gazed down past the gun at him. There was nothing at all in her expression except a cold, ruthless resolve.

That's when the riot started. There was a splintering of glass, a volley of shouts, and what seemed like about a hundred black-clad figures swarmed inside the building. They yelled at Maggie to 'drop it,' 'step away,' 'don't shoot'. Their boots were loud in the vaulted space. Some of them were splashing through the pool to my side.

They were too late.

Maggie was going to pull the trigger anyway, finish the job. But then I saw something flicker in her eyes and her lips move, as if she was running a series of fast permutations in her mind.

It took a few seconds before she lifted her arms slowly and let the gun hang loose around her finger as two armed police officers rushed in, tore the pistol from her, seized her arms and marched her away.

'Kate? Kate, can you hear me? Kate, I'm Officer Harris. We're bringing in some medical attention for you now.'

A female officer was kneeling down next to me. She had my hand in her hand and she was squeezing my thumb. Behind her, a tall black officer let go of a low whistle, staring at the scene that surrounded him.

'How did . . . How did you find me?'

'You sent a fax,' the officer told me. 'To your bosses? Their machine ran out of paper. One of them heard it making beeping noises when they got home tonight. They found your message and called us. And, well, let's just say it connected to a few other anomalies we've been dealing with here.'

I sank backwards into Mark's arms. I looked up at his face. My fingers were twisted in his shirt. I was holding on to him still. I didn't ever want to have to let him go again.

'Where's Luke?' I asked him.

And that's when I saw the darkness cross Mark's face and the dread swept back in again.

112

It was late the following morning when Officer Harris ventured into my hospital room. Luke had been taken to St Thomas' for emergency surgery for a gunshot to the head. I knew the prognosis was dire but I tried to take it as a good omen that he was being operated on in the same hospital where he worked. Everyone kept telling me that the surgical team would do everything they could.

Harris hesitated with her police hat under her arm. I was alone and exhausted, lying in bed with a heart rate monitor beeping beside me and a network of tubes running in and out of my body, flushing the toxins that Joel had poisoned me with from my system. Mark had wanted to be with me, but the detectives who'd appeared on scene at 55 Ludgate Hill had insisted he go with them to answer their questions. I felt oddly relieved about that. I don't know how to explain it. I had spent so long wishing and dreaming I could see him again and now I no longer knew if I could.

'How is your brother doing?' Harris asked.

I lifted my head from my pillow. It felt as if a giant elastic band was holding me down. 'They're still operating.'

'Listen, I can come back. We don't have to do this now.'

'No. Please. I'd like to talk.'

Harris nodded as though she understood, but she still looked uncertain as she pushed the door closed behind her. There was a chair opposite me and she debated for a moment before sitting down. I suspected her shift had finished hours ago. Thinking about it made me begin to well up.

'The man who held you . . .' she began.

'Joel.'

'Joel, yes. Did they tell you that he's—?'

'Dead.' I nodded. 'They said the impact with the car killed him outright.'

I didn't know how to feel about that. Of course, I wished that no one had died. But I had seen him murder Raul. I felt sure he'd killed Tony. His actions had very nearly cost me my life, too.

So no, I can't say I felt bad for him, but neither did I feel in any way relieved. I guess I was still processing. Too much had happened and was happening still.

'Did you find Tony's daughter?'

'We did. She's safe. If someone was watching her, there's no sign of them now. She's going to change her locks. Spend some time with her mum.'

'What about Maggie?'

'We're still working on that. For now I can tell you that Maggie is not her real name and there is no such company as Abacus Recruitment Services. Their website is bogus. She's in custody. She's asked for a lawyer but we have a good team who will be interviewing her. I'm sorry to have to tell you but before too long they'll want to talk to you, too.'

'Another interview?'

'Yes.'

I cried then. Everything just caught up to me. In the days and weeks ahead, I was going to learn that this was how it would be. Suddenly, out of nowhere, I'd be blindsided by the most overwhelming shock and horror. In my sleep, in my waking daydreams, I would relive my ordeal over and over. There were moments when I saw things turning out differently. When I told myself I could have said or done more. Most of all, my mind seemed to loop on the moment my heart stopped and Mark resuscitated me. In the very worst of my dreams, Maggie appeared before Mark could shock my heart back to life and my final seconds were spent watching her shoot him. I would wake gasping for breath and drenched in cold sweat.

For now, though, I didn't know any of that. But from the way Harris was looking at me, waiting patiently for me to gather myself, I'm pretty sure she understood something of what was to come.

'Something I wanted to tell you,' she said, when the worst of it had passed and I had myself almost under control again. She glanced back at the door behind her. It occurred to me that the doctors had probably warned her not to say anything that might distress me too much. 'You're a member of a Facebook support group for relatives and loved ones of those who were lost in the Global Air disaster. Is that right?'

The question came at me from left field. 'Yes, but I don't go on there very often. Maybe at the start . . .'

'He was streaming from your phone. To the group, I mean. Joel was streaming everything that happened in that parking garage. We found your phone attached to the wall with duct tape behind where he was standing. We think that's why he

424

made your husband talk. The video has been shared widely, all over the world. It's . . . Well, it's the lead story on the news right now. It's pretty much everywhere.'

I blinked at her. I wasn't sure what I was supposed to do with that information. I thought again about some of the things Joel had said to me at the end: about how he needed to get the truth out because that was the only way there could be true justice; that the authorities and the courts couldn't be relied upon when there was so much at stake.

At the time, I'd thought he was telling me that he was going to spread the word himself, maybe go to the press or circulate the information on social media. But now I began to see that this had always been his plan.

This is my job. My very last one.

It was Joel who'd warned me there would be a back-up in case he didn't fulfil his assignment. It was Joel who'd told me both our lives were on the line – that our fates were intertwined.

Did that mean that when he'd started our interview, he'd accepted the possibility that neither one of us would ever leave The Mirror alive? Had he decided it was a sacrifice he was willing to make in order to guarantee the full truth could be known?

Setting up the camera feed from my phone couldn't have been an instinctive reaction. He'd planned it, in all likelihood from the first moment Maggie had contacted me about the position at Edge. He must have decided that sharing everything Mark told him with the world directly, getting the information into the public domain before it could be manipulated or discredited by lawyers and spin doctors, was his best shot at bringing Sir Fergus Marsh down.

For a second, as I thought about what Harris had told me, an image flashed in my mind of the story being beamed into households throughout the globe, appearing on websites, hitting newspaper stands. But just then, it was no more than a fleeting consideration for me. I didn't care about how big the story was, or what the consequences might be. Outside, the world could go on turning, but for me, and for Luke, everything that mattered was taking place inside this hospital.

'He's an organ donor,' I whispered.

'Excuse me?'

'My brother. He carries a card. His job . . .' I raised my hand, felt the drag of the cannula attached to it. 'He sees people waiting on transplants all the time. They asked for my consent, if he doesn't make it. They don't need to, but they asked.'

'I'm sorry.' Harris touched my leg through the sheets. 'We're rooting for him. I want you to know that a lot of us are. I should let you rest now.'

She crossed the room, opened the door.

'Officer?'

She looked back at me.

'I never thanked you, and I should have. For what you did. For getting to me in time.' I clenched the sheets in my hands. 'I wanted to say thank you.'

'You're welcome, Kate.'

'Why didn't she shoot? Maggie, or whatever her name is – at the end, why did she hesitate?'

'Best guess?'

I nodded.

'It was already too late. Plus, if you want to get cynical about it, and usually I do, a good lawyer could spin her as a hero here. She drove that car. She killed Joel.'

'She was hired to kill me. To kill my husband.'

'Well, like I said, it's an argument. I'm not saying it will stick.'

113

At the same time, aboard a private jet waiting to push back from a rain-swamped runway apron at London City Airport, Sir Fergus Marsh wheezed as he patted himself dry with a soft white towel, watching with a weary sense of detachment at the way Dominic North was twisting around in the chair opposite him, his long fingers clenching and unclenching the armrests at his side.

His once fierce consigliere was beyond rattled, a cornered animal looking for help from the team of executives and lawyers who were making hurried phone calls and passing papers to one another around them.

The air smelled of damp clothing. They'd all got soaked on the short walk from their limos to the plane. The jet had been fuelled up and readied at short notice. At Dominic's insistence, the team would fly to Sir Fergus's home base in Monaco and from there they would plot their next move.

'Nathan!' Dominic screeched at Sir Fergus's personal pilot. 'Why haven't we pushed back yet?'

'We're just waiting for clearance, Mr North.'

'What's the hold-up?'

'No hold-up. We have our slot. It should only be a couple of minutes more.'

Sir Fergus remained aloof, silent. A powerful feeling of fatalism had fallen over him in the past half-hour. Of debts coming due.

Fifteen months ago, he'd allowed Dominic to persuade him that they risked losing everything if he didn't act and approve his plan to cripple one of their jets. Now he could see that he would lose so much more.

Ducking low, he peered out of the rain-streaked window beside him. A Swiss Air passenger jet (not one of theirs) was tearing along the sodden runway, its wheels parting company with the ground in a misty spray. Other planes were stacked nose-in to the terminal building. He counted eight of his aircraft, looking worryingly inert. A portent, he suspected. The sky was dreary, wet.

In his mind, moving achingly slowly, he pictured the blanket coverage on the twenty-four-hour news channels, the devastating morning headlines to come, the dangers and disgrace that were closing in on him like the purple storm clouds massing outside.

'How are we coming with that statement?' Dominic snapped.

Their media adviser, an ex-BBC journalist, jerked up from behind an open laptop screen, his face as taut and translucent as his rain-spattered work shirt.

'I'm still finessing what we're trying to say, Mr North.'

'What's to finesse? It's a denial. You deny everything in that video.'

'Right. Only . . .' The man quailed. 'Some people are going to think that by flying out of the country like this we have something to hide.'

'We have a scheduled business meeting.'

Scheduled as of ten minutes ago.

'I understand that. The point I'm making is that others might not see it that way.'

'Well, that's what we pay you for, isn't it? All of you. *Make* them see it that way.'

Sir Fergus pressed two fingers against his throat. He hadn't said a word but the scorching pain was relentless. Every breath hurt worse than the one before. And wasn't that a kind of reckoning, too? His own personal punishment.

He signalled to Nancy, his regular flight attendant, to fetch him his morphine. When he looked back at Dominic, his CFO's face was flickering an odd bluish white.

'What is it?' Dominic asked him. 'Why are you looking at me like that?'

He didn't answer, preferring to gaze to his right, where his team were crowding the oval windows, their bodies grown rigid, faces awed.

'Will somebody tell me what is happening,' Dominic shouted.

Sir Fergus eased forwards in his chair, placing his towel down to one side. He stepped into the aisle and buttoned his jacket.

'What are you doing?' Dominic asked him. 'Why are you standing like that?'

Fergus faced forwards, drew back his shoulders and walked stiffly towards the front of the cabin, where he nodded at Nancy to open the aircraft door.

Gusty rain swept in as a phalanx of police vehicles slewed to a halt in front of the jet, their tyres screeching damply, their emergency lights popping and smeared in the murky afternoon.

'Don't you go down there, you mad old bastard,' Dominic yelled at him. 'Don't you dare.'

The front doors of a dark saloon car clunked open and two plainclothes officers in cheap suits emerged. One of them contemplated Sir Fergus from beneath a black umbrella, paperwork fluttering in her hand. The other one strode towards the base of the steps, raised his ID and waited for Sir Fergus to descend.

EPILOGUE

Eight weeks have gone by. Eight weeks without Luke. He didn't make it out of surgery. He died in the operating theatre, not long after Officer Harris had finished talking with me.

Part of me still has trouble accepting that my brother really is gone. I guess that's a consequence of having Mark returned to me against all odds. But this time, I know there can be no miracle reprieve. I viewed Luke's body in the mortuary. I kissed his forehead. I told him goodbye. I also whispered a thank you for everything he'd done for me – everything he'd *tried* to do – and I told him that I forgave him and loved him. I told him that he should rest now.

Set against how much I miss him, and the future he's been denied, it's difficult to engage with the idea that anything else really matters. But of course it does, and not just for me but for so many others, too. So I guess the first thing to say is that MarshJet has collapsed. The wider MarshJet board and management team disavowed the actions of Sir Fergus and Dominic North early on, but it made little difference. All MarshJet planes have been grounded on a worldwide basis, pending an emergency redesign and refit.

In the wake of Joel's video going viral, the Melanie Turner court case against MarshJet has been postponed. Most commentators now view it as almost redundant. With my publicist hat on, it's easy to see that the reputational damage MarshJet has sustained is irreversible.

I have mixed feelings about that. I suppose, on the one hand, it removes any likelihood of MarshJet's team of expensive lawyers deflecting blame from the company. On the other hand, many legal and business experts are already suggesting that the millions of pounds of compensation owed to Melanie and the other flight crew who became ill after flying on MarshJet planes, or who develop symptoms in the years to come, may now never be paid.

Then there's the Global Air disaster. The UK and US governments quickly announced that the investigation into the air crash had been intensified based on new information. In the media, there is speculation of what the investigation will now uncover (as well as plenty of insinuations about how it could possibly have missed evidence of sabotage before now). With the right witnesses called, and the right pressure applied, I am hopeful the families and loved ones of those who lost their lives will finally get the truth and perhaps even the justice they deserve.

The upshot, for now, is that the success or otherwise of the civil cases against MarshJet (and there seem to be more each and every day) does not in any way shield the company's directors from criminal liability. That's where Maggie (real name Theresa Murphy) comes in. Like everybody else, she's cutting deals where she can. The last I heard, she's giving the CPS the ammo they need to convict Sir Fergus Marsh and Dominic North directly for the plot against me and Mark.

There are some people who are calling Joel a hero. I'm afraid I can't go along with that. He may have broadcast the truth to a worldwide audience but he murdered Raul and Tony, a shot from his gun killed my brother, and he terrorized me. There are even stories appearing of other suspicious deaths and illnesses linked to interviews he conducted in the past, from as far away as Shanghai to LA.

The woman who left the voicemail on his phone was his lover, Sarah Walker, a thirty-six-year-old media analyst based in New York. She was separated from her husband, Alex, and had been involved with Joel in secret for at least two years before she died in the Global Air disaster. I've spoken to Alex on the phone. He told me he suspected his wife had been seeing someone but he had no idea who she was dating or how serious it had been. He asked me if Joel had said anything to me about Sarah when we spoke. He was a little hesitant about how to phrase that and I understood his predicament. It wasn't as if I'd had any real choice in what Joel had forced me to discuss and I could tell he still wasn't over the loss of his wife.

As it happens, I lied and said that we had both talked about how broken we'd been following the Global Air crash. I told him Joel had told me how special Sarah was to him but that she'd talked about ending their relationship in a phone call shortly before the flight. It's ironic, I guess, that Joel had pushed so hard to get the truth he wanted from me, when a lie like that can, I hope, go some way towards healing the deepest of wounds.

I went to the funerals for Raul and Tony. It was hard. I still don't know if going was the right thing to do. I do know that seeing their loved ones so hopelessly grieving broke me in ways I hadn't been prepared for, and that I still don't know how to begin to heal from.

After taking some time to recuperate and grieve for Luke, I'm back at work at Simple, grateful to be working with Simon and Rebecca again. I owe them more than I can say, but whenever I have a spare moment and I'm feeling strong enough, I'm dedicating myself to helping to promote the campaign agenda of the support group set up for the MarshJet victims – both those who got ill and those who lost loved ones in the Global Air disaster. It hasn't escaped my notice that by doing that, I'm helping to do what Joel wanted, in a way, though I try not to let it trouble me. I imagine some people might suspect I'm motivated by guilt and to a certain extent, I am. Deceived like so many others, I helped to tell the world that MarshJet's planes were safe when they weren't. Hundreds of people died in a plane crash because, in part, my husband couldn't bring himself to confide in me. Am I trying to make amends? I'm not foolish enough to believe I ever could. But I do intend to commit myself to the quest for justice for as long as it takes.

Edge Communications' stock has tumbled. They've been losing multiple clients and key accounts – including, of course, MarshJet and Sir Fergus Marsh. In the midst of the damage limitation exercise they're engaged in, they've already announced that their London offices inside The Mirror will be shuttered and closed.

And then there is Mark.

It's a Tuesday morning in August. We're walking along the South Bank of the Thames together. The sky is blue and cloudless, the sun high overhead. The river shimmers in a golden hue. It's a perfect summer's day.

Mark spent the night with me last night. We woke together this morning. Every time I touch him I get this feeling inside – this topsy-turvy sense that anything is possible. Perhaps even us.

But then there are other moments. Moments when I think of the secrets he kept from me, how he hid from me, of the pain and the hurt he is responsible for in the hearts of so many people I will never know or meet. And he is responsible. Perhaps he was doing the only thing he could when he ran. Maybe he was right to think that he had to stay hidden until he could appear as a witness in court and get the whole truth out. Or perhaps he made mistake after mistake.

He tells me he tried to do the right thing. Sometimes, when I can't see that, he begs me to understand. He pleads with me and tells me that too many people have lost so much already that it makes no sense for the two of us to forfeit what we can have as well.

It's messy. And in all honesty, I can't tell you how things will turn out between us. There are so many moments when I still don't feel like I know my own mind. I do know that seeing Mark reunited with his daughter, Rosie, was one of the happiest moments of my life. Perhaps, when it comes down to it, that will be enough.

'You don't have to do this alone,' he says to me now. 'I could come with you?'

I look away from him. Shake my head no. And then I shudder.

'Nerves?' he asks.

And yet again – sorry, Joel – I don't tell the truth. I don't say that my shudder is because I have looked across the river to the peak of 55 Ludgate Hill, that the memories are crashing over me again, that I still wonder, sometimes, if I ever really did escape that office.

Instead I nod, and then I squeeze his hand. 'Wait for me?'

I find Anna ten minutes later, in the shade under one of the trees outside the Tate Modern art gallery where we've arranged to meet. She's thin and delicate-looking, wearing a pretty summer dress and sitting in a wheelchair. She doesn't see me approach because her face is tilted to the sky in what appears to be a kind of rhapsody, as discs of sunlight sprinkle her face.

It takes me a long time to get to her, and as I do I think about Luke and what he would have made of all this. I think about how he was there for me when I needed him. Every time. And I think about how often he mentioned Anna to me in the days before I lost him, if he was even aware of it – how he'd tried to conceal the way he was so obviously attracted to one of his patients; because, I suspect, he hadn't wanted to admit his true feelings when he'd known how vulnerable she was.

'Anna?'

She opens her eyes and gives me this smile. The most amazing, most full-of-life smile. And it's what finally breaks me. Her smile is what starts the tears I cannot stop.

'You came,' she says.

I nod because I can't speak. Because it should be Luke that's here with her instead of me.

There's the faint whisper of wind in the trees overhead,

and for a second I allow myself to indulge the fantasy that the wind is my brother's voice whispering to me, telling me it's OK, that he's at peace, that staying in touch with Anna is somehow the right thing to do.

'How are you feeling?' I ask her.

'Better. I get stronger every day.'

There's a stone bench next to her. Whoever has brought her here, whoever has made themselves scarce for this moment – her parents, I will later find out – is obviously intending for me to sit down.

I feel so light suddenly that the solidity of the bench under my legs jars me.

'You probably think this is silly, my asking you here,' she tells me. 'It's not as if I was his girlfriend or anything. But, I don't know, the last time I saw him he brought me this ridiculous pink balloon. Instead of flowers. He was kind of awkward about it, but I sort of hoped that if I got a transplant, he might ask me out. Or I'd ask him out. I never thought . . .'

'He would have, Anna. He really liked you. So no, it's not silly. And he'd be so glad to know you got your heart. I wish it could have been his, in a way. I think that would have been more bearable for me, to know who got it. To be able to talk to them, sometimes.'

She squeezes my hand.

'They tell me I'll get a letter eventually,' I say to her. 'I'll get to hear a little bit about who he helped.'

'*Saved*,' she whispers.

And I nod. Because I get it. Because in those last seconds before my brother was shot, he saved me, too. And I know that it's my responsibility to make that count.

438

AUTHOR'S NOTE

This book was written before and during lockdown in the UK, at a time when it was unclear quite how far or how dramatically the global Covid pandemic would change all our lives. As a result, eagle-eyed readers might have spotted some discrepancies between certain travel restrictions, social-distancing rules and other factors that were in place in reality during the timeline covered by events in *The Interview* and how I have portrayed them in this novel. My hope is that this has not caused any offence. I also hope that wherever you are when this note finds you, things have improved and life is back, or on its way back, to being something like normal again.

ACKNOWLEDGEMENTS

An enormous thank you to Vicki Mellor, my editor, who made this book better in many and crucial ways. Thanks also to Gillian Green for her valuable input and guidance, and to Samantha Fletcher, Claire Gatzen, Matthew Cole and the brilliant teams in Sales, Marketing and Publicity at Pan Macmillan.

Camilla Bolton, my agent, gave me all the wisdom, enthusiasm and support any writer could dream of, backed by everyone I owe huge thanks to at Darley Anderson, including Mary Darby, Kristina Egan, Georgia Fuller, Sheila David and Jade Kavanagh, as well as Sylvie Rabineau at WME.

Thanks for their help with queries to Lucy Hanington and Dominic Jones, and to Clare Donoghue and Tim Weaver for laughter and support.

Mum, Allie, Jessica and Jack – well done on putting up with me while I'm writing (and when I'm not).

And to my wife, Jo – thank you for everything again, and always.

Discover C. M. Ewan's nerve-shredding thriller
A Window Breaks.

They were supposed to be getting away from their troubles . . .

Still recovering from their son's death eight months before, Tom and Rachel Sullivan take their daughter to a remote Scottish lodge in the hope that spending time together will begin to heal the rifts between them.

But at 2 a.m. on their first night, downstairs a window breaks.

Someone is inside their holiday home, intent on causing them harm.

They don't know why they have been targeted and with nowhere to run, their choices are limited.

With only each other to rely on, can they escape?

'Fantastic' **Lee Child**

'Totally addictive' **Ann Cleeves**

'A thrill-a-minute page-turner' **Simon Kernick**